Mar 19

GRAVEYARD SHAKES

LAURA TERRY

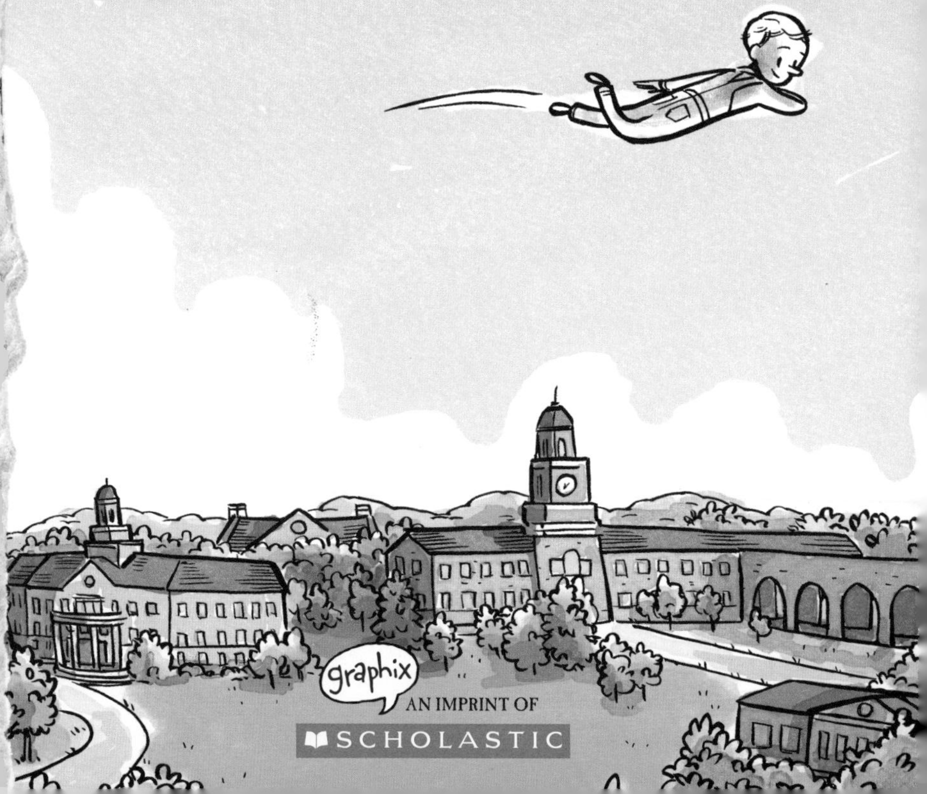

graphix
AN IMPRINT OF
SCHOLASTIC

Graveyard Shakes was painted using a combination of hand-painted and digital watercolor. The hand-painted watercolor was done on Saunders Waterford 140-pound cold-press paper and quinacridone rose, Prussian blue, and cadmium yellow pigments. The digital art was created using Kyle T. Webster brushes.

Library of Congress Control Number: 2016960079

ISBN 978-0-545-88955-1 (hardcover)
ISBN 978-0-545-88954-4 (paperback)

10 9 8 7 6 5 4 3 2 1 17 18 19 20 21

Printed in China 38
First edition, October 2017
Edited by Cassandra Pelham
Book design by Phil Falco
Creative Director: David Saylor

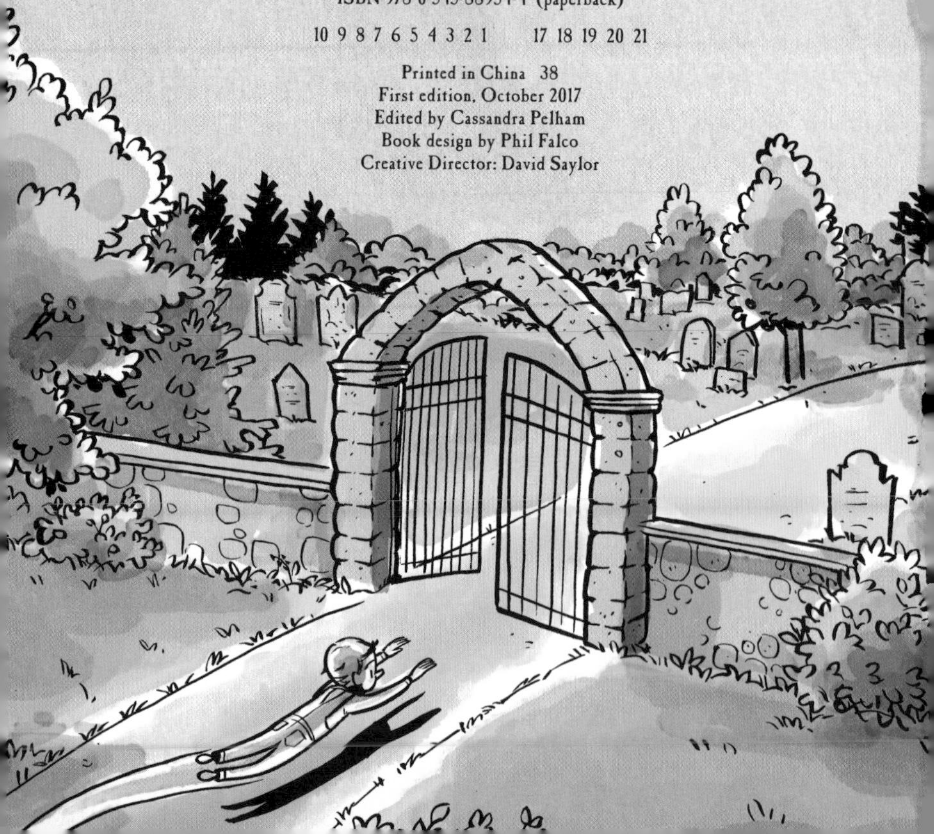

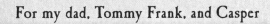
For my dad, Tommy Frank, and Casper

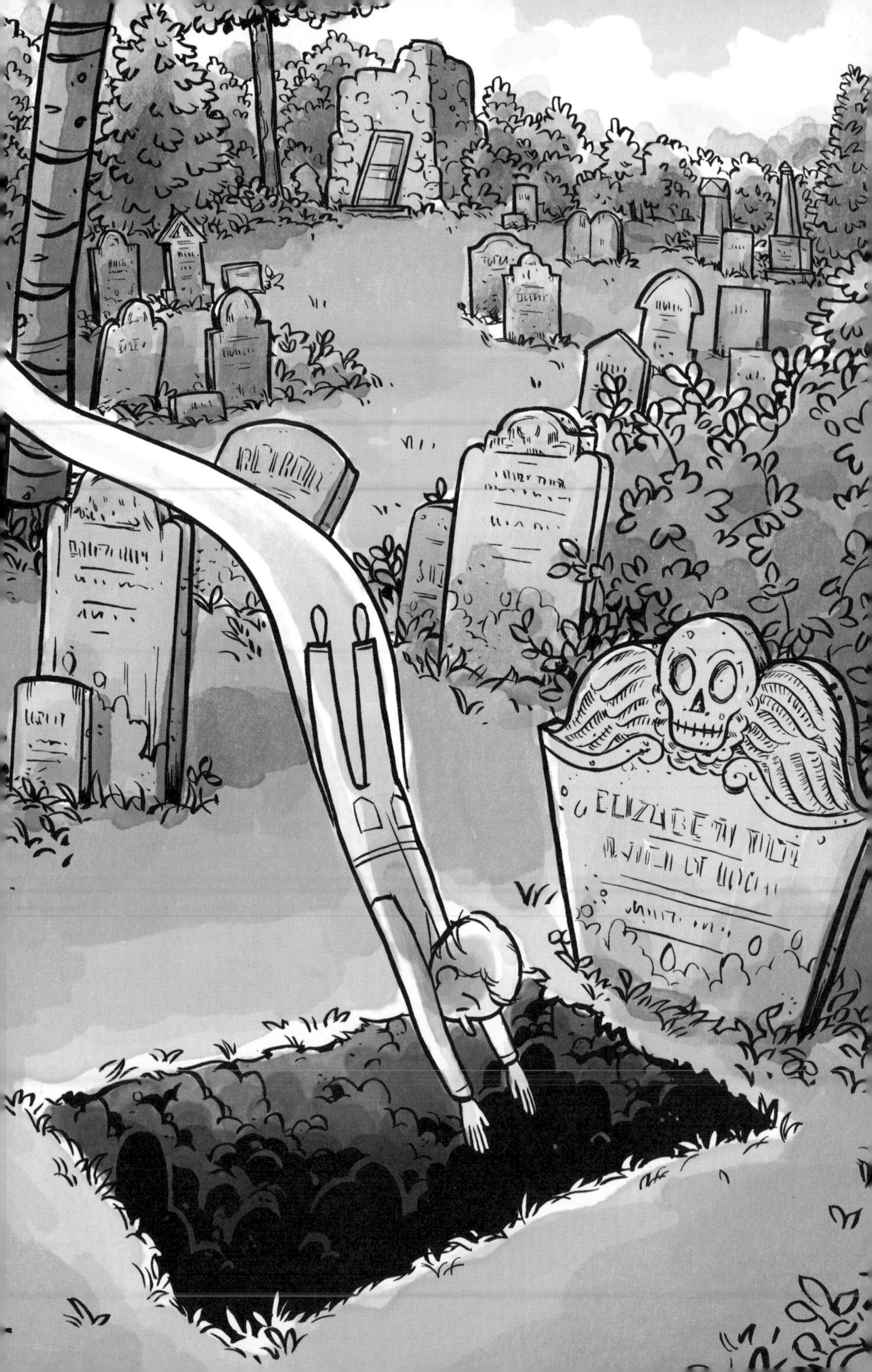

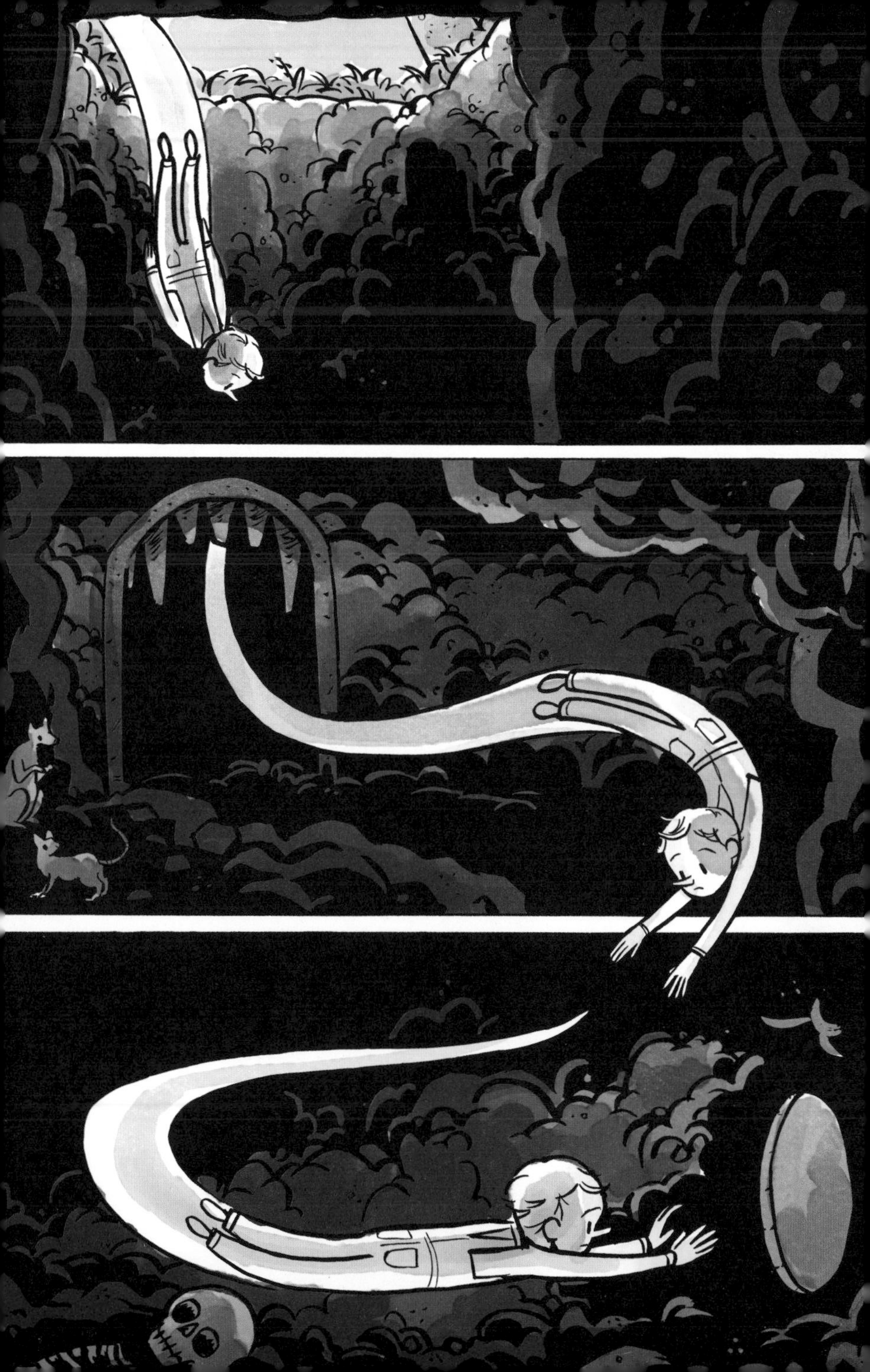

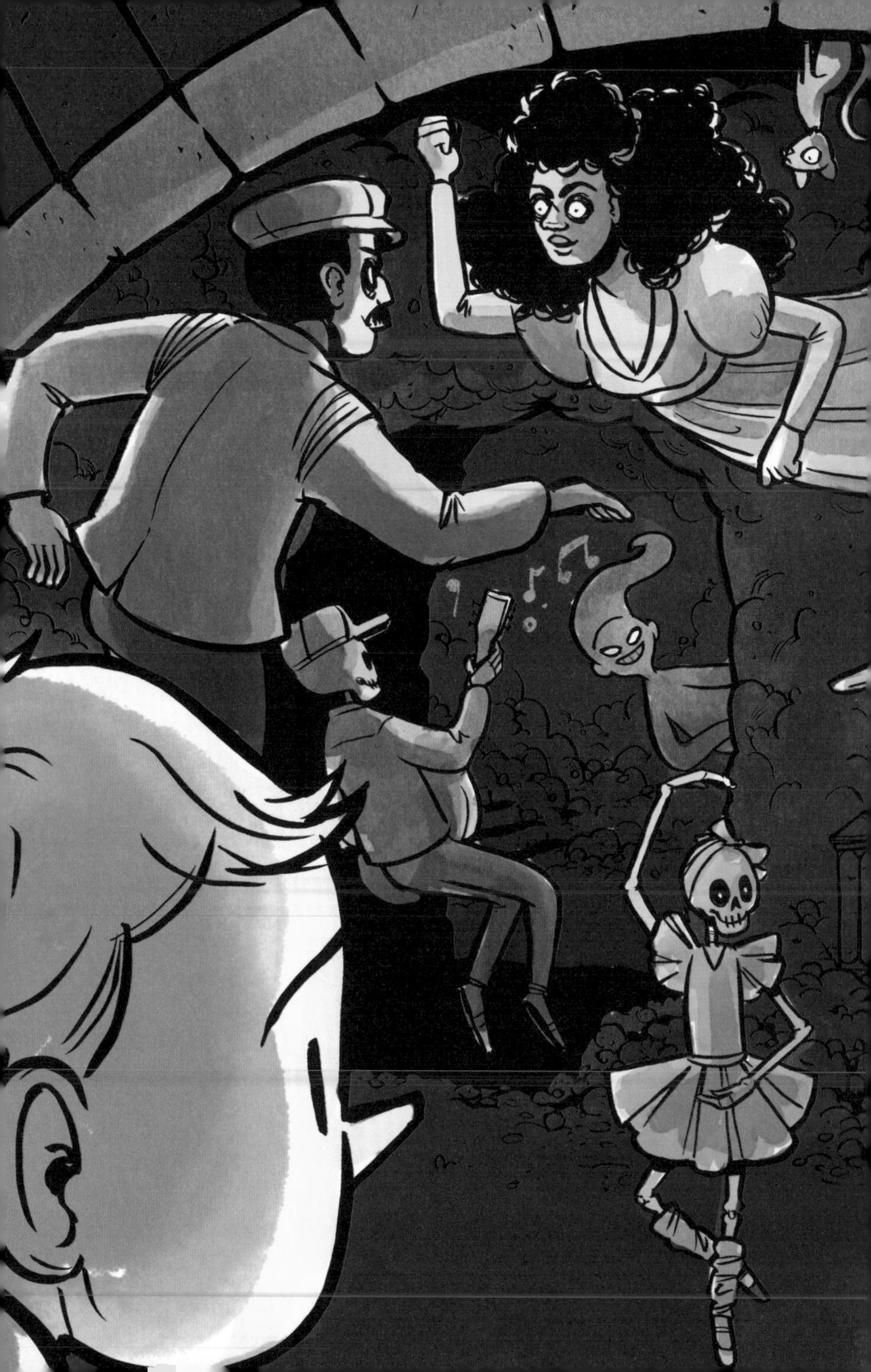

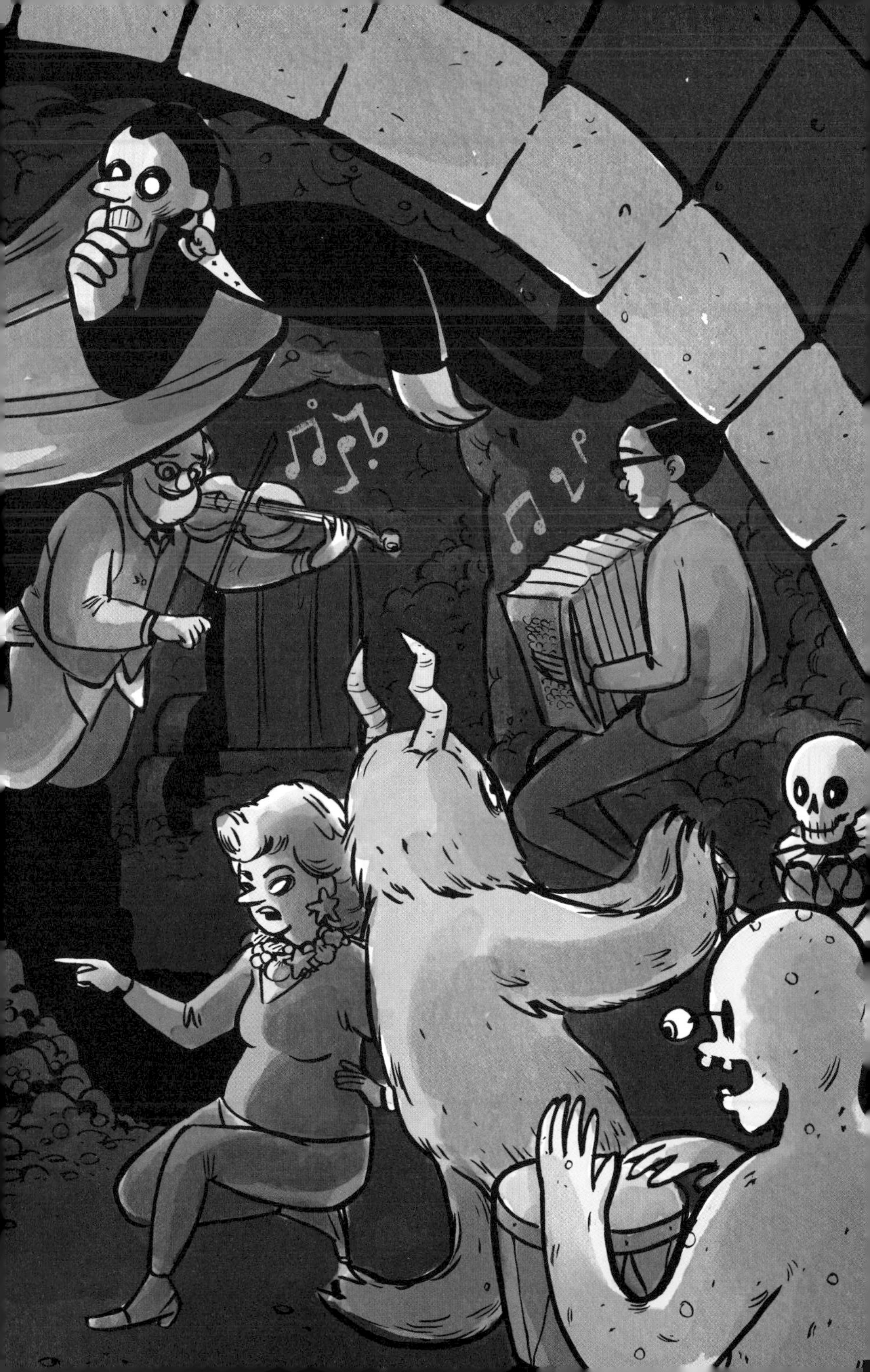

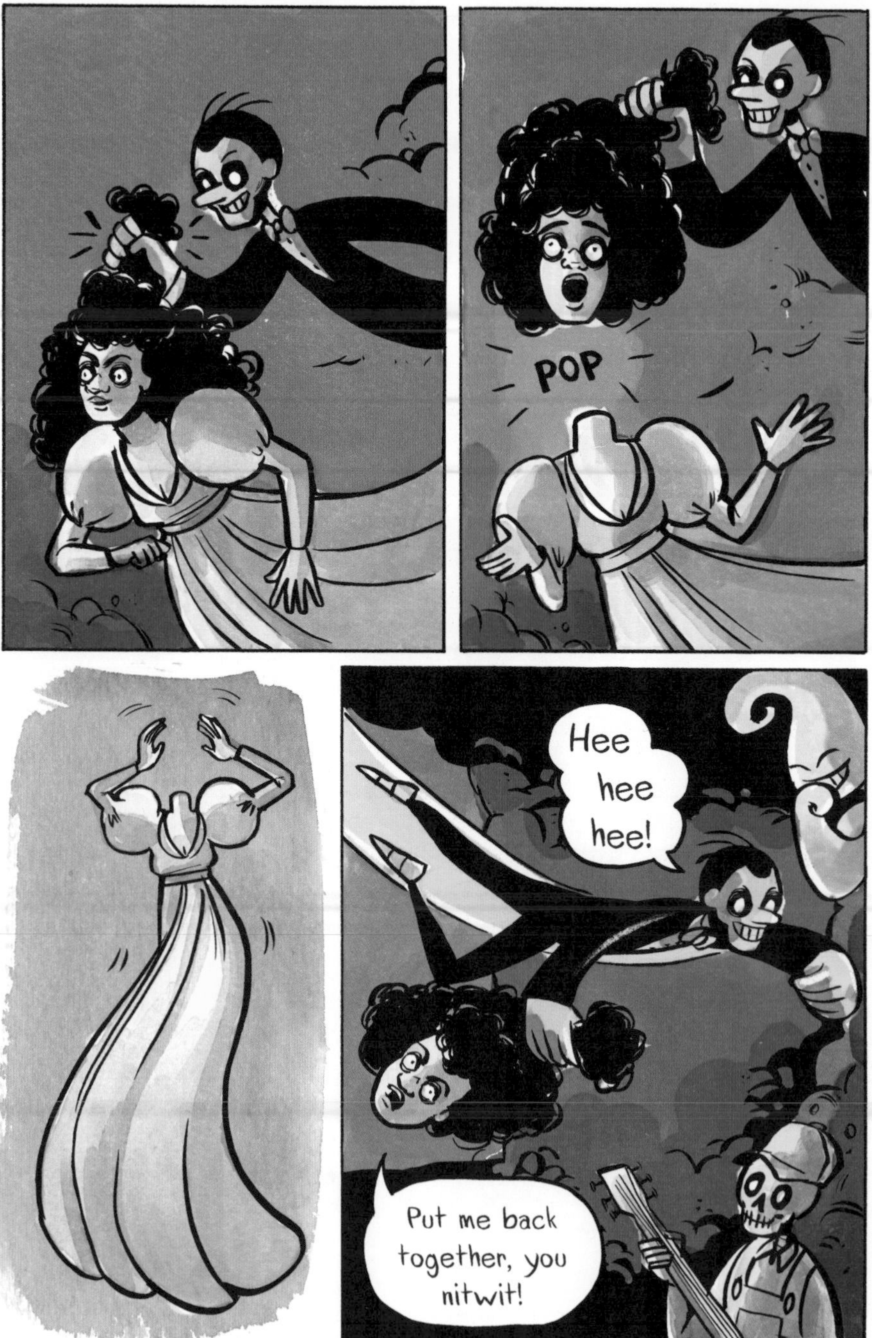
POP
Hee hee hee!
Put me back together, you nitwit!

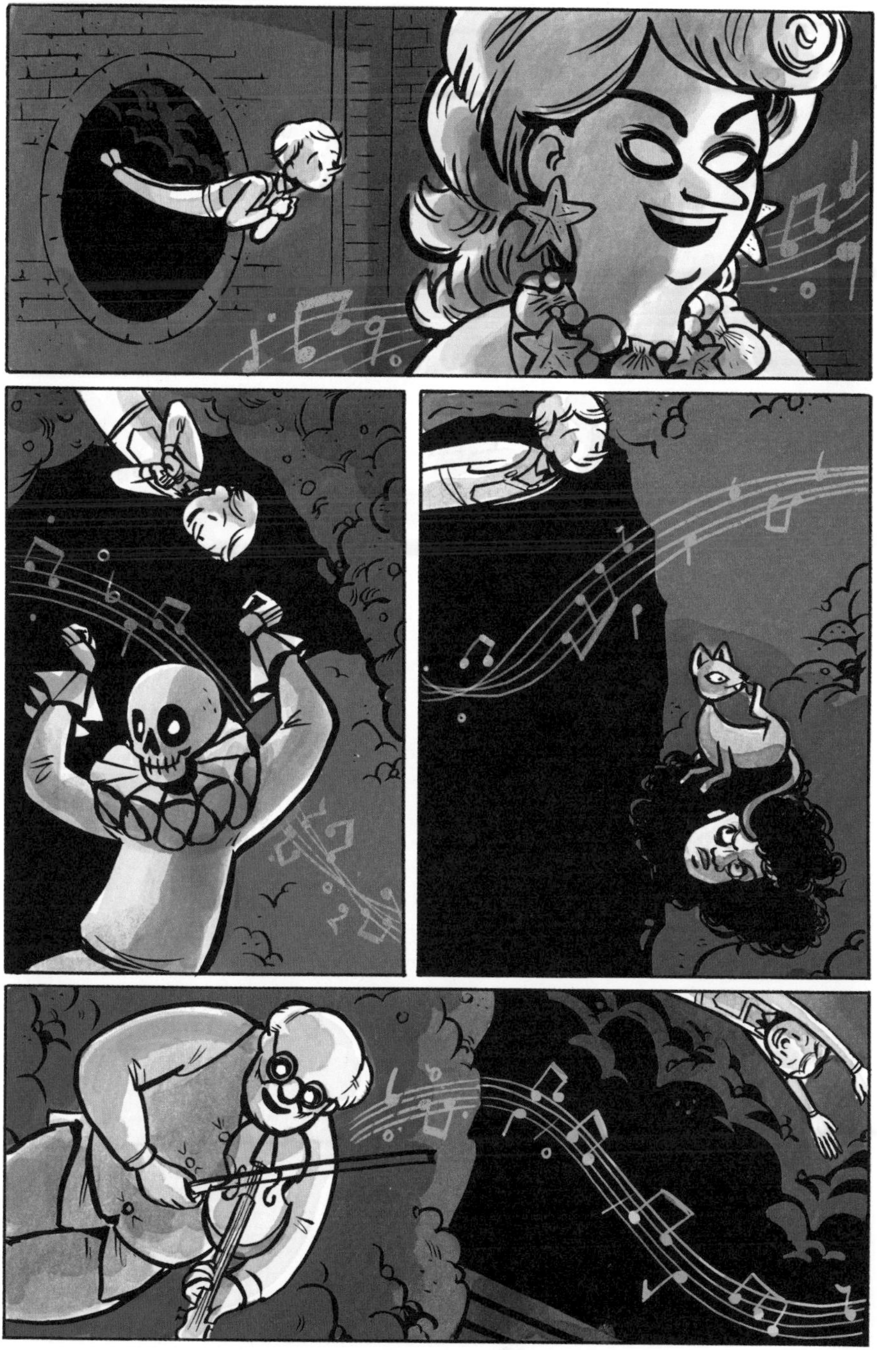

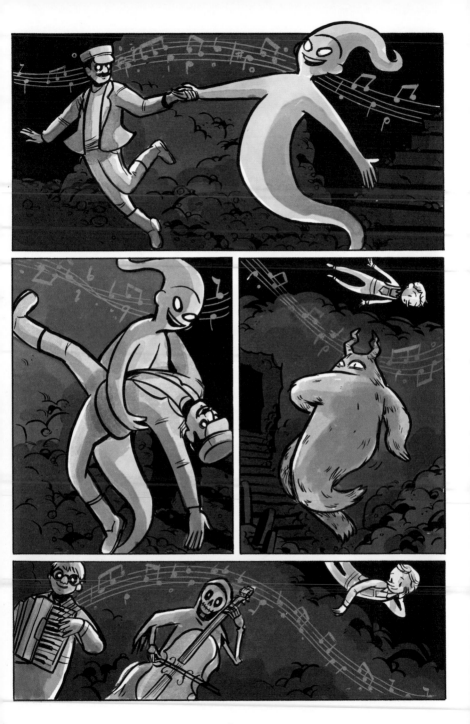

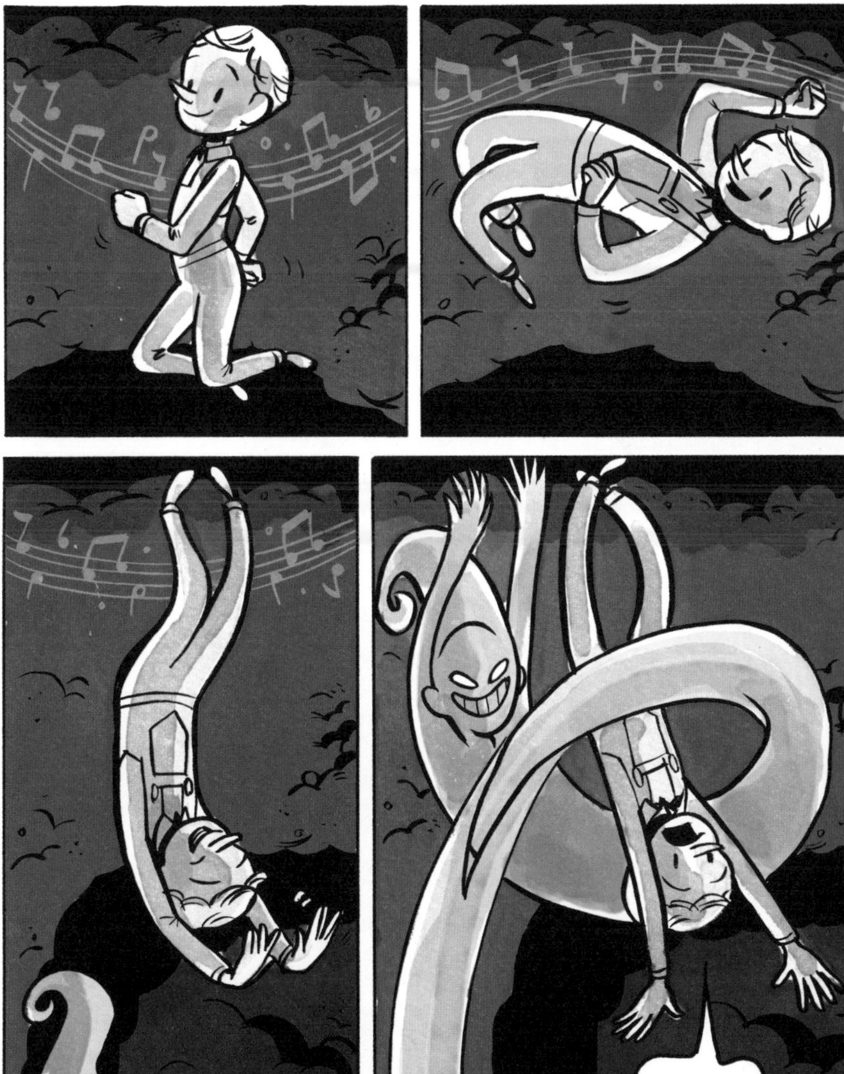
Gasp!

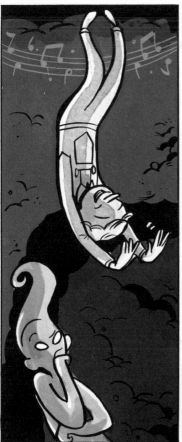

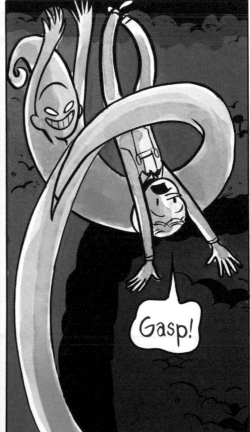

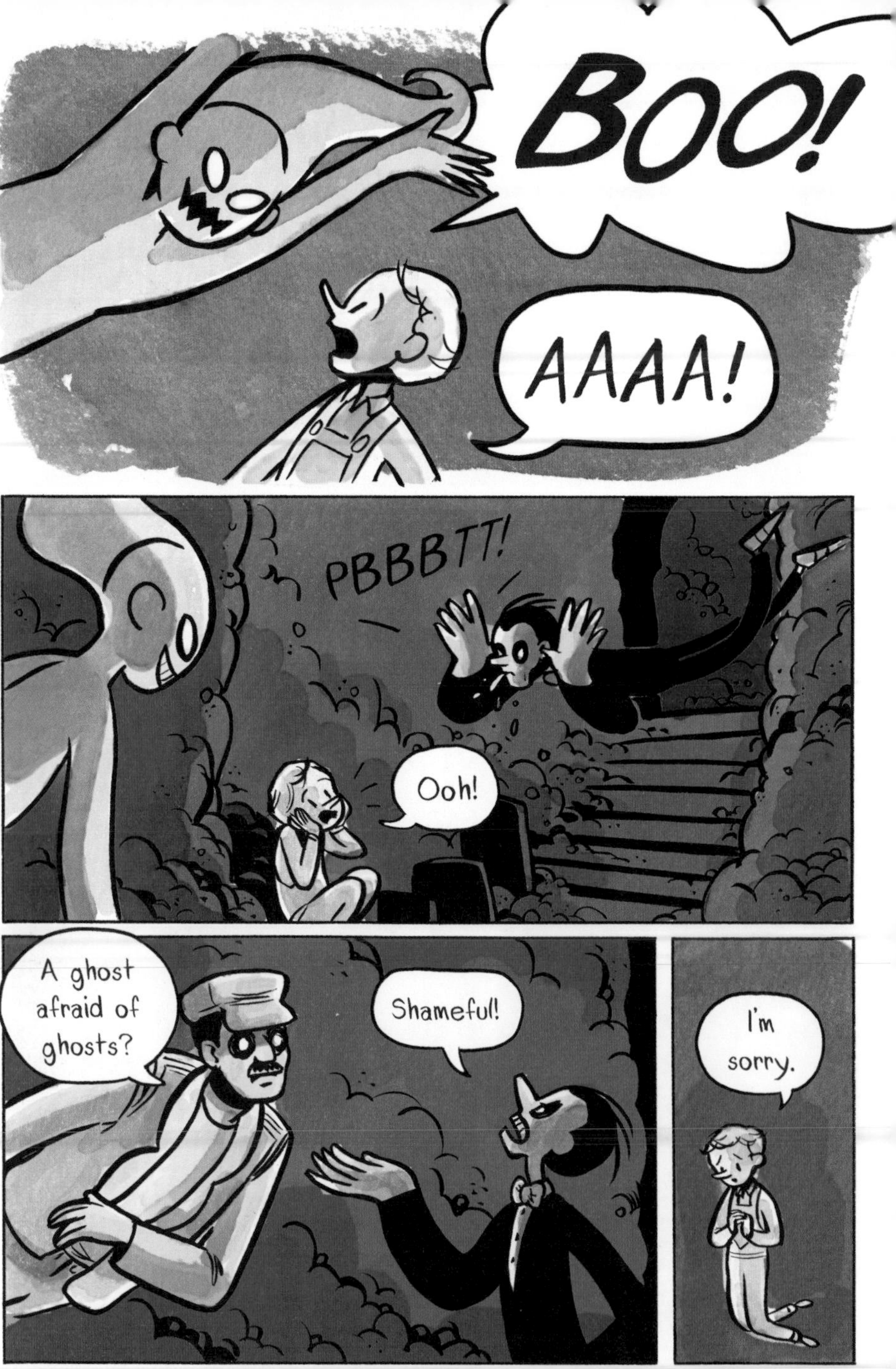
BOO!
AAAA!
PBBBTT!
Ooh!
A ghost afraid of ghosts?
Shameful!
I'm sorry.

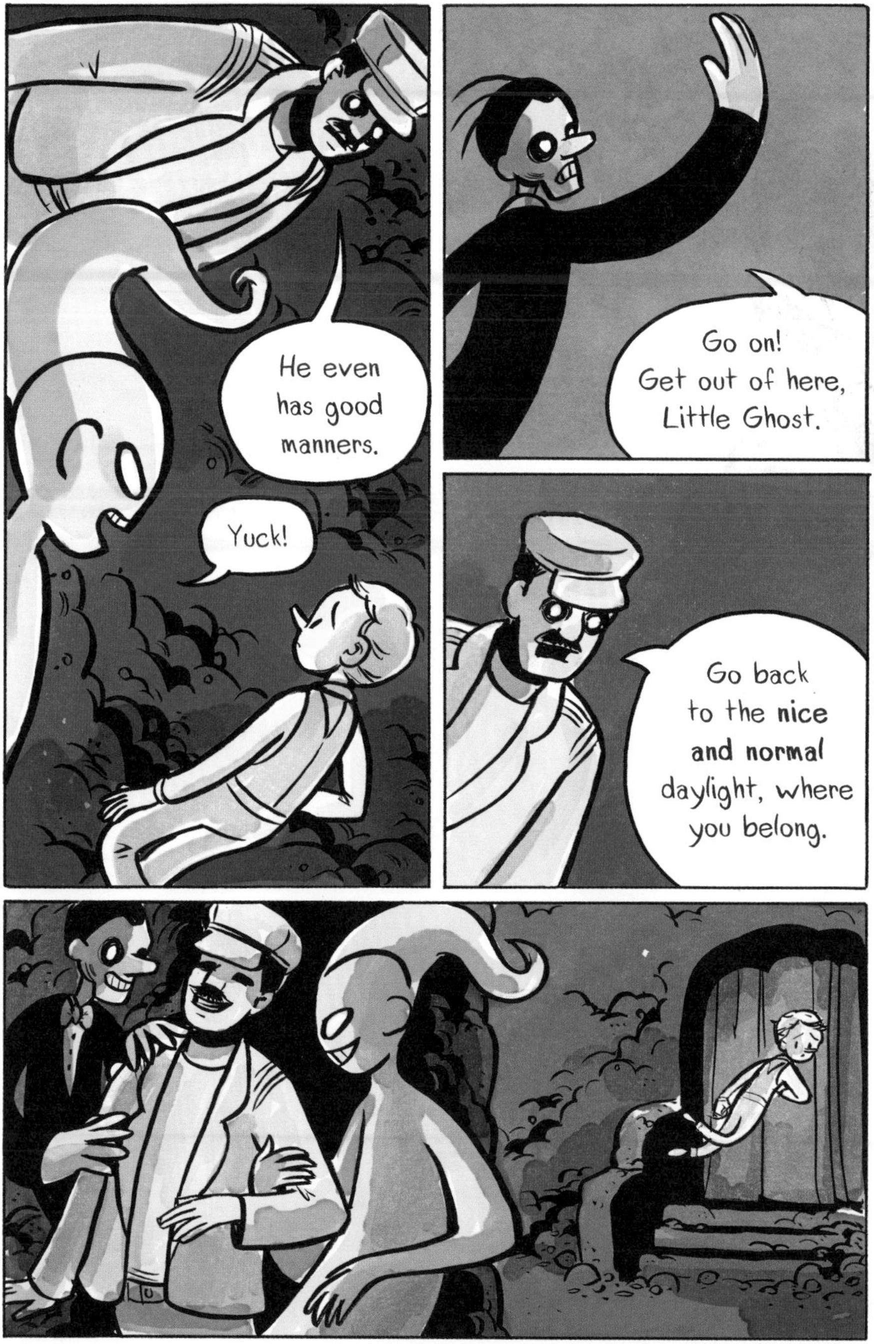
He even has good manners.
Yuck!
Go on! Get out of here, Little Ghost.
Go back to the **nice and normal** daylight, where you belong.

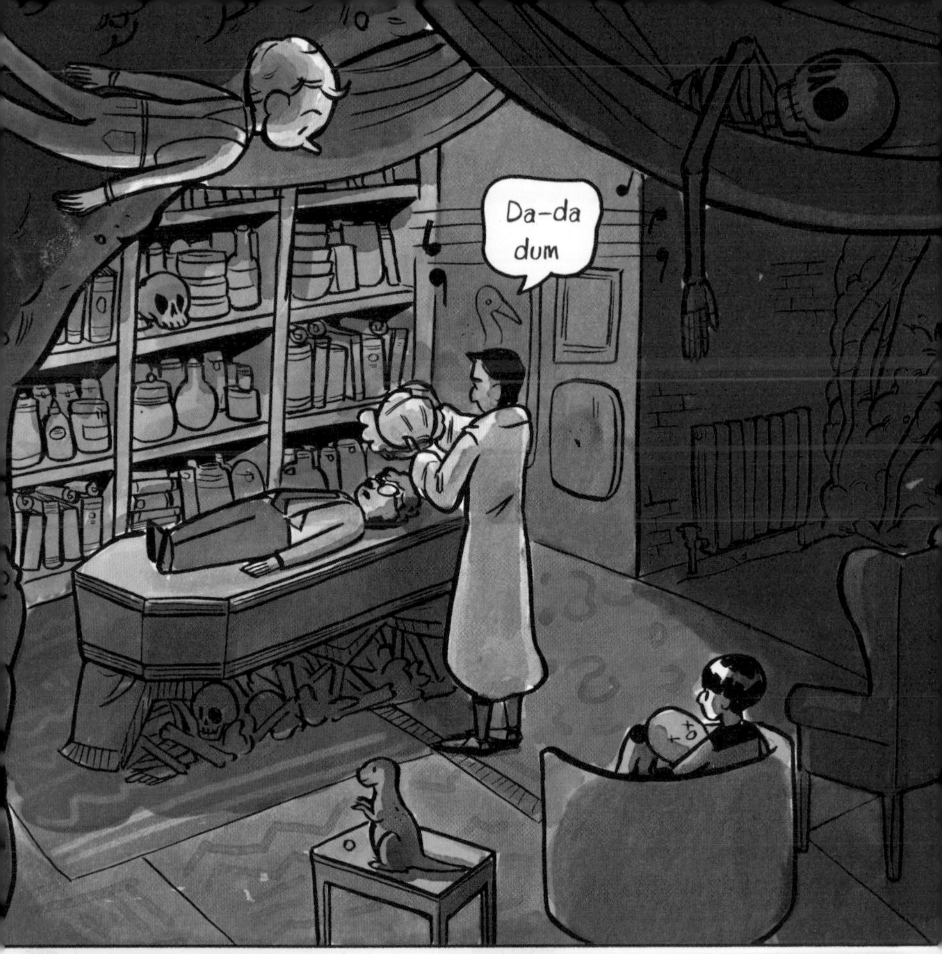
Da-da
dum

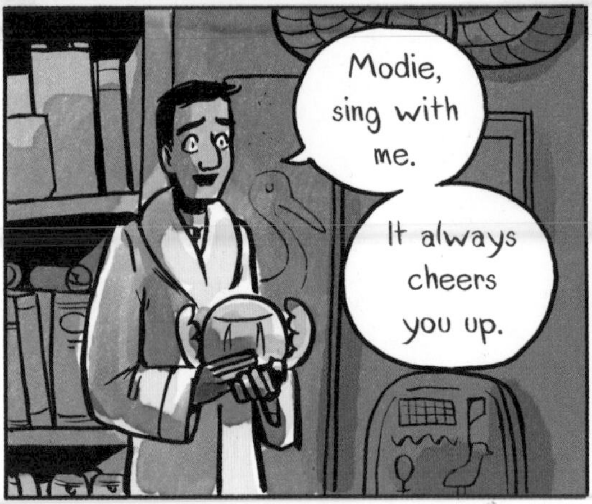
Modie, sing with me.
It always cheers you up.

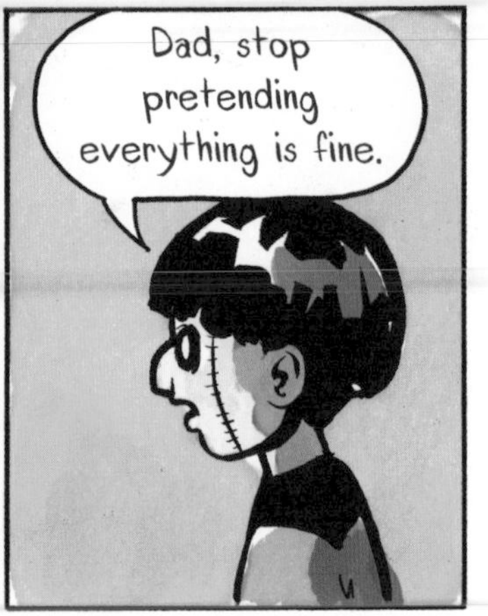
Dad, stop pretending everything is fine.

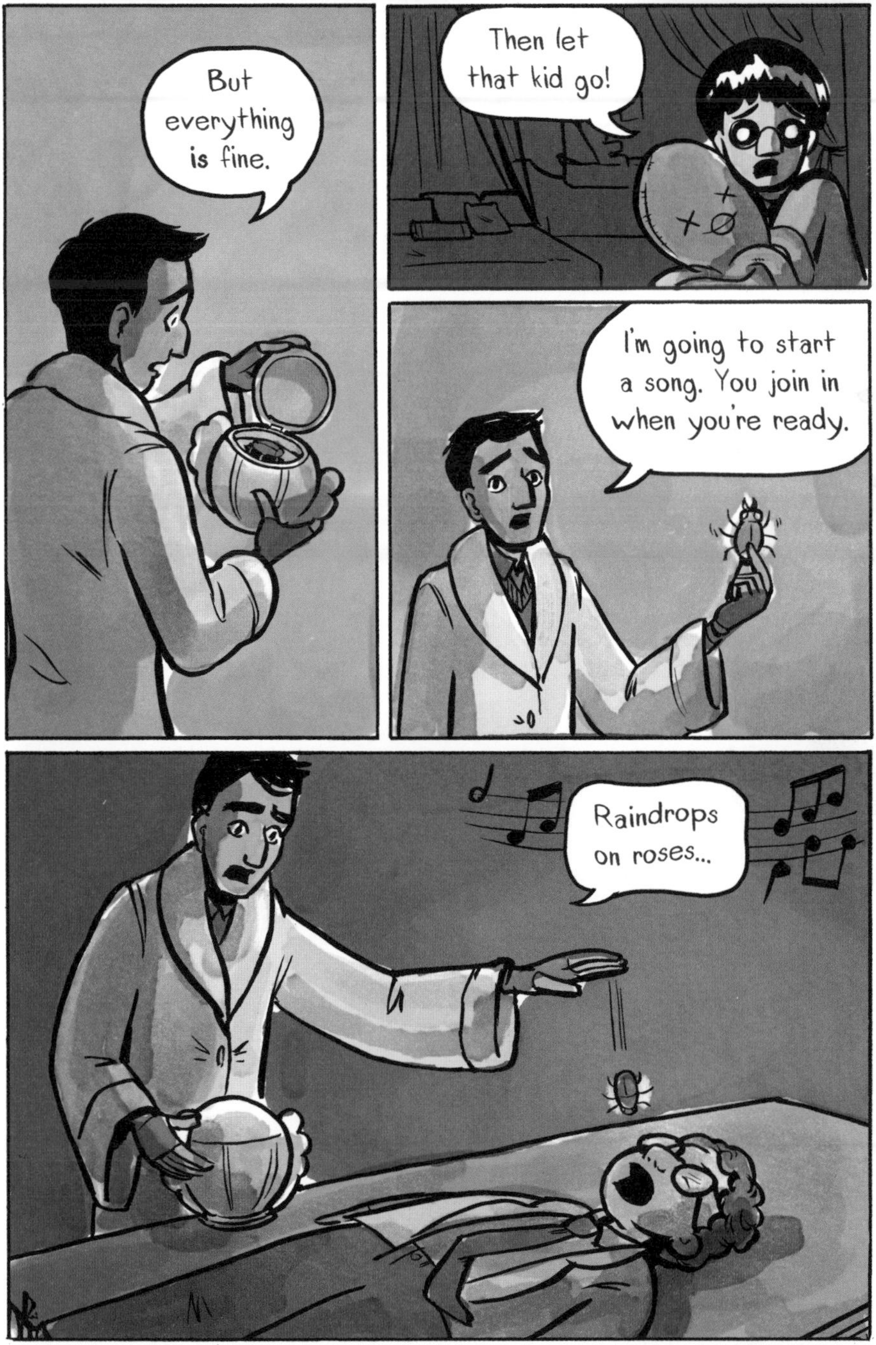
But everything is fine.
Then let that kid go!
I'm going to start a song. You join in when you're ready.
Raindrops on roses...

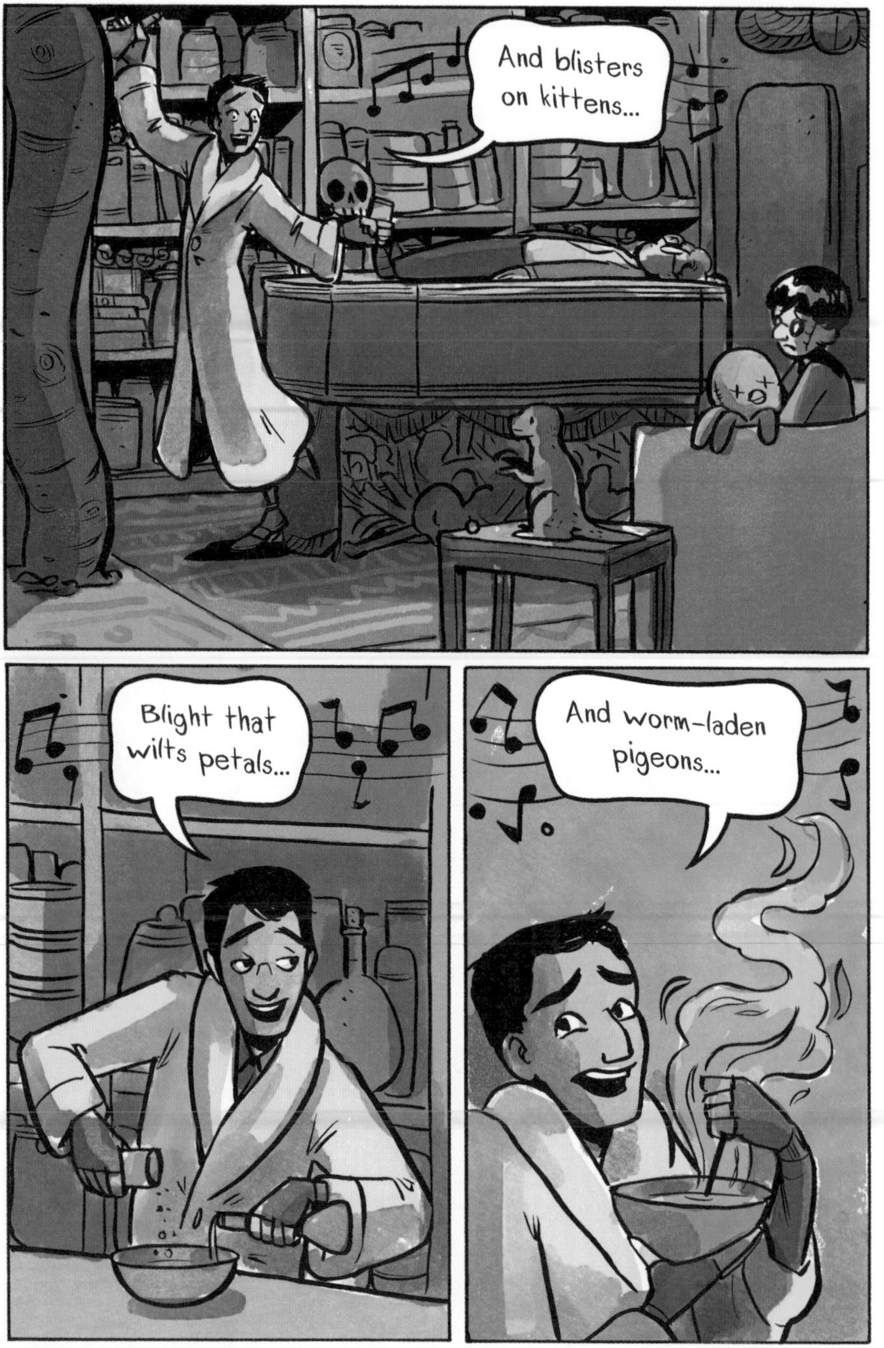
And blisters on kittens...
Blight that wilts petals...
And worm-laden pigeons...

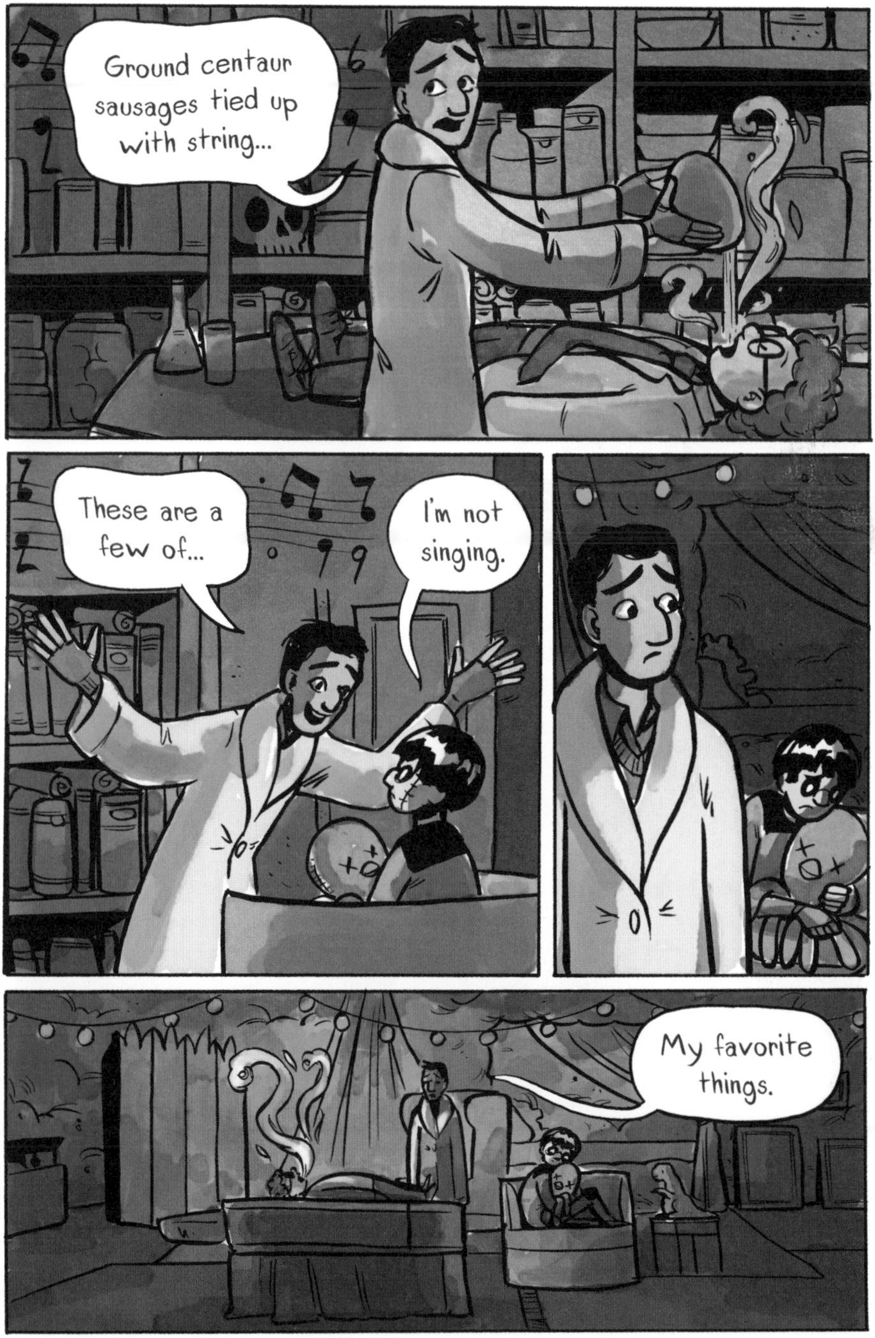
Ground centaur sausages tied up with string...
These are a few of...
I'm not singing.
My favorite things.

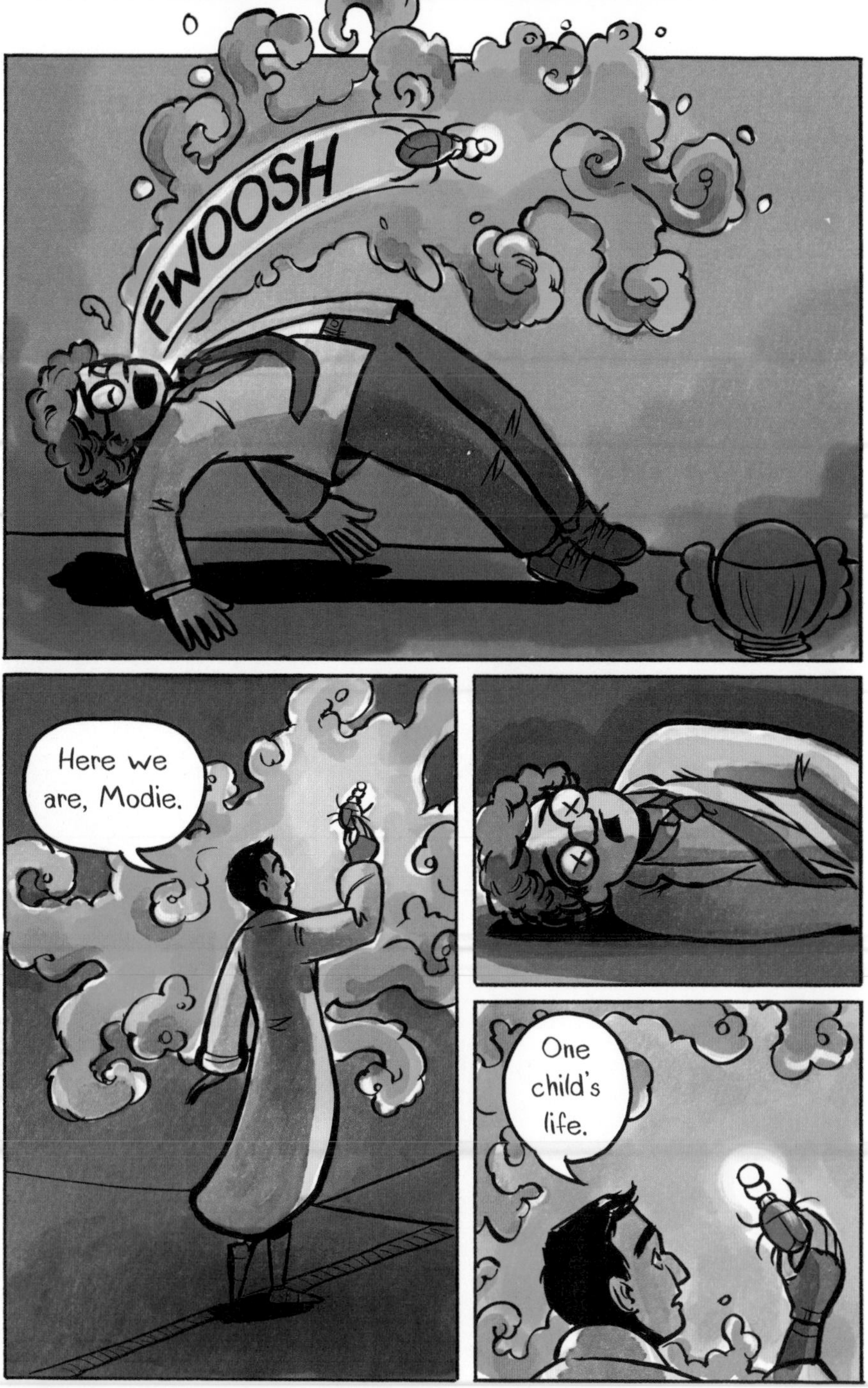
FWOOSH
Here we are, Modie.
One child's life.

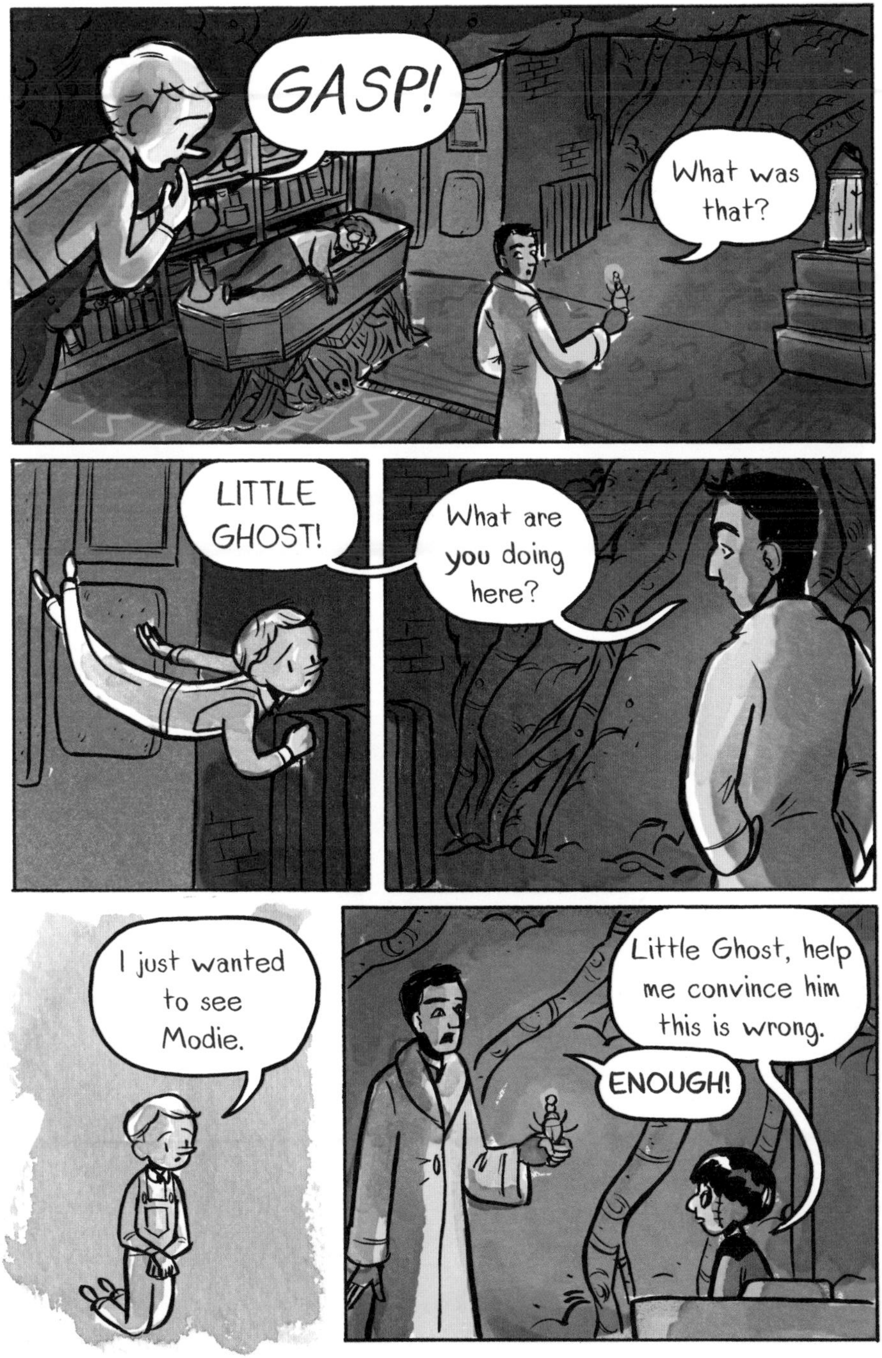
GASP!
What was that?
LITTLE GHOST!
What are you doing here?
I just wanted to see Modie.
Little Ghost, help me convince him this is wrong.
ENOUGH!

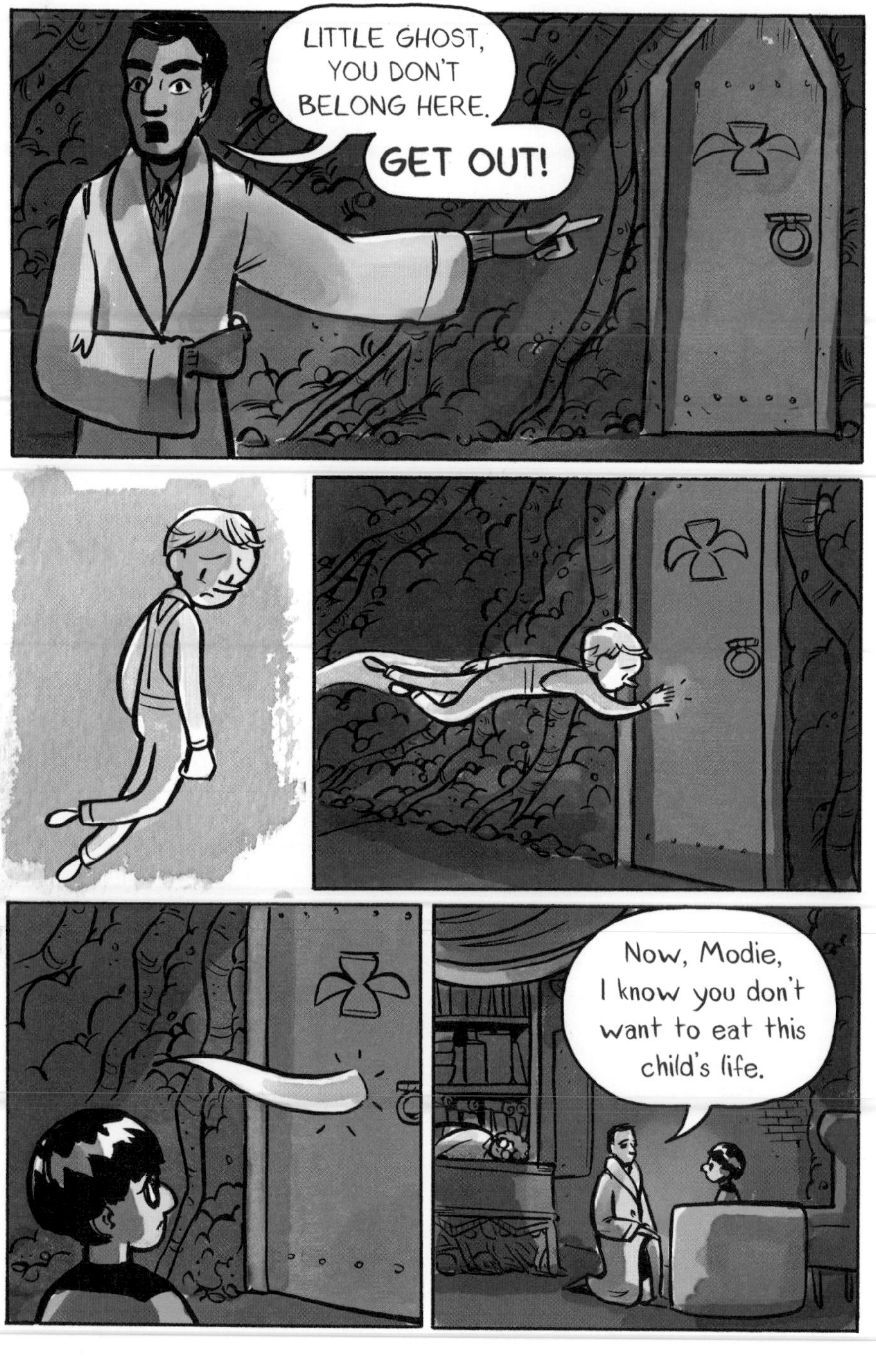
LITTLE GHOST, YOU DON'T BELONG HERE.
GET OUT!
Now, Modie, I know you don't want to eat this child's life.

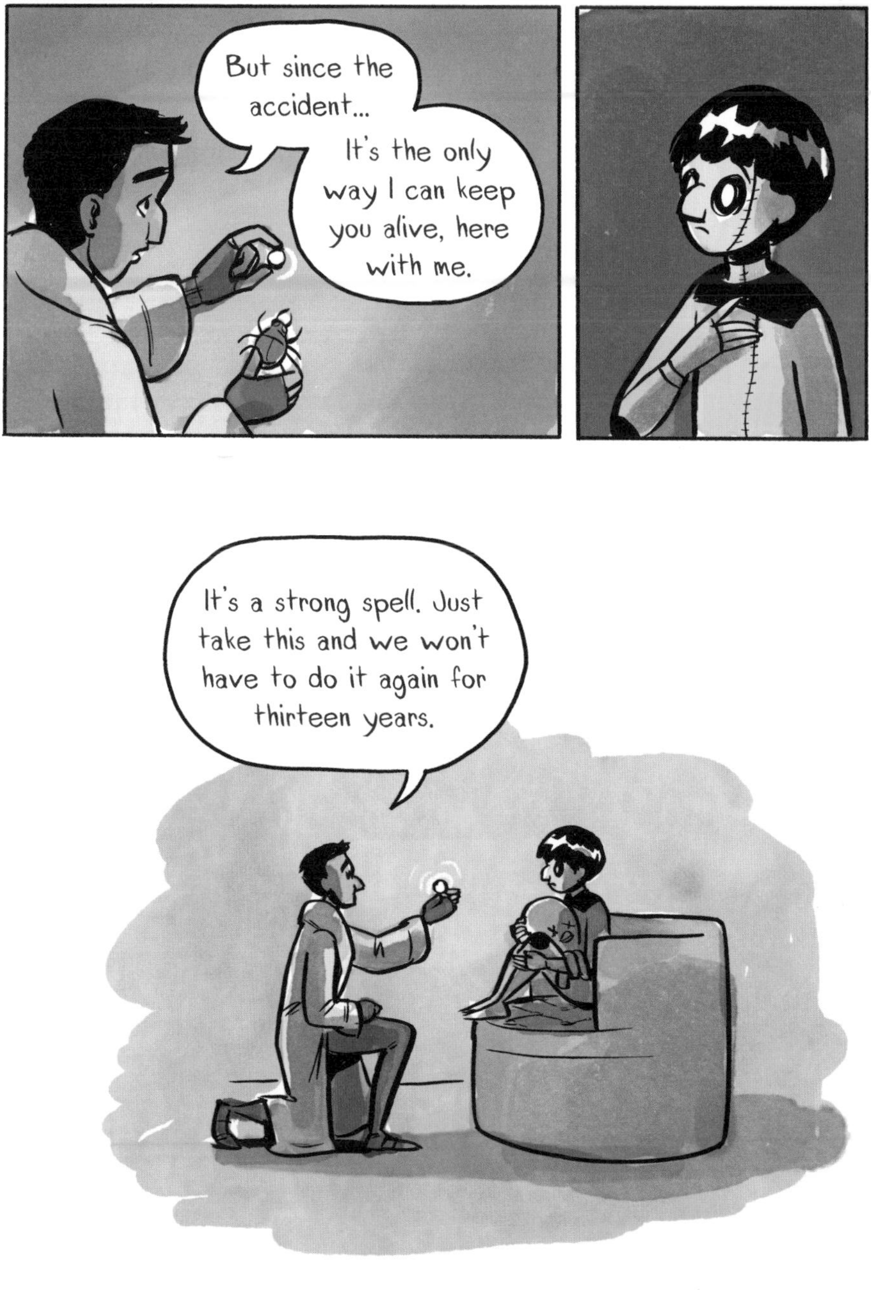
But since the accident...
It's the only way I can keep you alive, here with me.
It's a strong spell. Just take this and we won't have to do it again for thirteen years.

Twelve years and eleven months later . . .

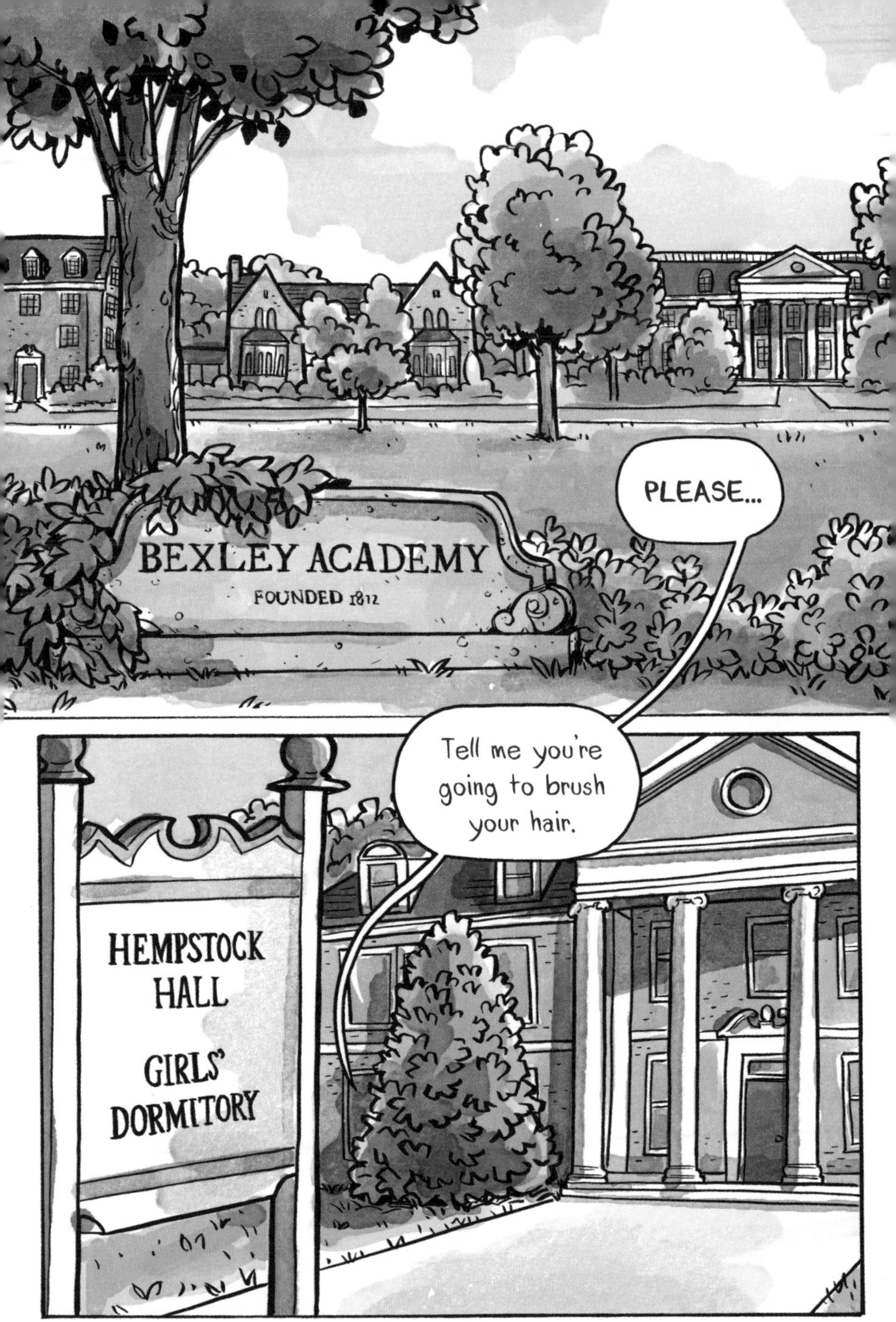
BEXLEY ACADEMY
FOUNDED 1812
PLEASE...
Tell me you're going to brush your hair.
HEMPSTOCK HALL
GIRLS' DORMITORY

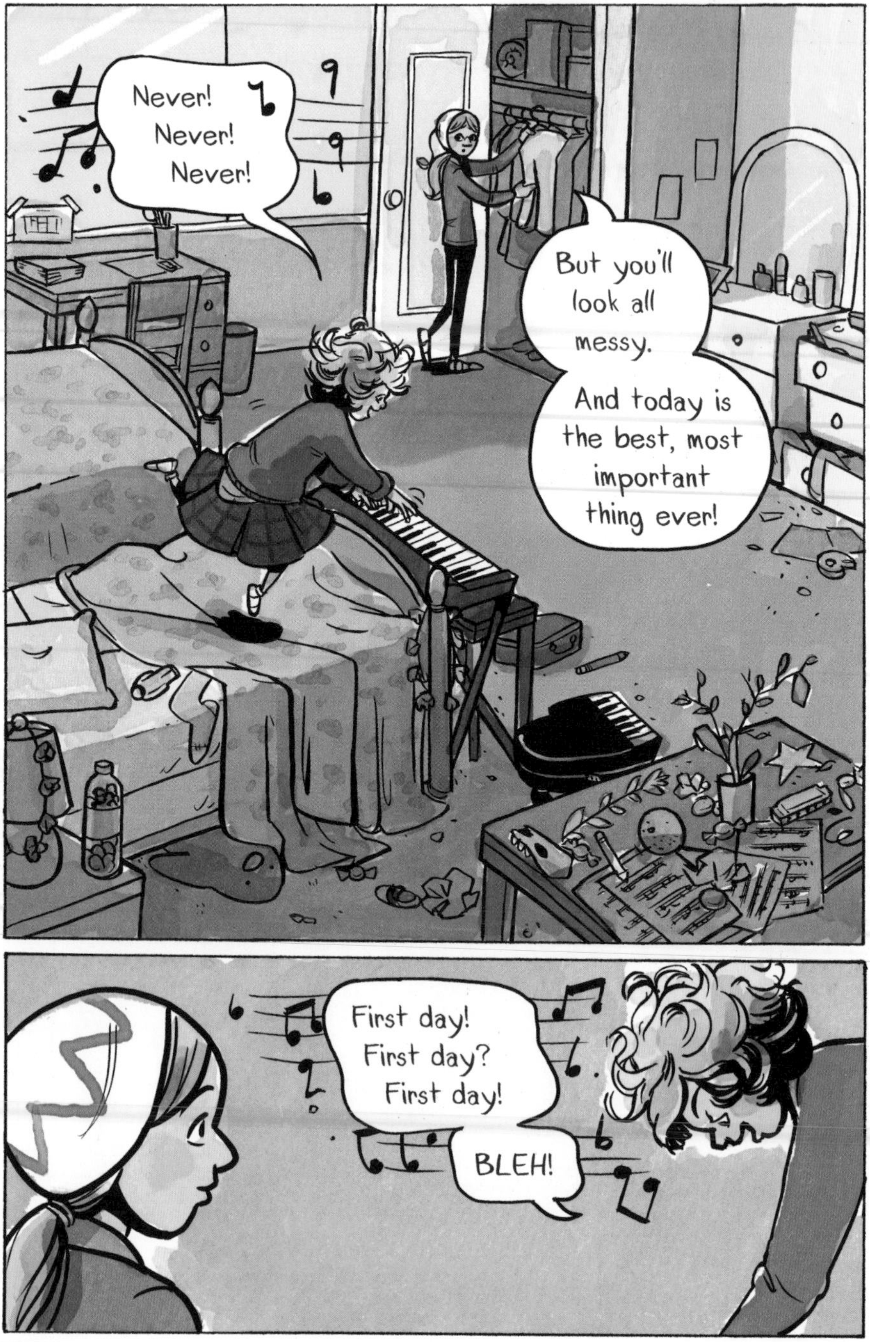
Never! Never! Never!
But you'll look all messy.
And today is the best, most important thing ever!
First day! First day? First day!
BLEH!

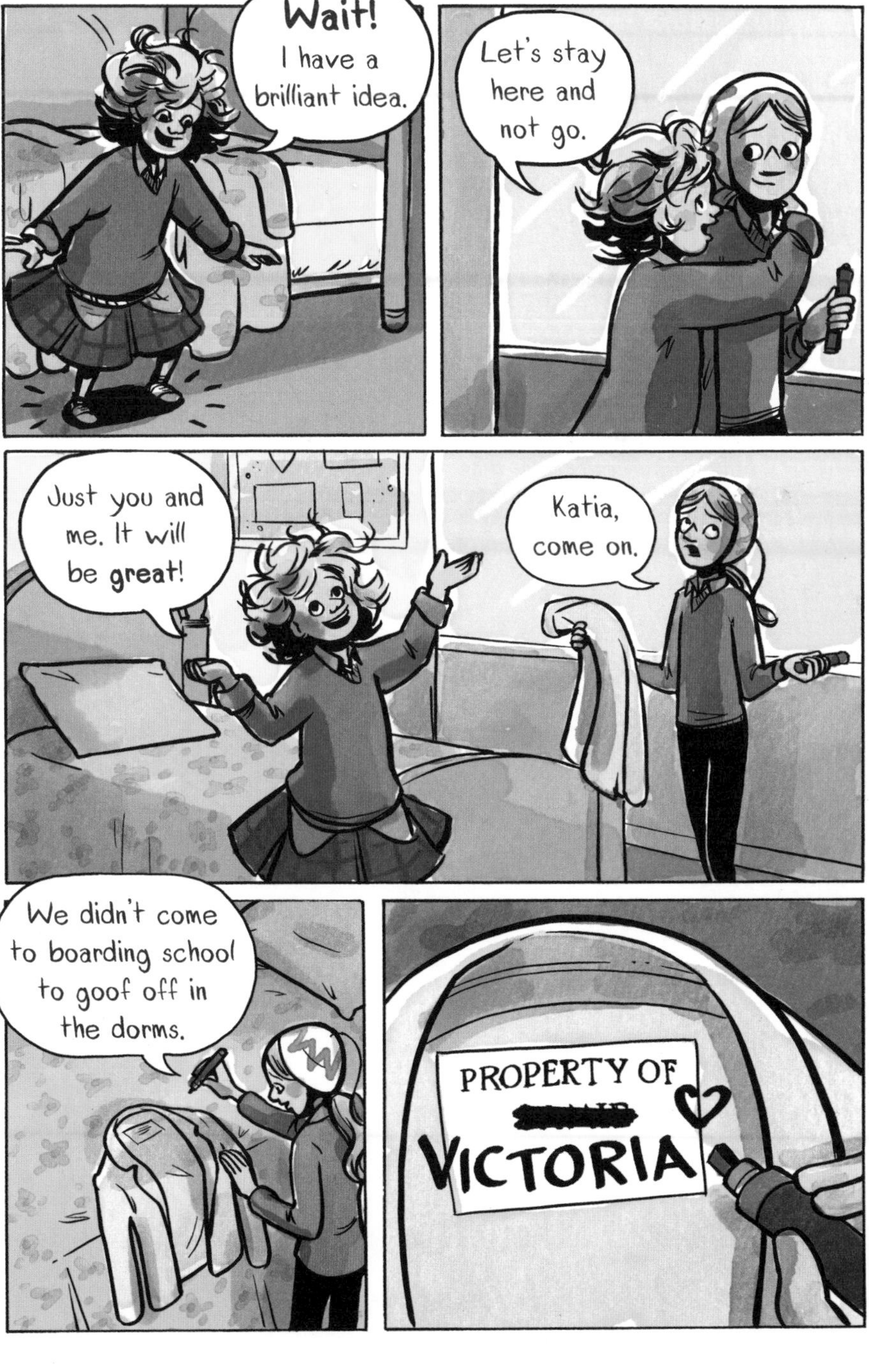
Wait! I have a brilliant idea.
Let's stay here and not go.
Just you and me. It will be **great**!
Katia, come on.
We didn't come to boarding school to goof off in the dorms.
PROPERTY OF
[redacted]
VICTORIA

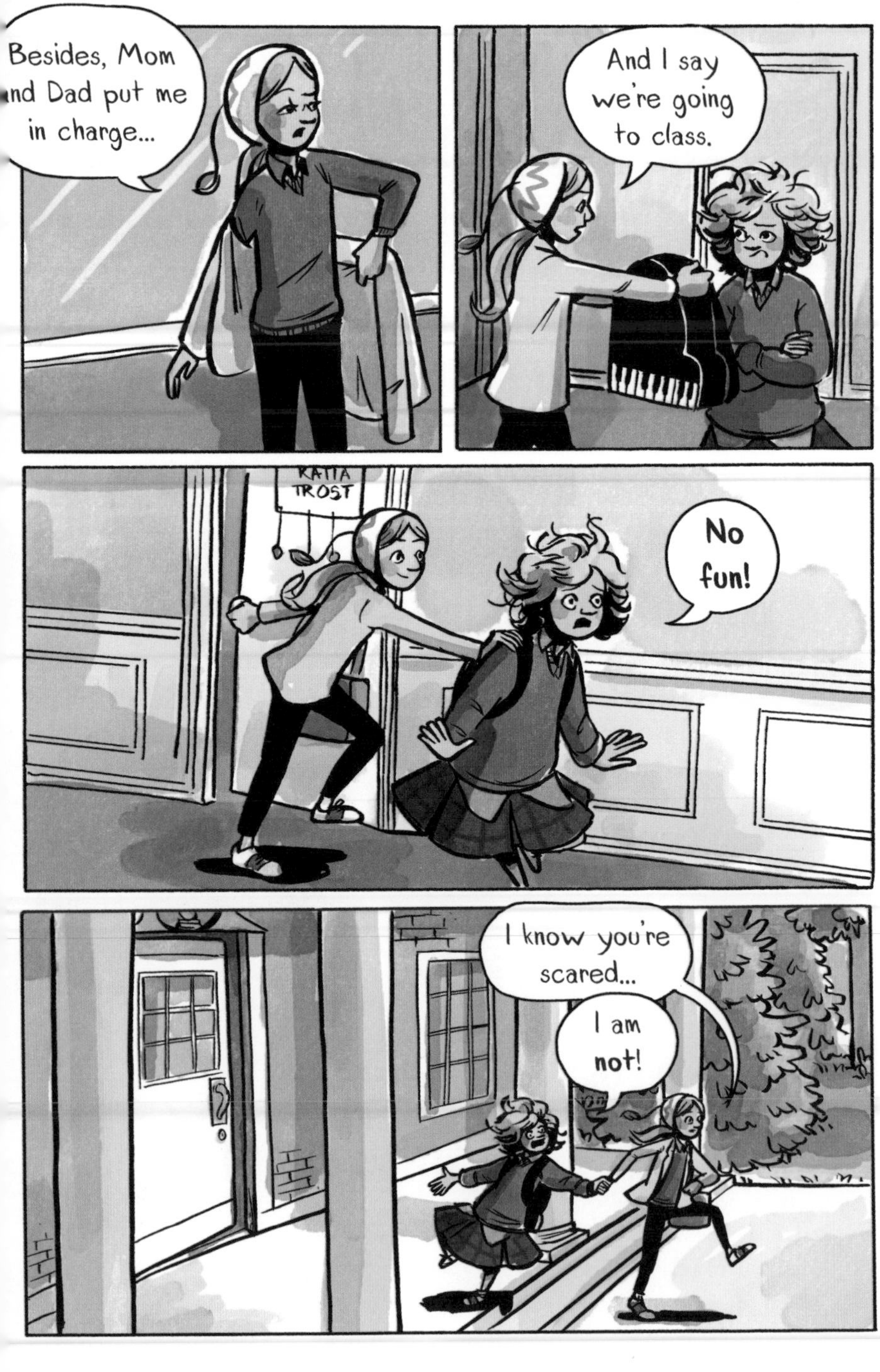
Besides, Mom and Dad put me in charge...
And I say we're going to class.
KATIA TROST
No fun!
I know you're scared...
I am not!

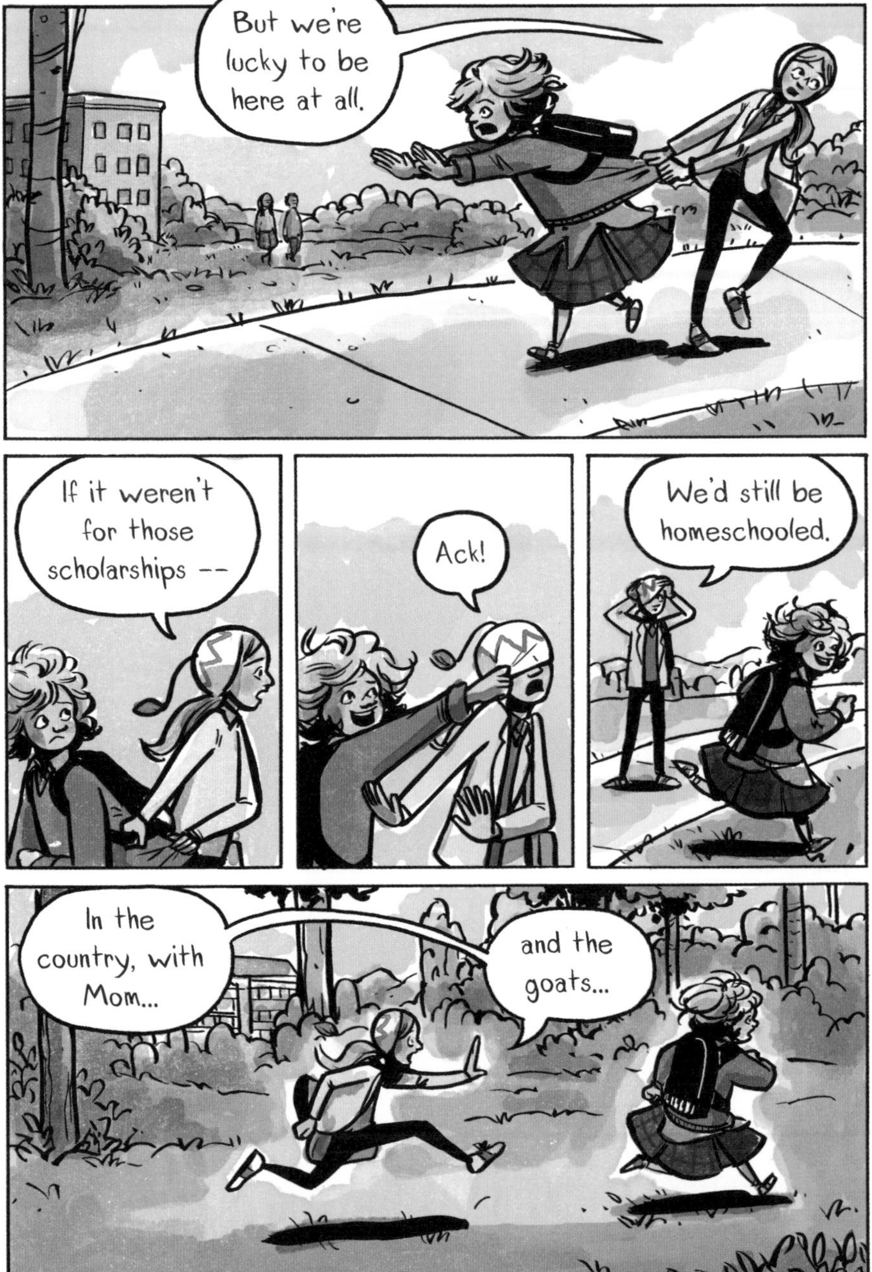
But we're lucky to be here at all.
If it weren't for those scholarships --
Ack!
We'd still be homeschooled.
In the country, with Mom...
and the goats...

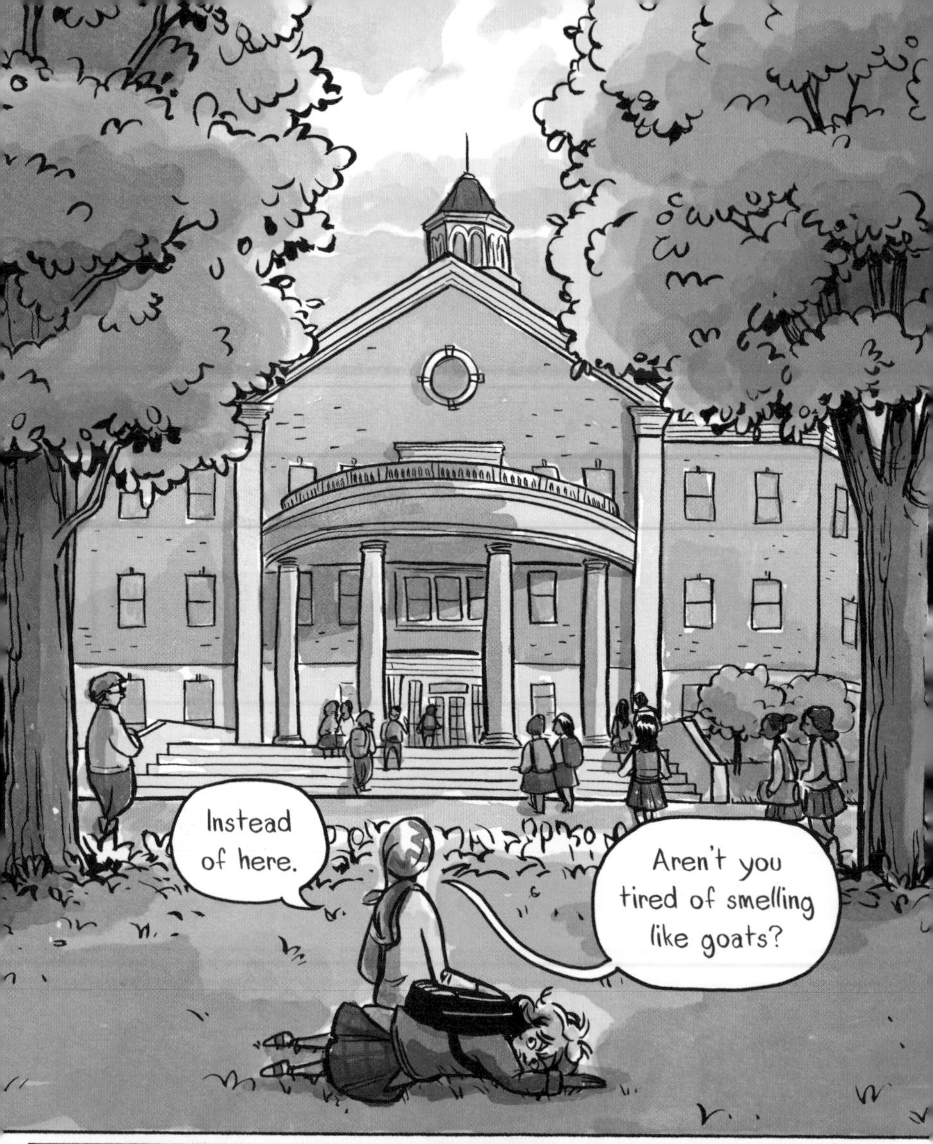
Instead of here.
Aren't you tired of smelling like goats?

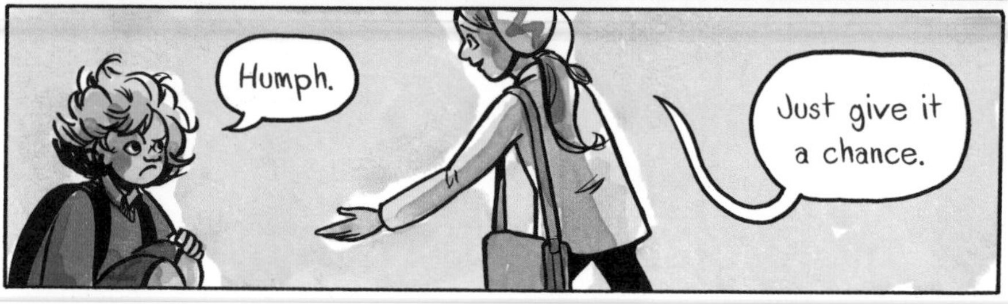
Humph.
Just give it a chance.

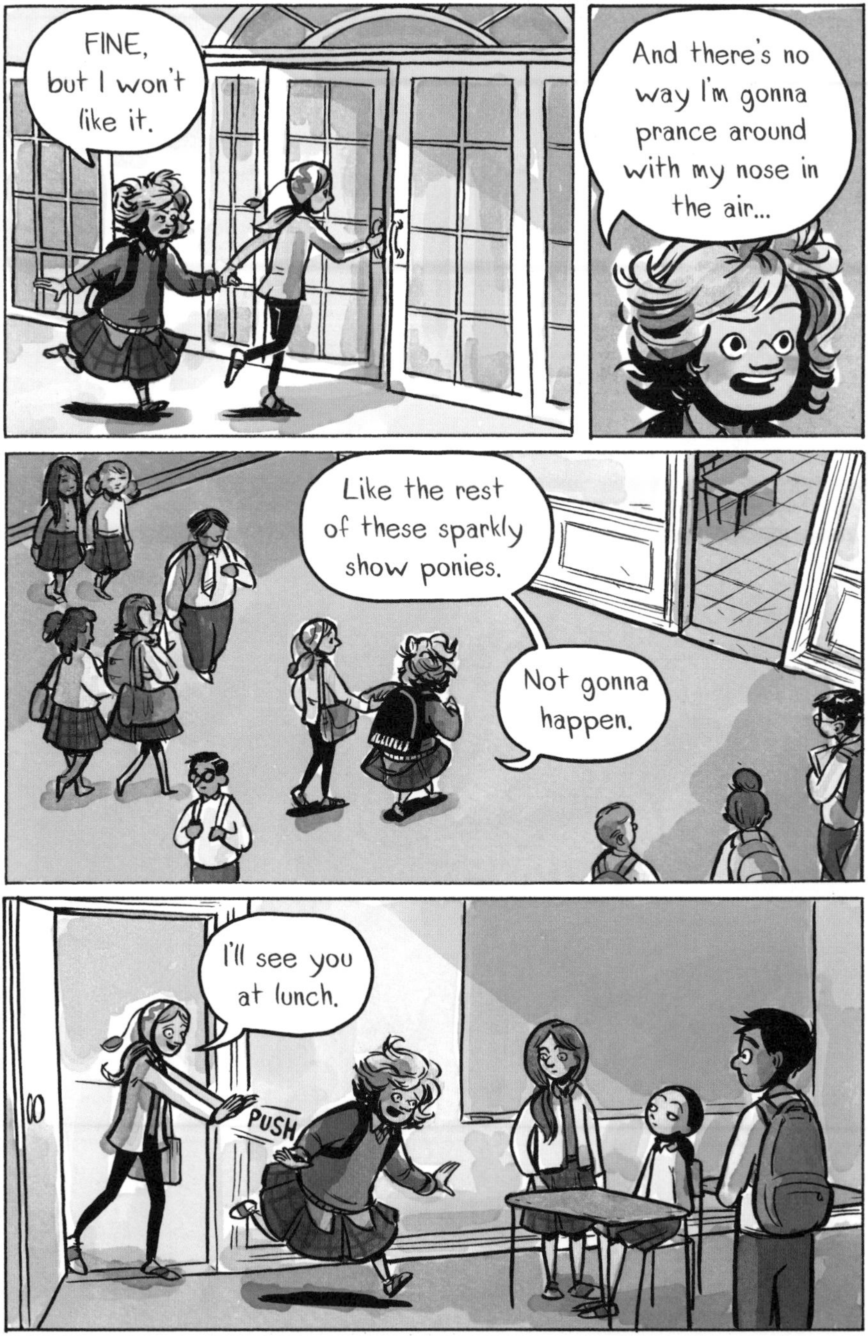
FINE, but I won't like it.
And there's no way I'm gonna prance around with my nose in the air...
Like the rest of these sparkly show ponies.
Not gonna happen.
I'll see you at lunch.
PUSH

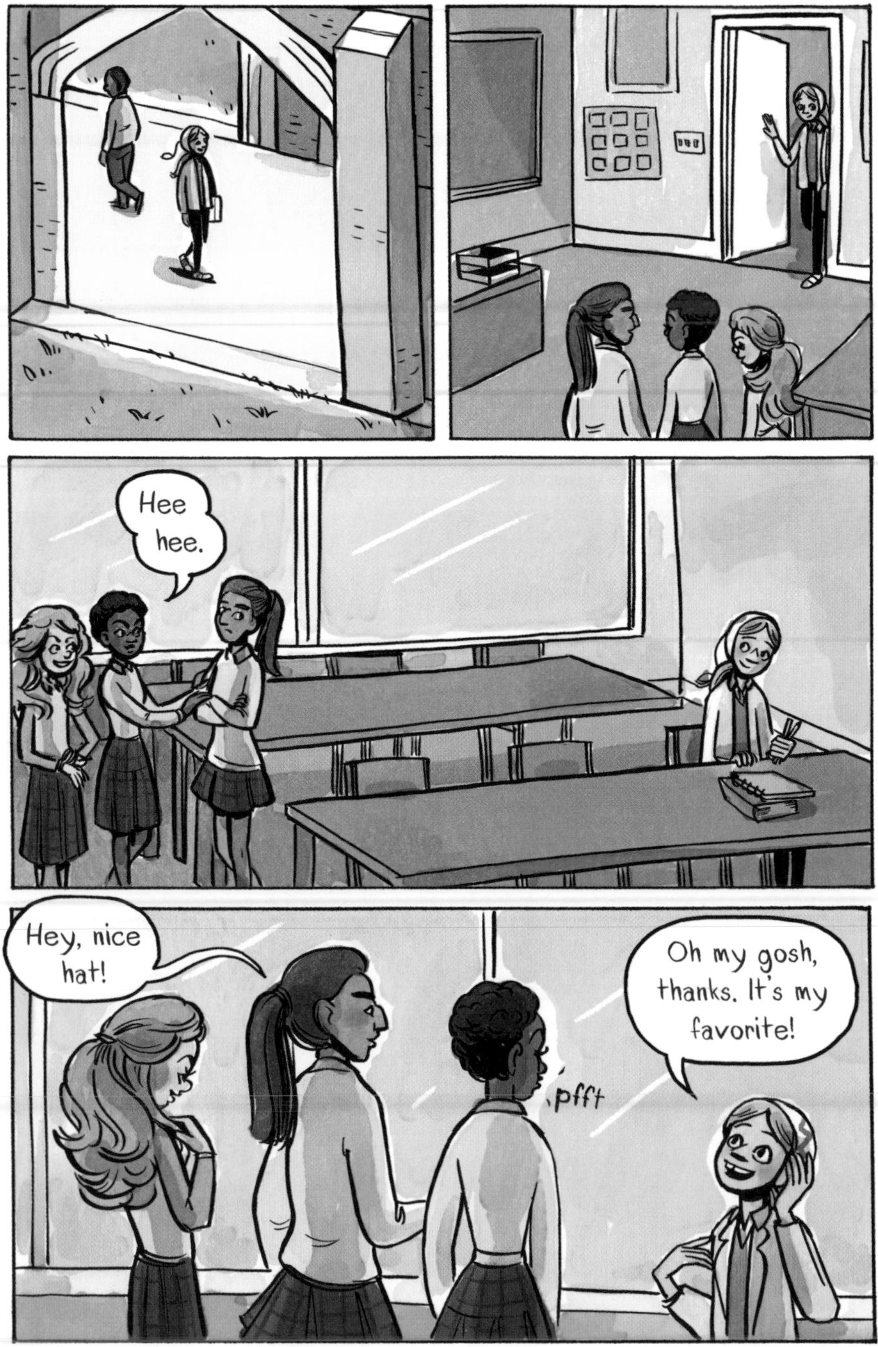
Hee hee.
Hey, nice hat!
pfft
Oh my gosh, thanks. It's my favorite!

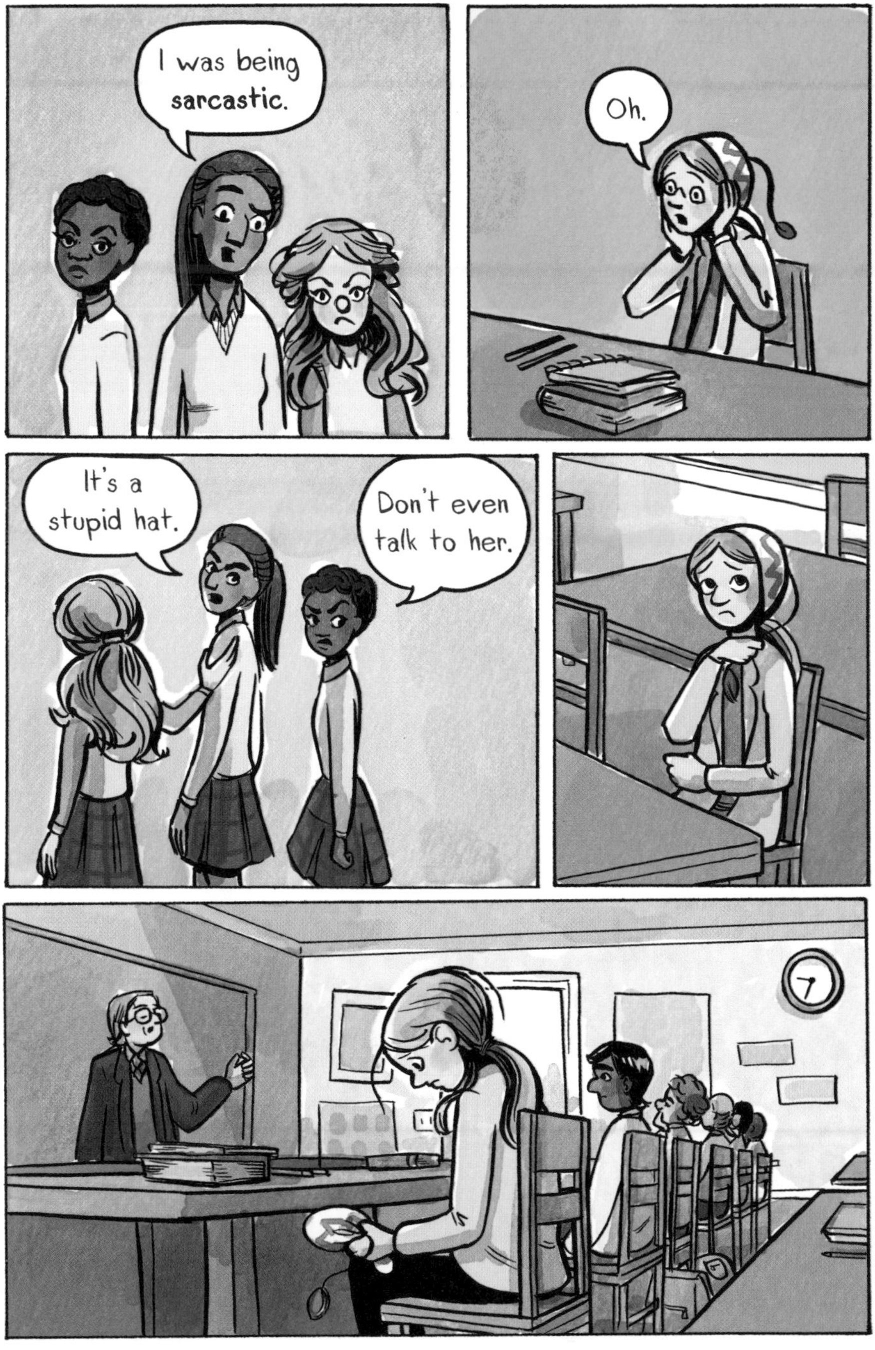
I was being **sarcastic**.
Oh.
It's a stupid hat.
Don't even talk to her.

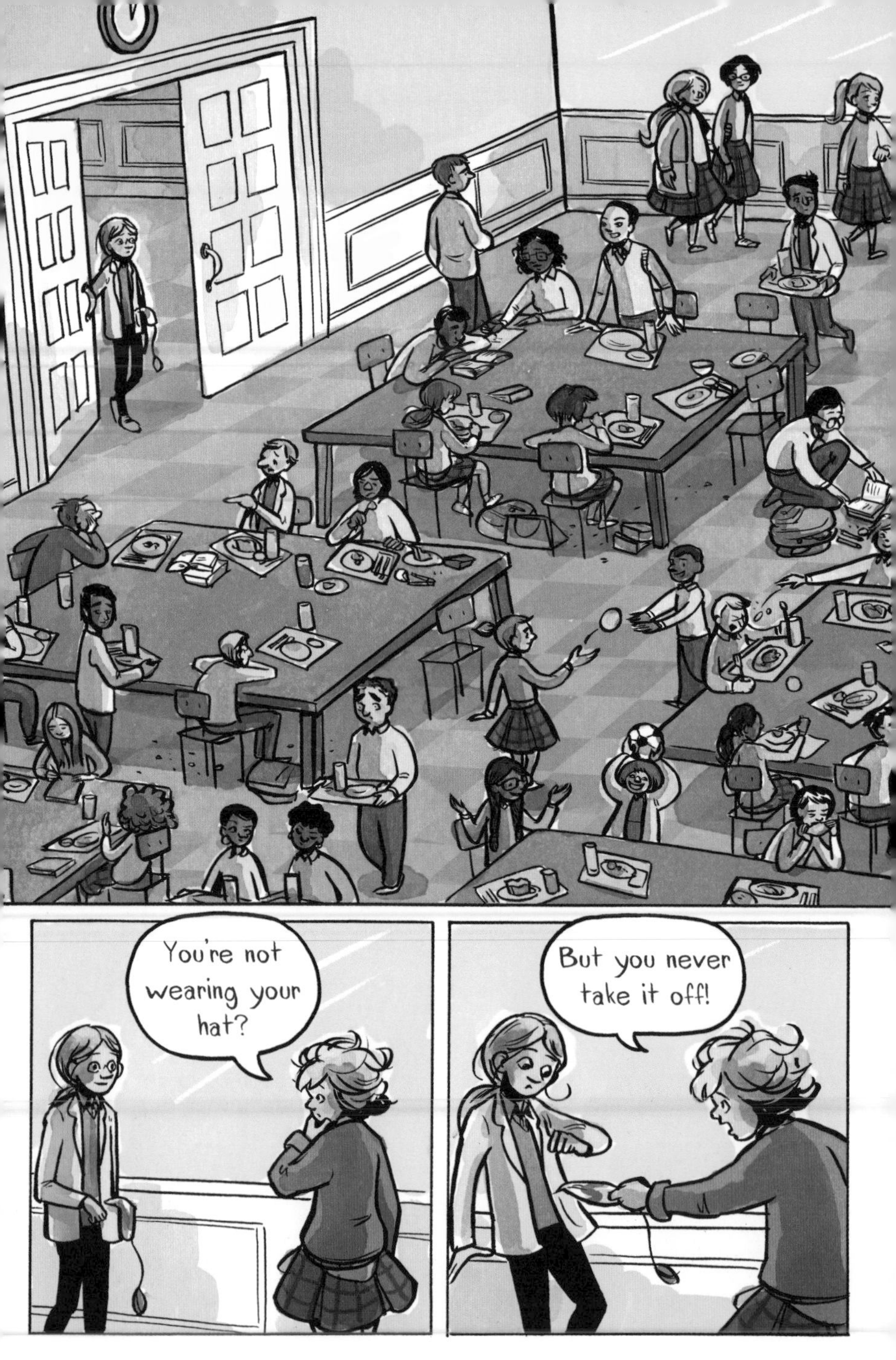
You're not wearing your hat?
But you never take it off!

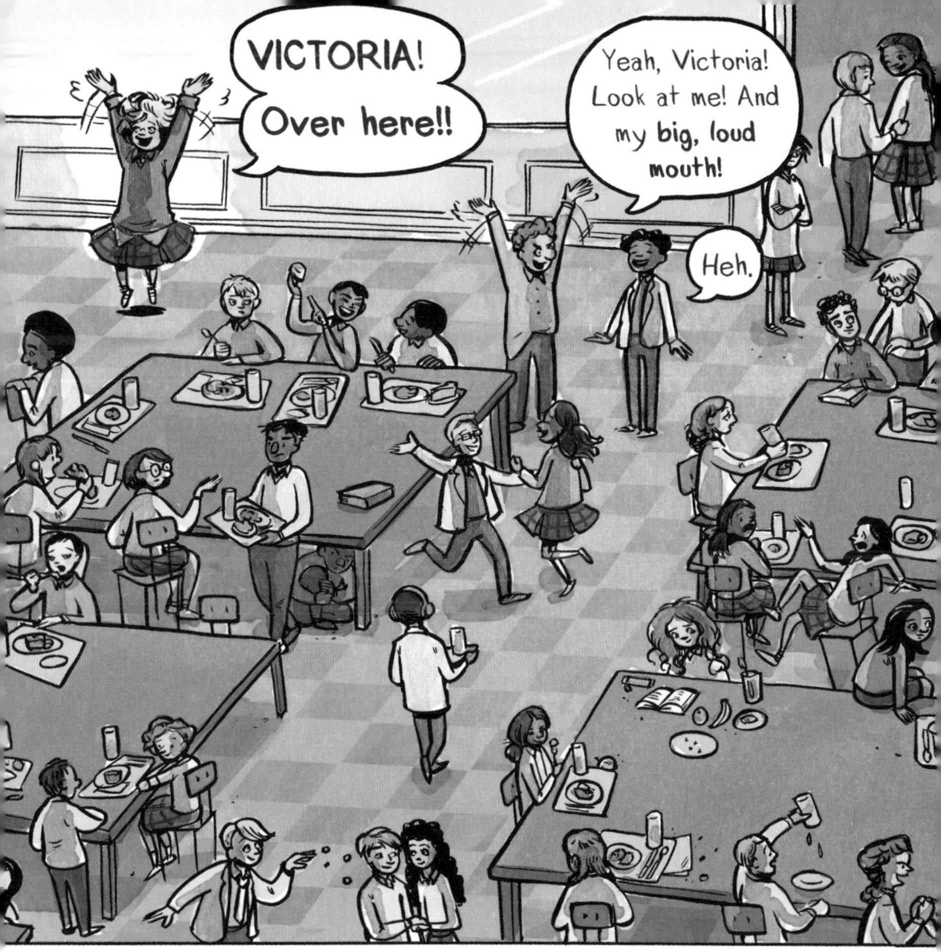
VICTORIA!
Over here!!
Yeah, Victoria! Look at me! And my big, loud mouth!
Heh.

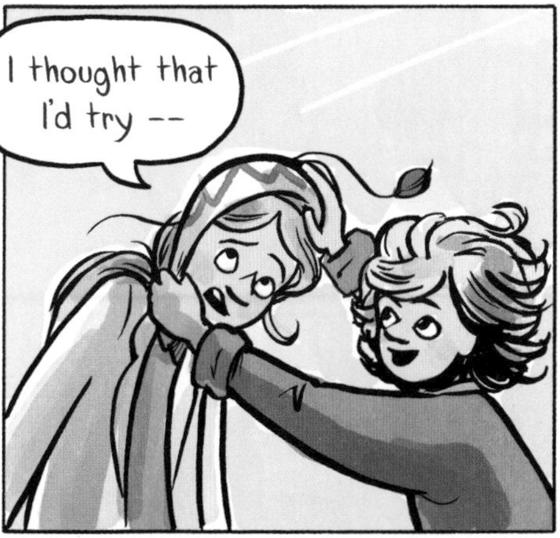
I thought that I'd try --

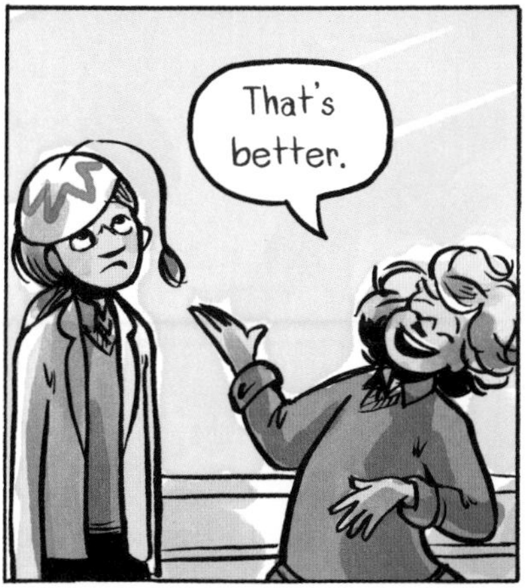
That's better.

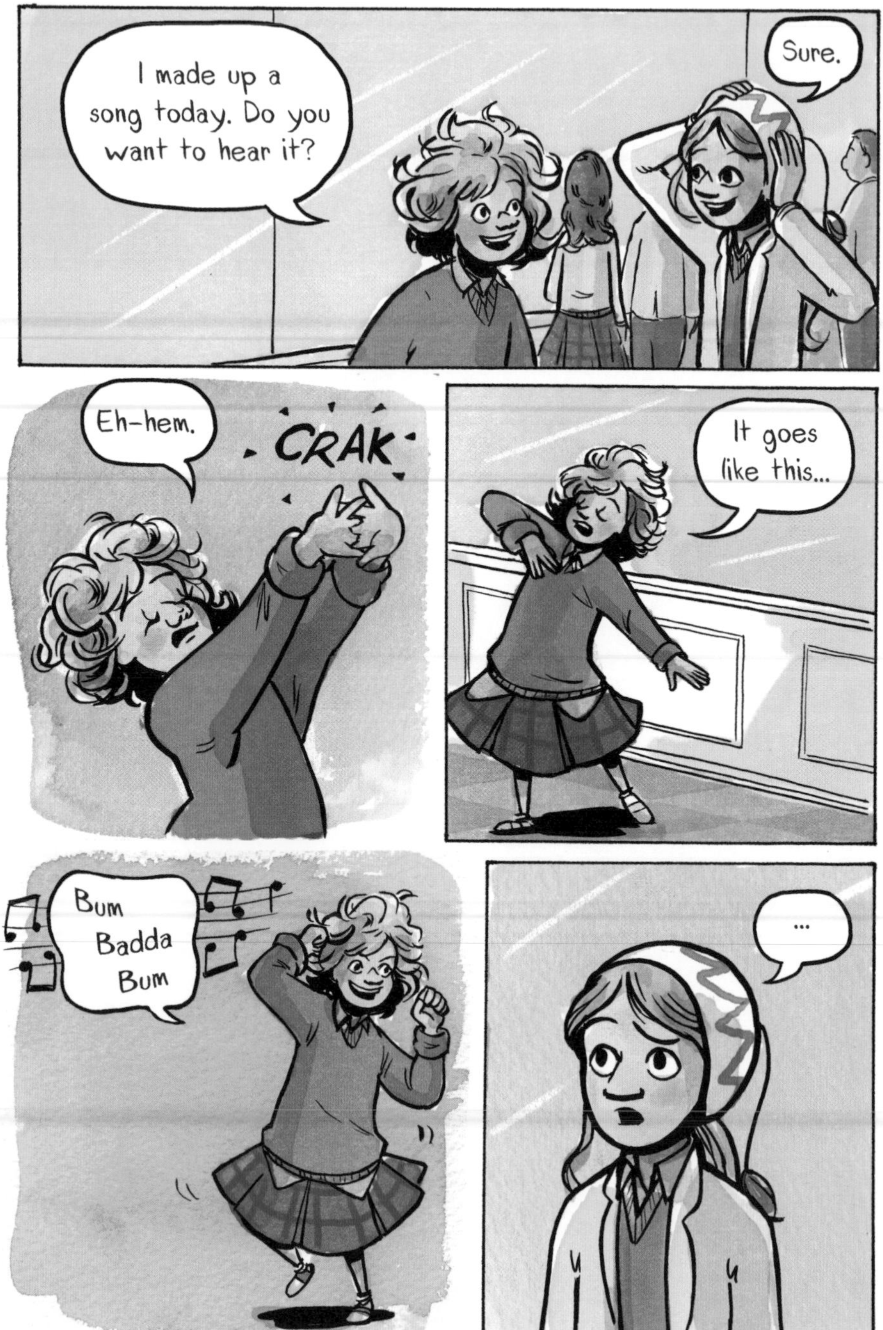
I made up a song today. Do you want to hear it?
Sure.
Eh-hem.
CRAK
It goes like this...
Bum Badda Bum
...

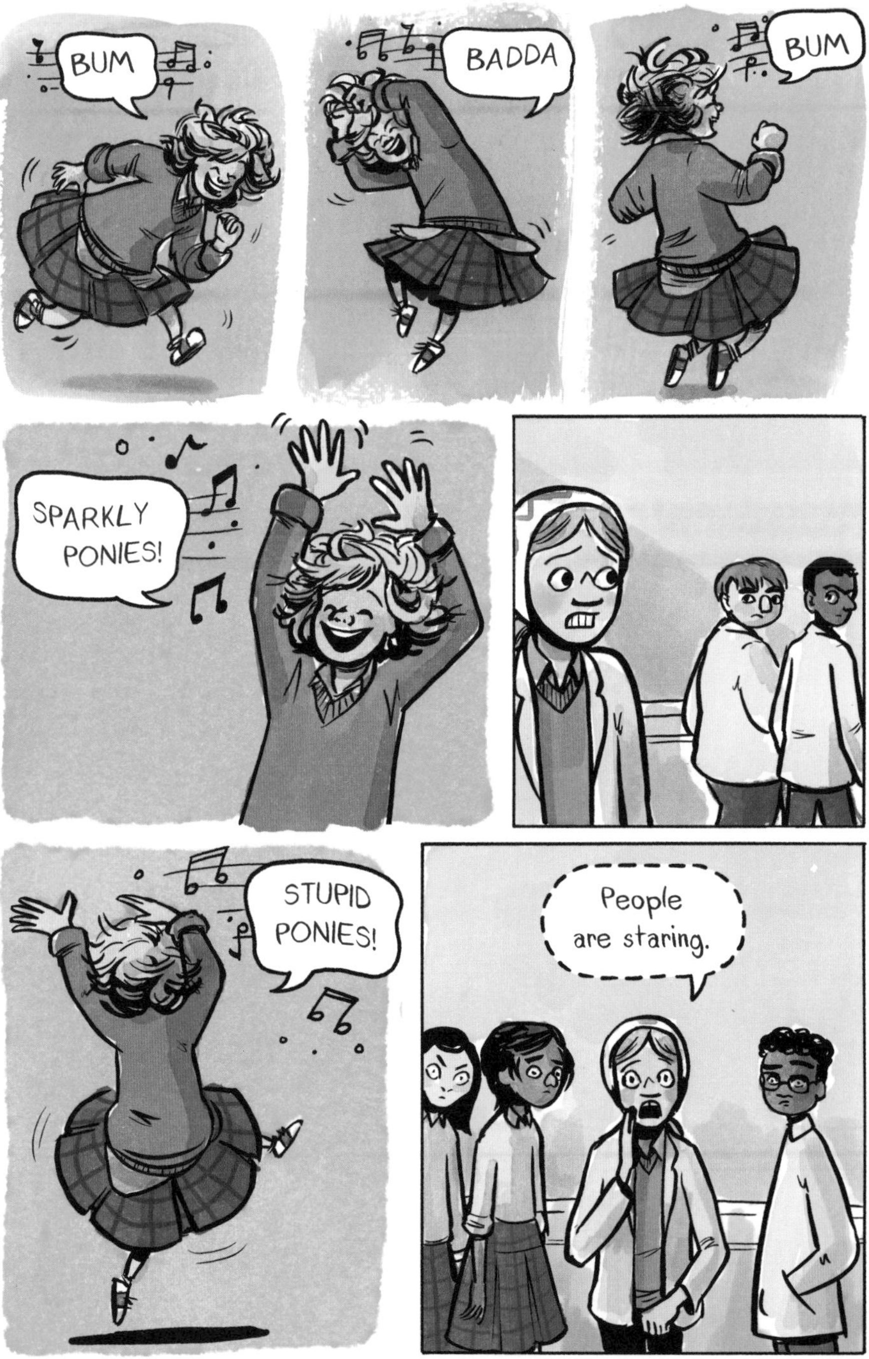
BUM
BADDA
BUM
SPARKLY PONIES!
STUPID PONIES!
People are staring.

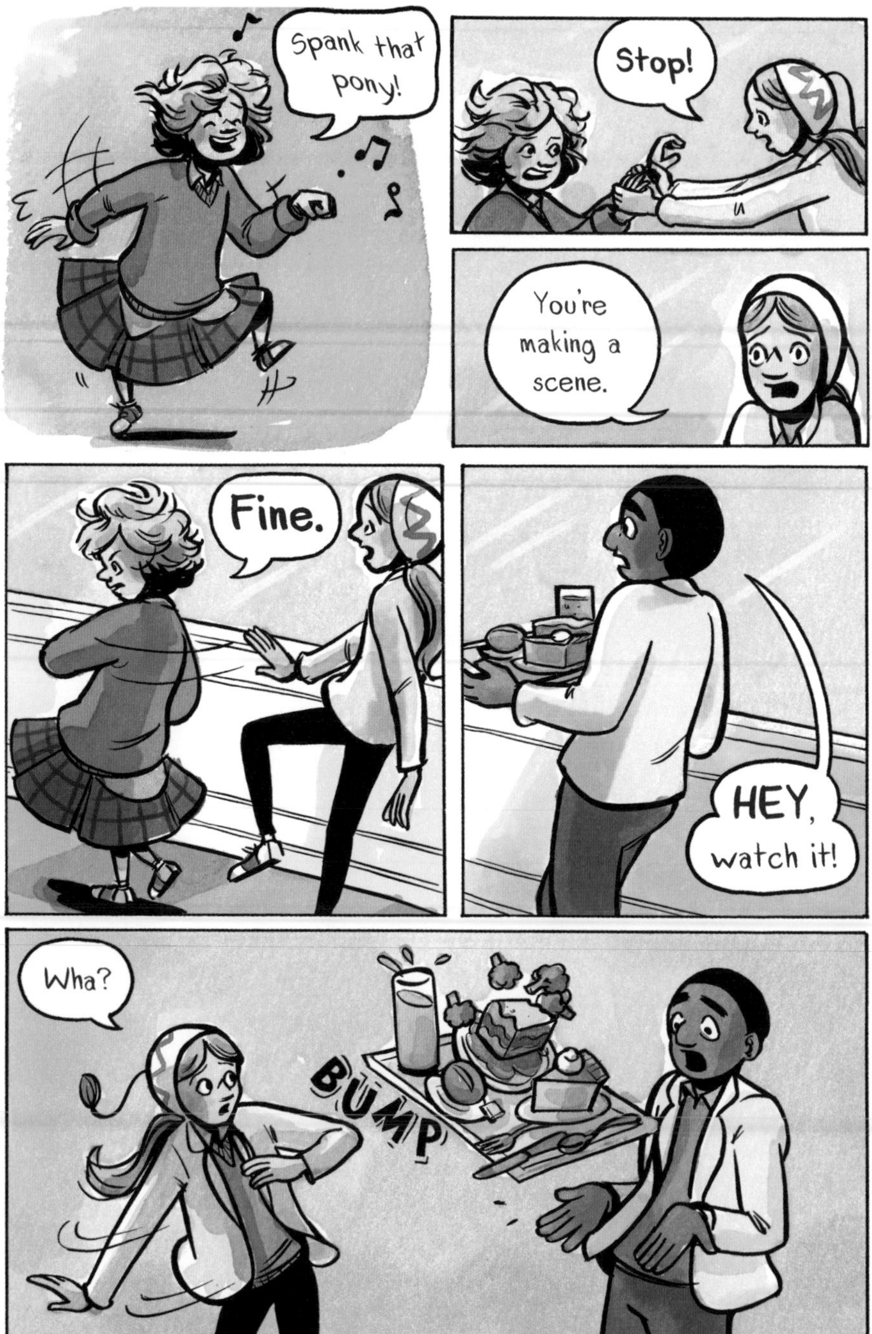
Spank that pony!
Stop!
You're making a scene.
Fine.
HEY, watch it!
Wha?
BUMP

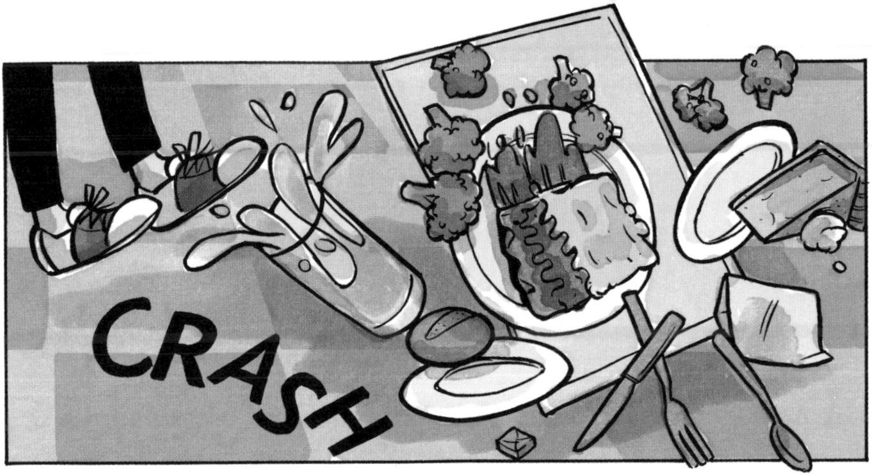
CRASH

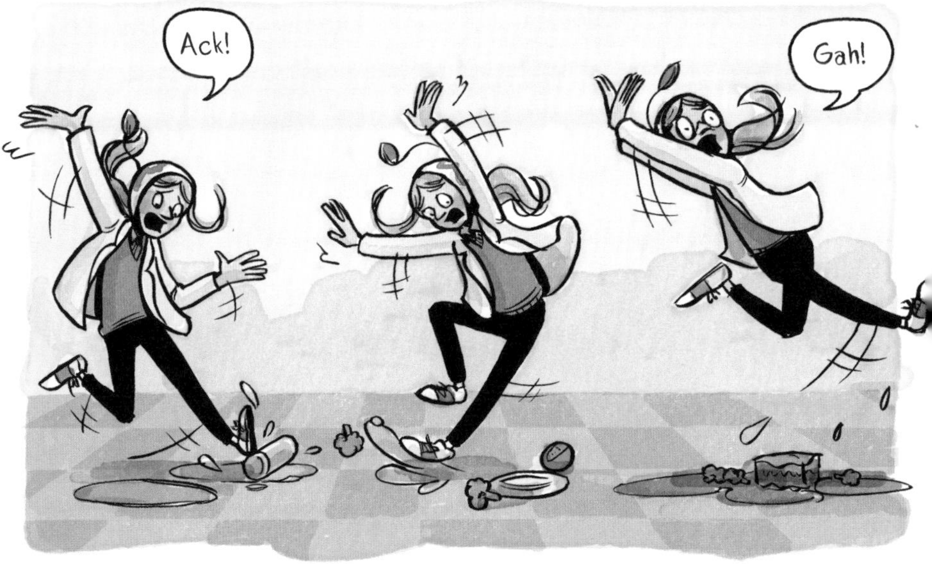
Ack!
Gah!

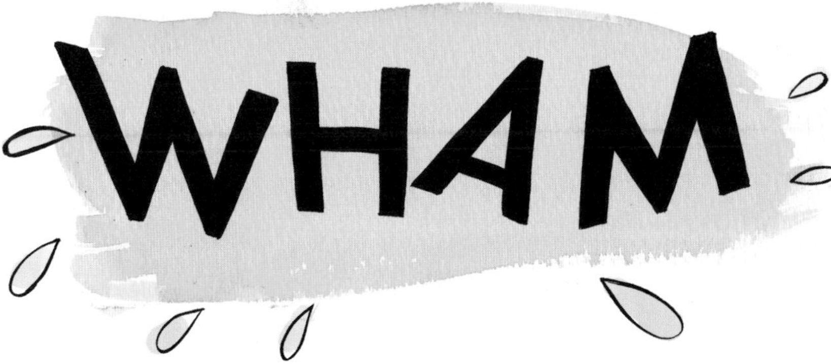
WHAM

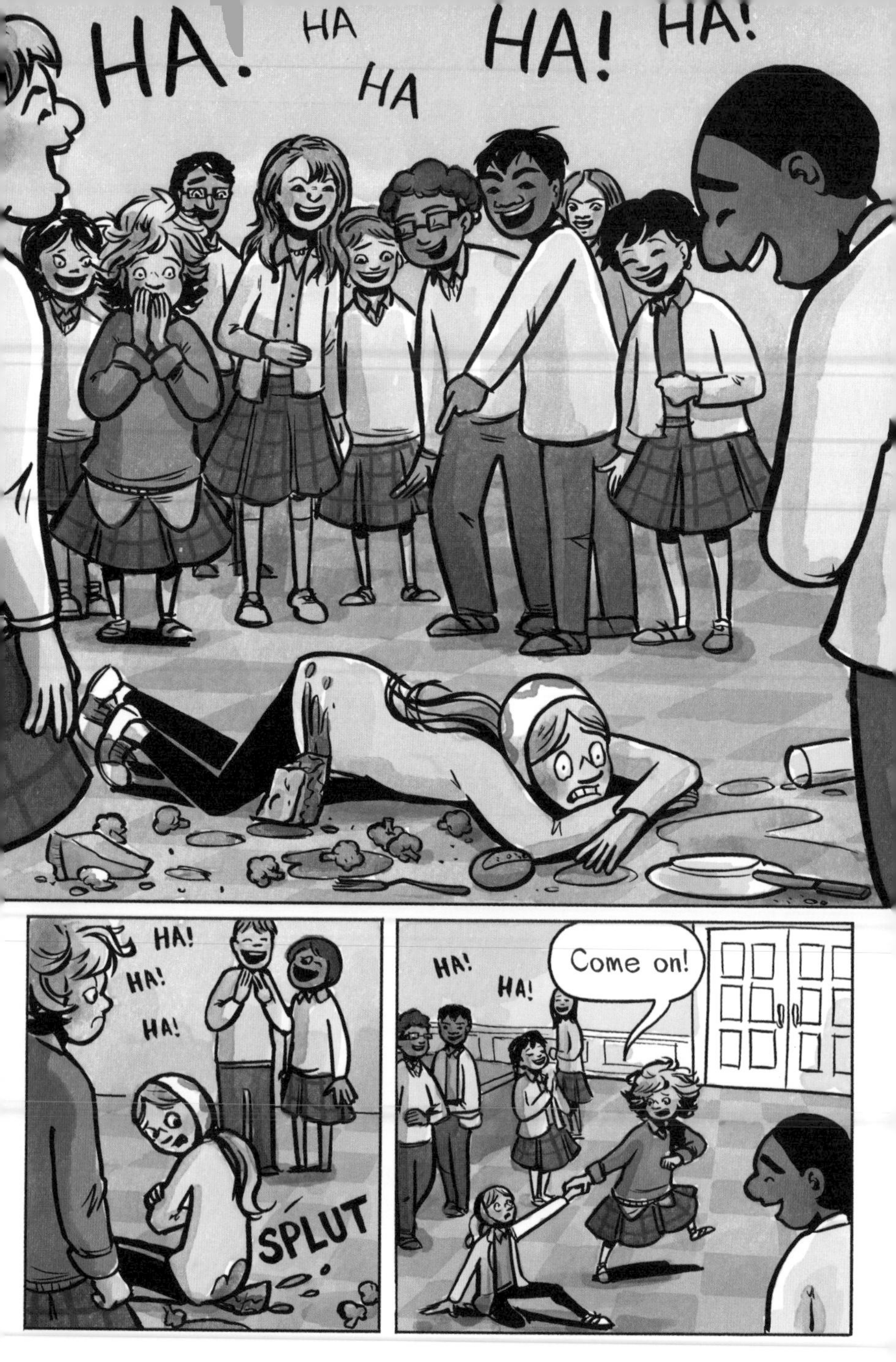

HA!
HA
HA
HA!
HA!
HA!
HA!
HA!
SPLUT
HA!
HA!
Come on!

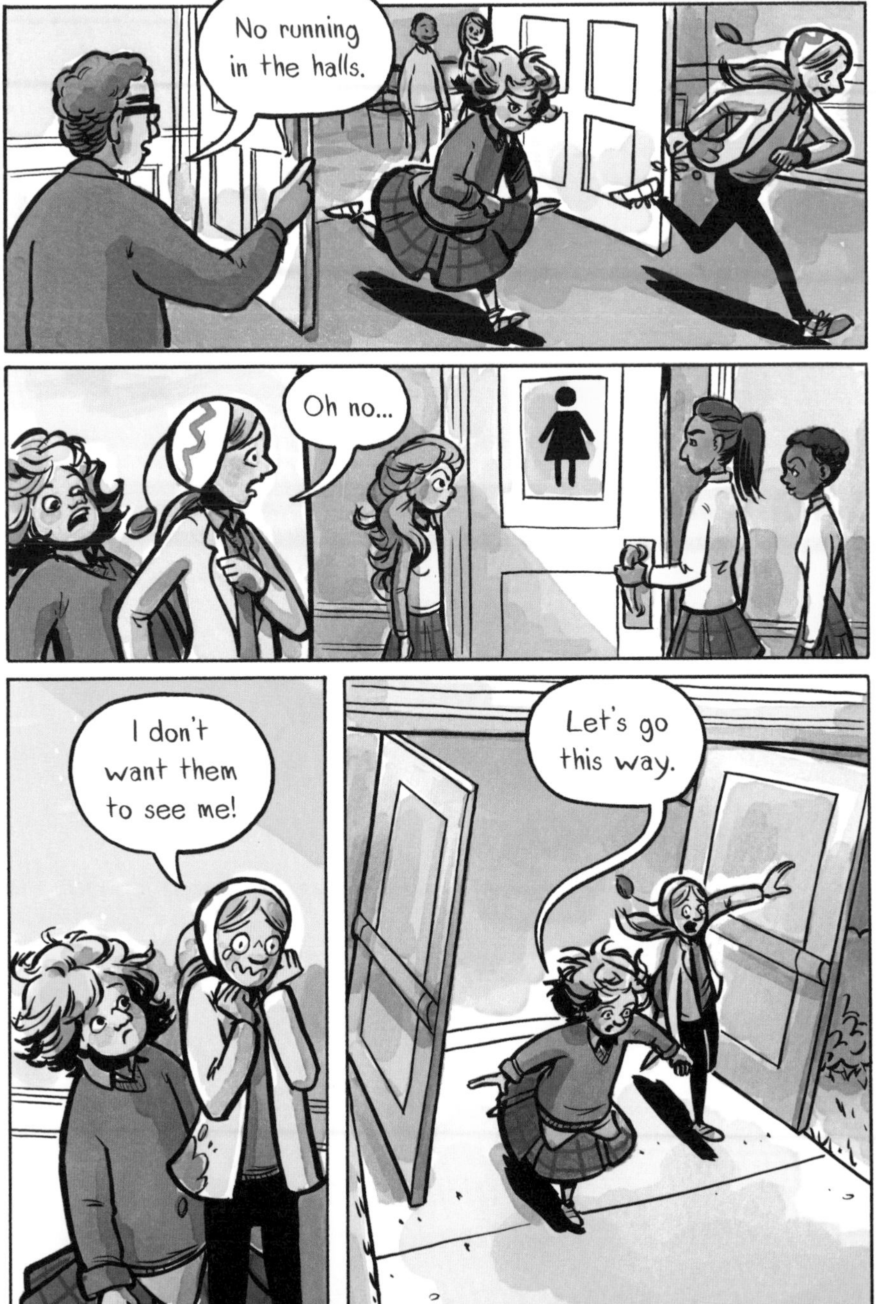
No running in the halls.
Oh no...
I don't want them to see me!
Let's go this way.

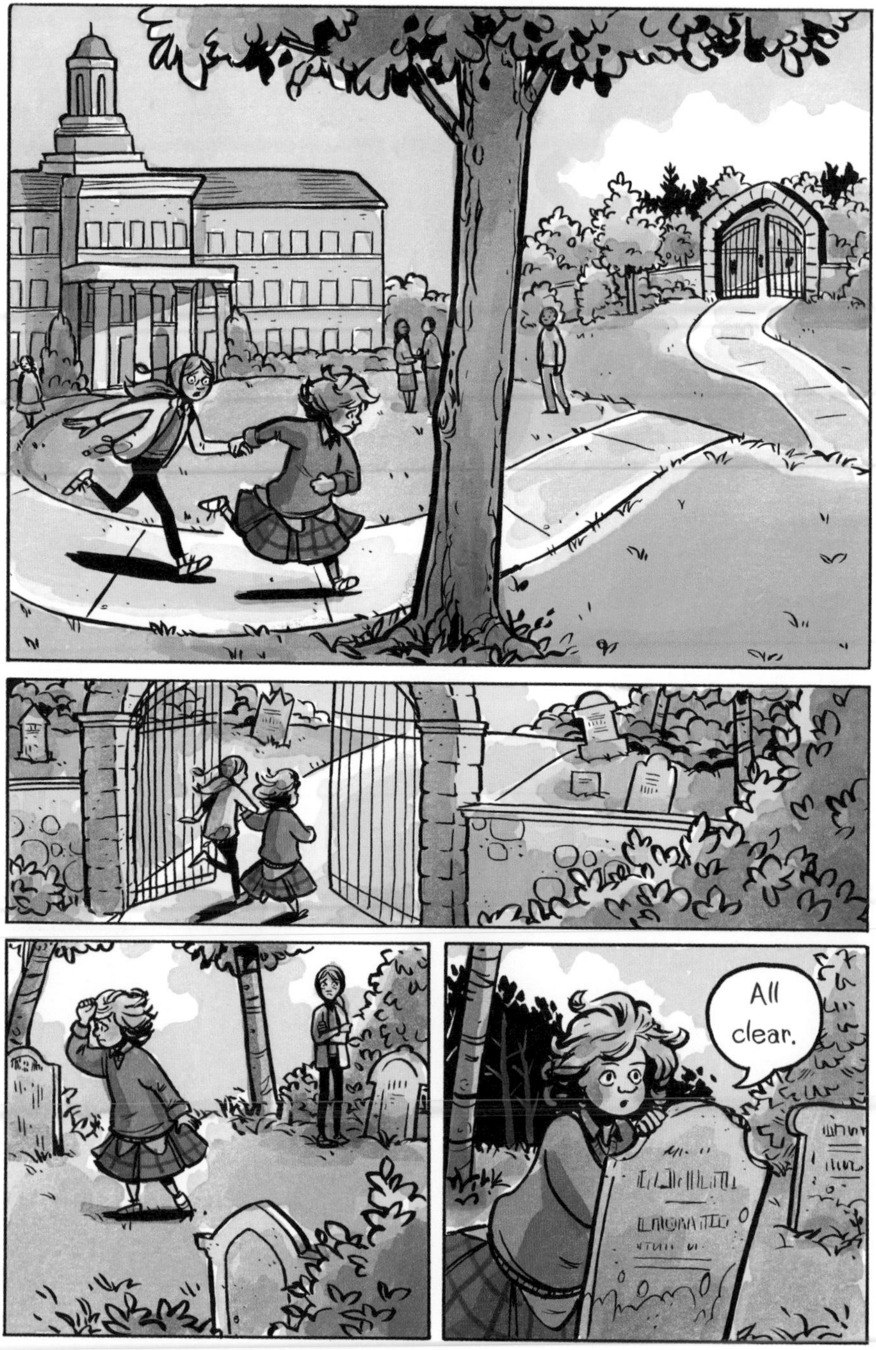
All clear.

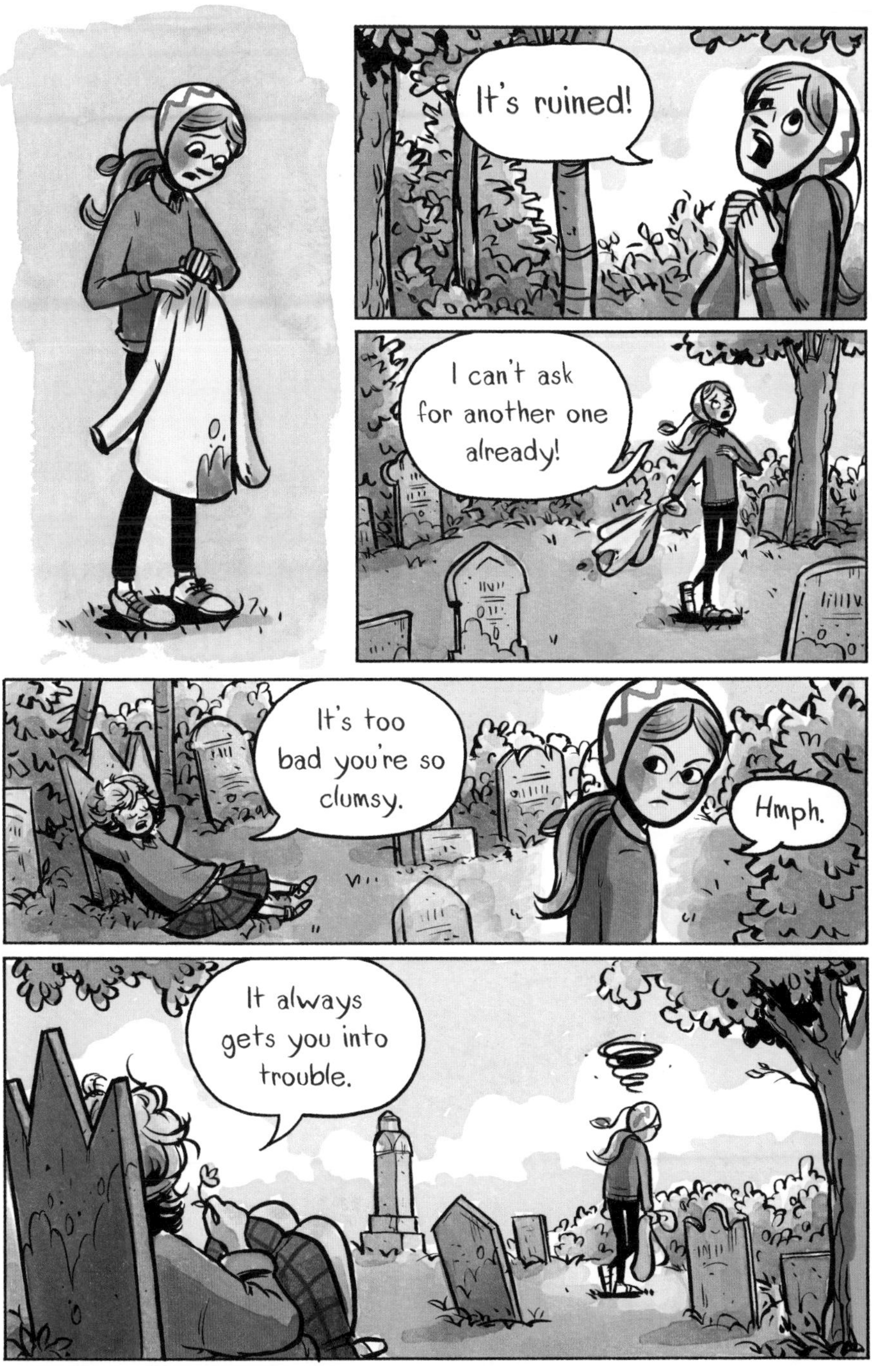
It's ruined!
I can't ask for another one already!
It's too bad you're so clumsy.
Hmph.
It always gets you into trouble.

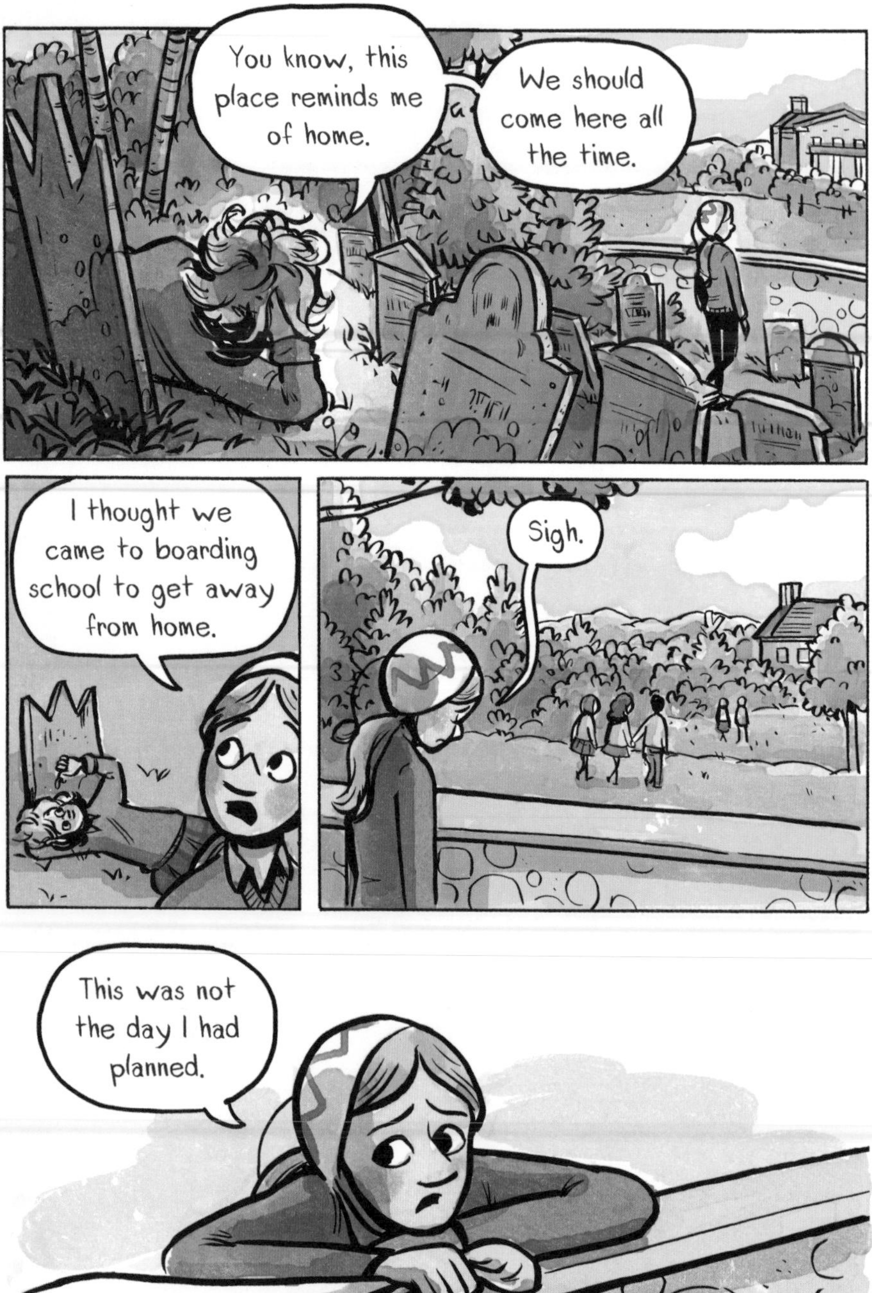
You know, this place reminds me of home.
We should come here all the time.
I thought we came to boarding school to get away from home.
Sigh.
This was not the day I had planned.

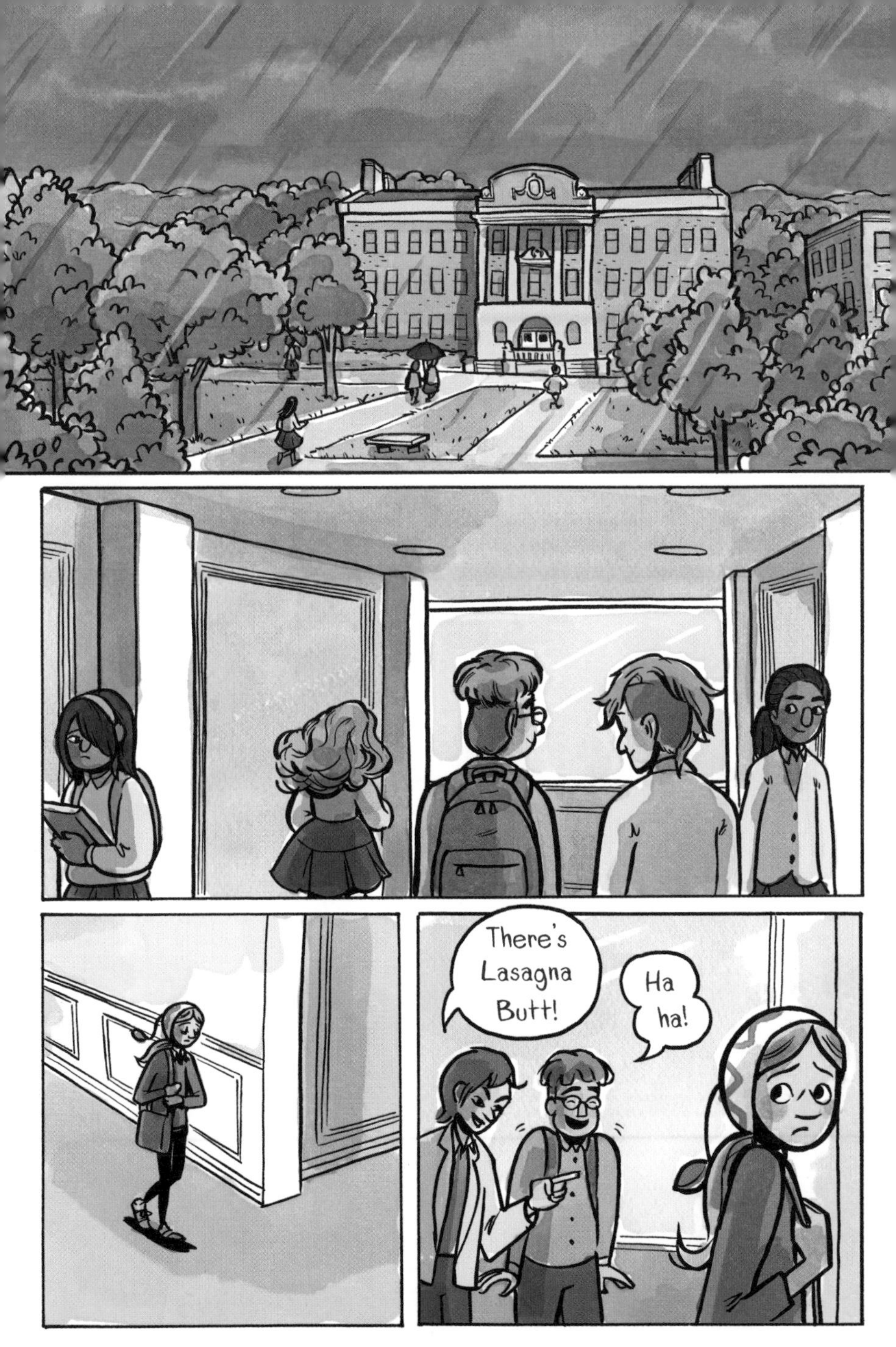

There's Lasagna Butt!
Ha ha!

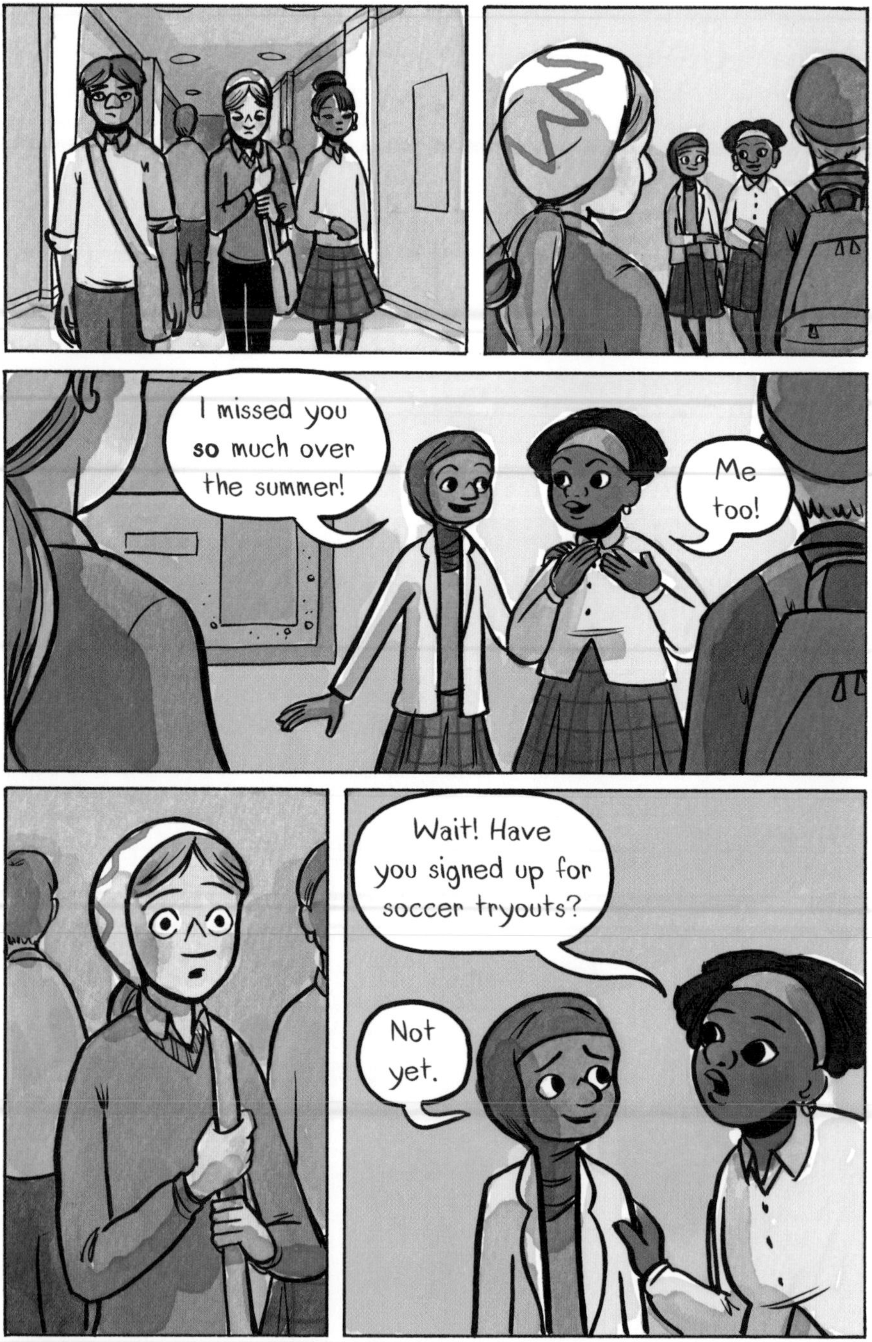
I missed you **so** much over the summer!
Me too!
Wait! Have you signed up for soccer tryouts?
Not yet.

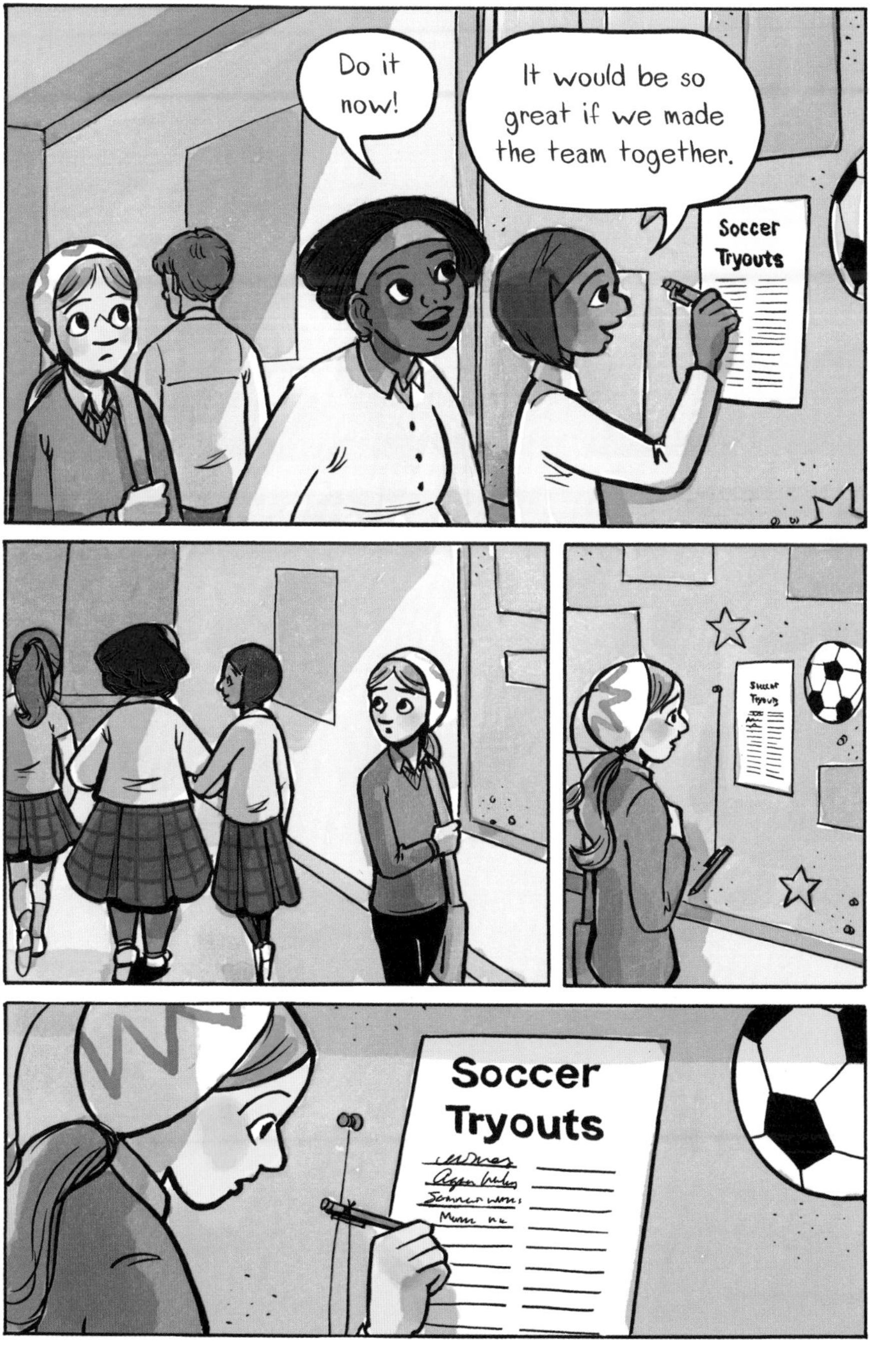
Do it now!
It would be so great if we made the team together.
Soccer Tryouts
Soccer Tryouts

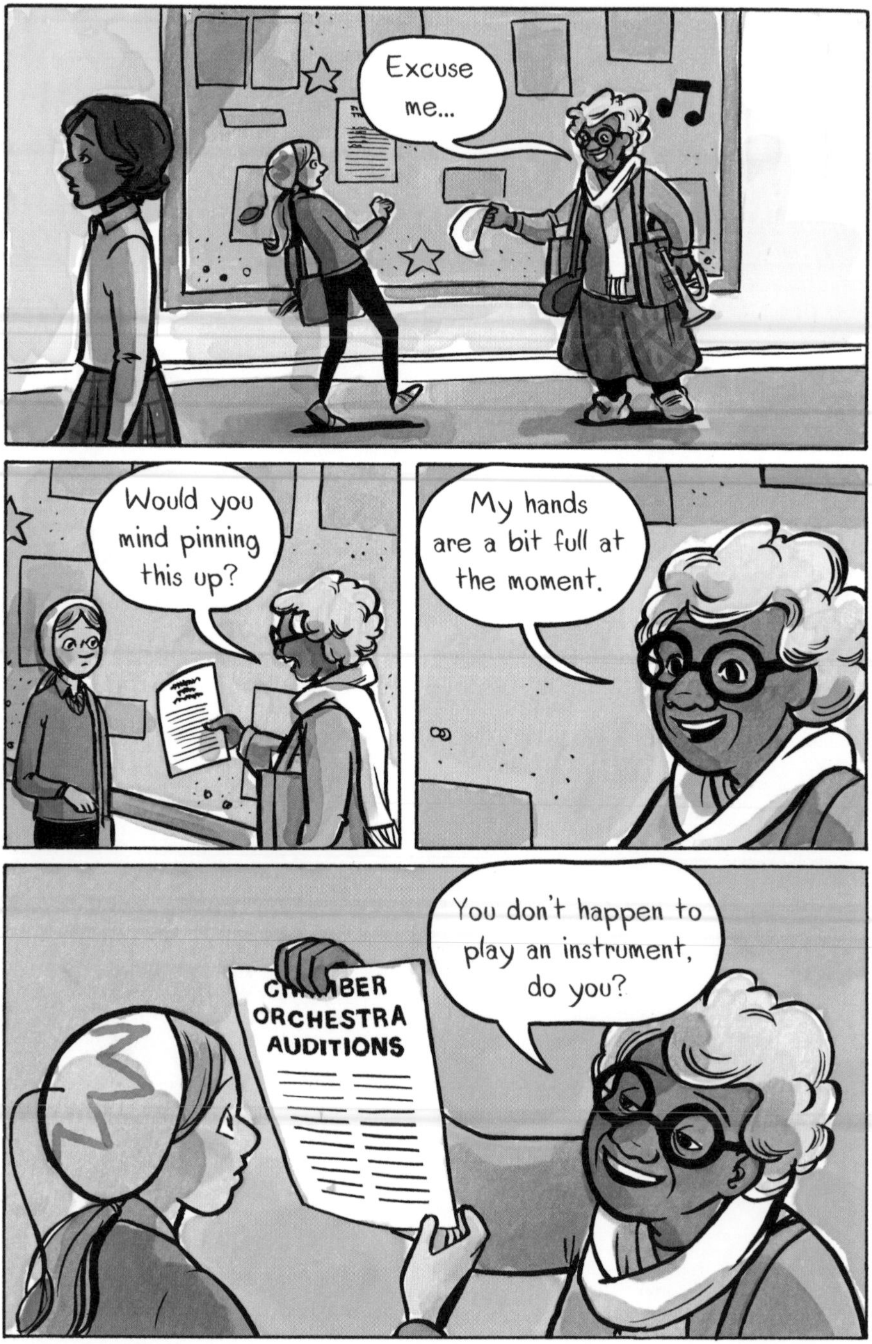

Excuse me...
Would you mind pinning this up?
My hands are a bit full at the moment.
CHAMBER ORCHESTRA AUDITIONS
You don't happen to play an instrument, do you?

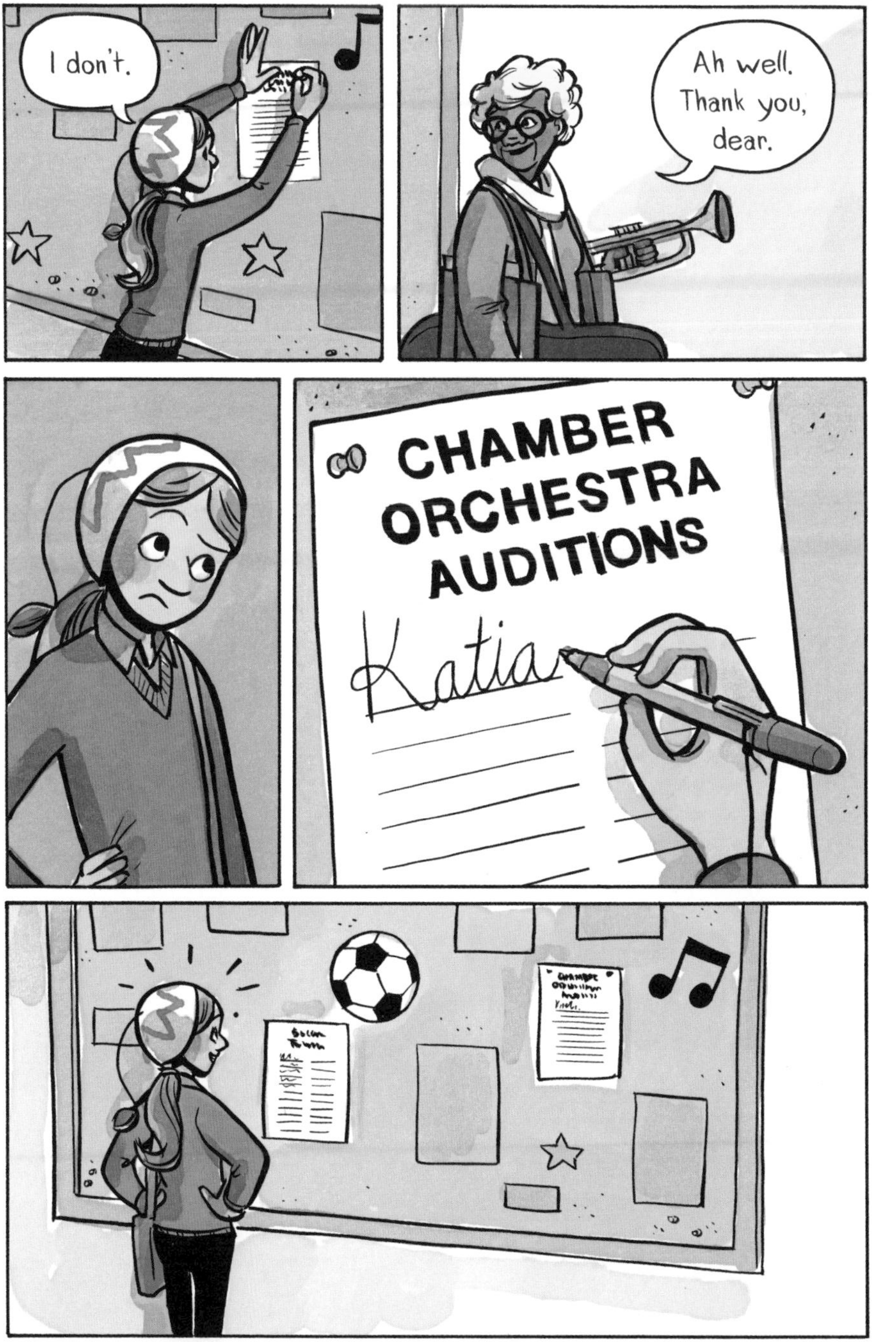
I don't.
Ah well. Thank you, dear.
CHAMBER ORCHESTRA AUDITIONS
Katia

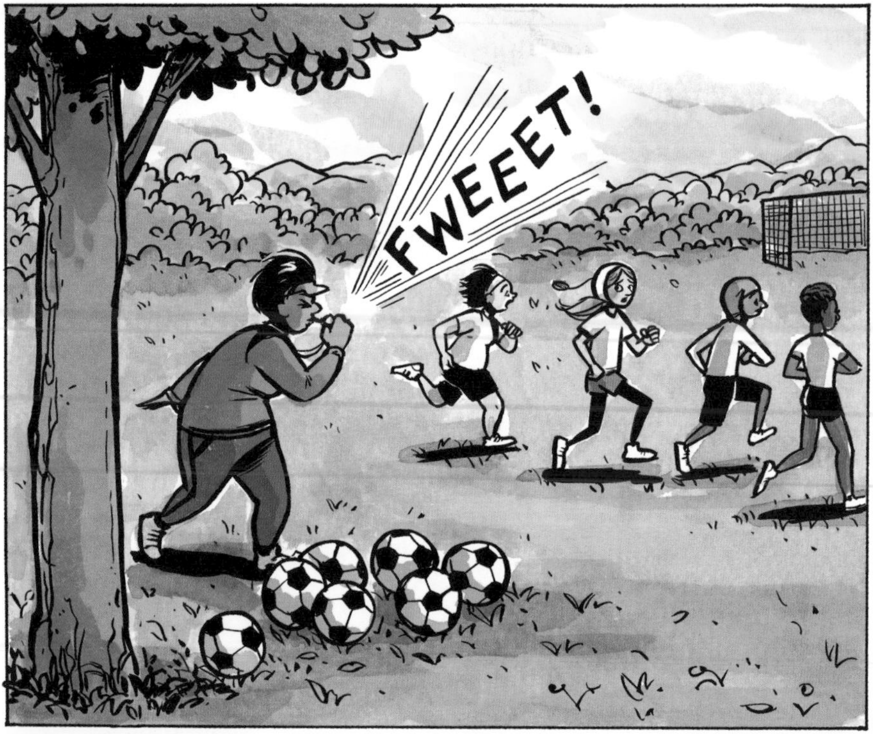
FWEEET!

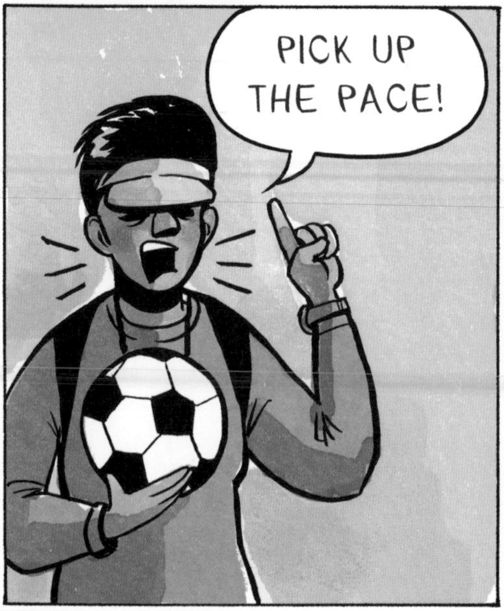
PICK UP
THE PACE!

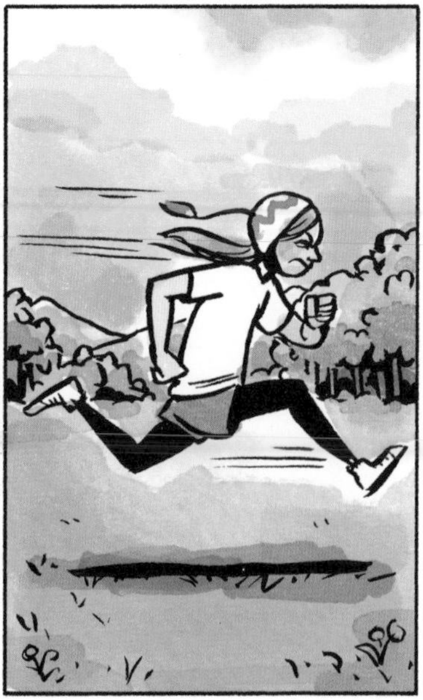

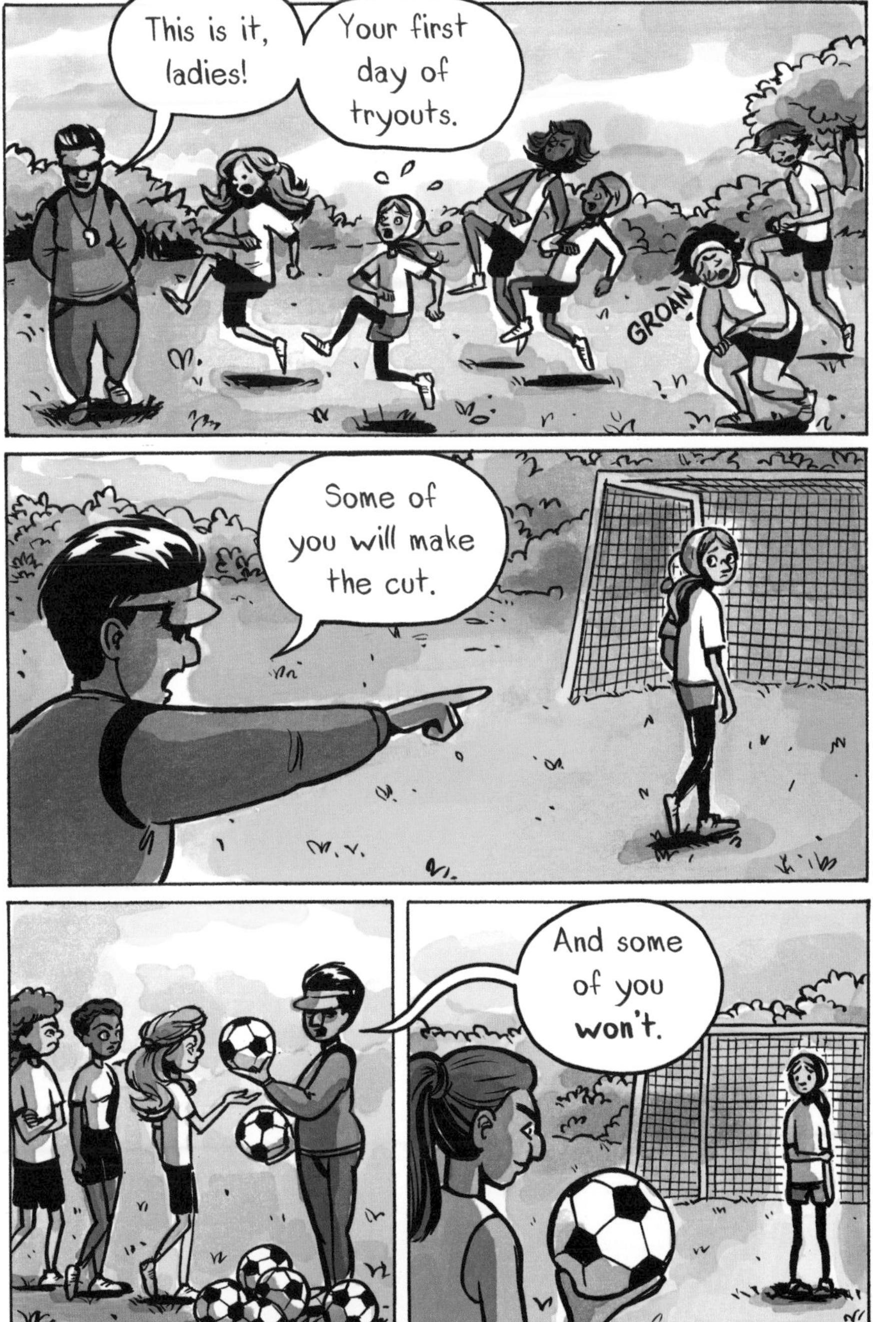
This is it, ladies!
Your first day of tryouts.
GROAN
Some of you will make the cut.
And some of you **won't**.

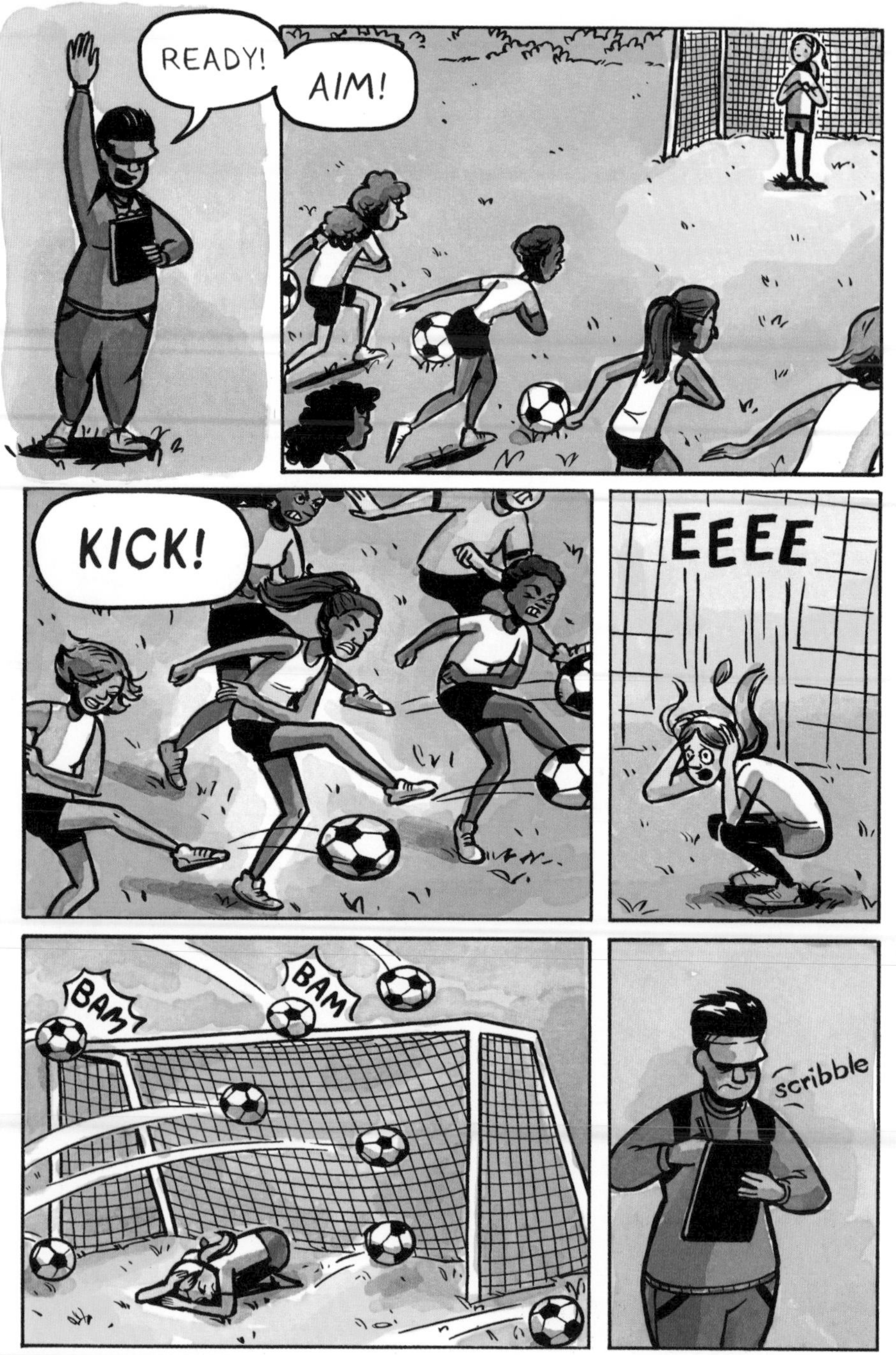
READY!
AIM!
KICK!
EEEE
BAM
BAM
scribble

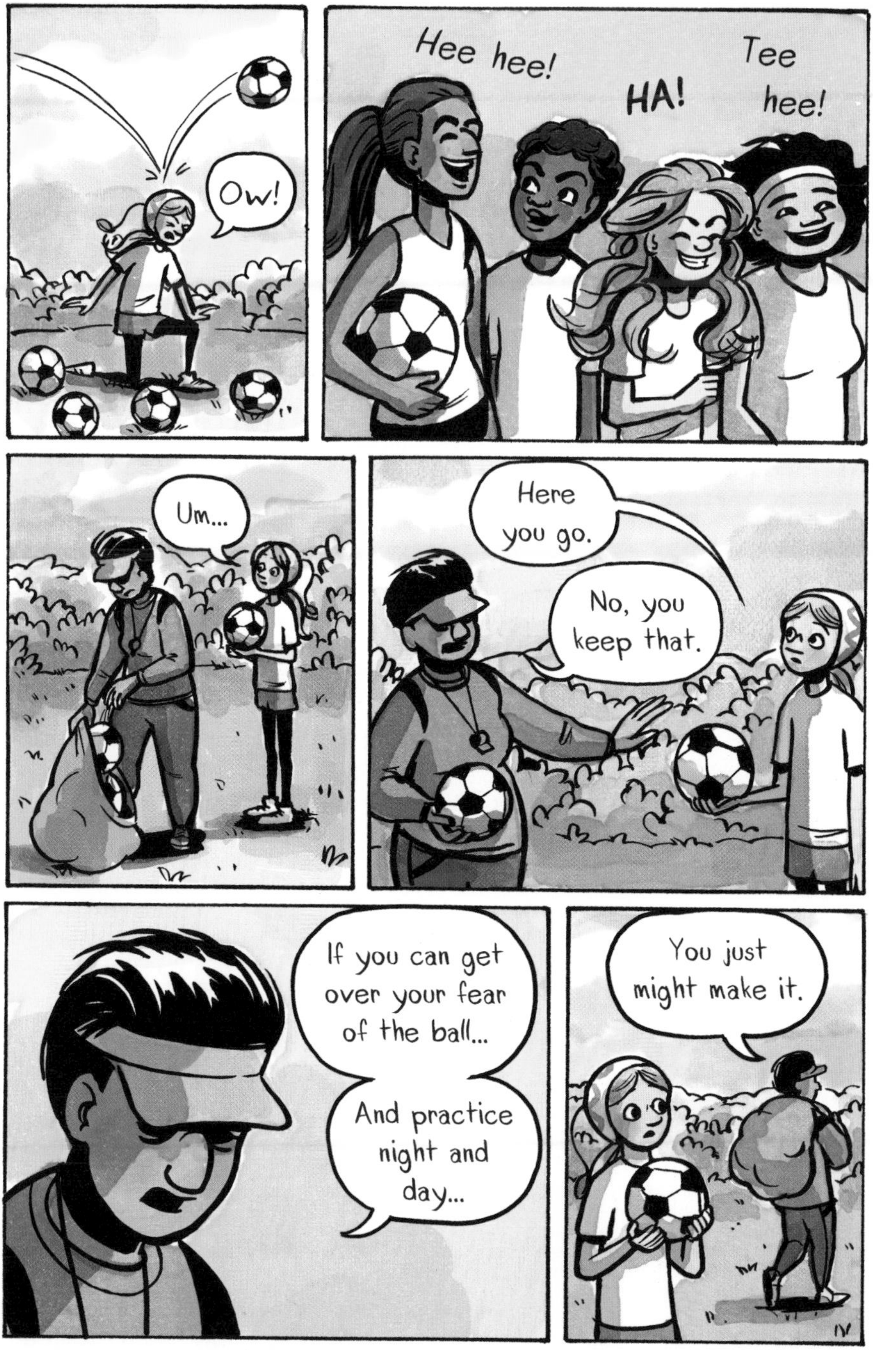
Ow!
Hee hee!
HA!
Tee hee!
Um...
Here you go.
No, you keep that.
If you can get over your fear of the ball...
And practice night and day...
You just might make it.

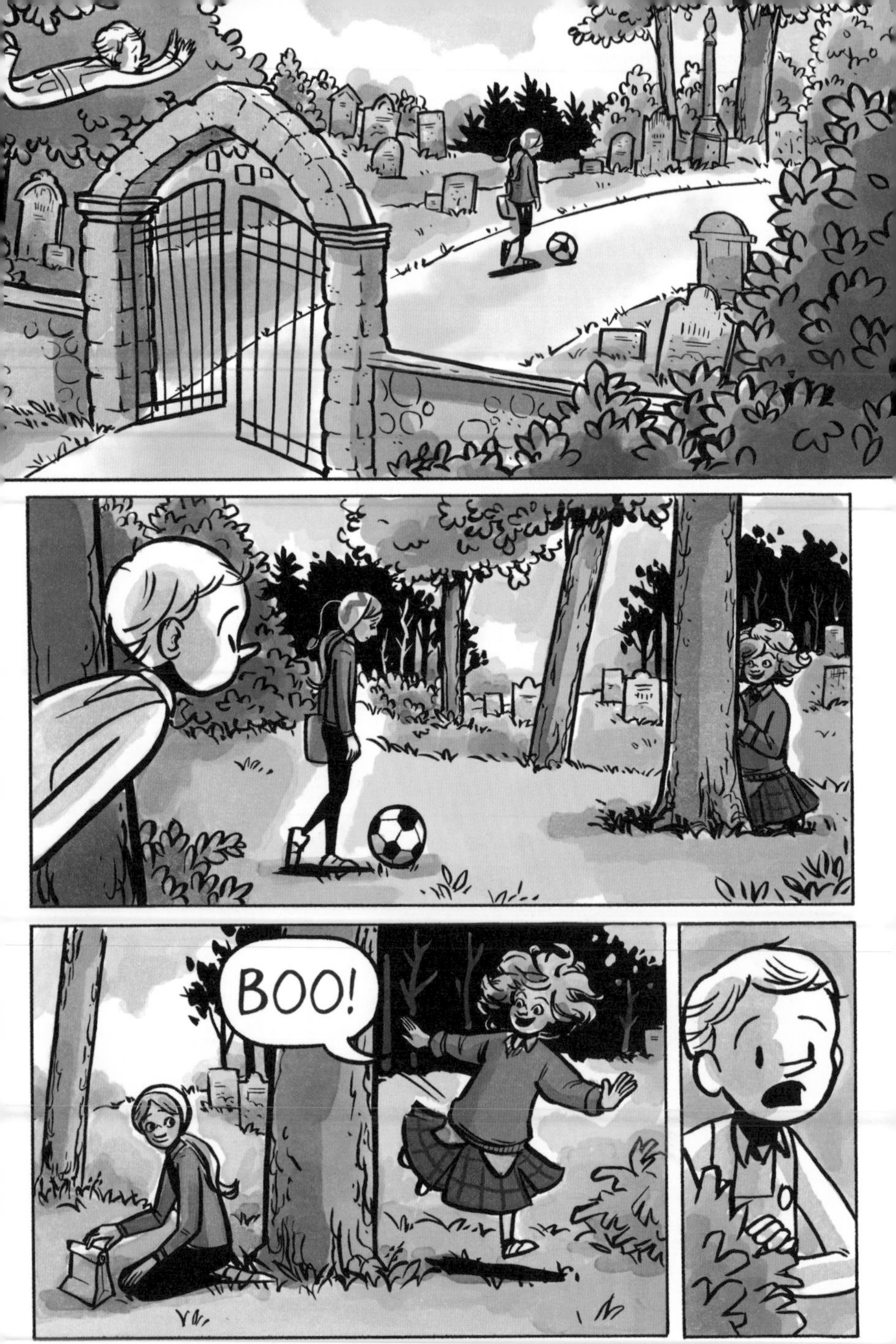
BOO!

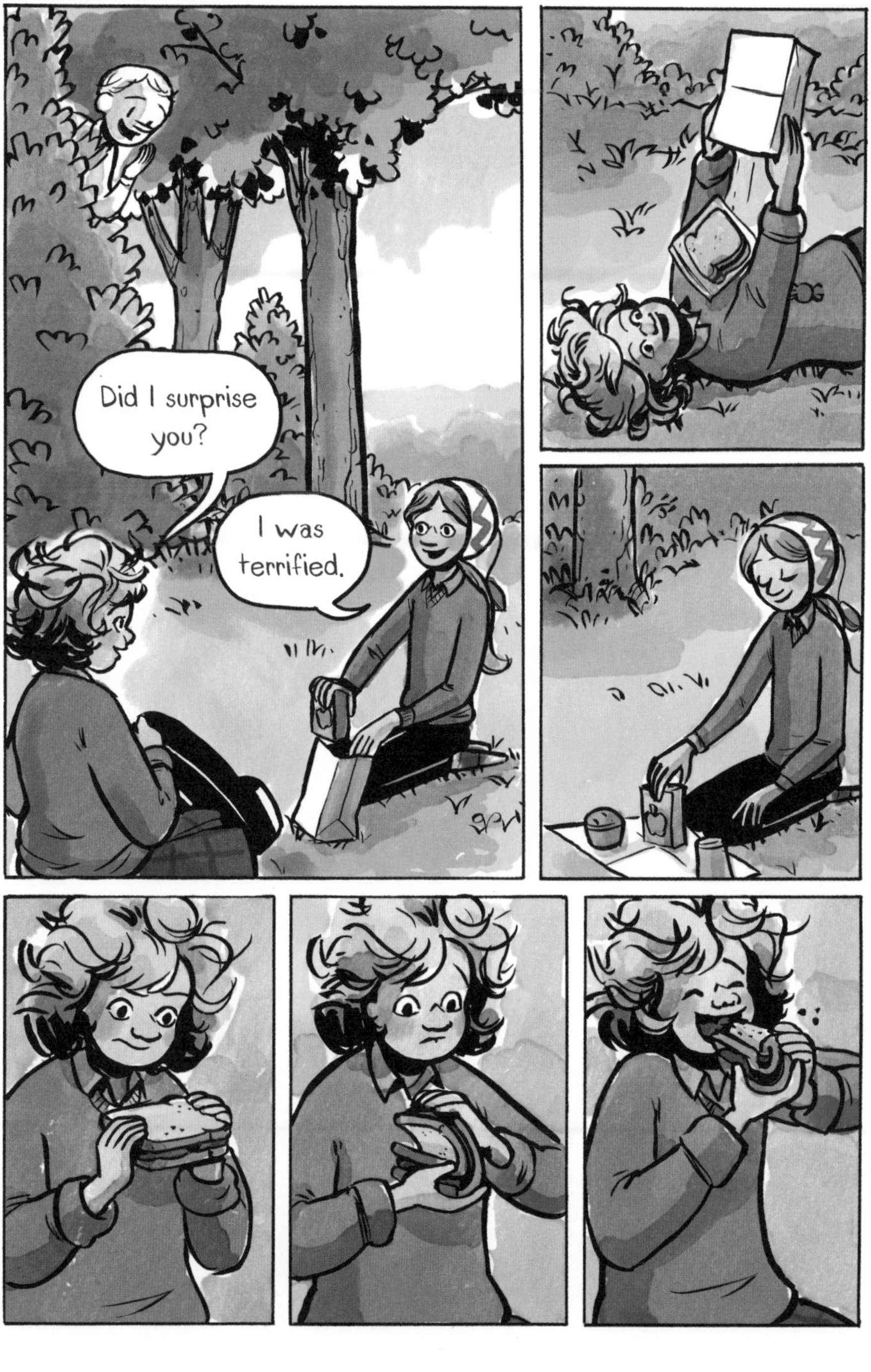
Did I surprise you?
I was terrified.

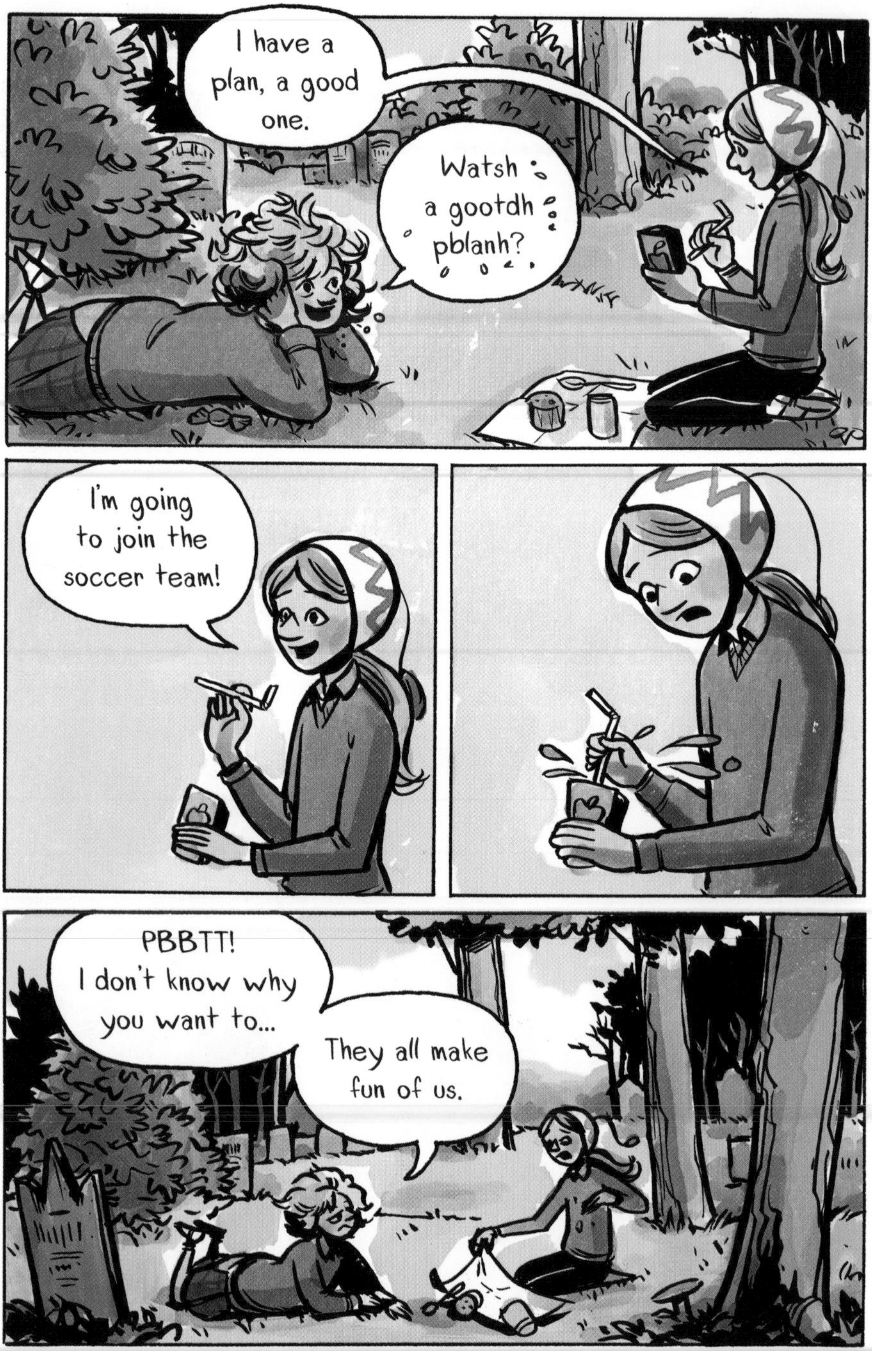

I have a plan, a good one.
Watsh a gootdh pblanh?
I'm going to join the soccer team!
PBBTT! I don't know why you want to...
They all make fun of us.

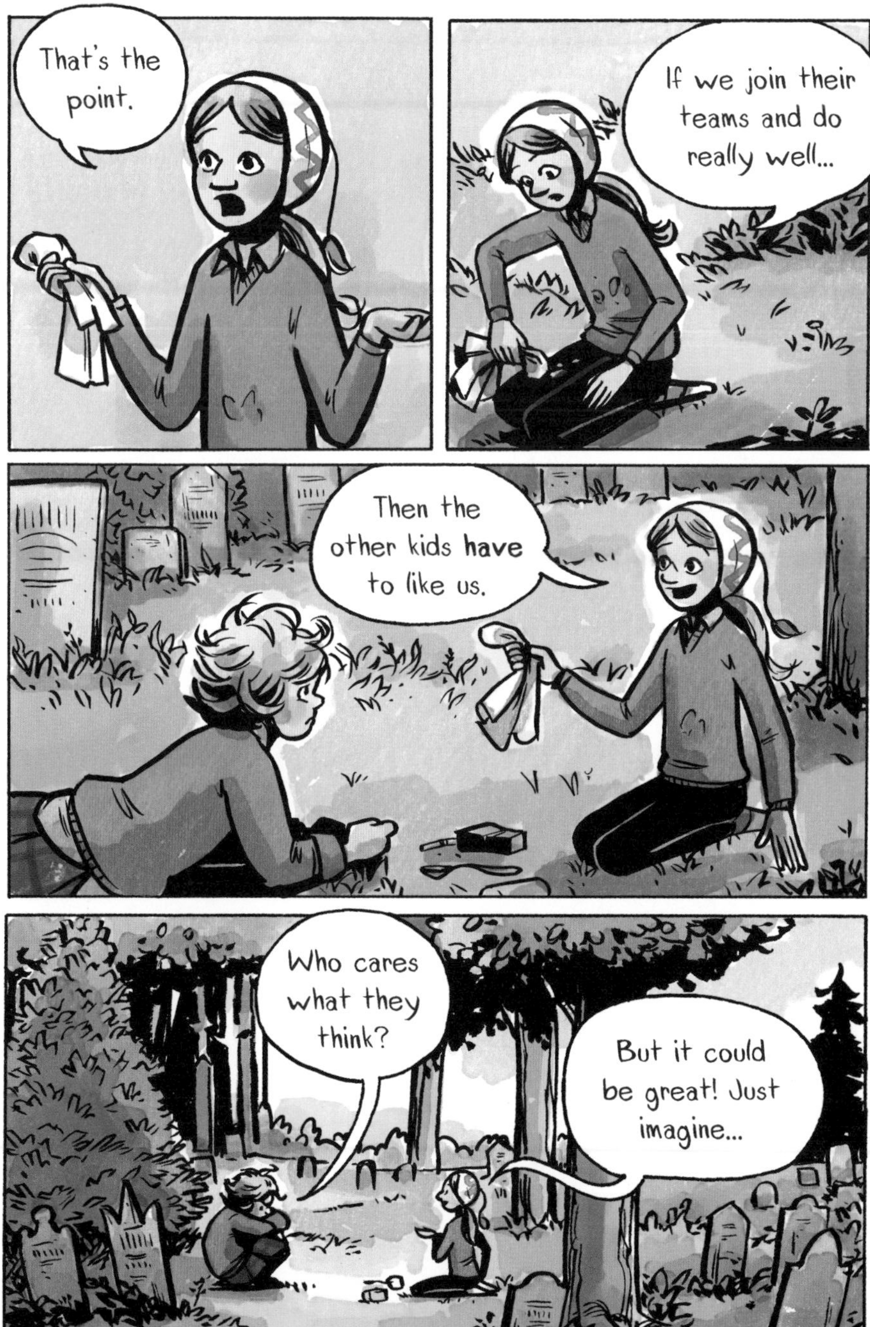
That's the point.
If we join their teams and do really well...
Then the other kids **have** to like us.
Who cares what they think?
But it could be great! Just imagine...

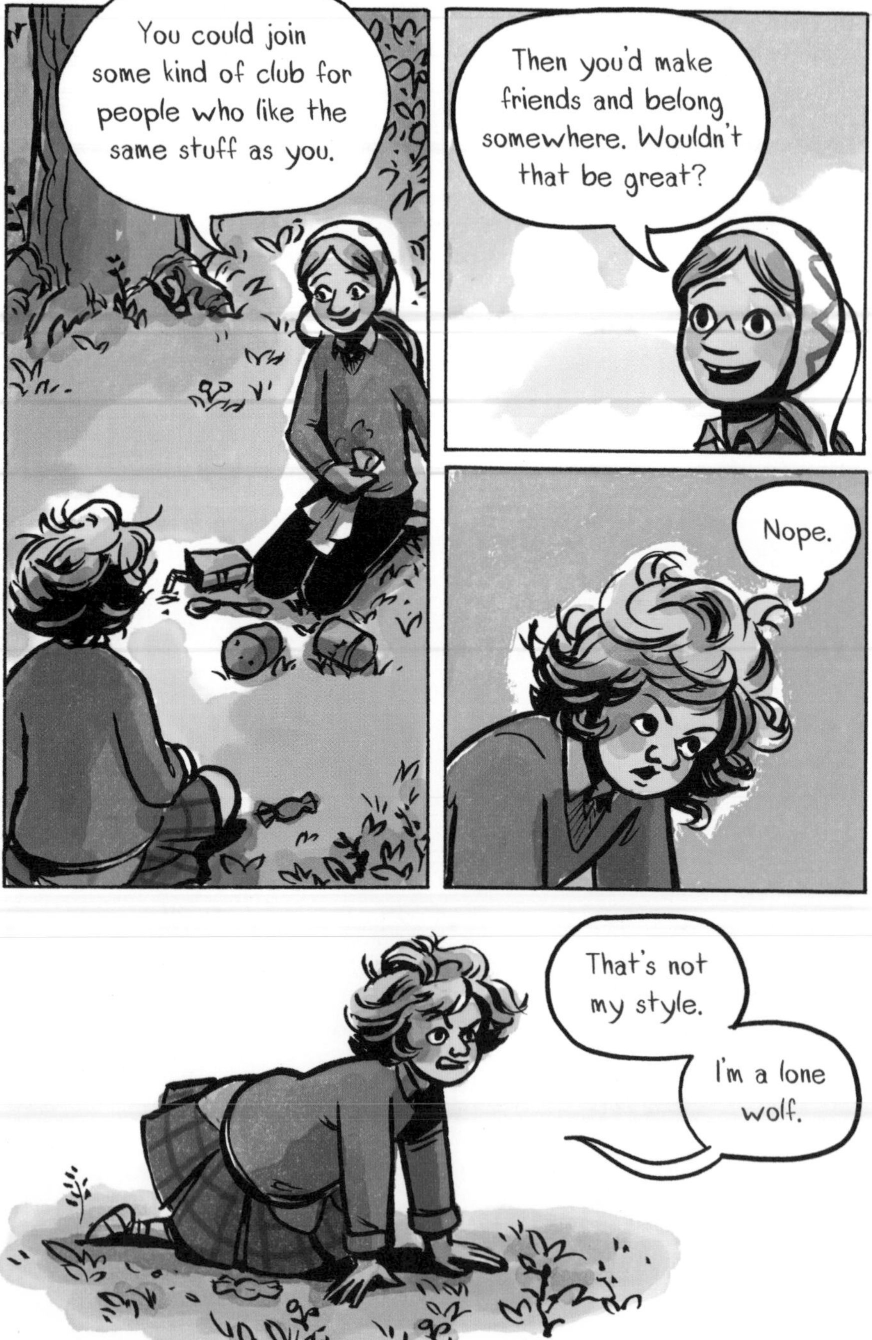
You could join some kind of club for people who like the same stuff as you.
Then you'd make friends and belong somewhere. Wouldn't that be great?
Nope.
That's not my style.
I'm a lone wolf.

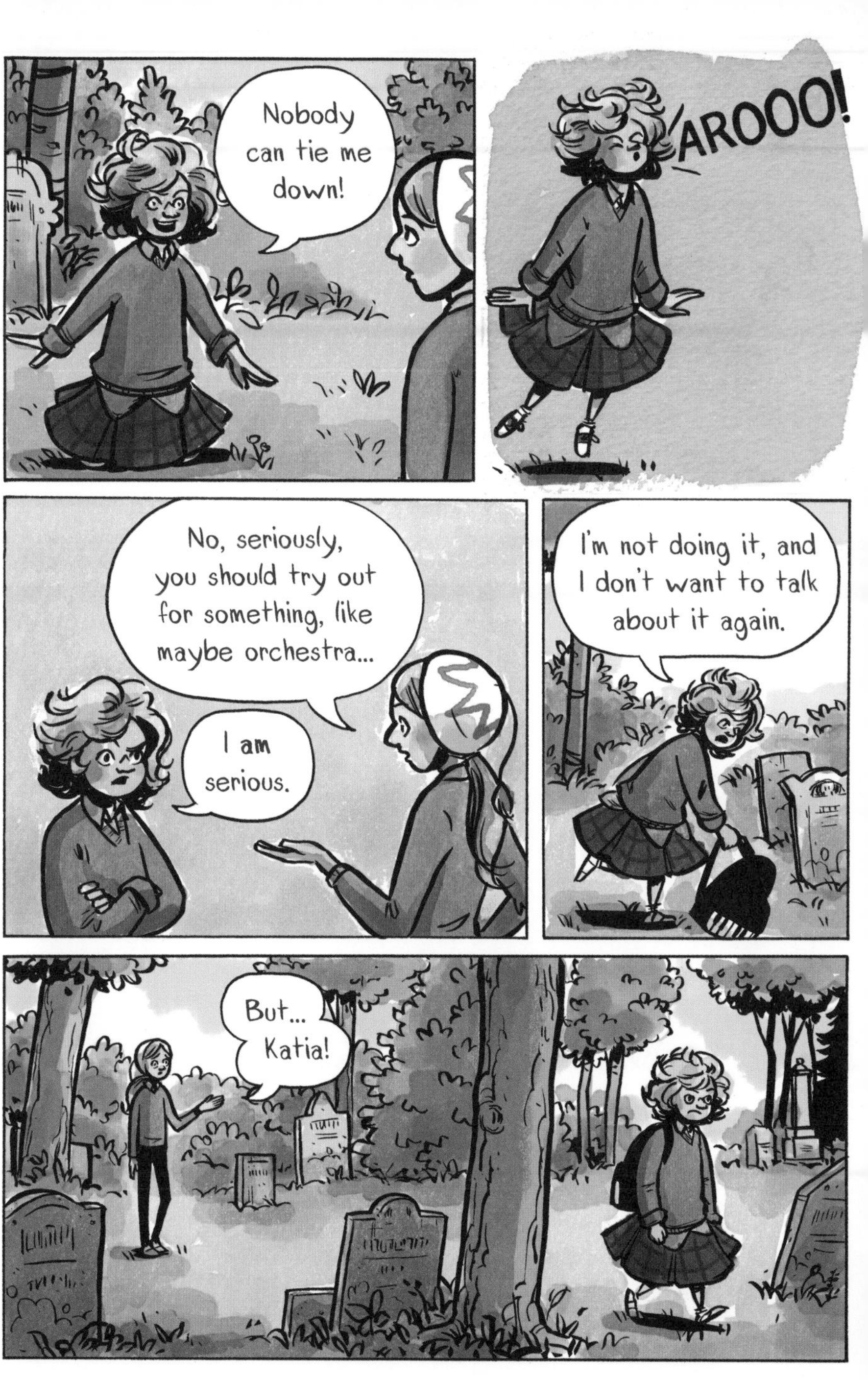
Nobody can tie me down!
AROOO!
No, seriously, you should try out for something, like maybe orchestra...
I am serious.
I'm not doing it, and I don't want to talk about it again.
But... Katia!

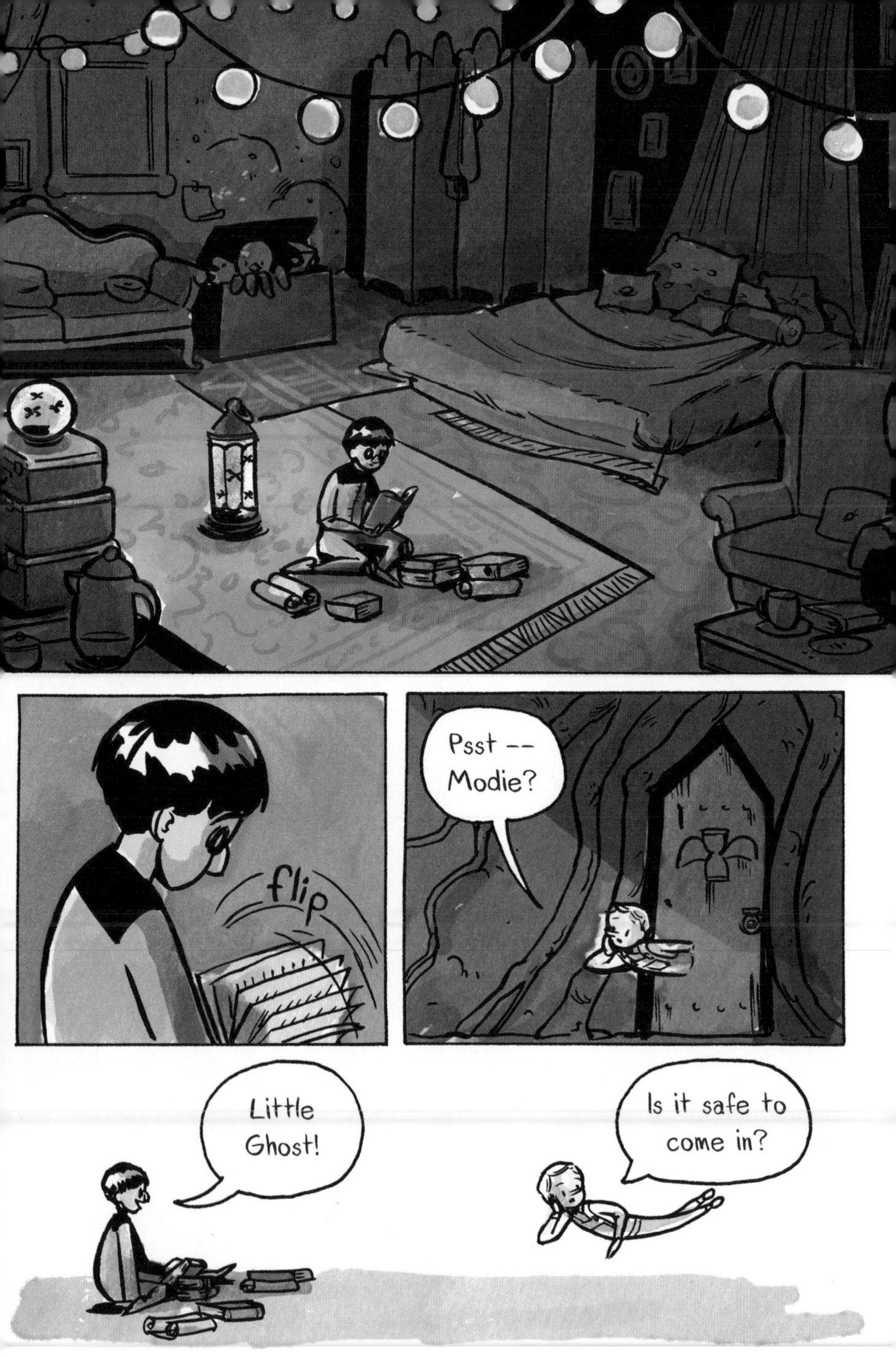
flip
Psst -- Modie?
Little Ghost!
Is it safe to come in?

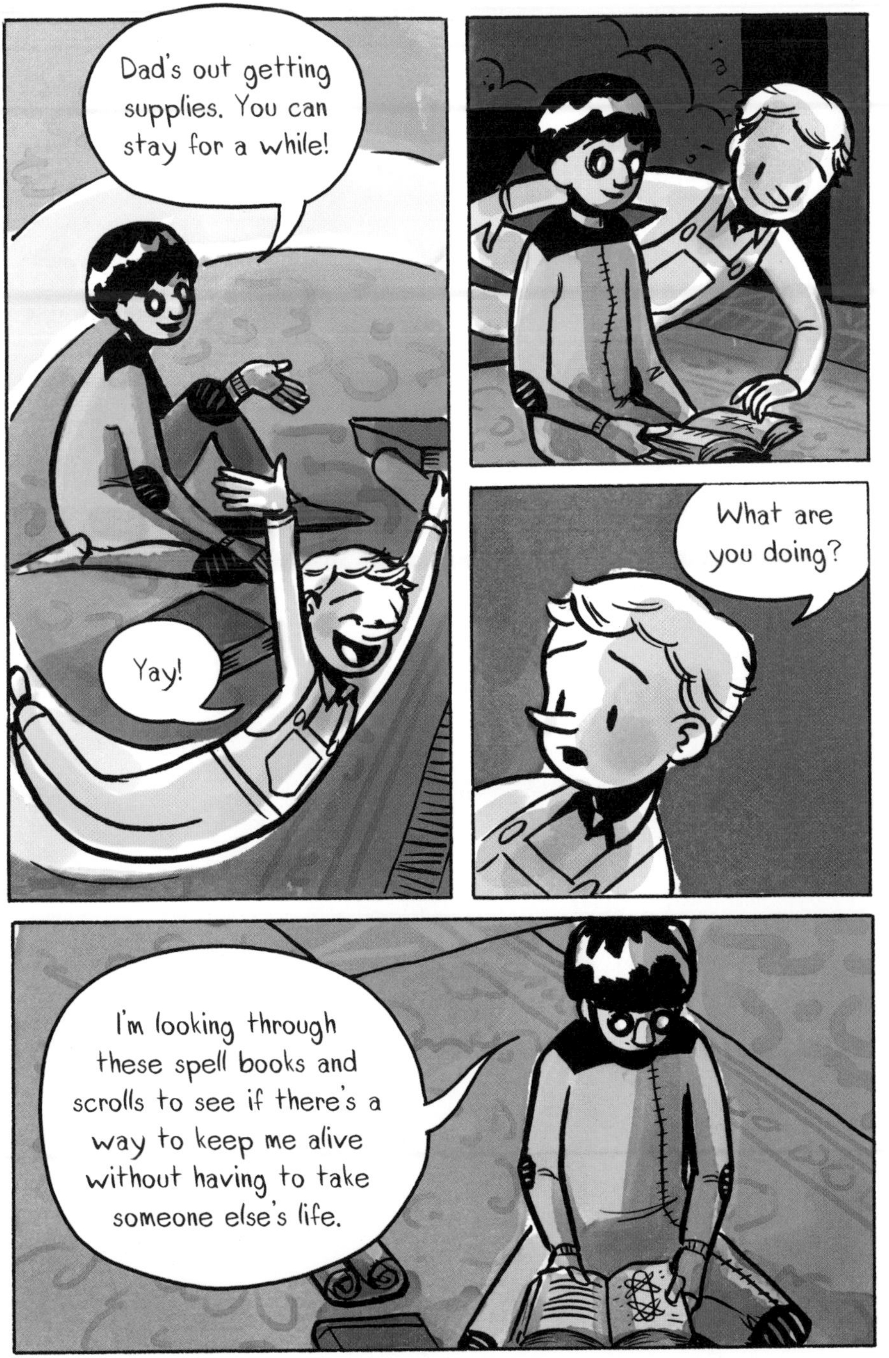
Dad's out getting supplies. You can stay for a while!
Yay!
What are you doing?
I'm looking through these spell books and scrolls to see if there's a way to keep me alive without having to take someone else's life.

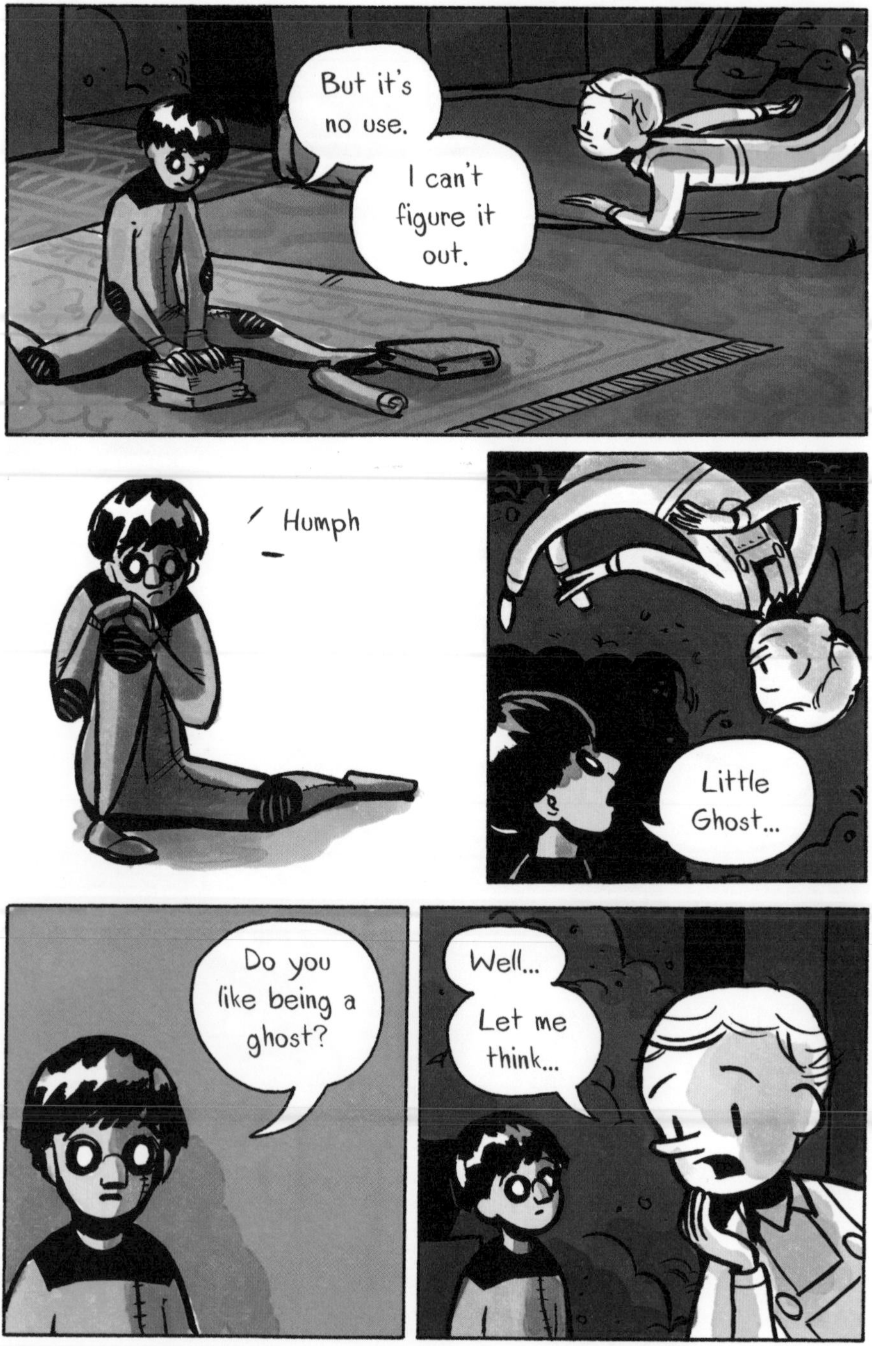
But it's no use.
I can't figure it out.
Humph
Little Ghost...
Do you like being a ghost?
Well...
Let me think...

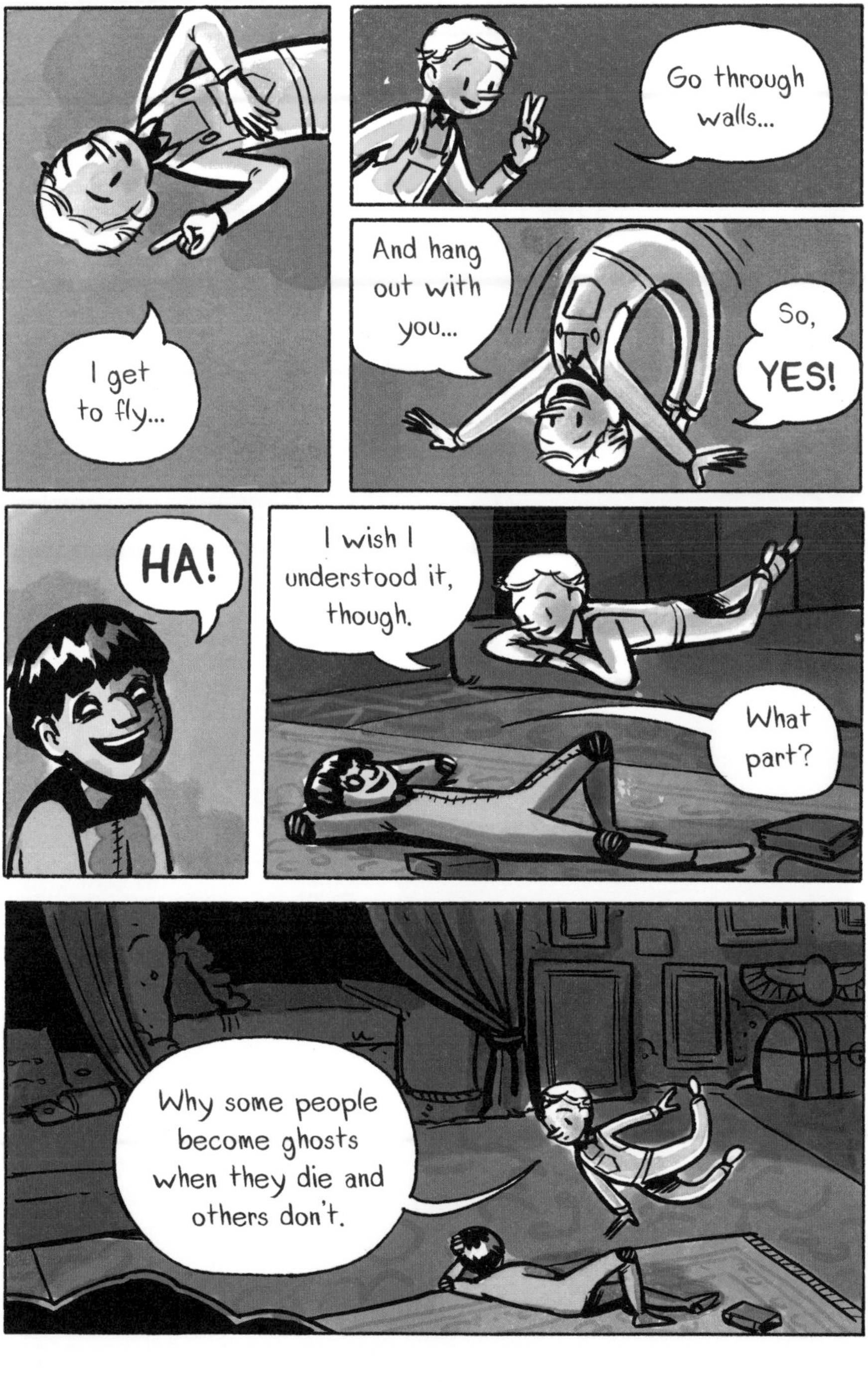
I get to fly...
Go through walls...
And hang out with you...
So, YES!
HA!
I wish I understood it, though.
What part?
Why some people become ghosts when they die and others don't.

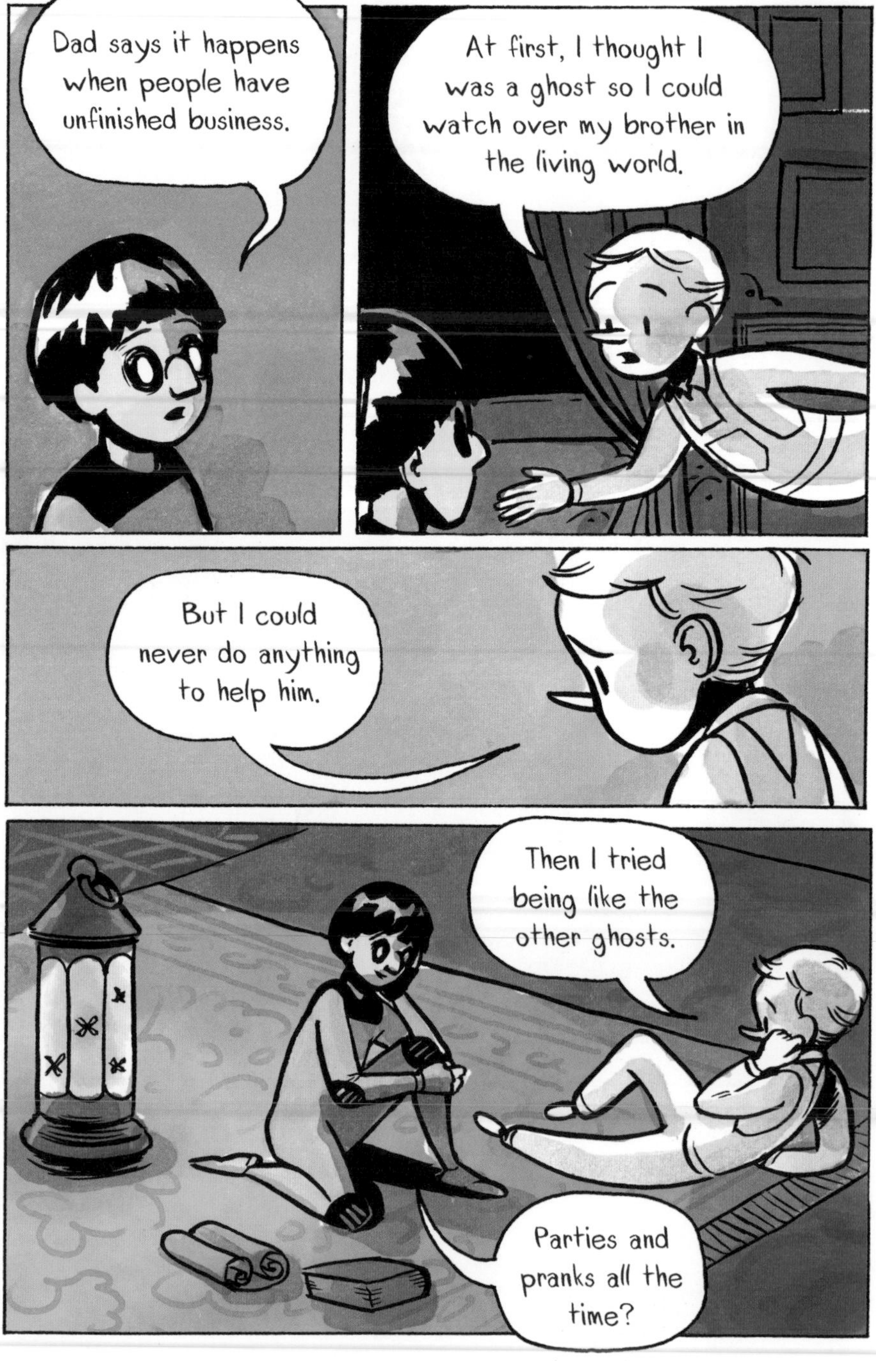
Dad says it happens when people have unfinished business.
At first, I thought I was a ghost so I could watch over my brother in the living world.
But I could never do anything to help him.
Then I tried being like the other ghosts.
Parties and pranks all the time?

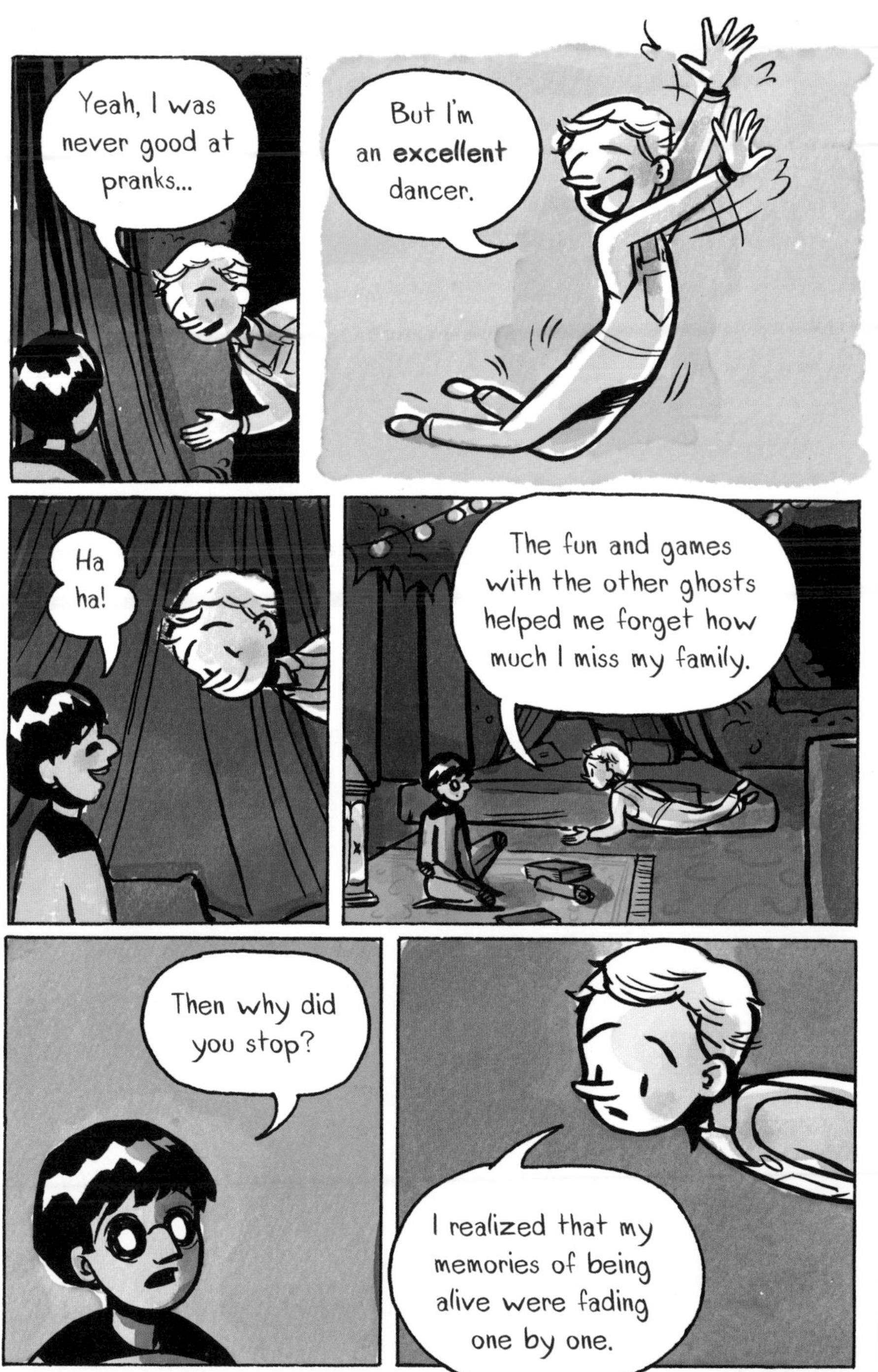
Yeah, I was never good at pranks...
But I'm an **excellent** dancer.
Ha ha!
The fun and games with the other ghosts helped me forget how much I miss my family.
Then why did you stop?
I realized that my memories of being alive were fading one by one.

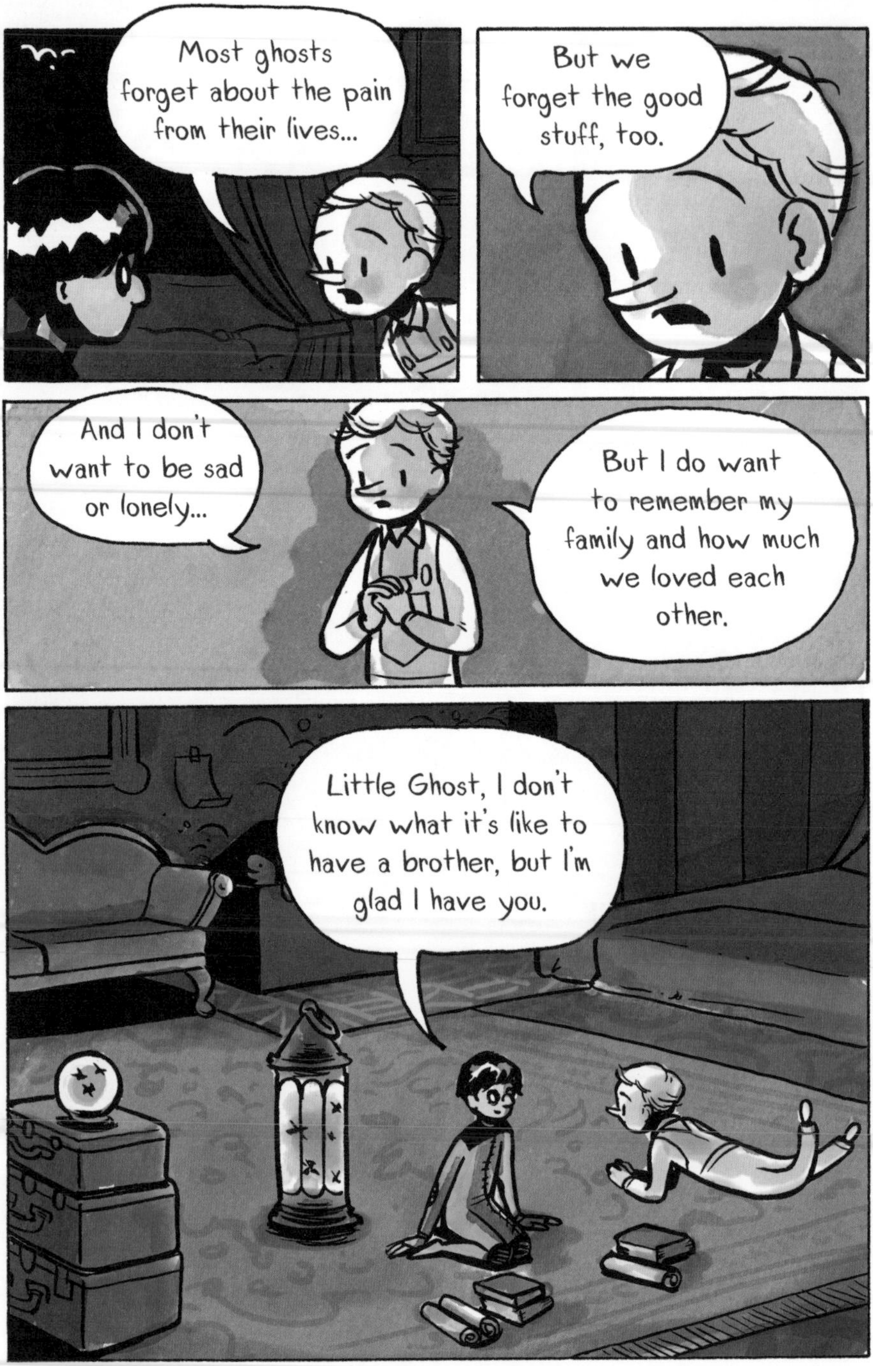
Most ghosts forget about the pain from their lives...
But we forget the good stuff, too.
And I don't want to be sad or lonely...
But I do want to remember my family and how much we loved each other.
Little Ghost, I don't know what it's like to have a brother, but I'm glad I have you.

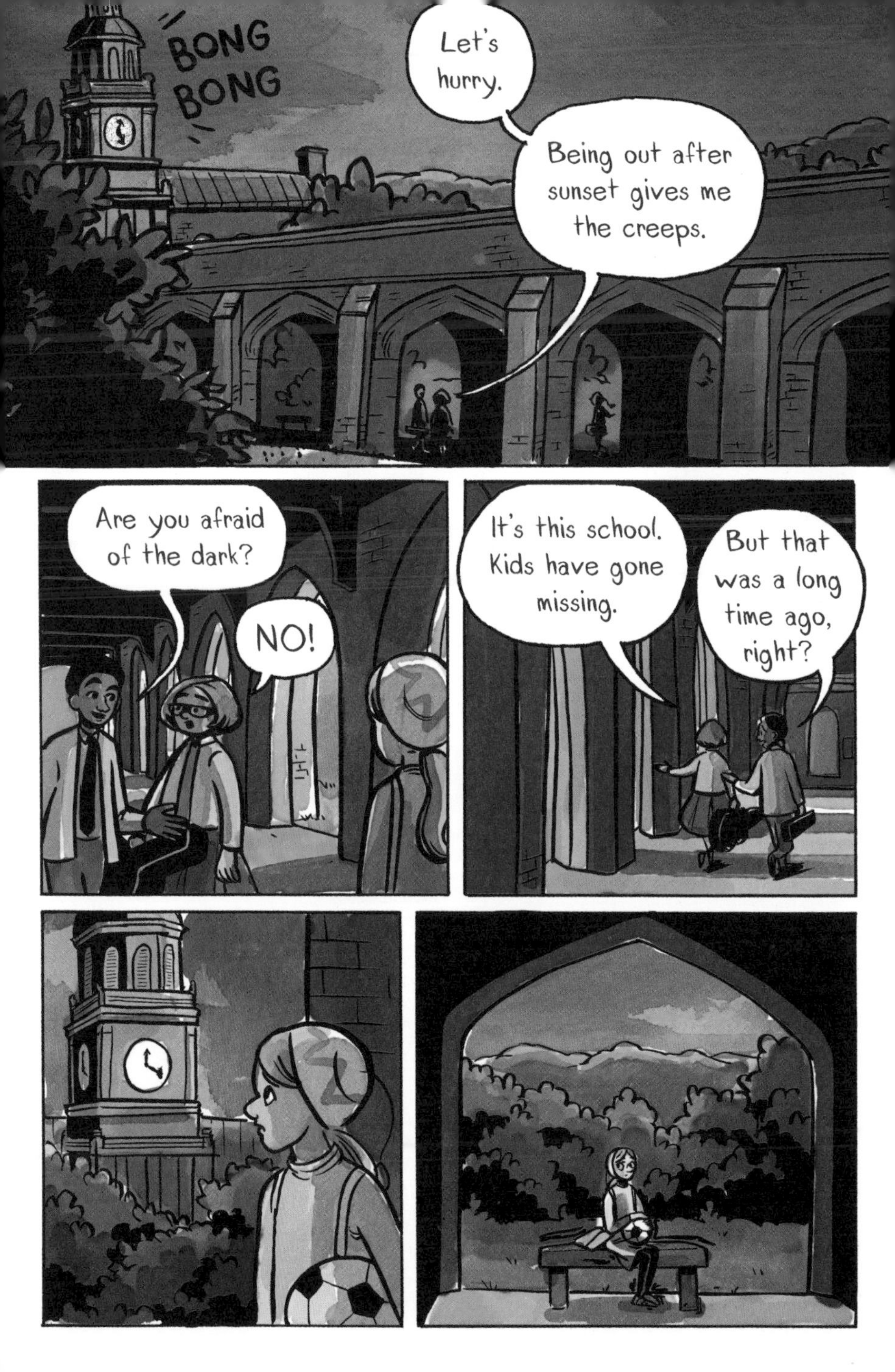
BONG
BONG
Let's hurry.
Being out after sunset gives me the creeps.
Are you afraid of the dark?
NO!
It's this school. Kids have gone missing.
But that was a long time ago, right?

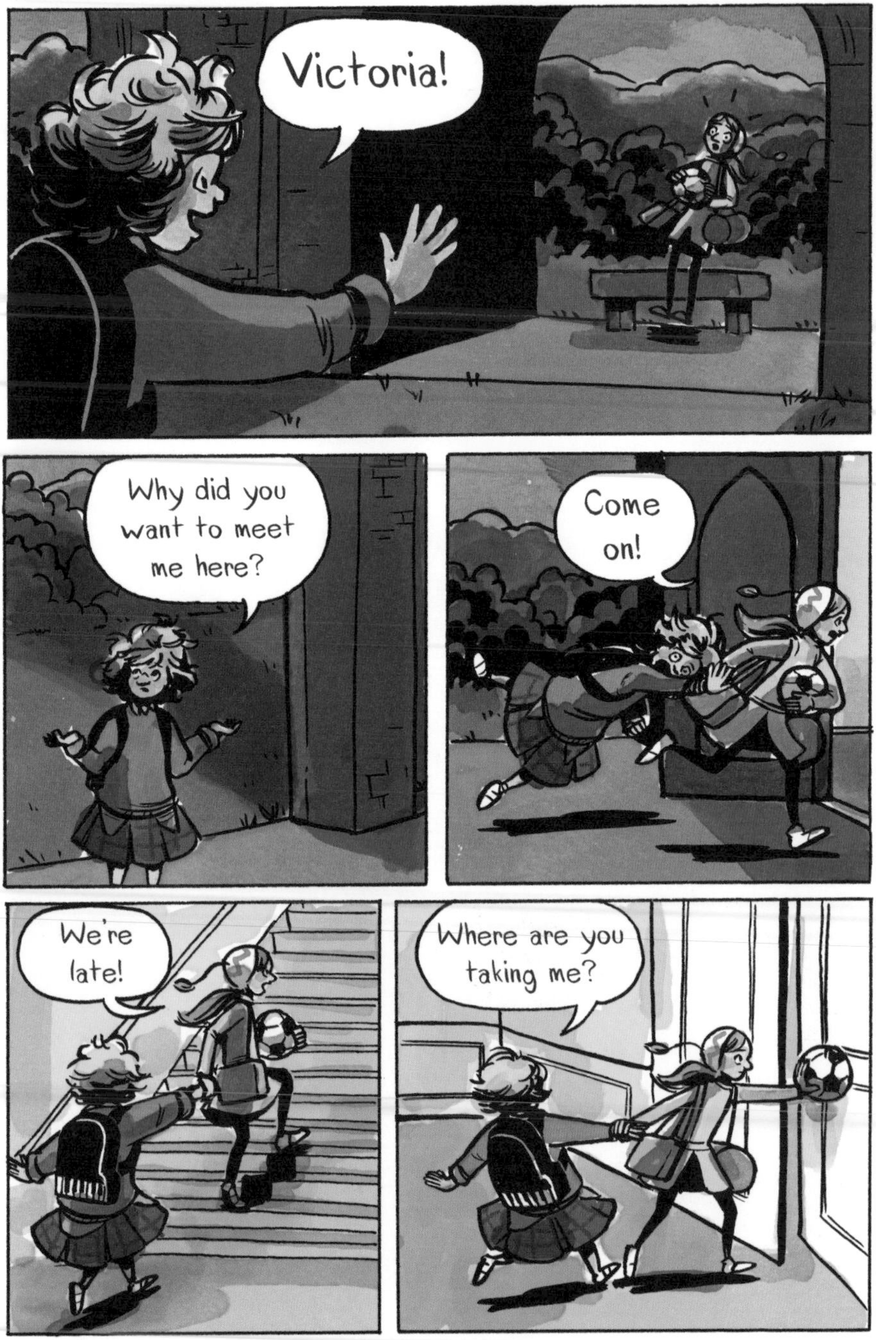
Victoria!
Why did you want to meet me here?
Come on!
We're late!
Where are you taking me?

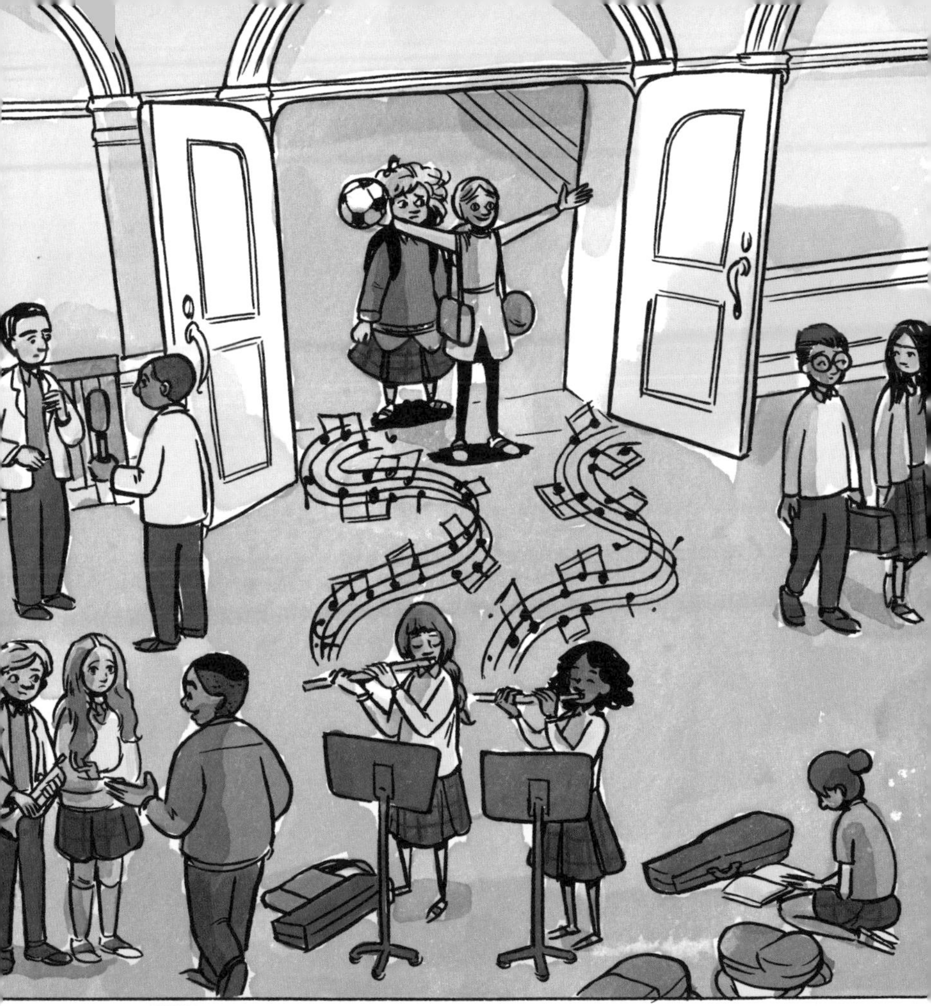

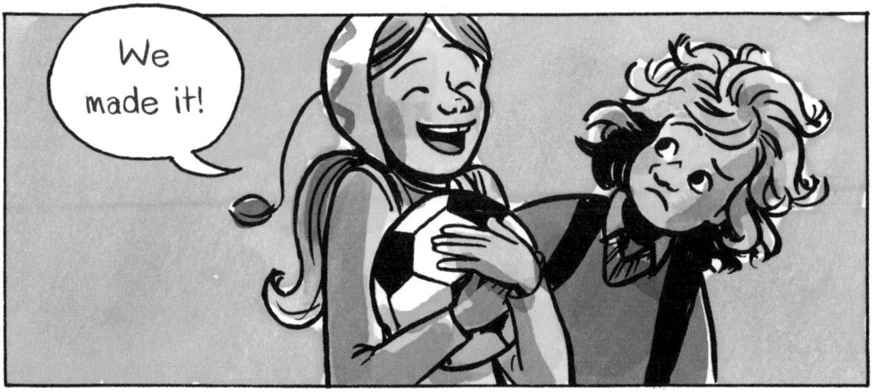
We made it!

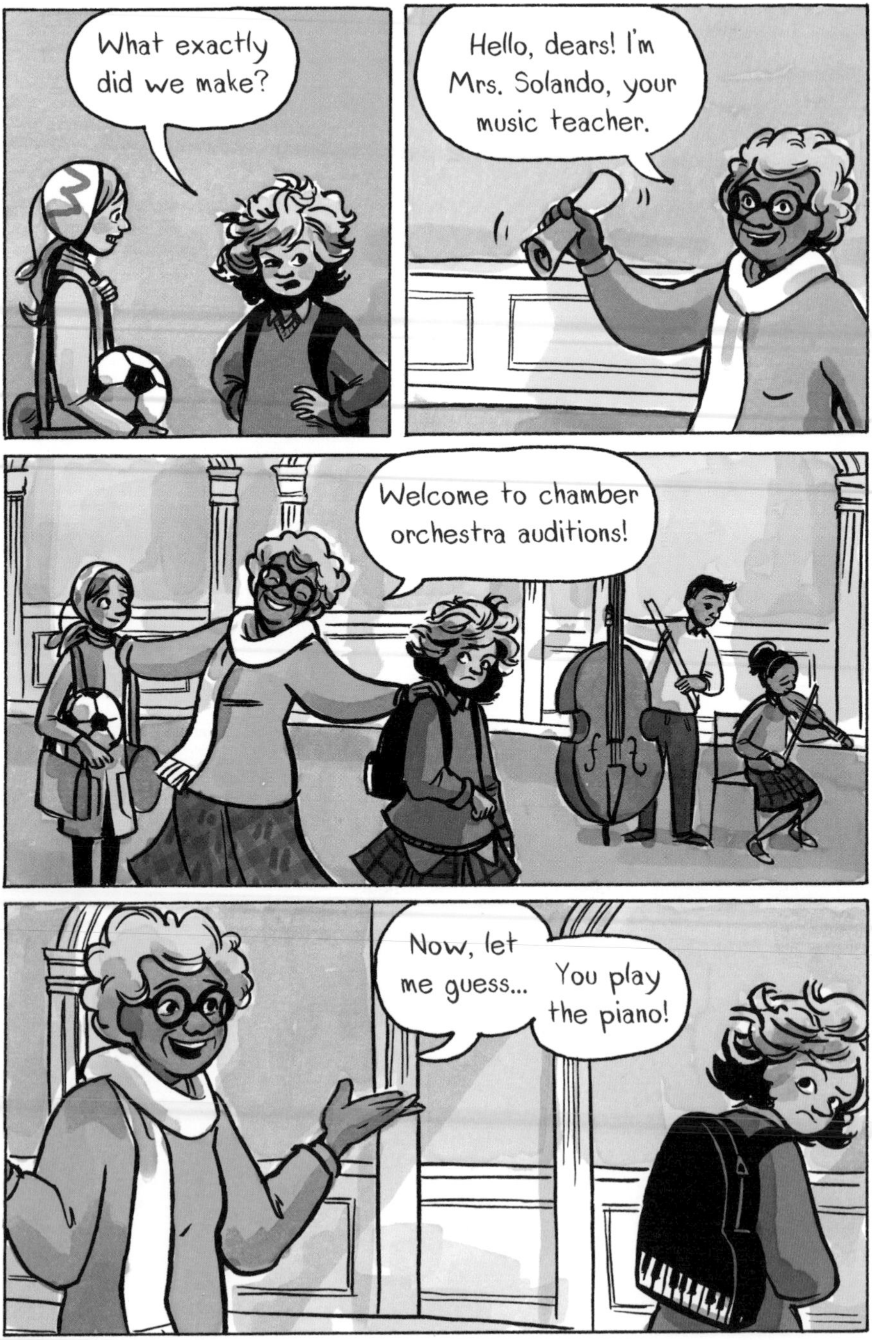
What exactly did we make?
Hello, dears! I'm Mrs. Solando, your music teacher.
Welcome to chamber orchestra auditions!
Now, let me guess...
You play the piano!

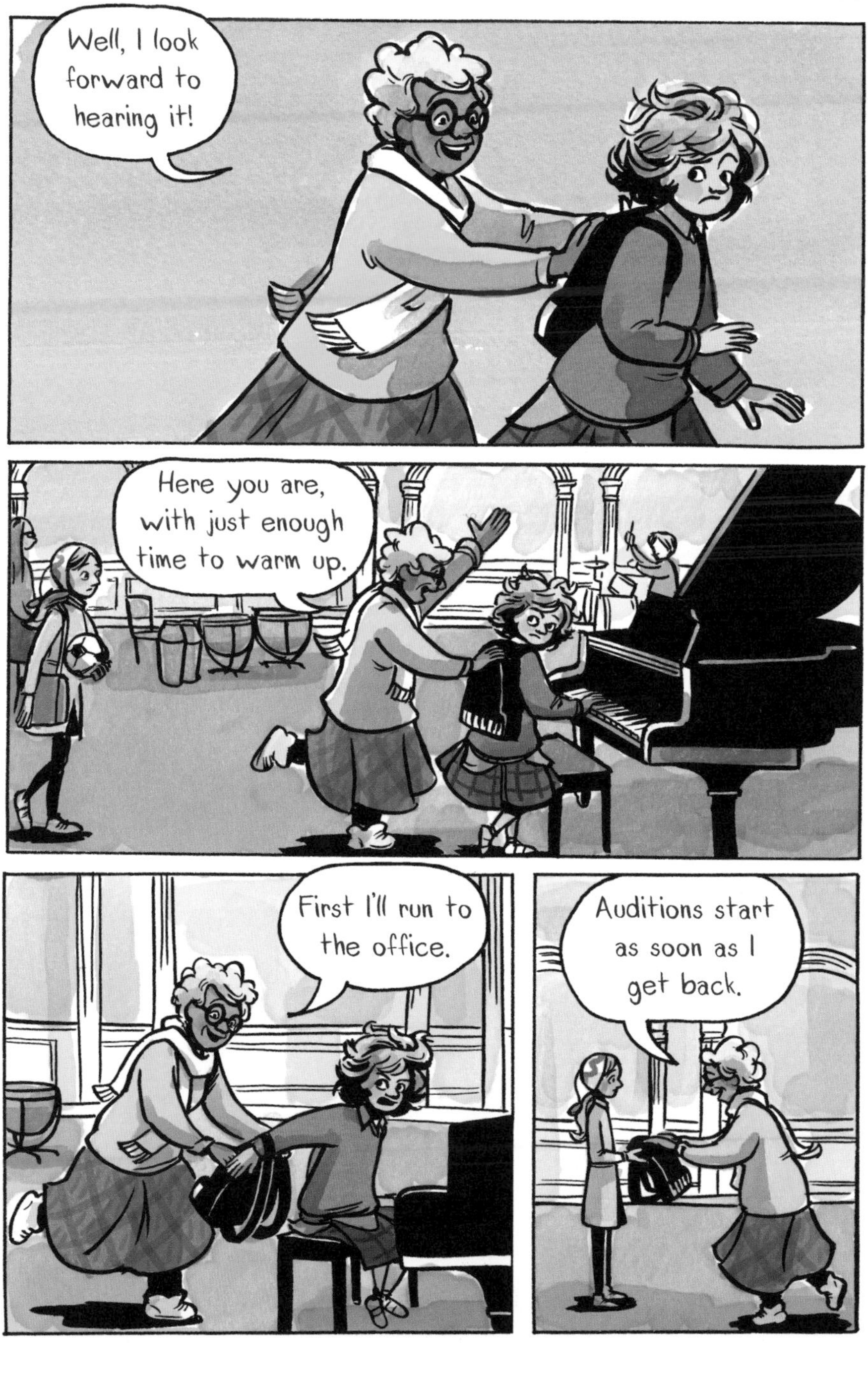
Well, I look forward to hearing it!
Here you are, with just enough time to warm up.
First I'll run to the office.
Auditions start as soon as I get back.

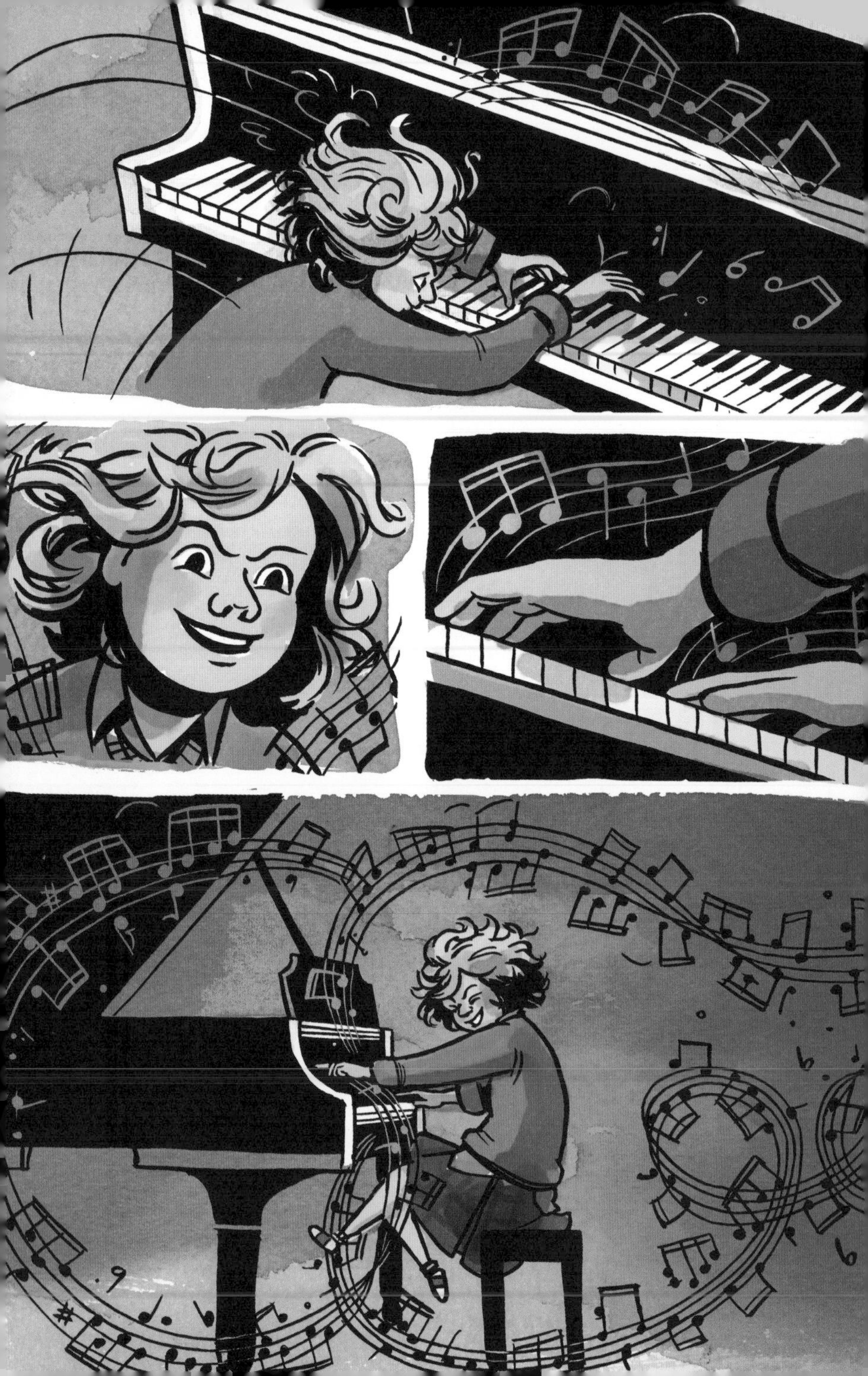

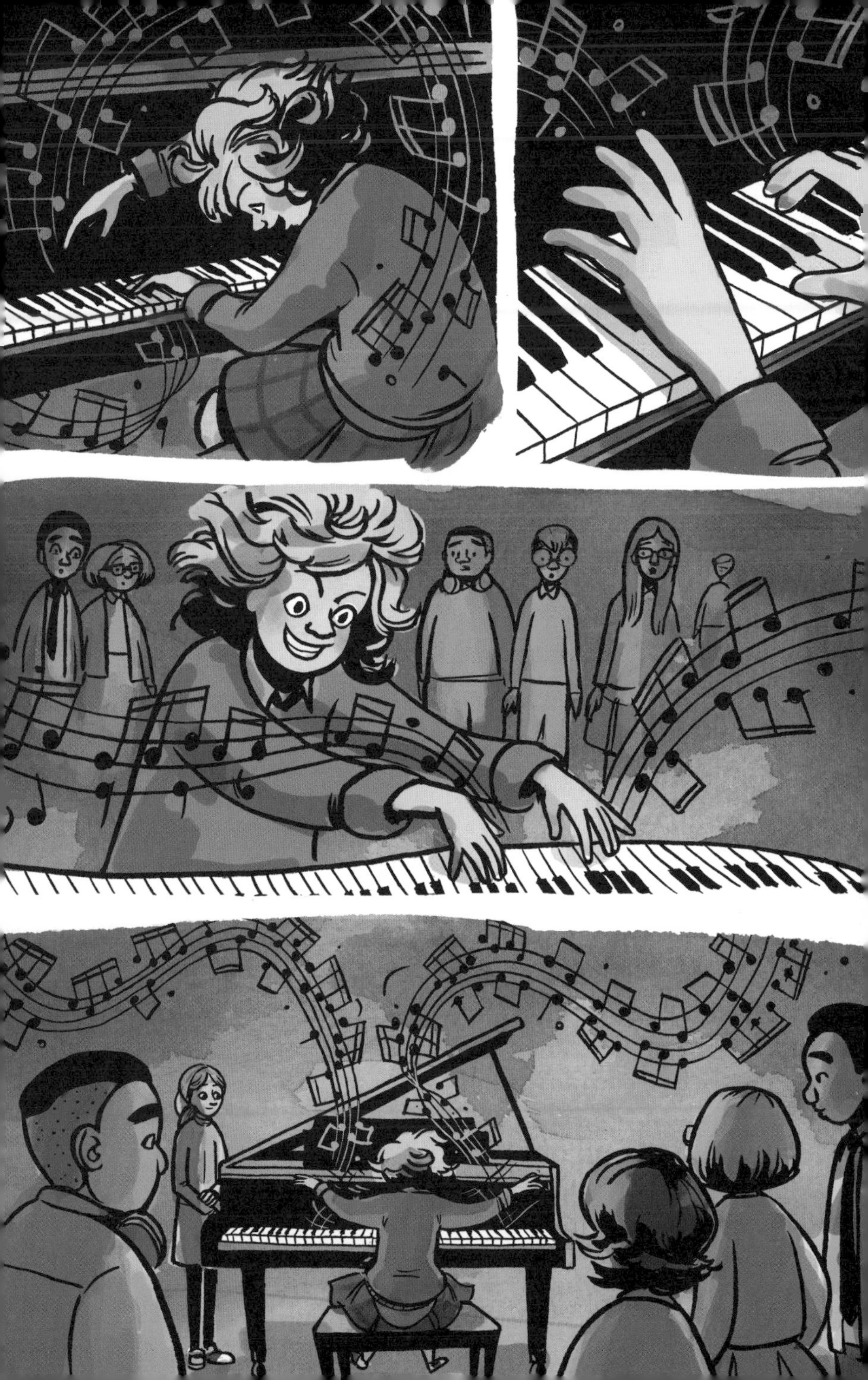

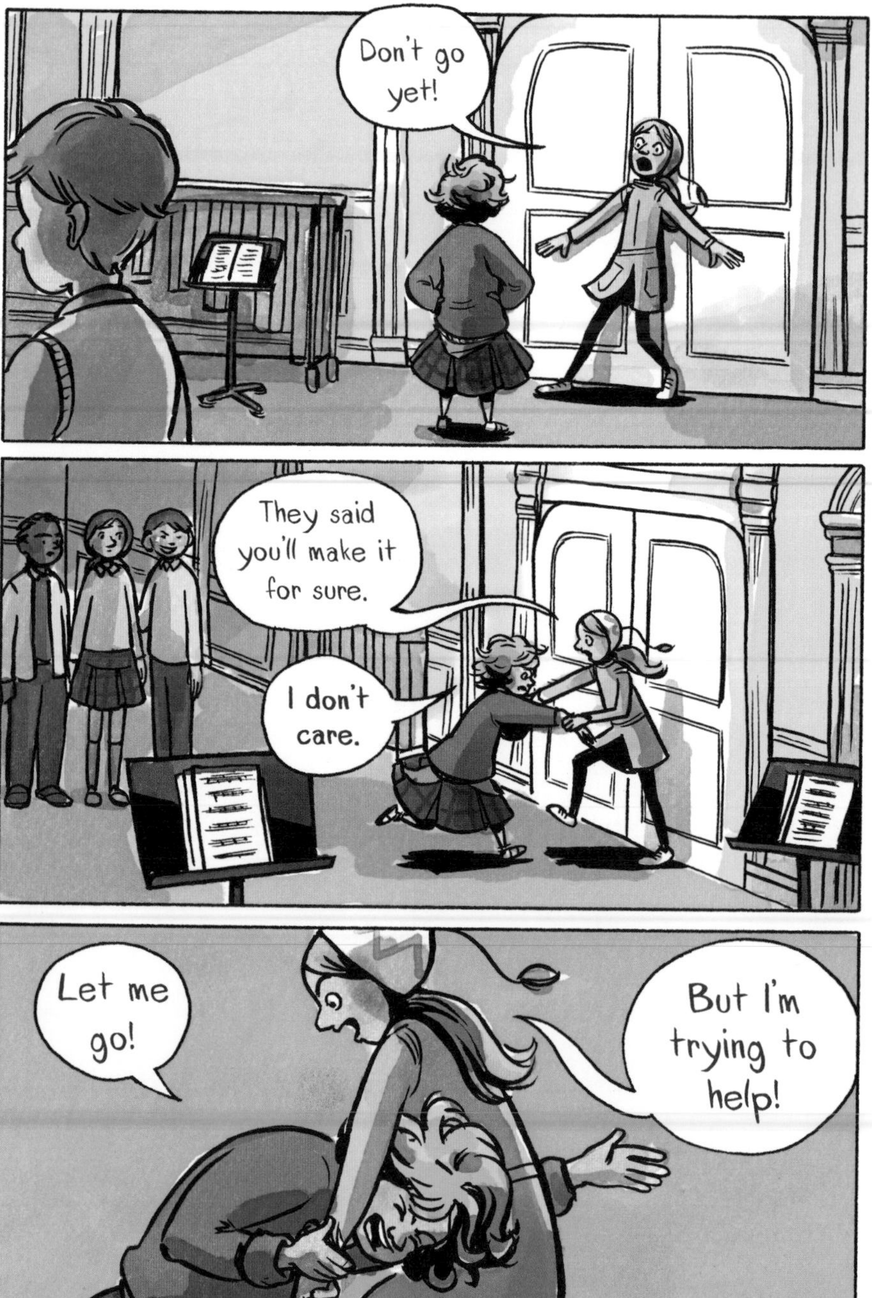

Don't go yet!
They said you'll make it for sure.
I don't care.
Let me go!
But I'm trying to help!

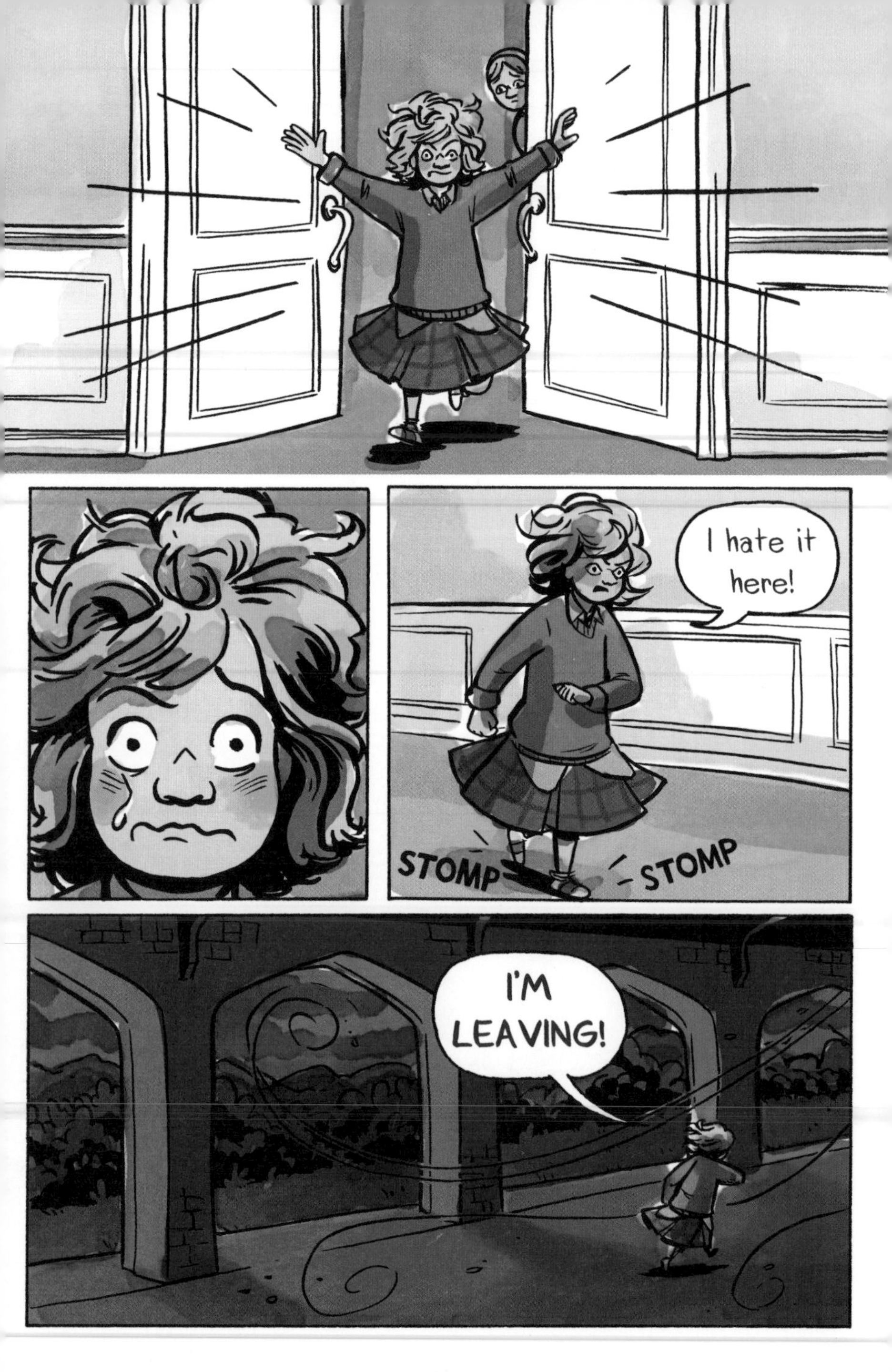
I hate it here!
STOMP
STOMP
I'M LEAVING!

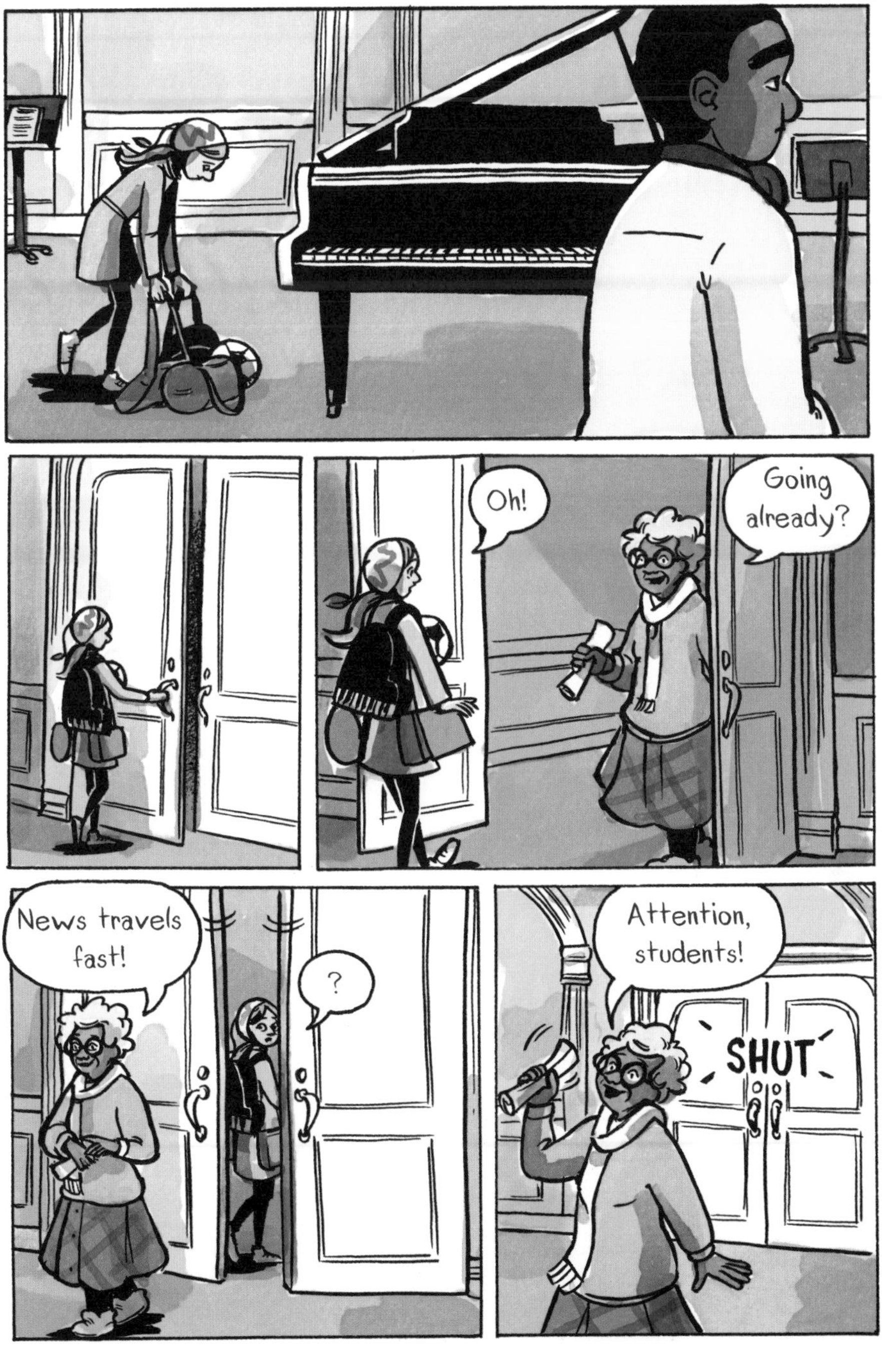
Oh!
Going already?
News travels fast!
?
Attention, students!
SHUT

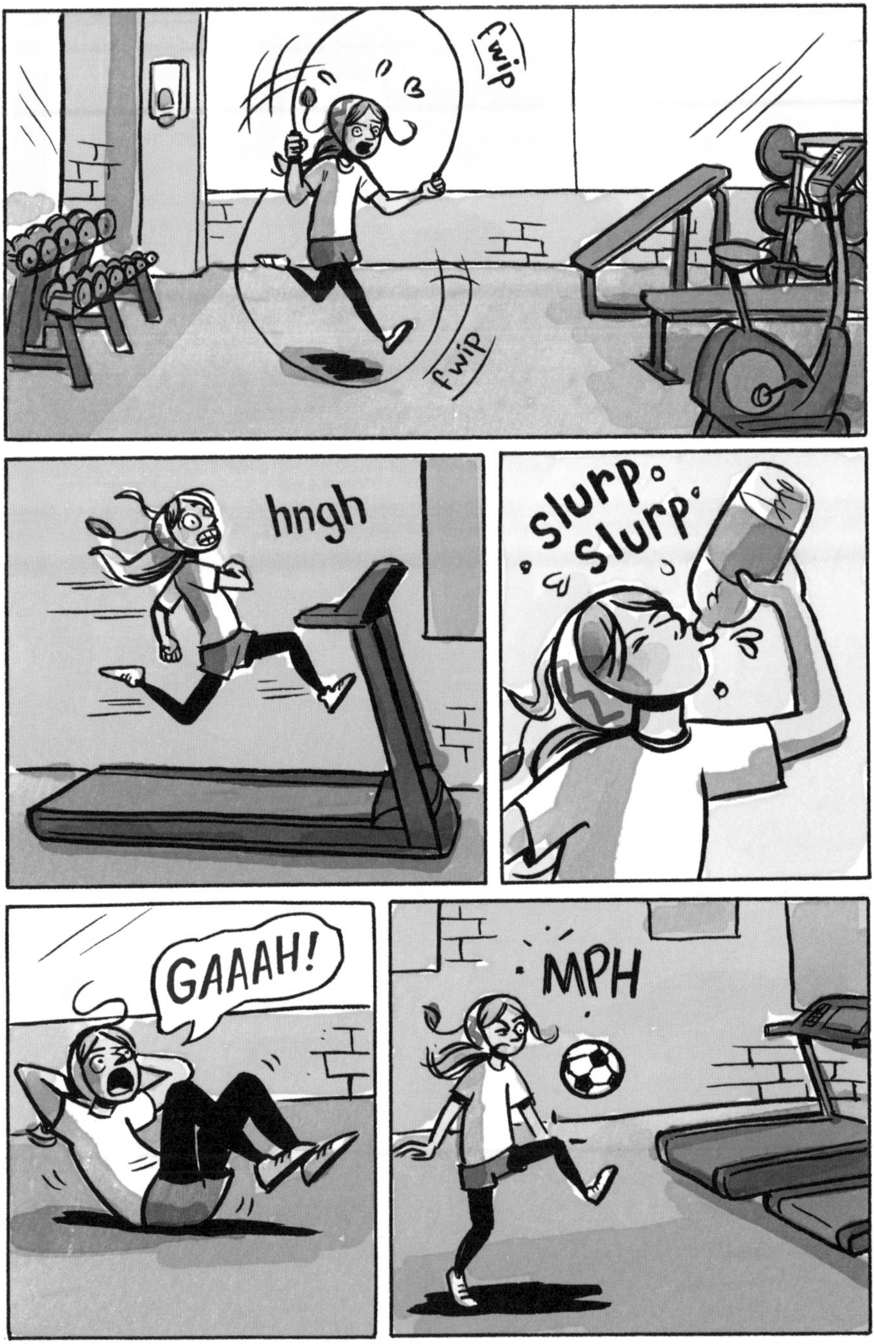
fwip
fwip
hngh
slurp
slurp
GAAAH!
MPH

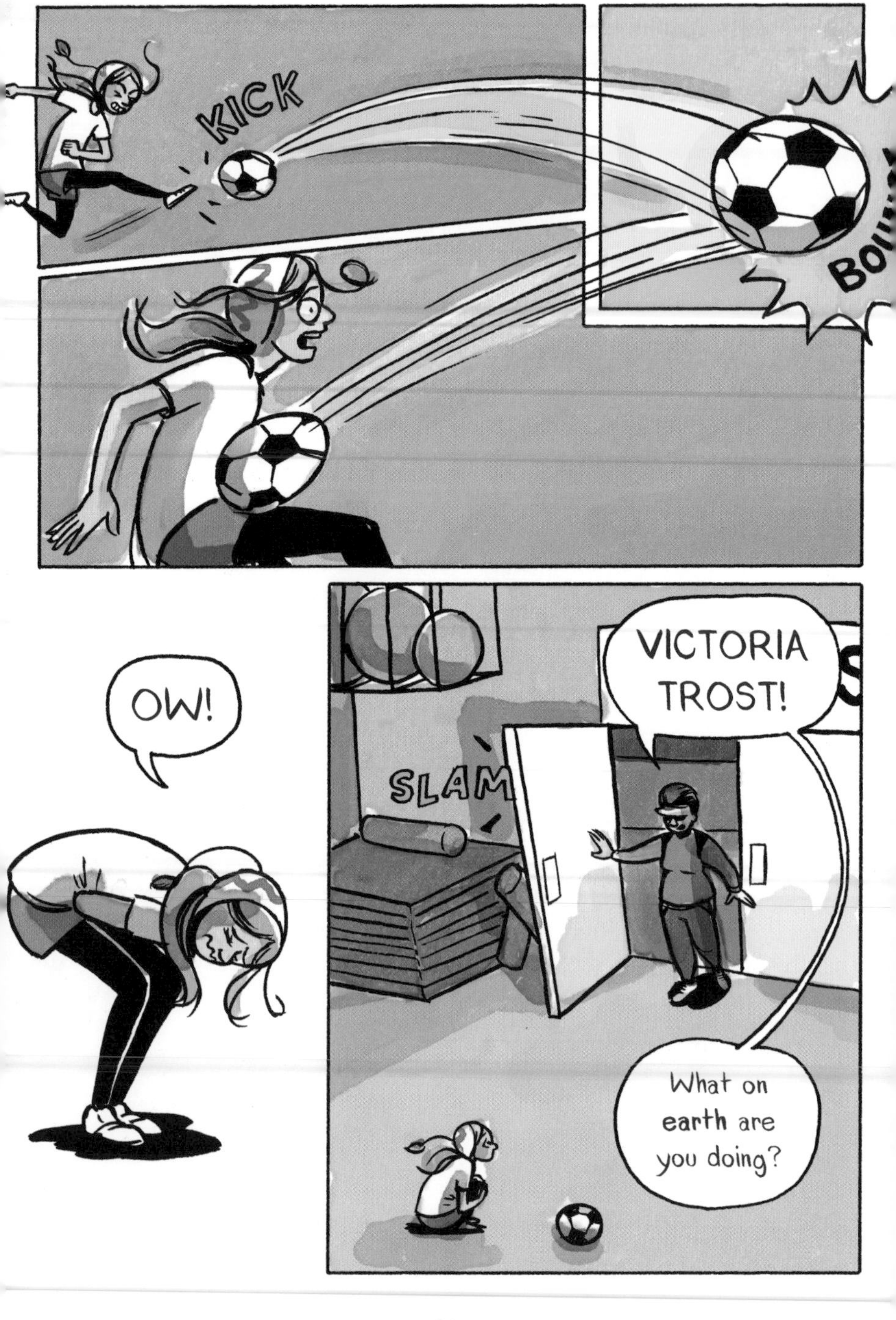
KICK
BOU
OW!
SLAM
VICTORIA TROST!
What on earth are you doing?

81

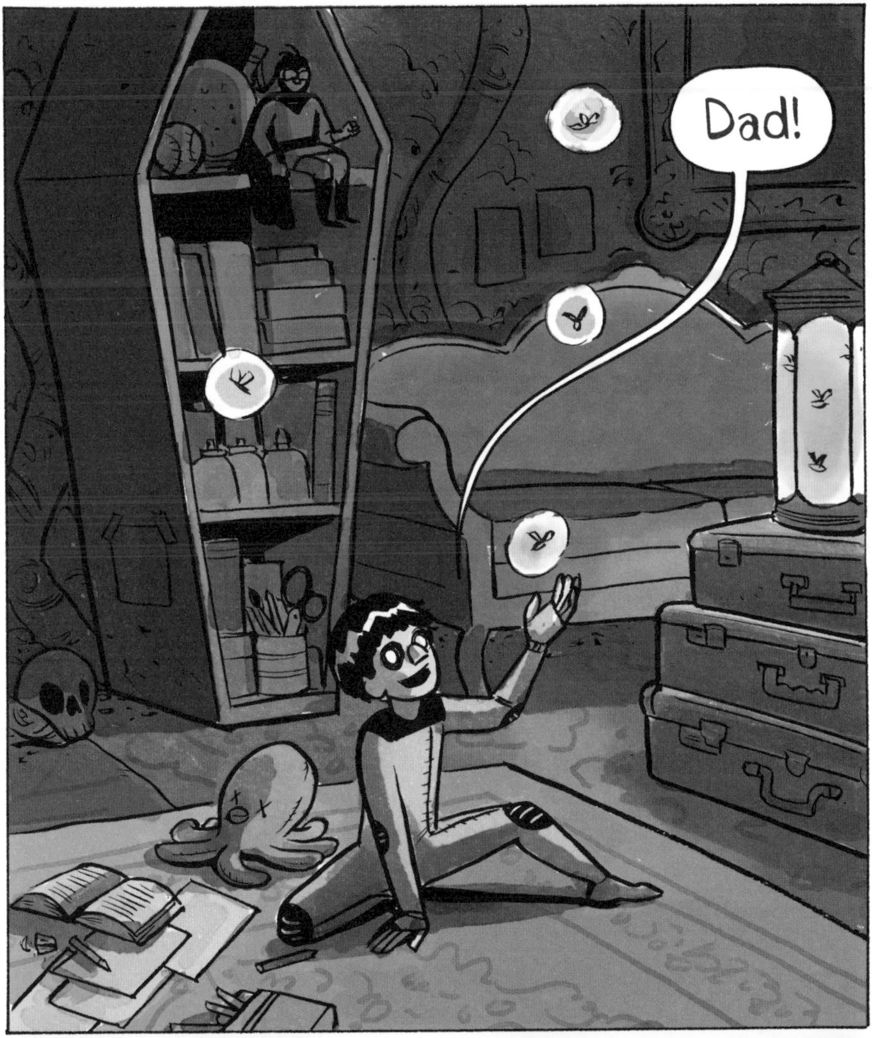
Dad!

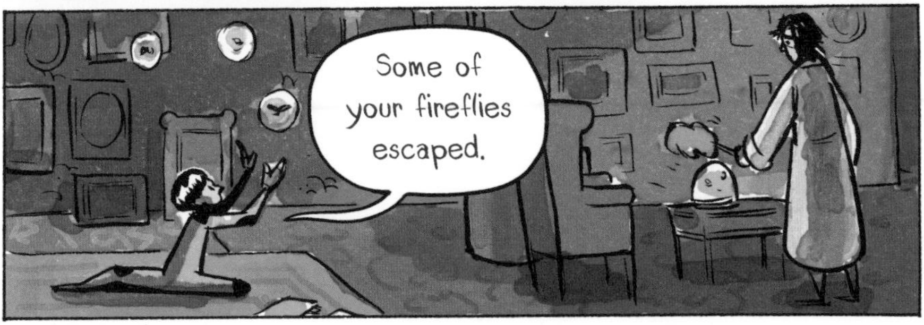
Some of your fireflies escaped.

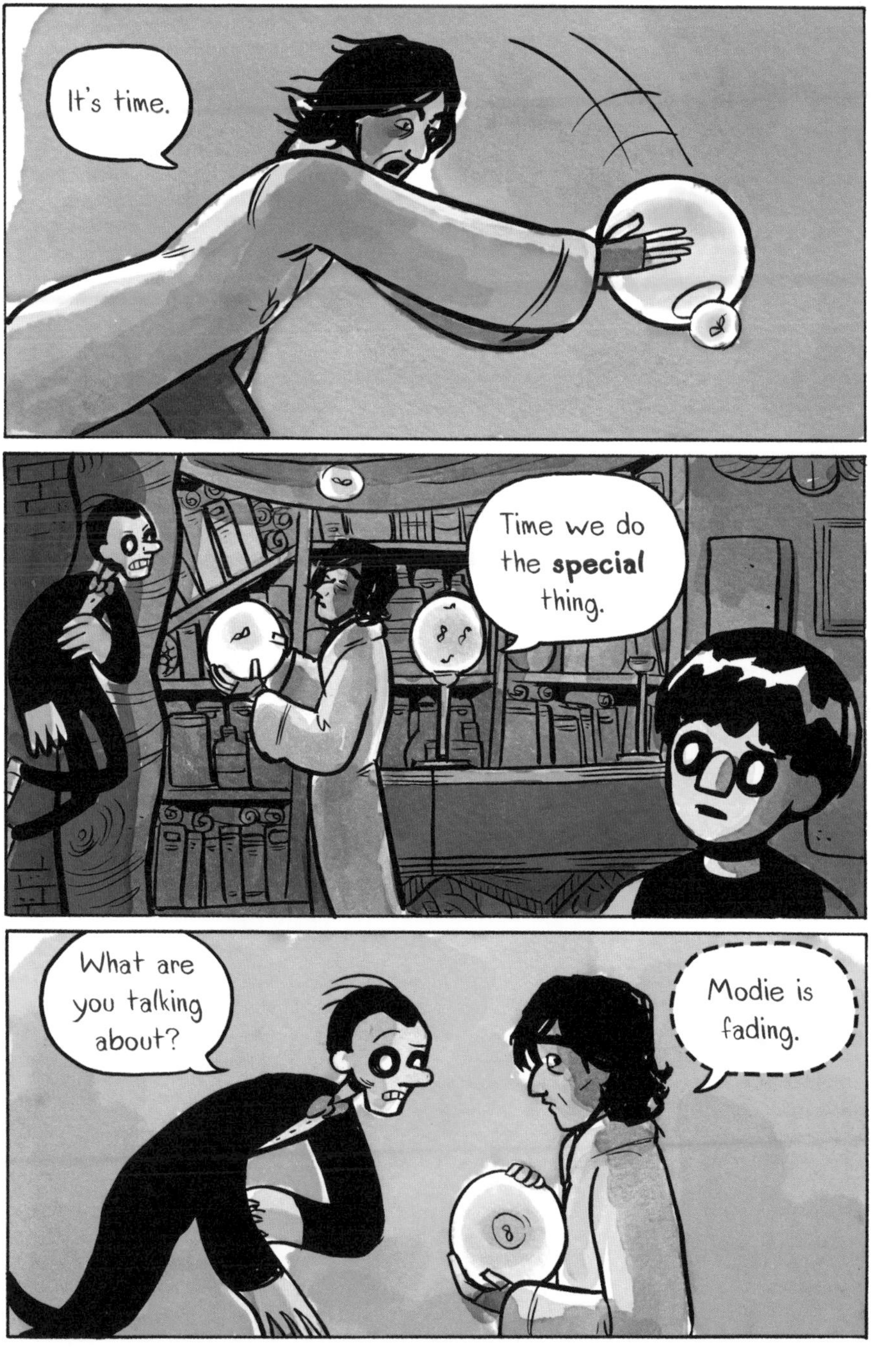
It's time.
Time we do the **special** thing.
What are you talking about?
Modie is fading.

86

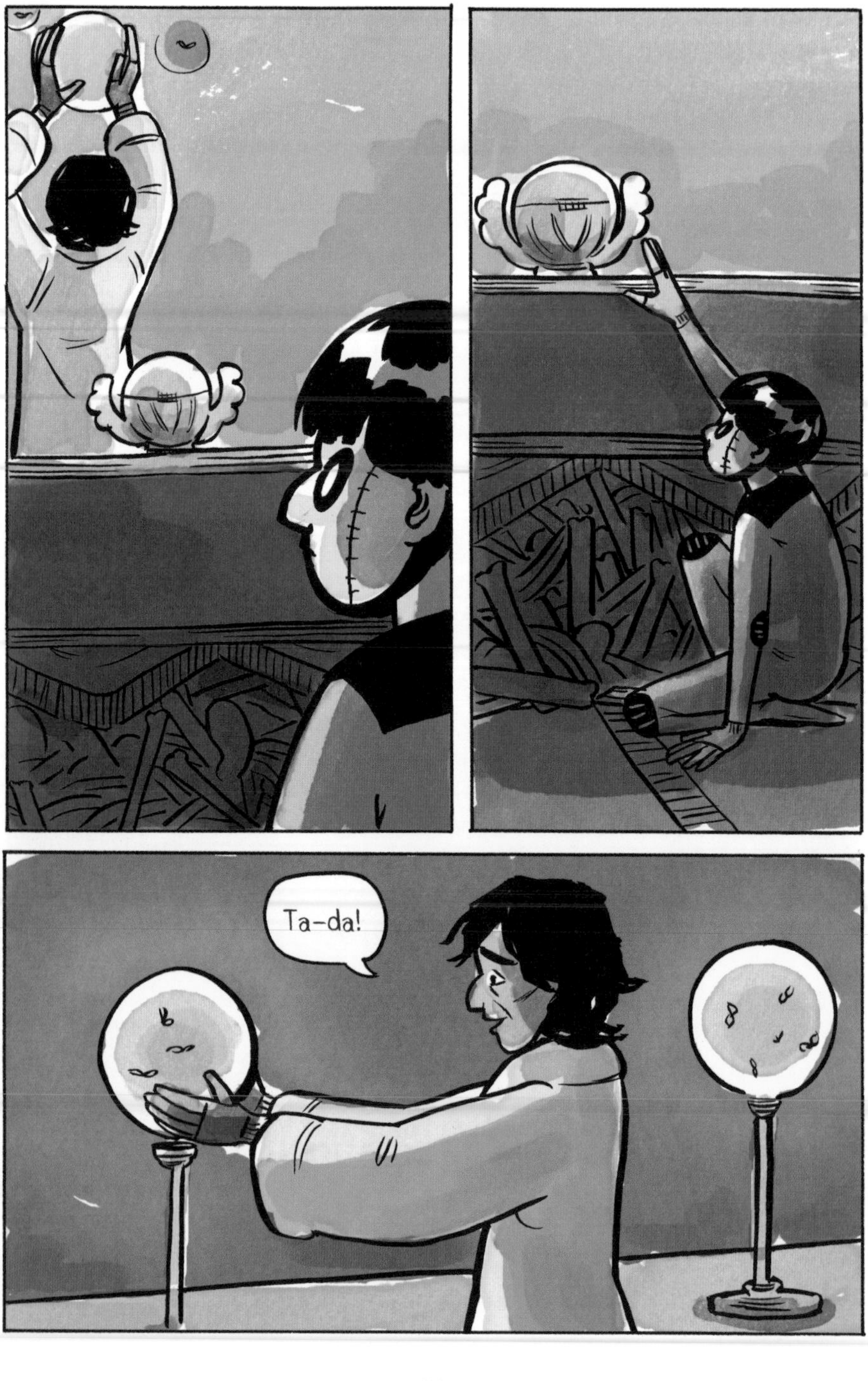
Ta-da!

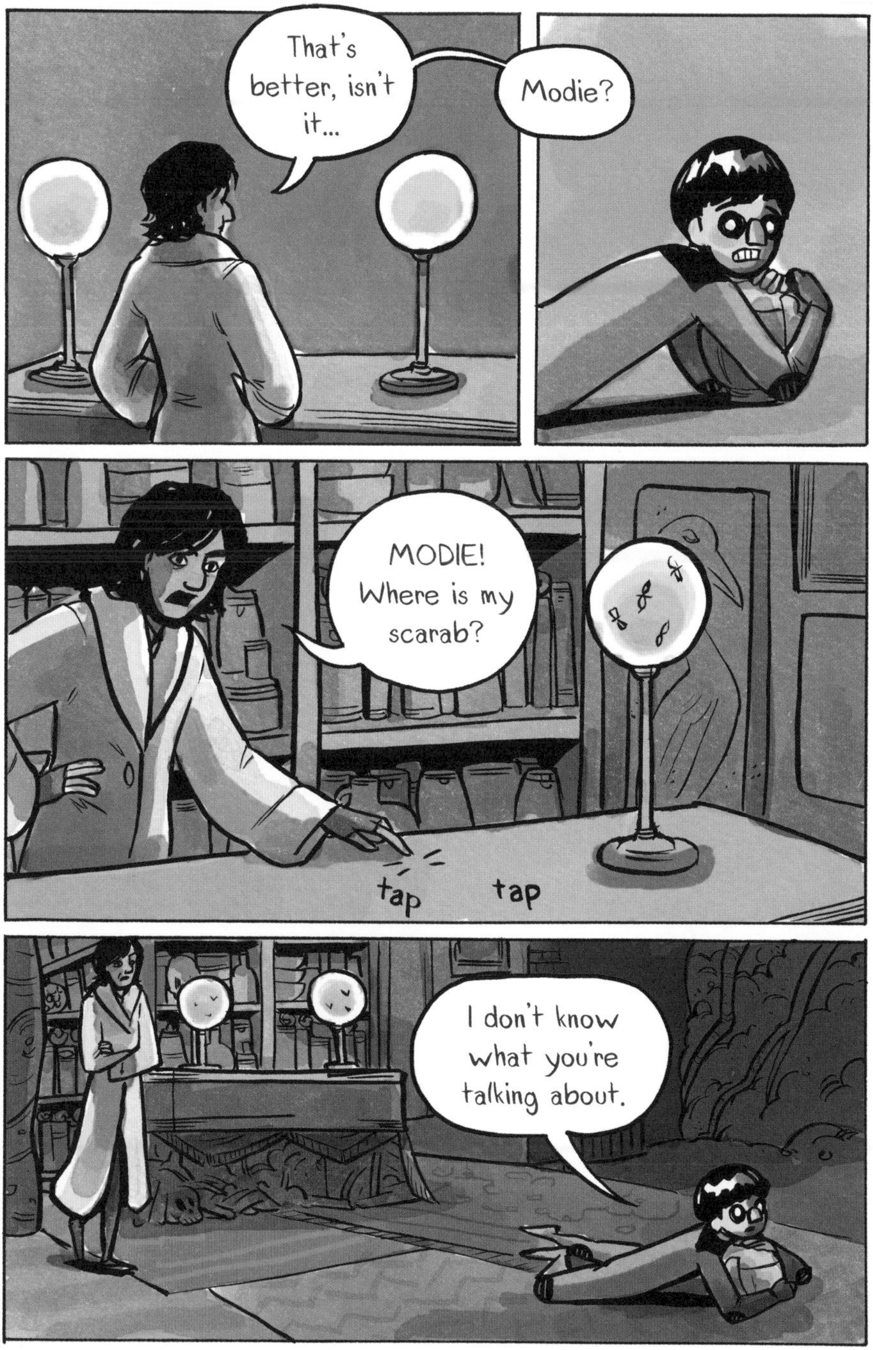
That's better, isn't it...
Modie?
MODIE! Where is my scarab?
tap
tap
I don't know what you're talking about.

90

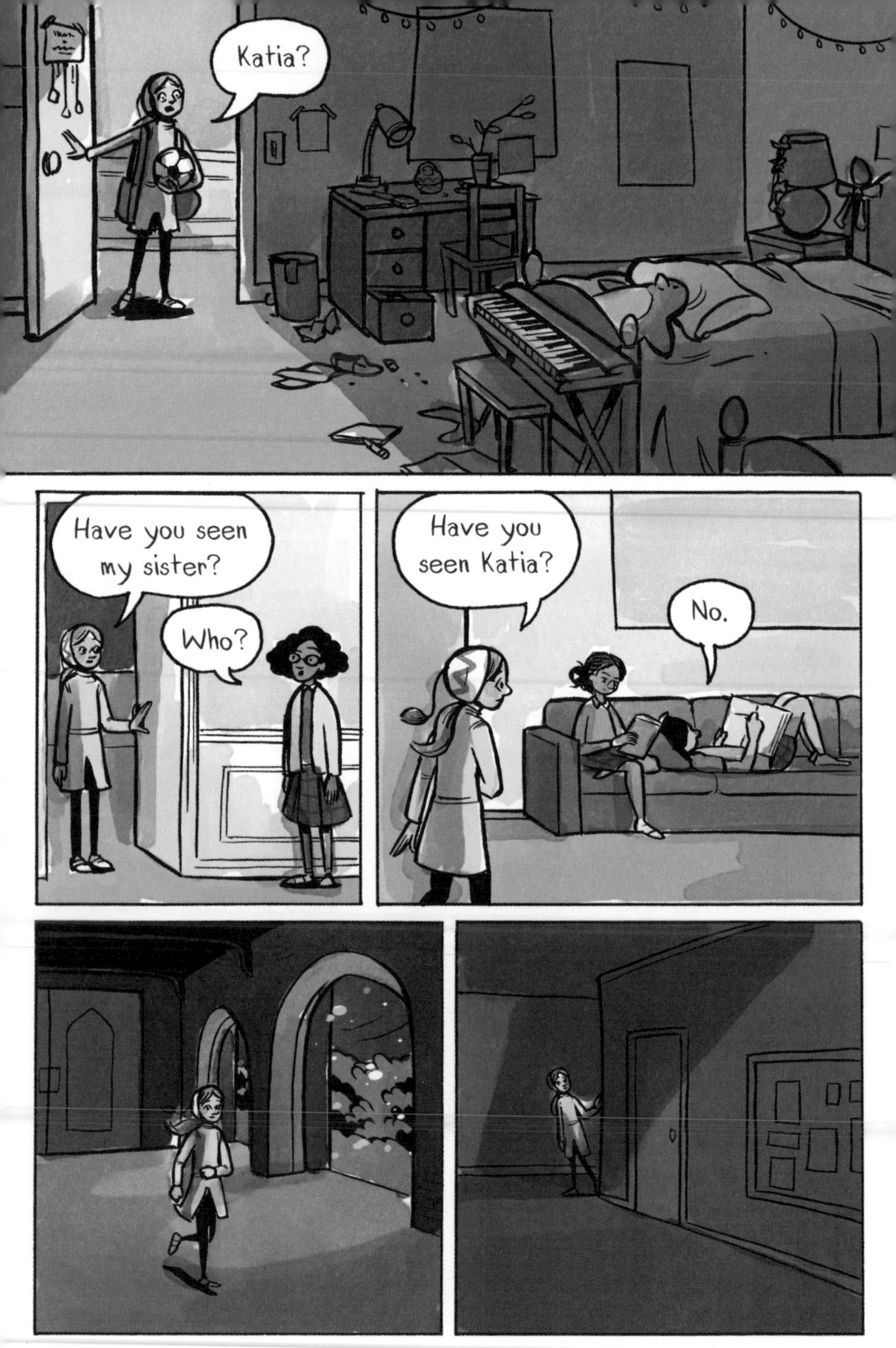
Katia?
Have you seen my sister?
Who?
Have you seen Katia?
No.

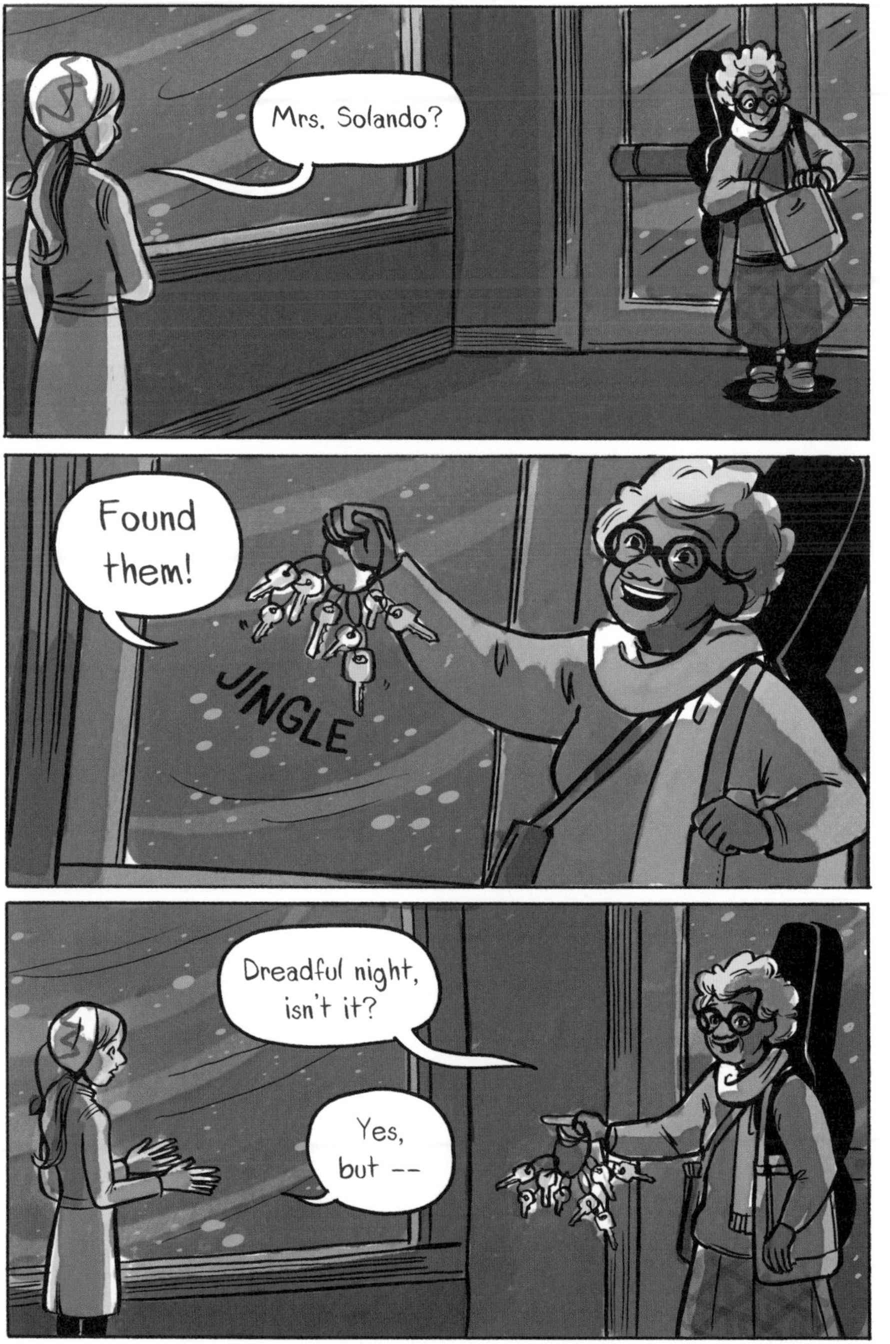
Mrs. Solando?
Found them!
JINGLE
Dreadful night, isn't it?
Yes, but --

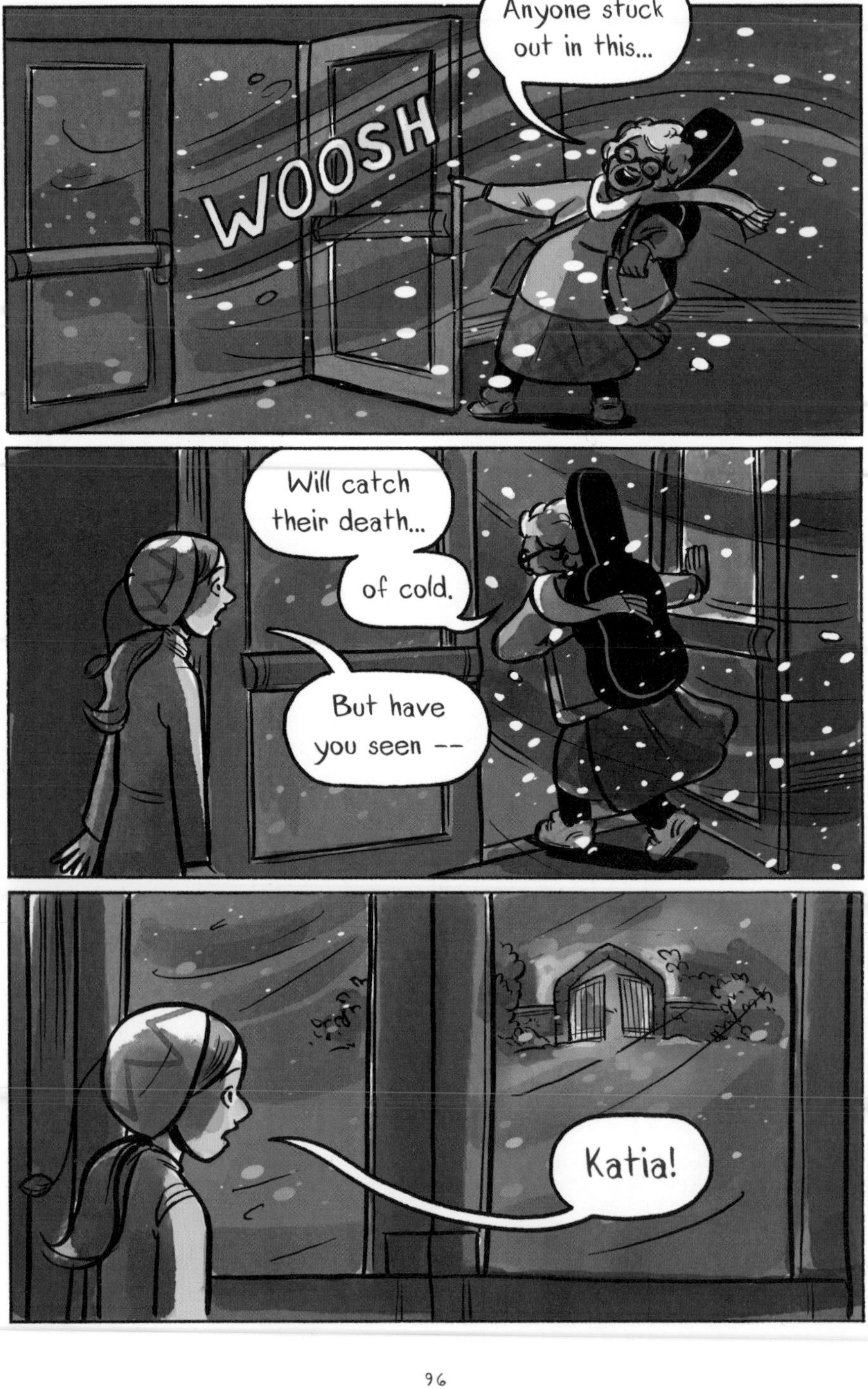

Anyone stuck out in this...
WOOSH
Will catch their death...
of cold.
But have you seen --
Katia!

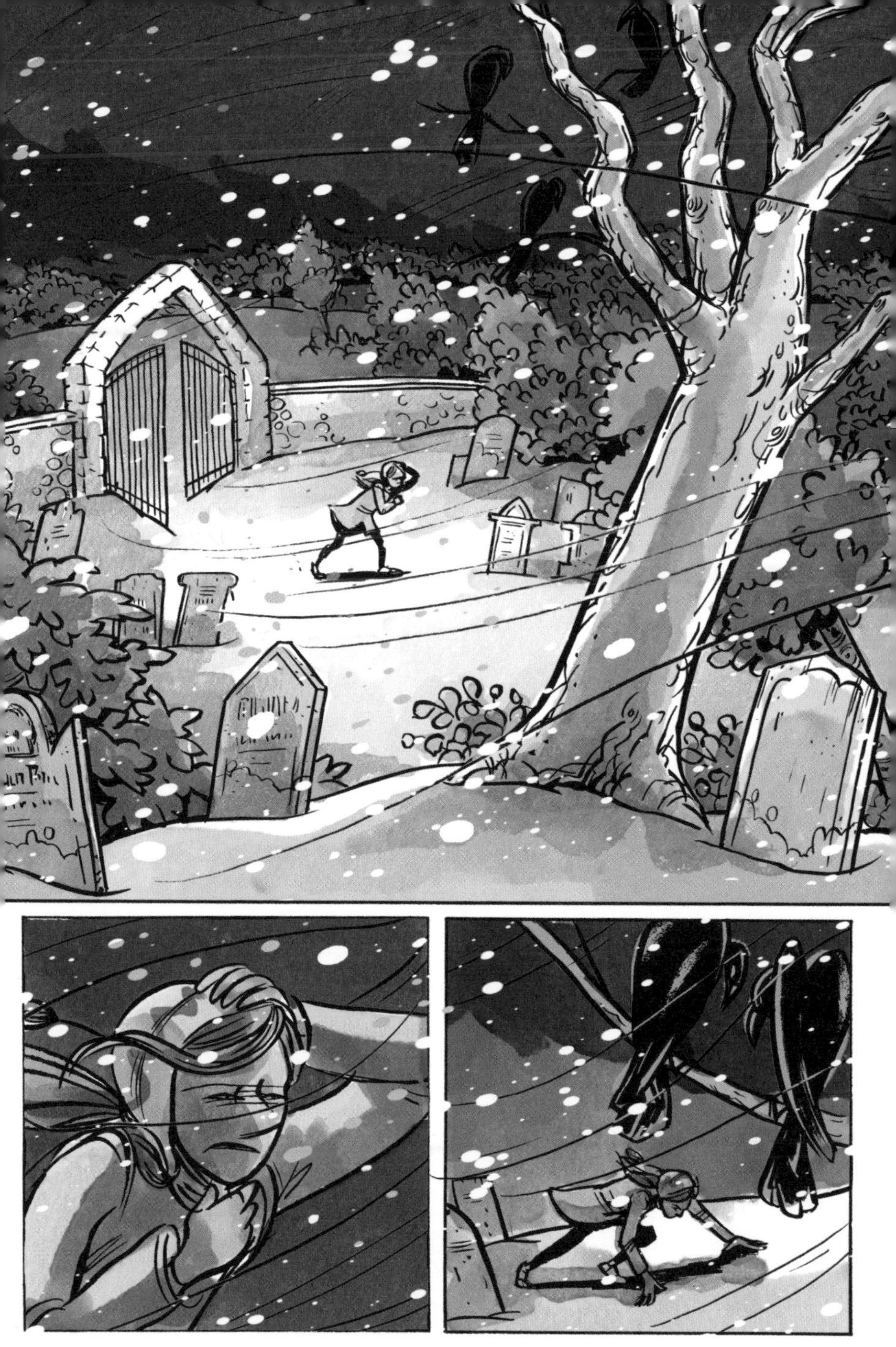

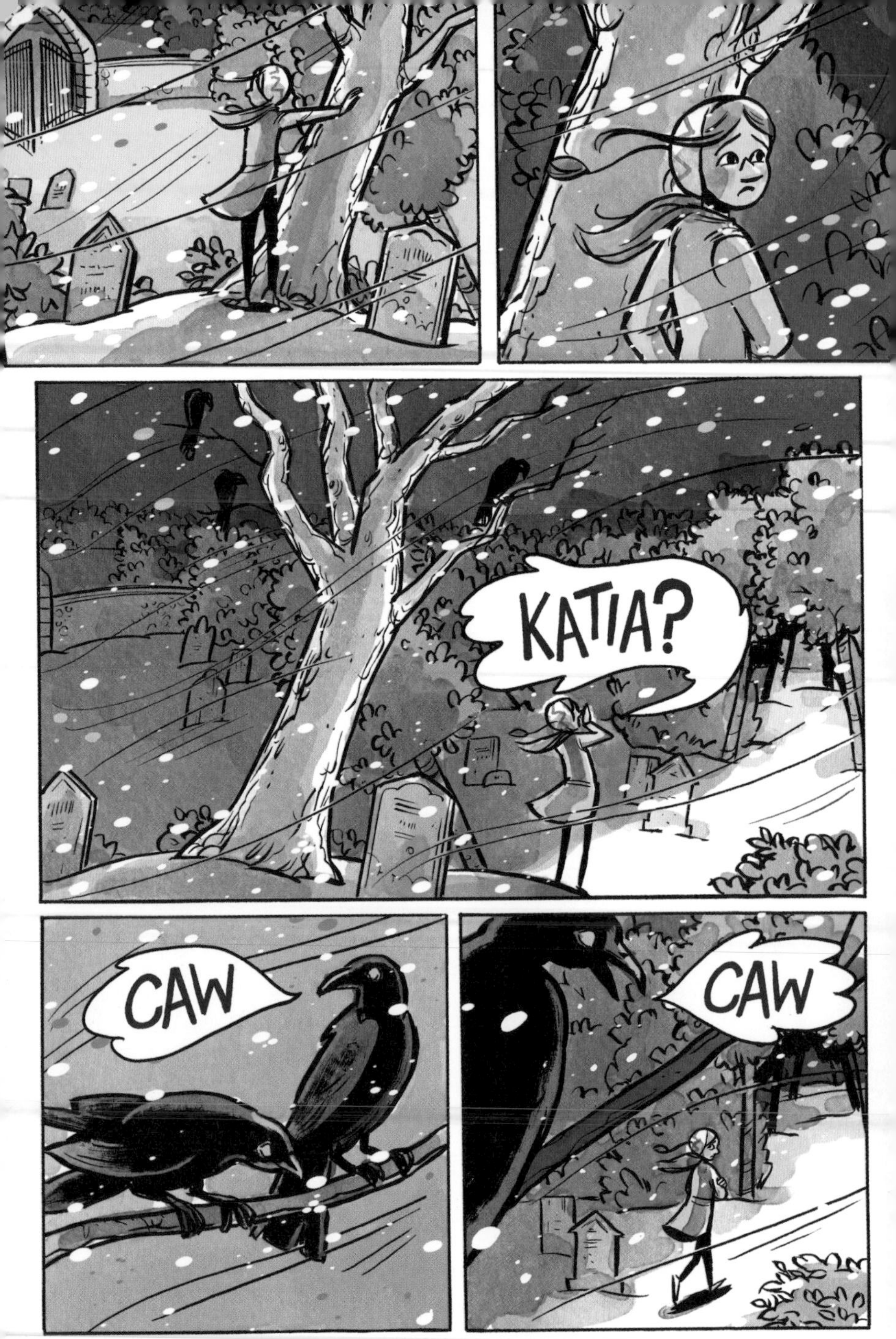
KATIA?
CAW
CAW

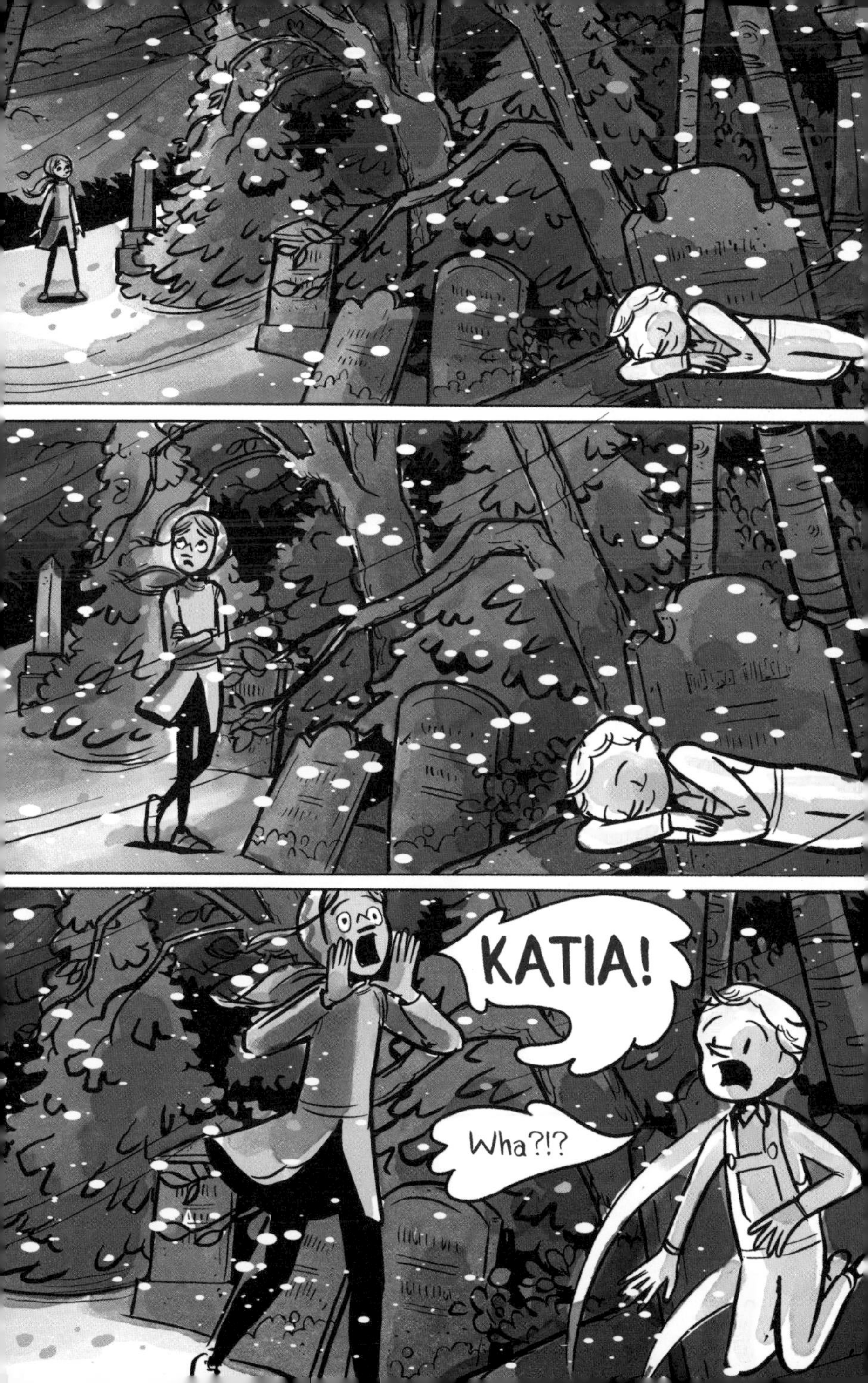
KATIA!
Wha?!?

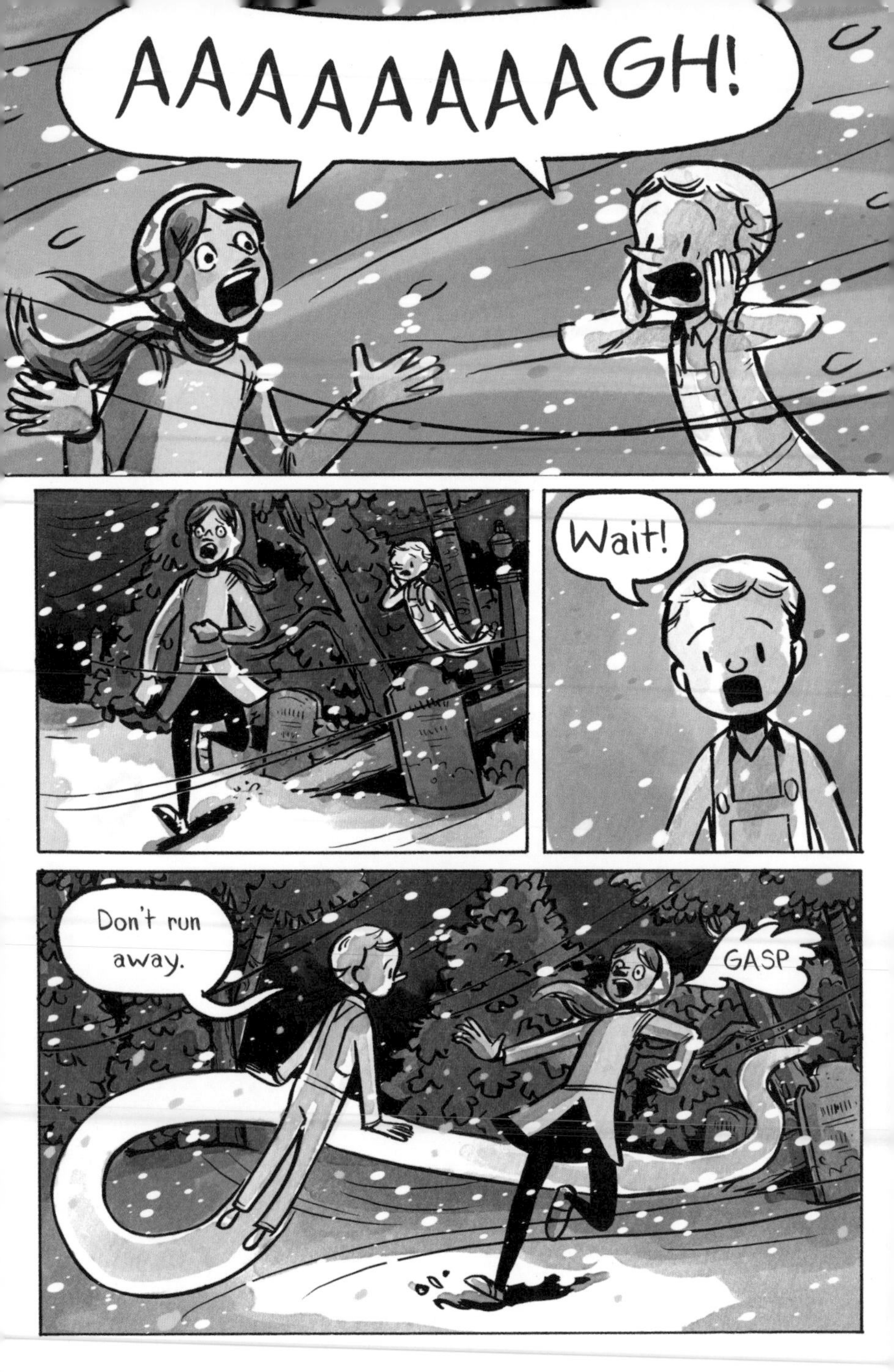
AAAAAAAAAGH!
Wait!
Don't run away.
GASP

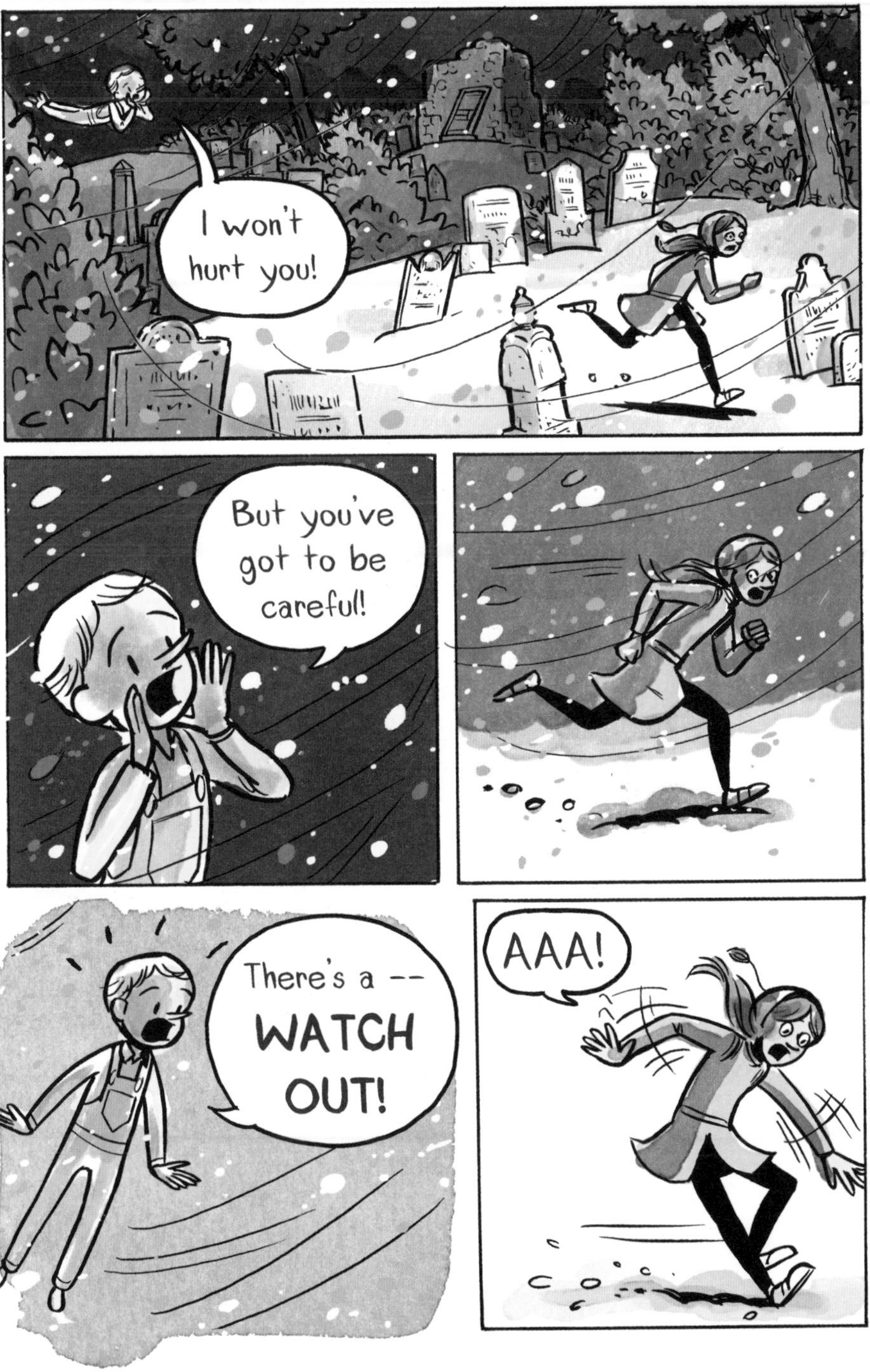
I won't hurt you!
But you've got to be careful!
There's a -- WATCH OUT!
AAA!

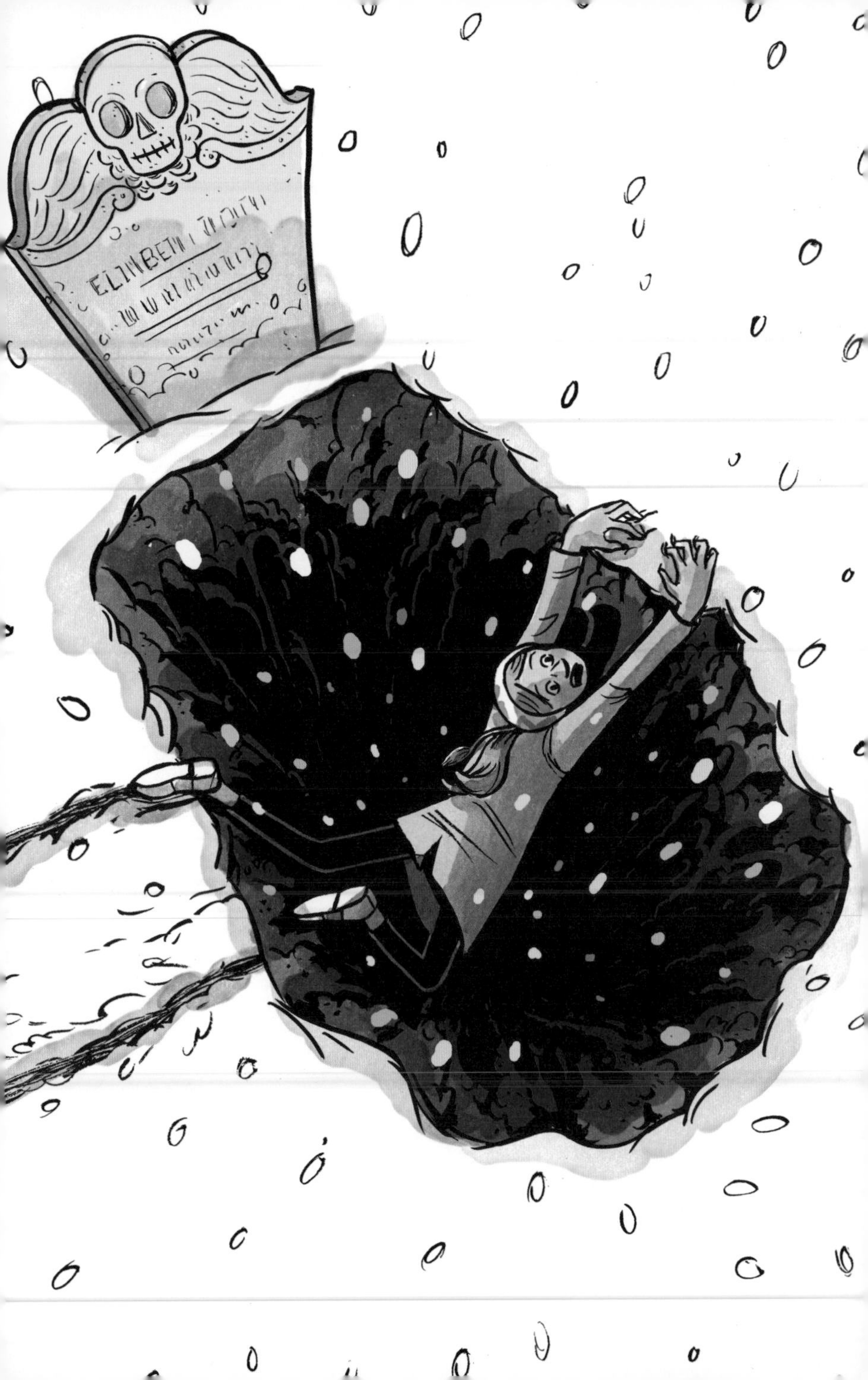

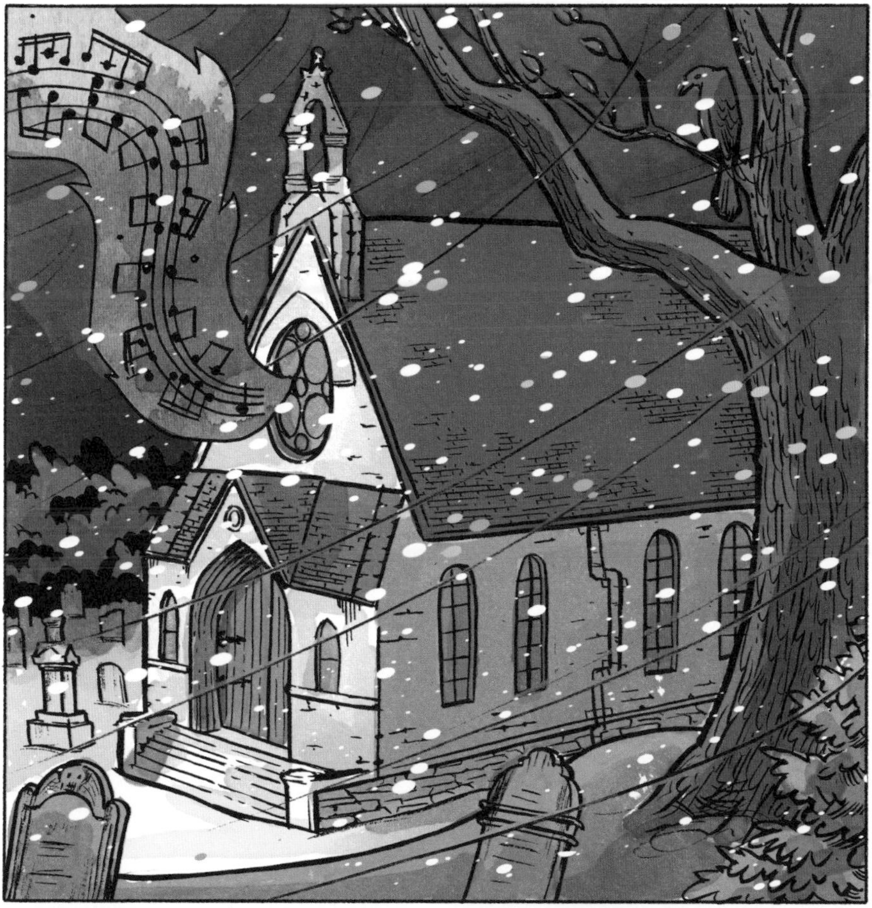

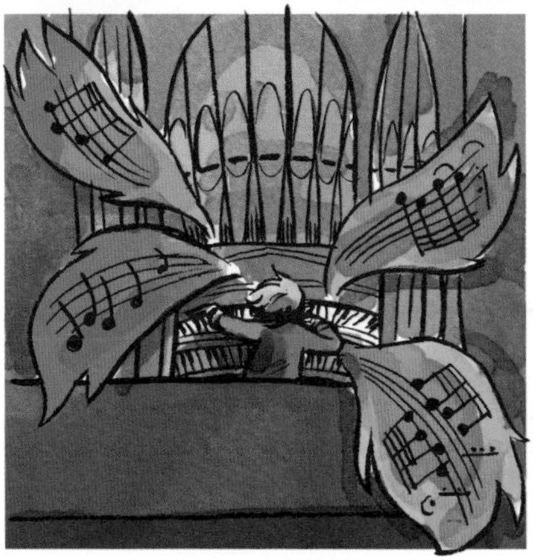

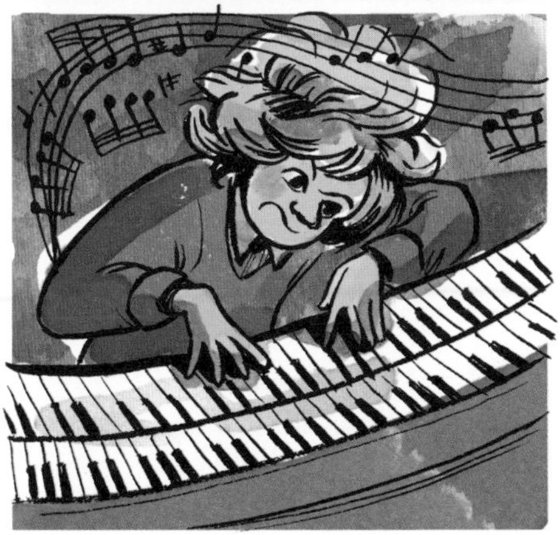

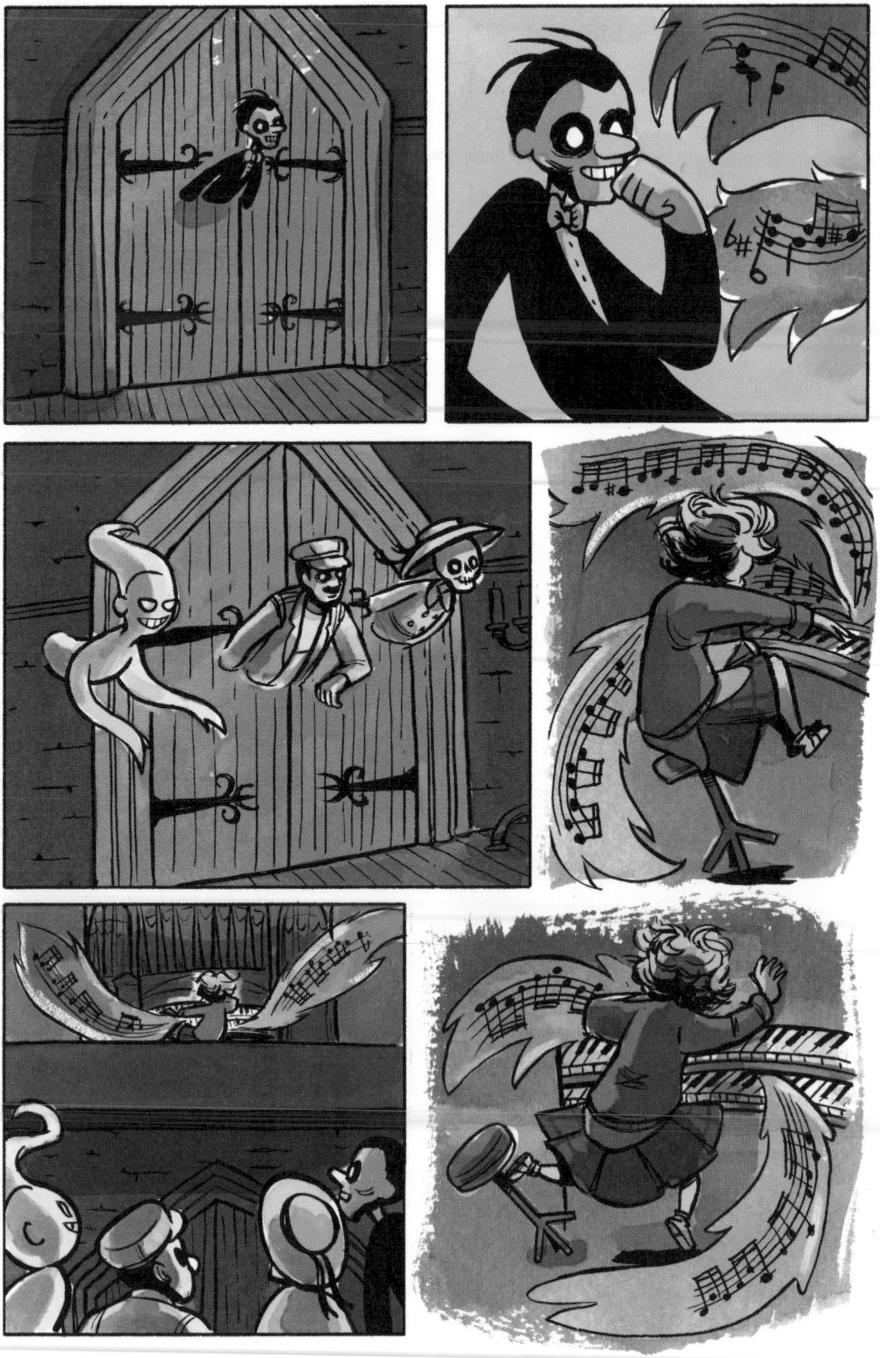

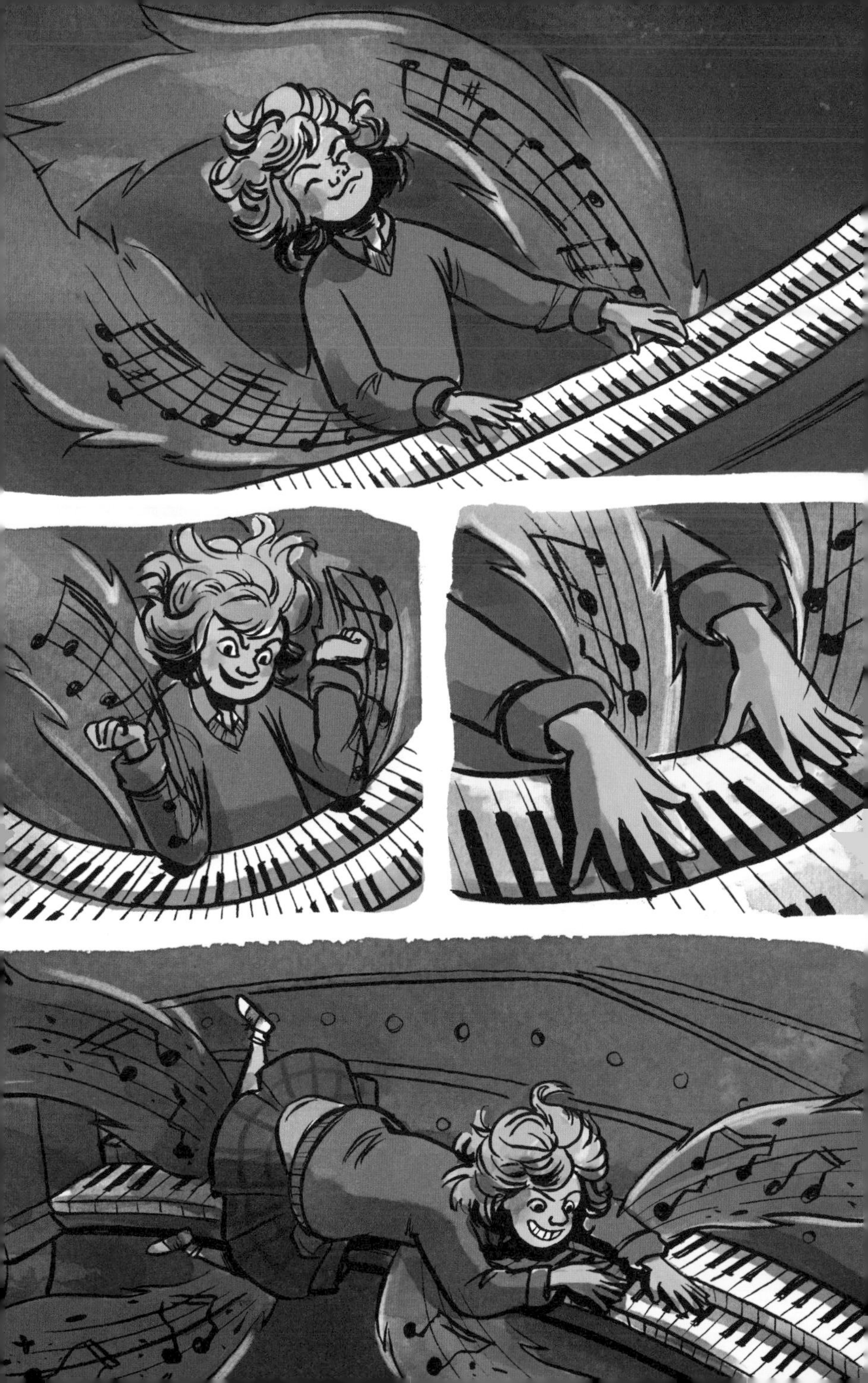

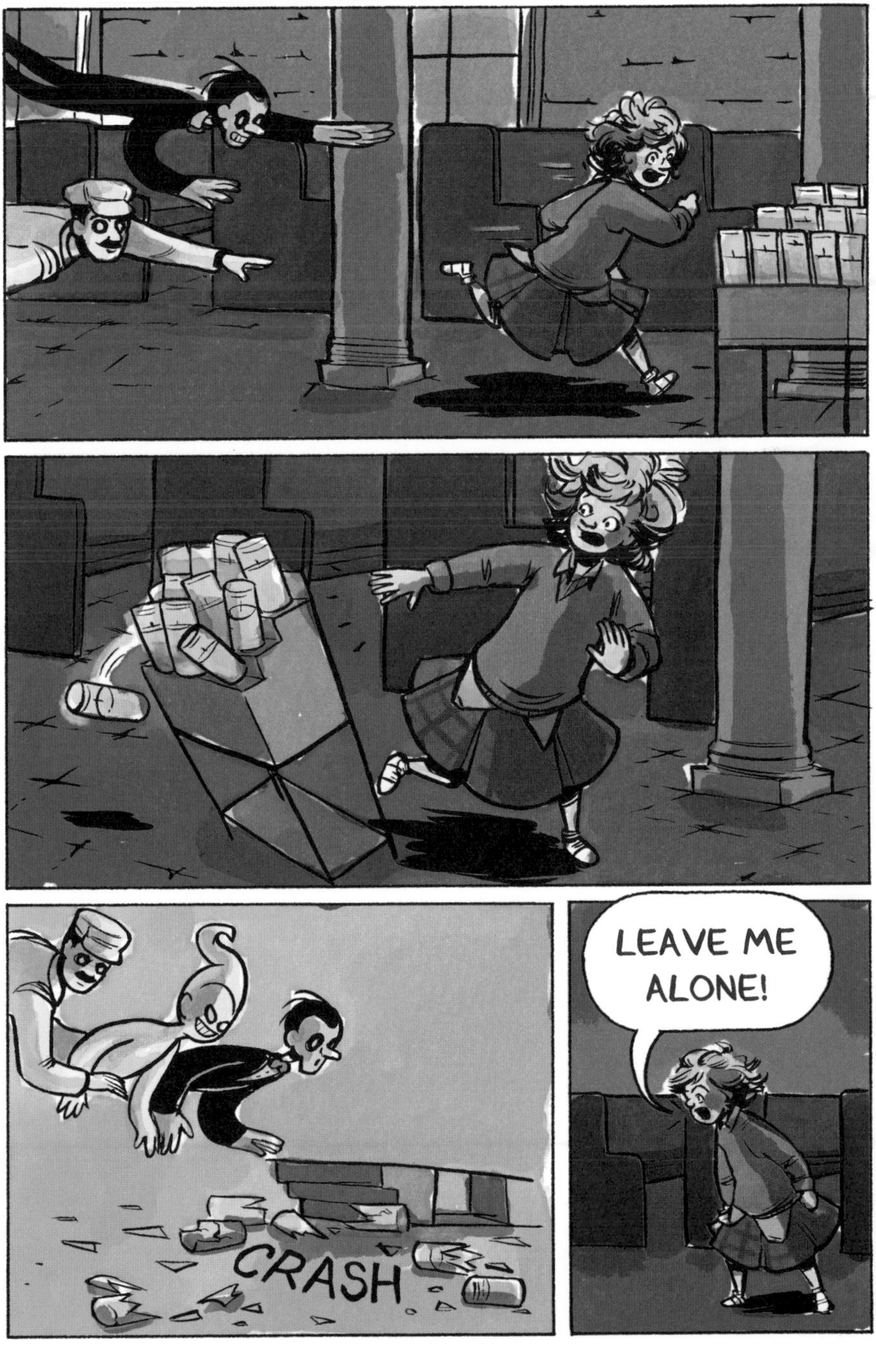
CRASH
LEAVE ME ALONE!

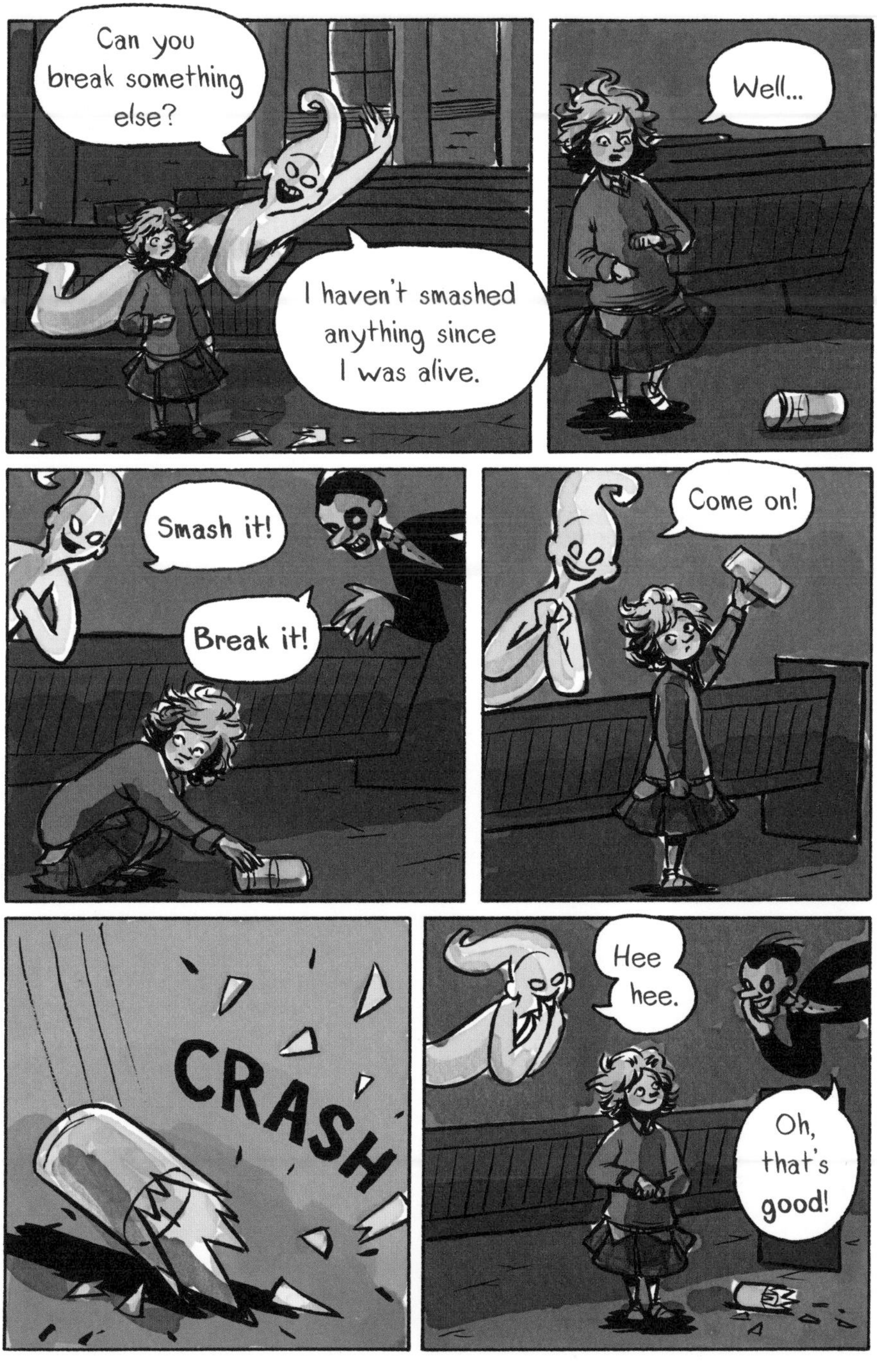
Can you break something else?
I haven't smashed anything since I was alive.
Well...
Smash it!
Break it!
Come on!
CRASH
Hee hee.
Oh, that's good!

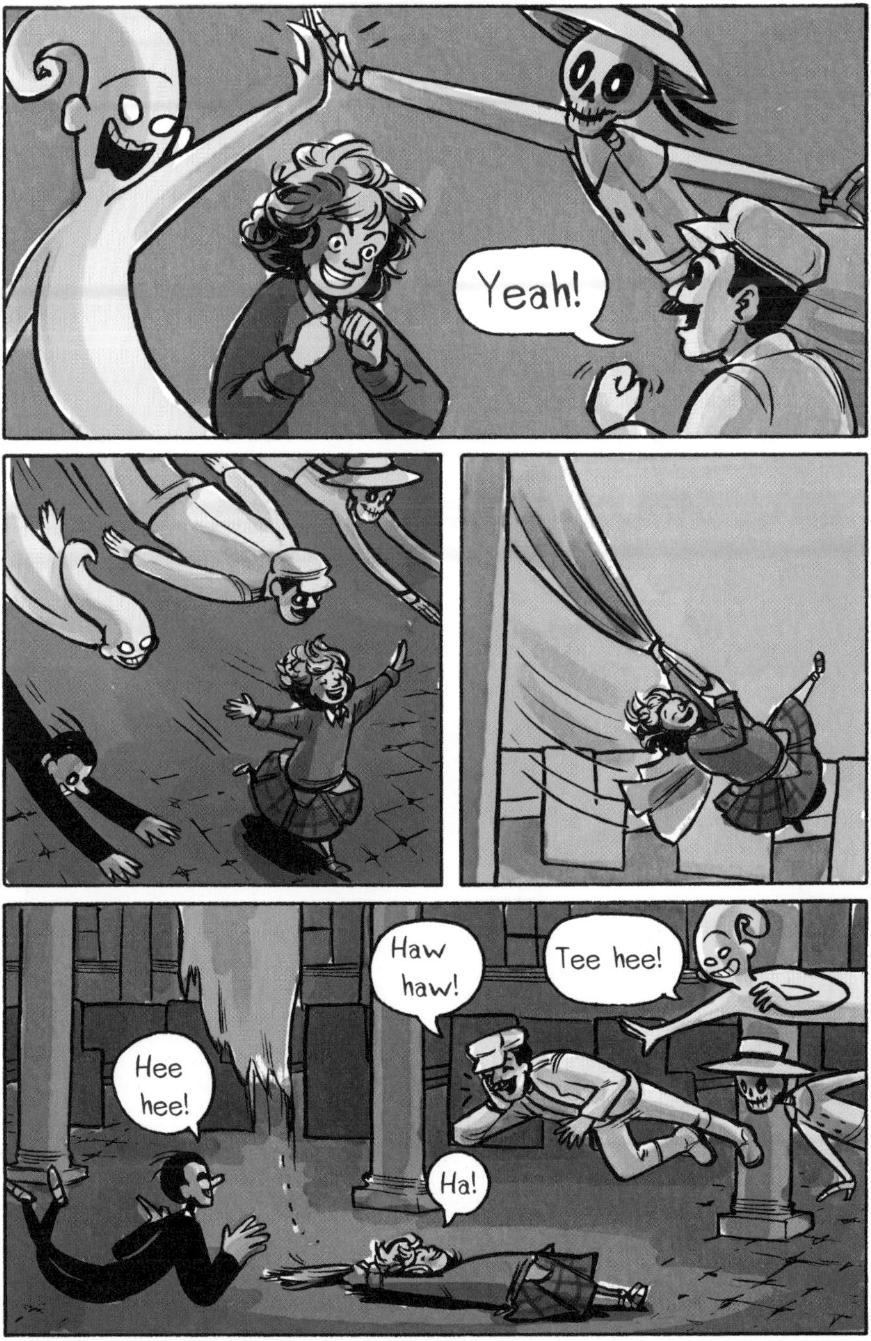
Yeah!
Haw haw!
Tee hee!
Hee hee!
Ha!

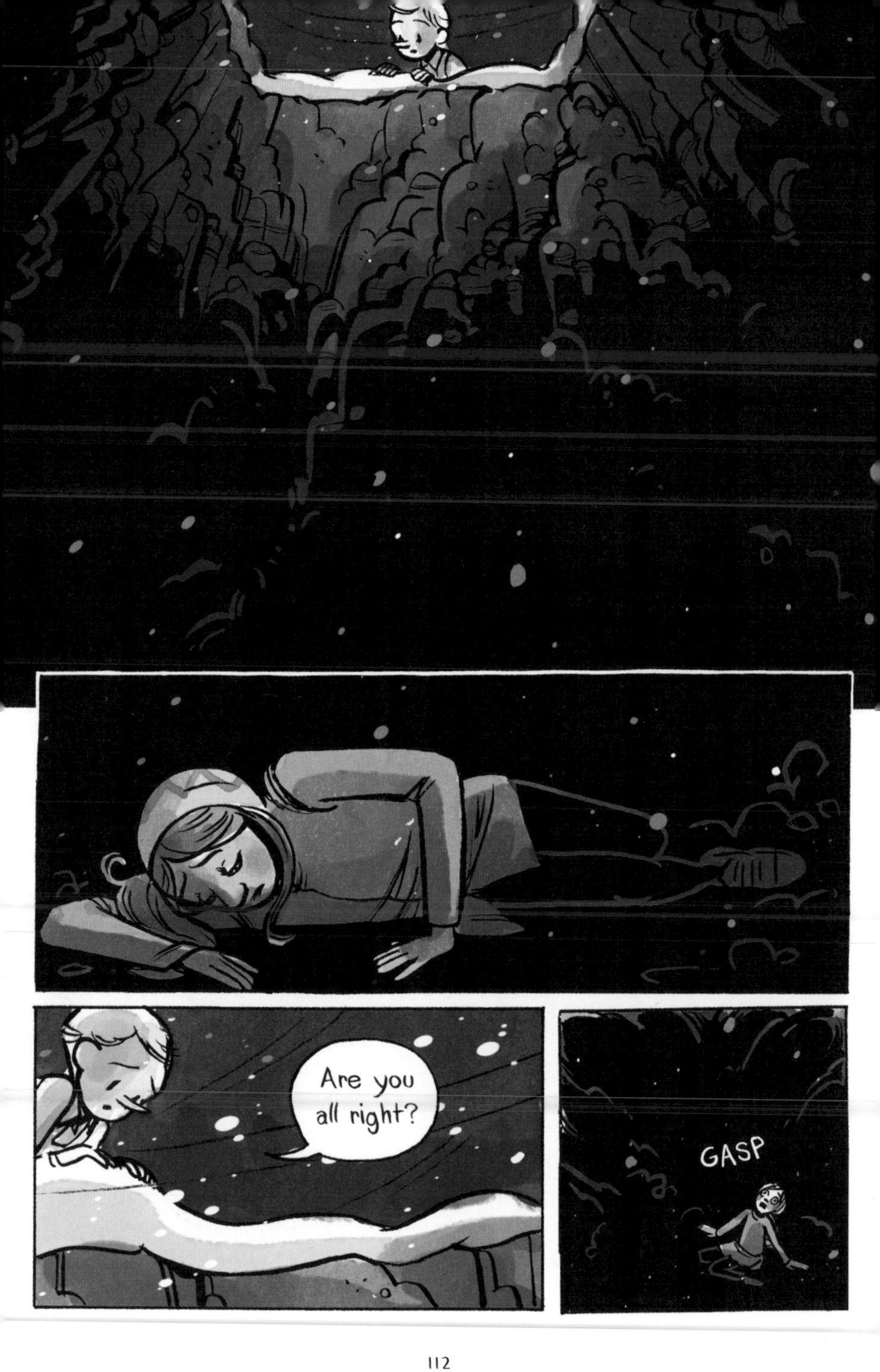
Are you all right?
GASP

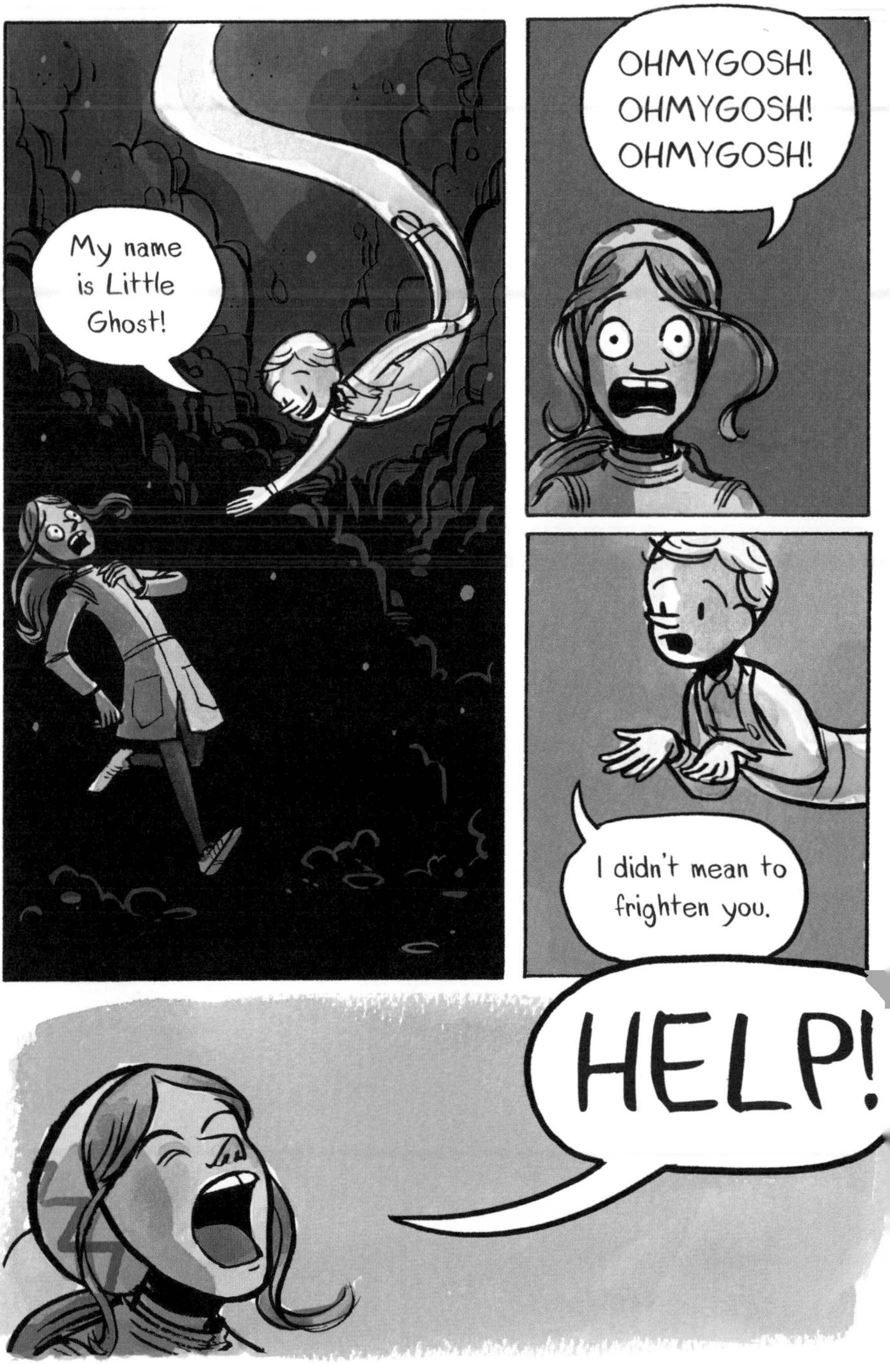
My name is Little Ghost!
OHMYGOSH! OHMYGOSH! OHMYGOSH!
I didn't mean to frighten you.
HELP!

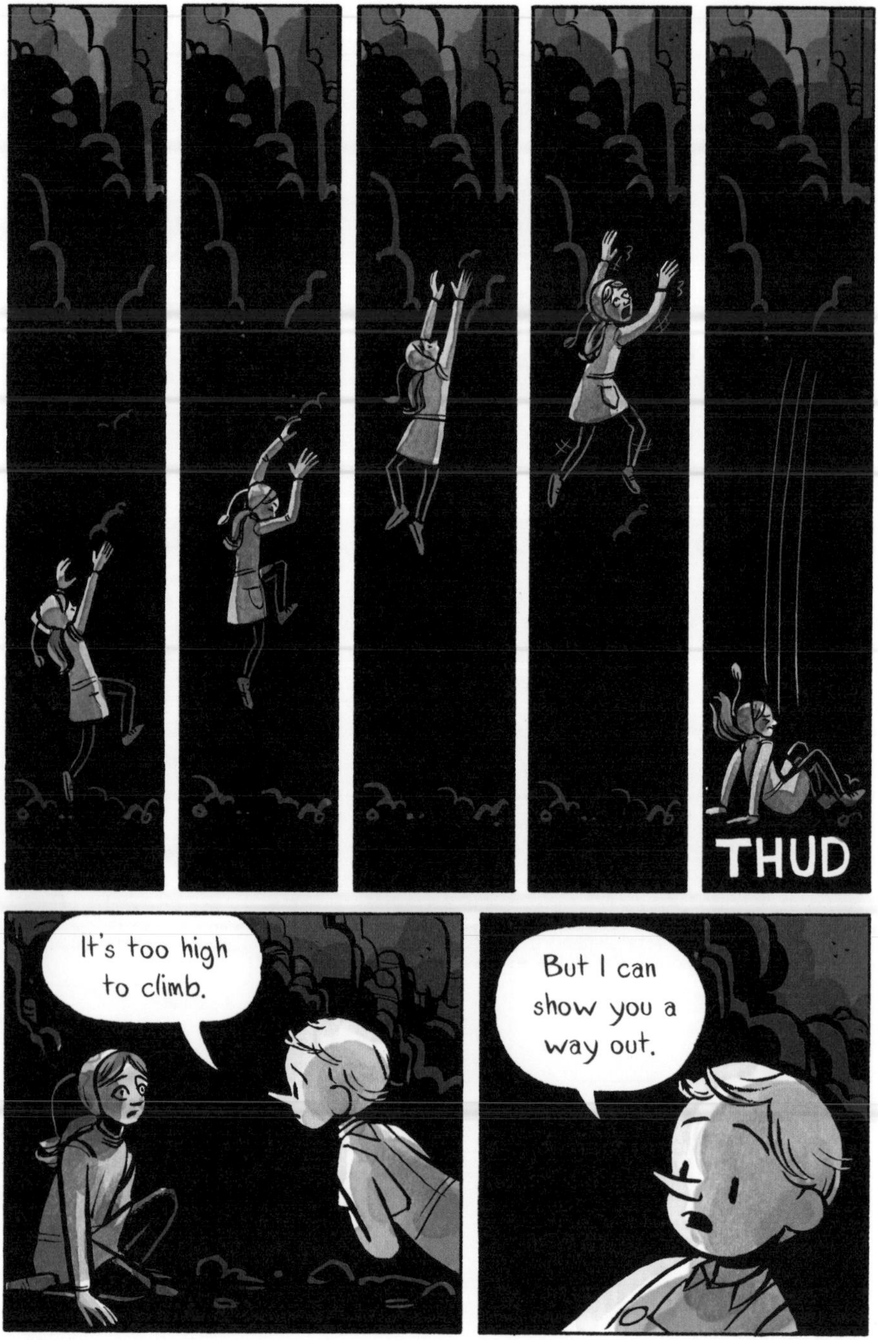
THUD
It's too high to climb.
But I can show you a way out.

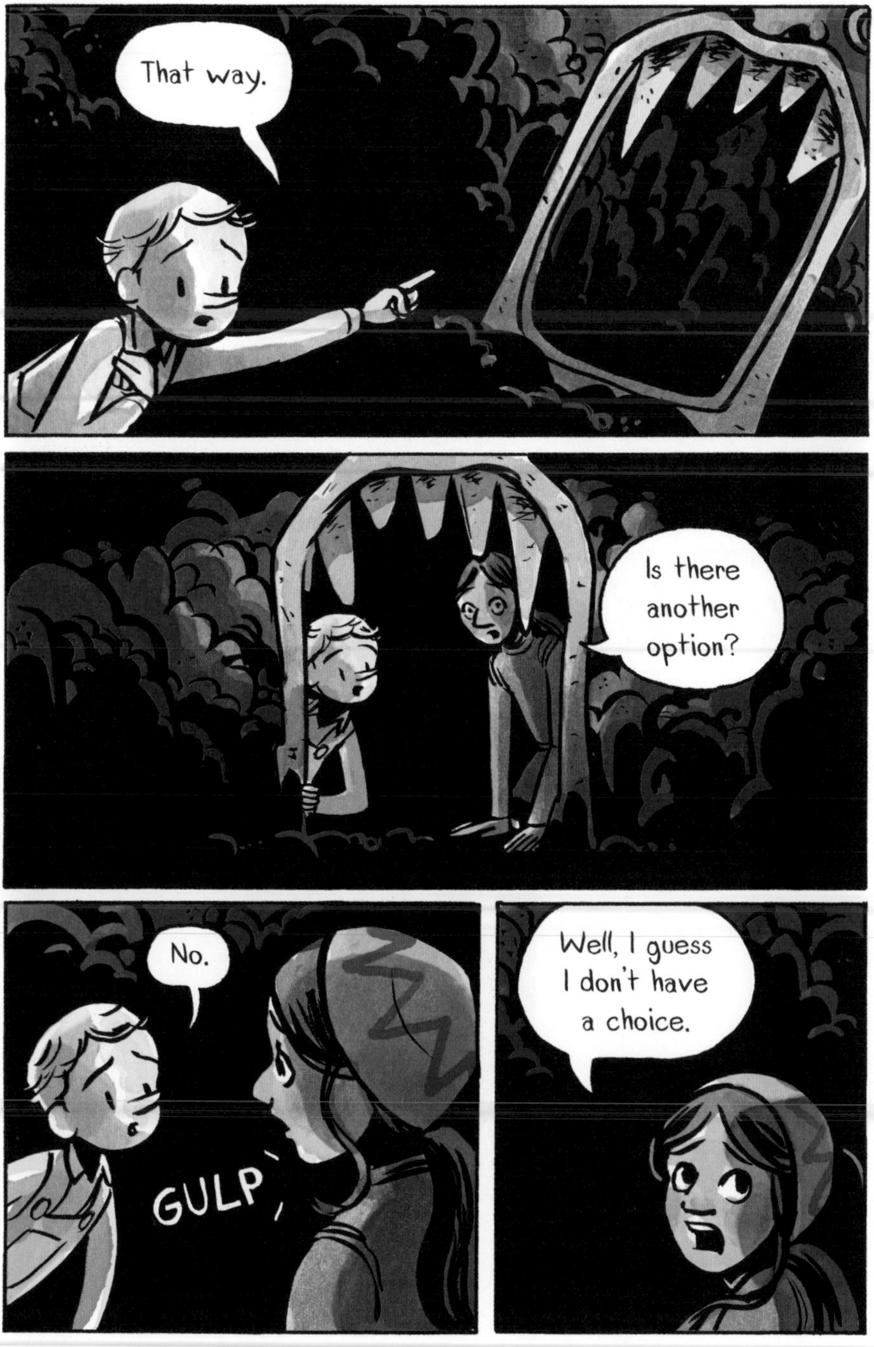
That way.
Is there another option?
No.
GULP
Well, I guess I don't have a choice.

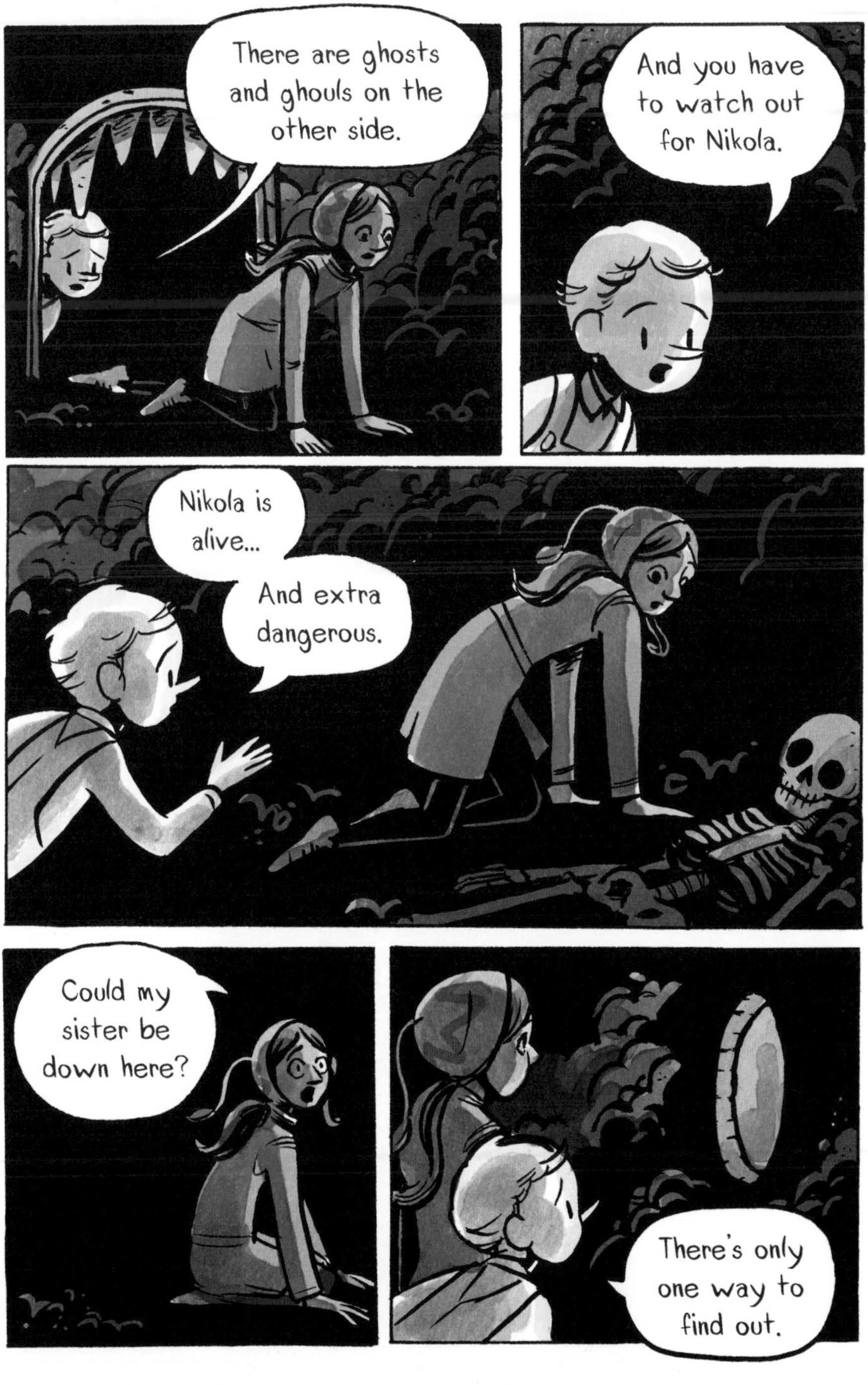

There are ghosts and ghouls on the other side.
And you have to watch out for Nikola.
Nikola is alive...
And extra dangerous.
Could my sister be down here?
There's only one way to find out.

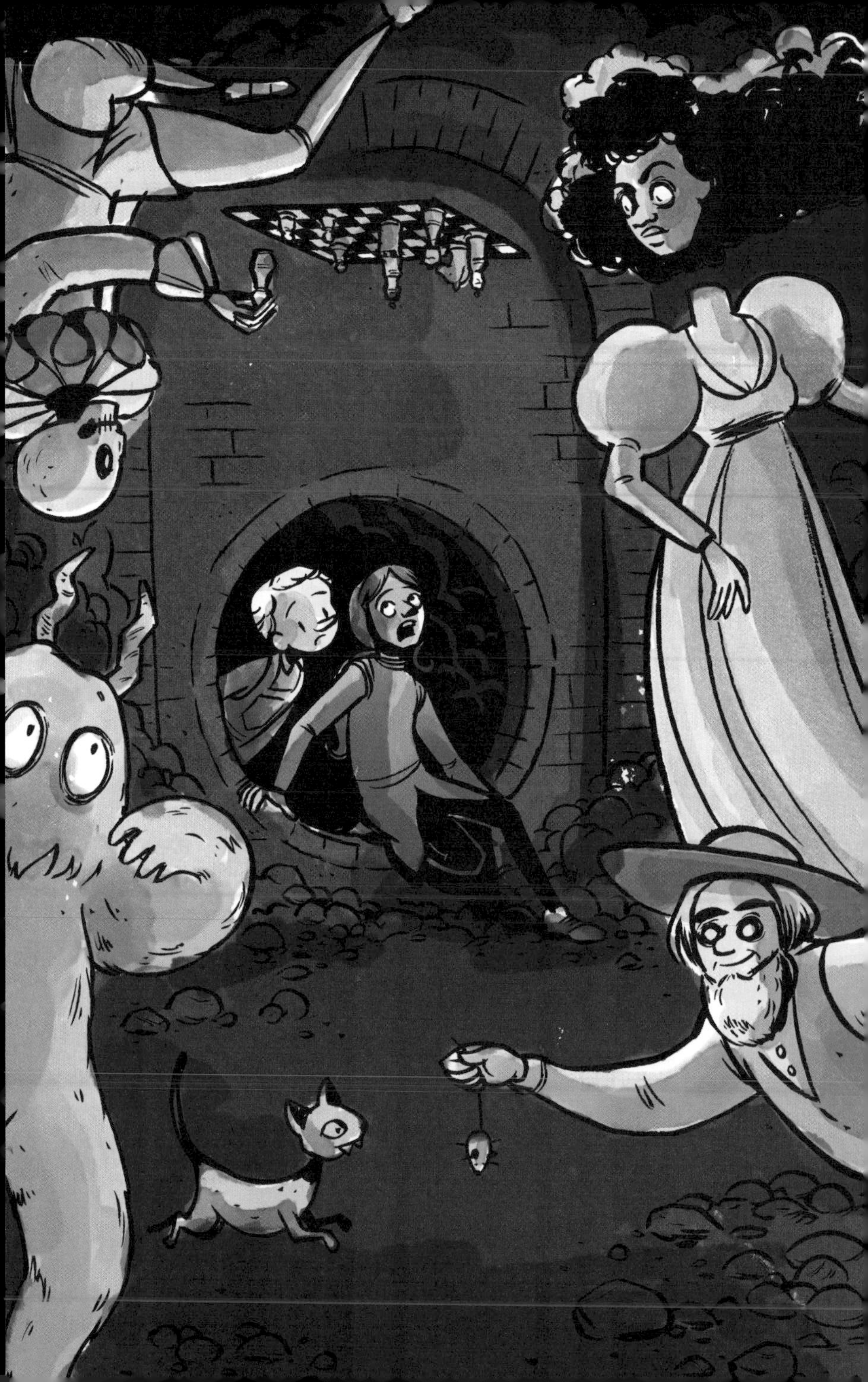

119

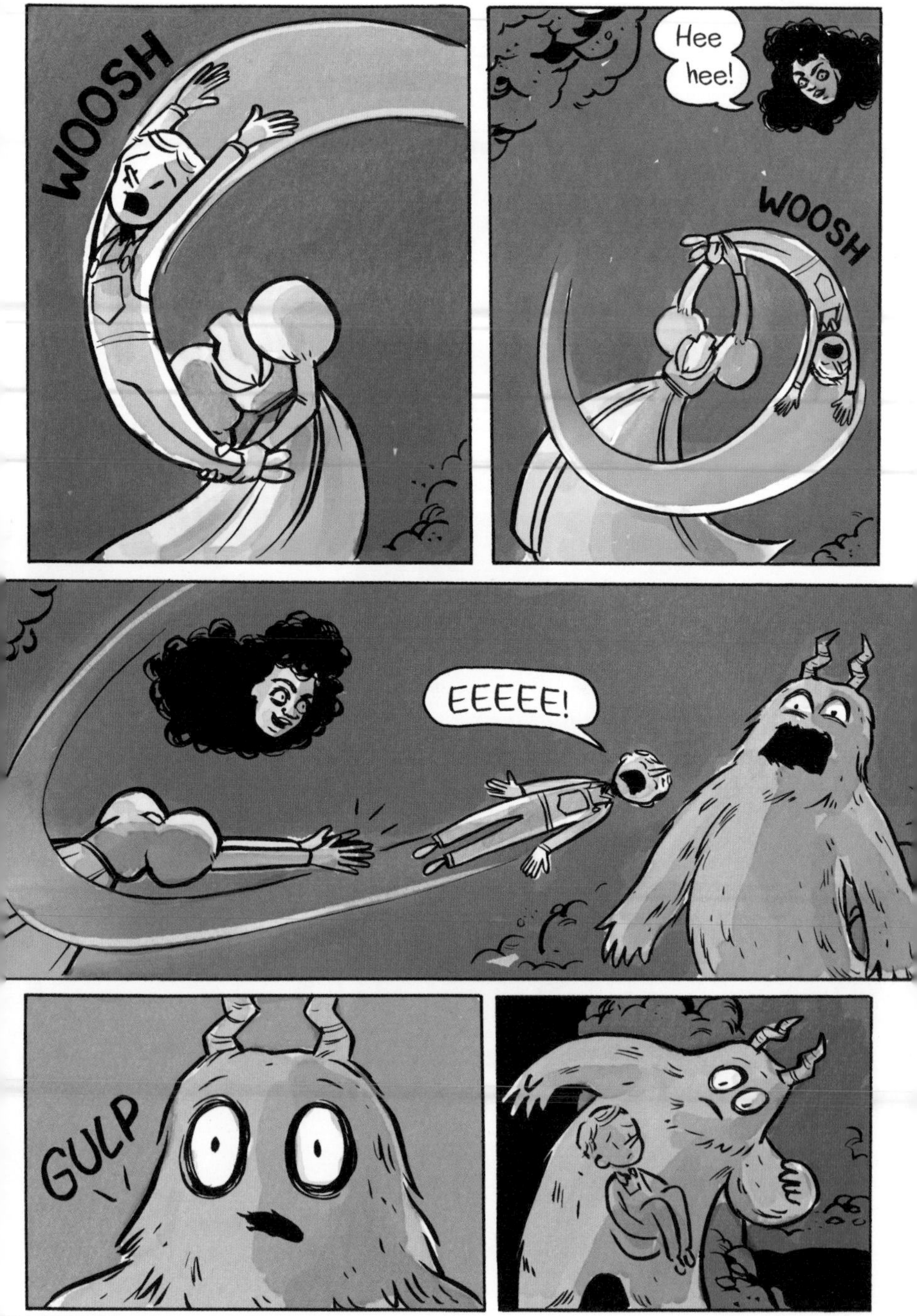
WOOSH
Hee hee!
WOOSH
EEEEE!
GULP

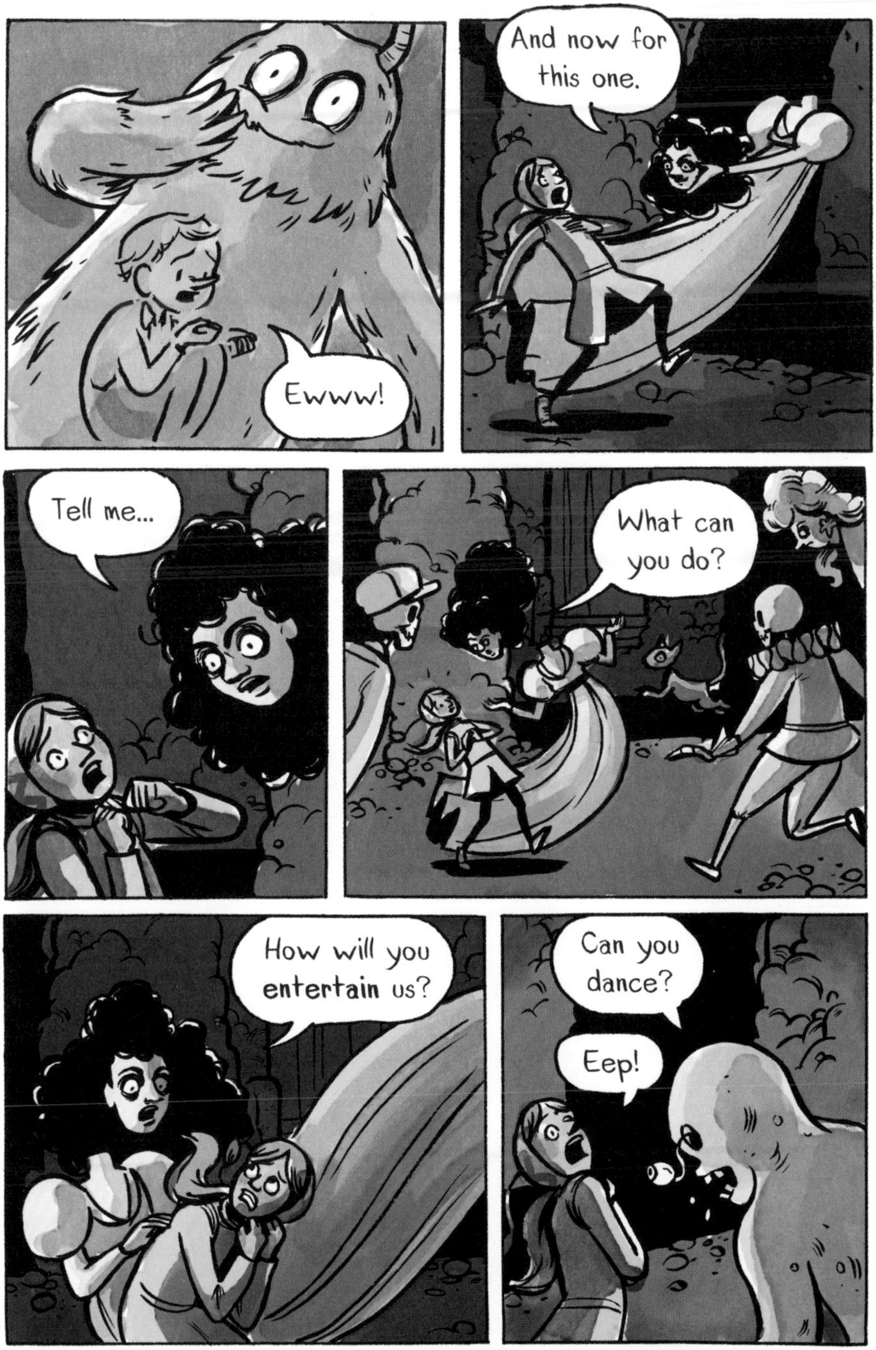
Ewww!
And now for this one.
Tell me...
What can you do?
How will you **entertain** us?
Can you dance?
Eep!

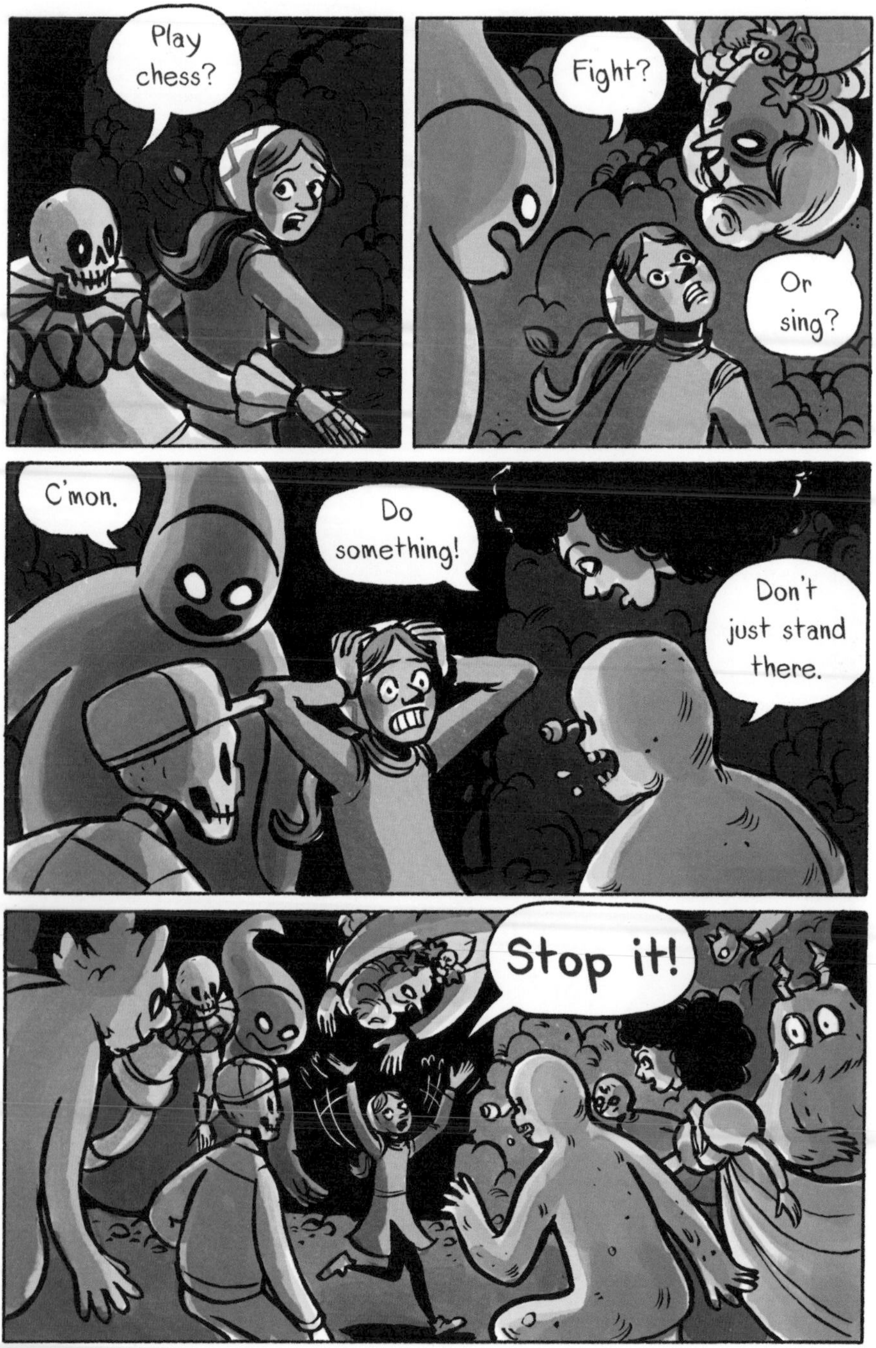
Play chess?
Fight?
Or sing?
C'mon.
Do something!
Don't just stand there.
Stop it!

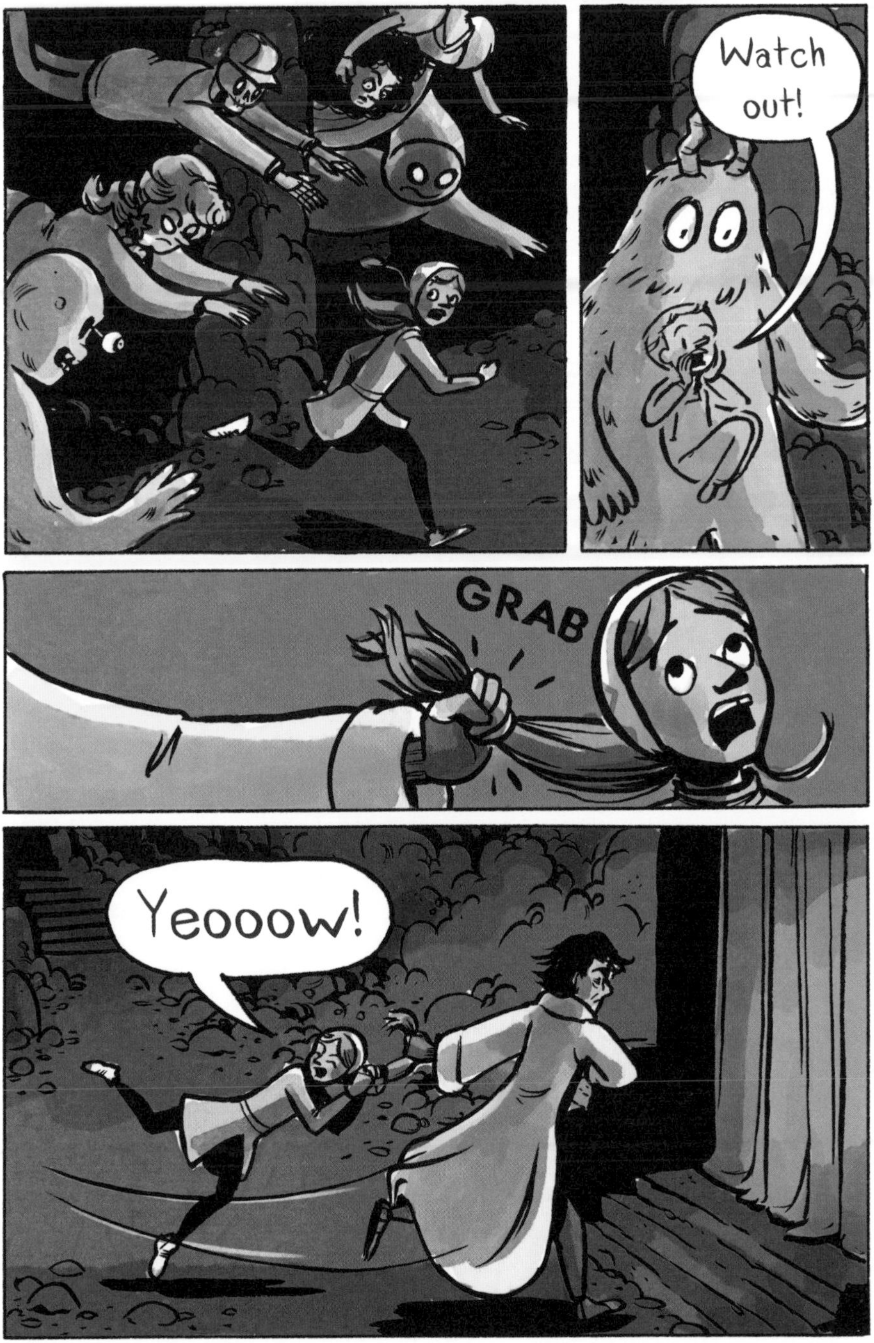
Watch out!
GRAB
Yeooow!

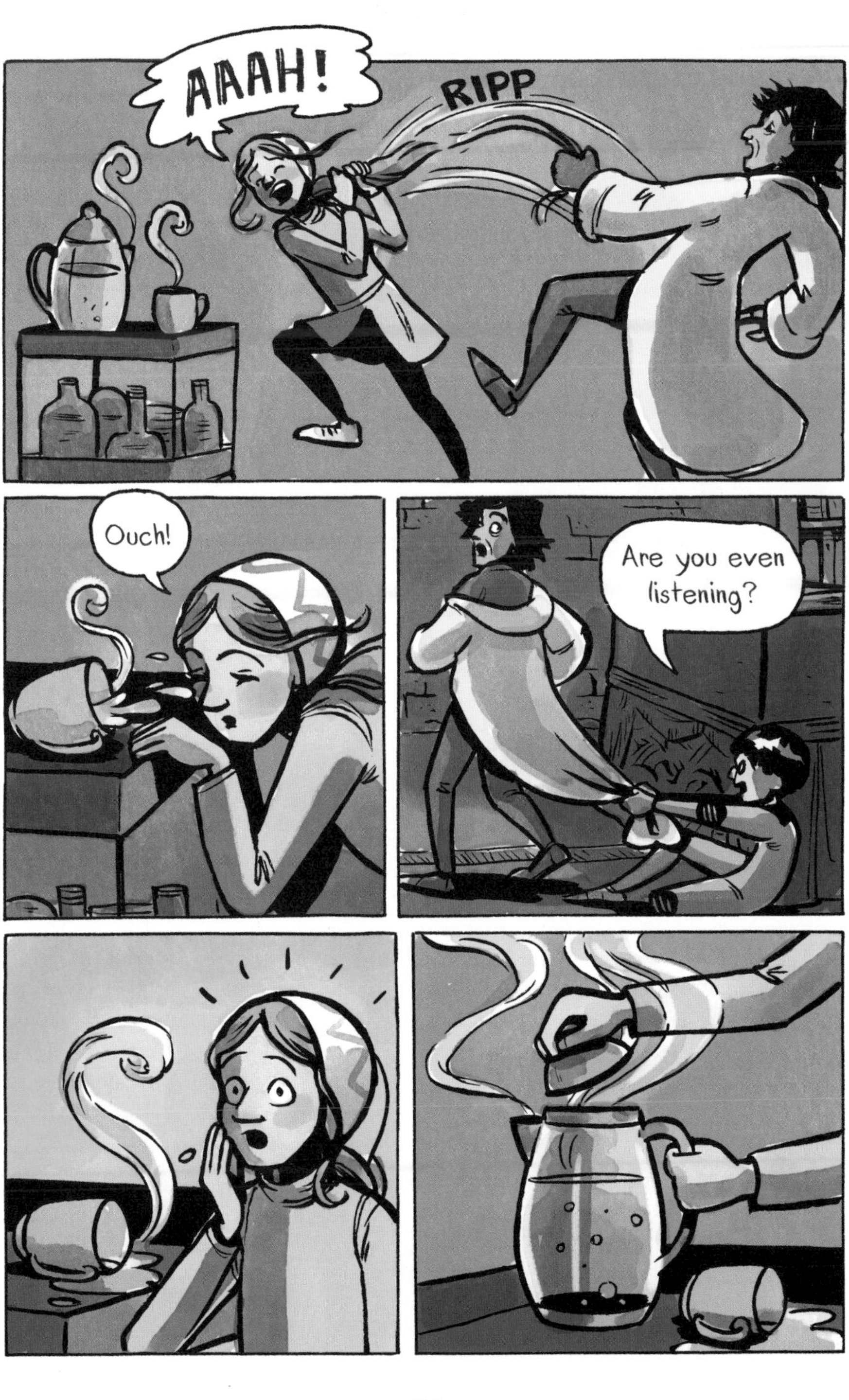
AAAH!
RIPP
Ouch!
Are you even listening?

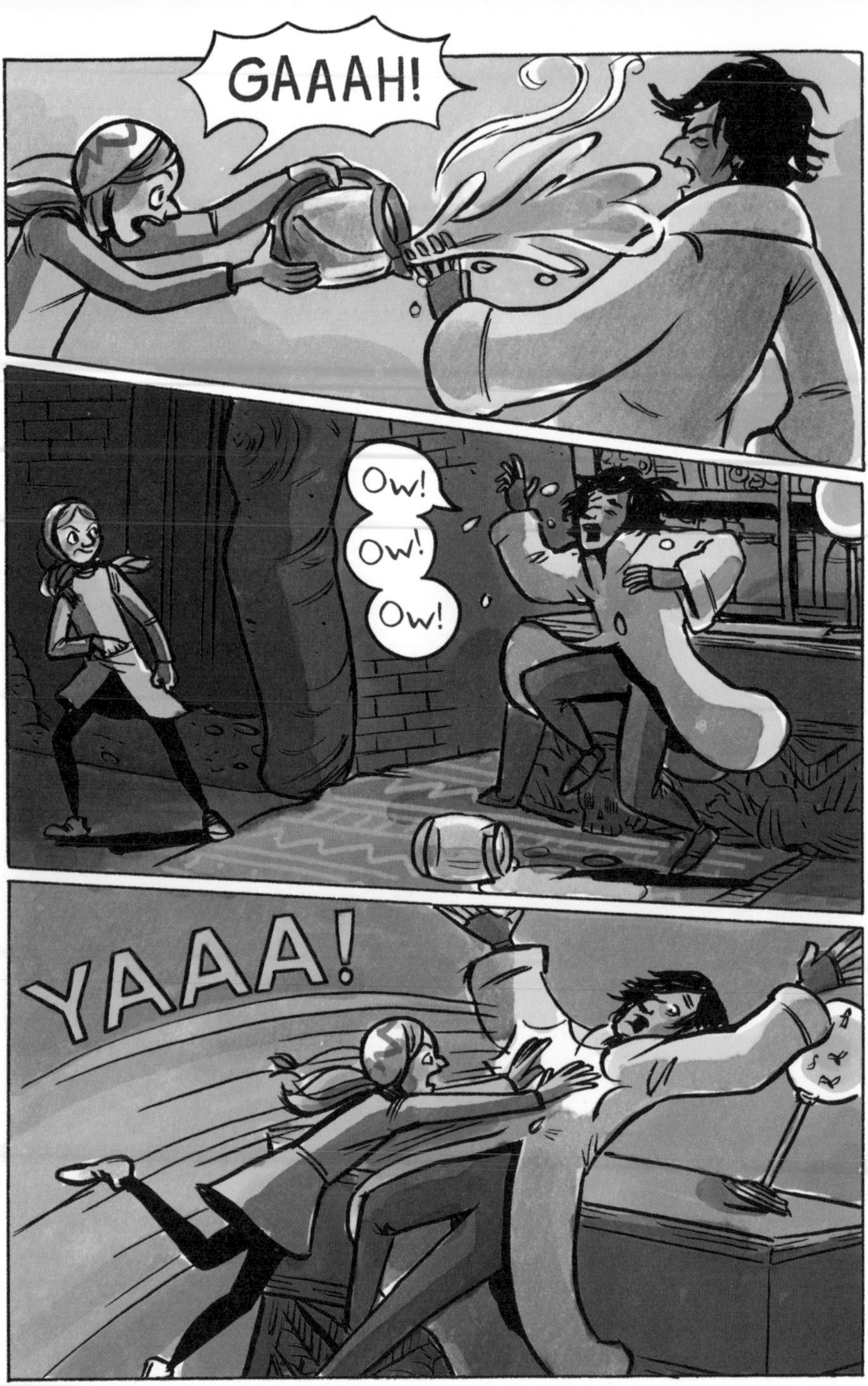
GAAAH!
Ow!
Ow!
Ow!
YAAA!

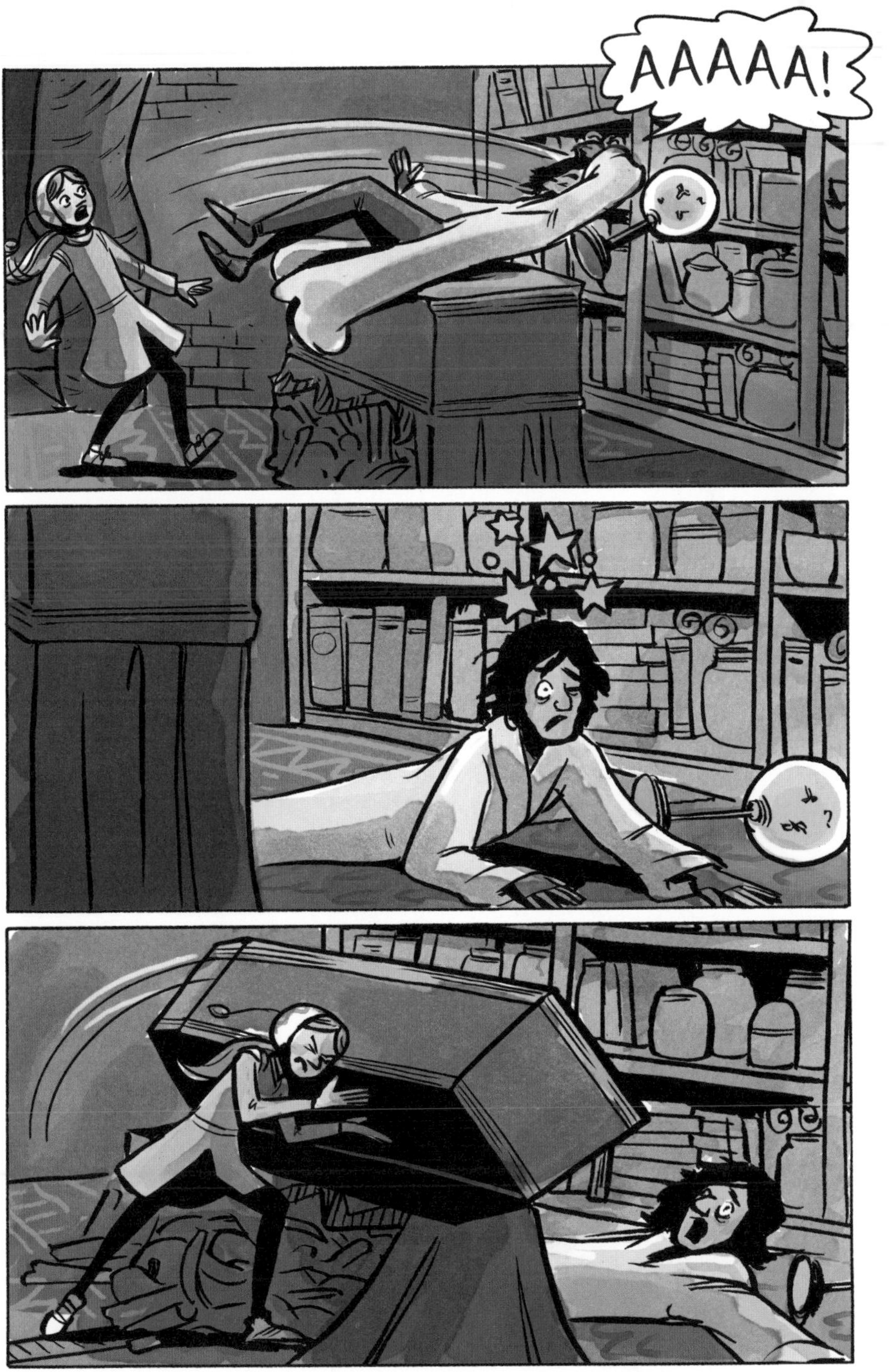
AAAAA!

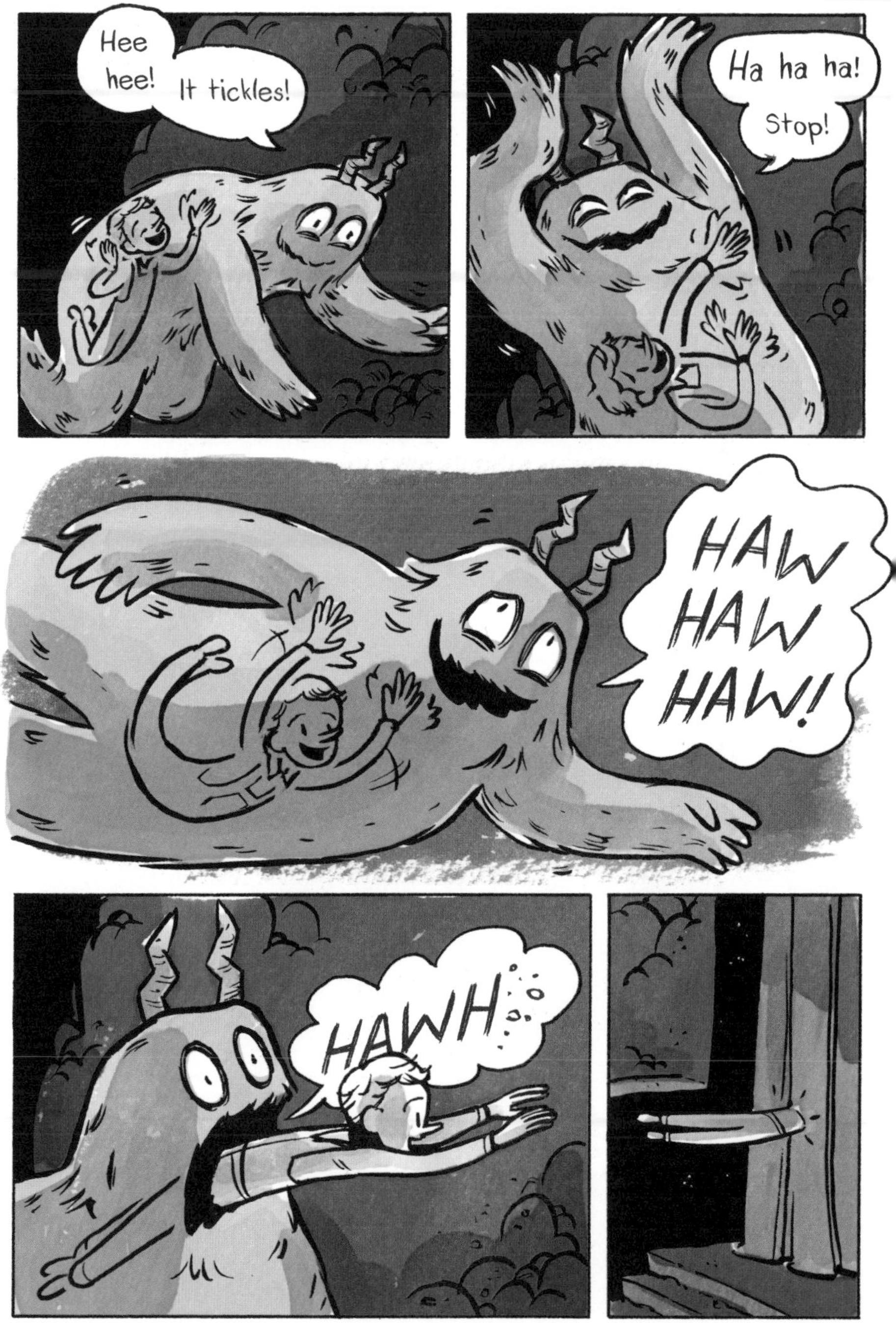
Hee hee!
It tickles!
Ha ha ha!
Stop!
HAW HAW HAW!
HAWH

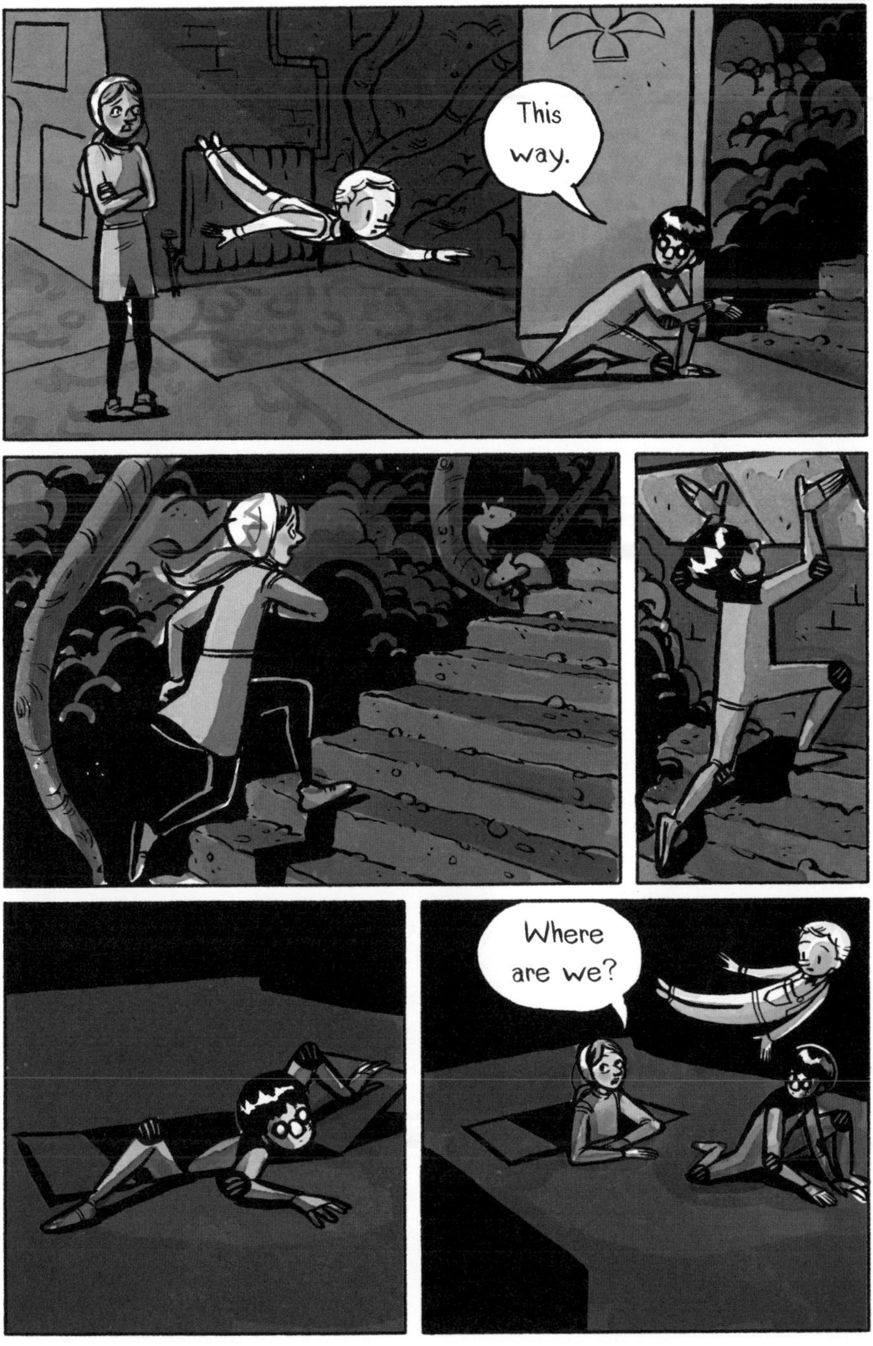
This way.
Where are we?

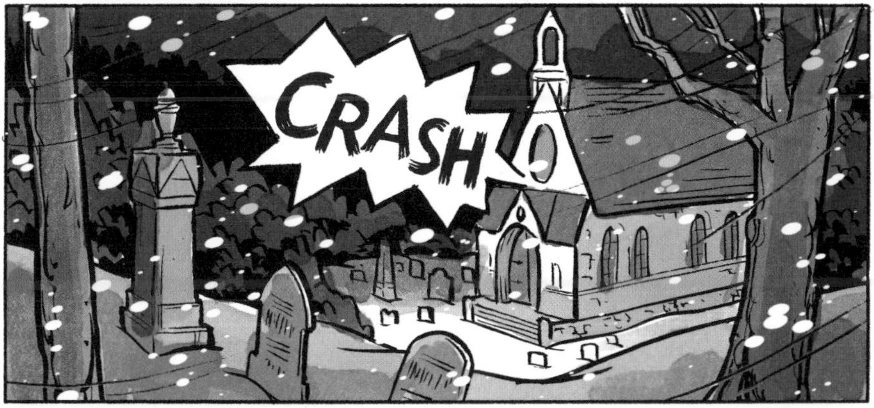
CRASH

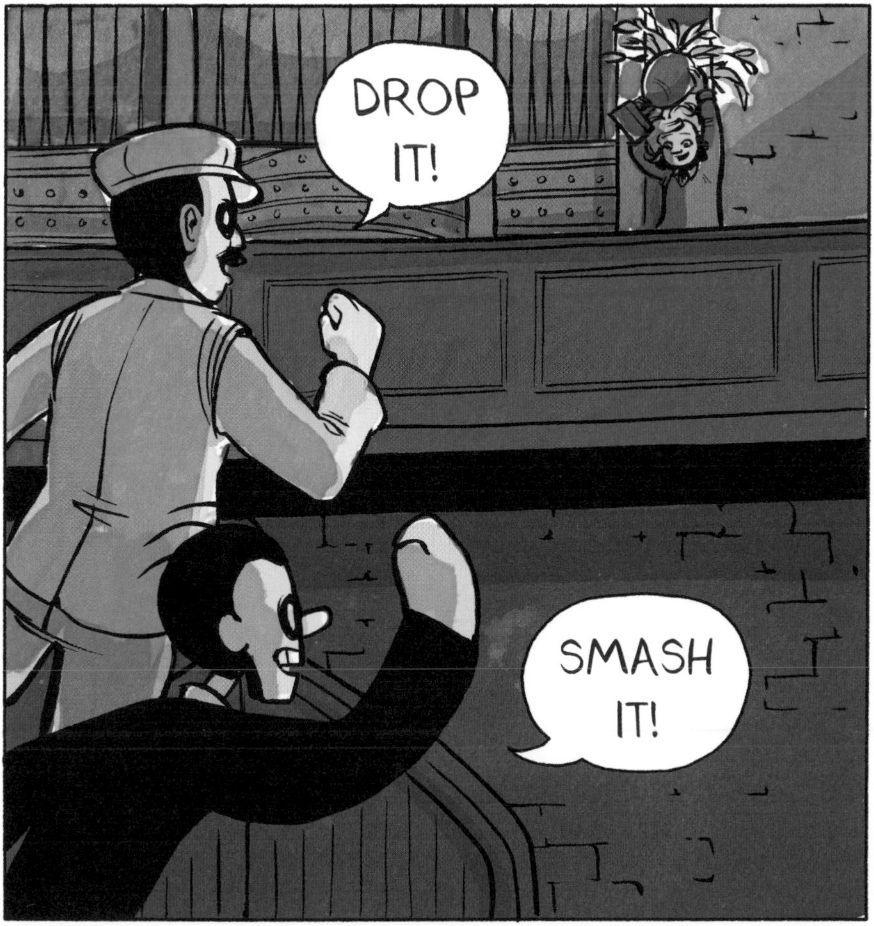
DROP IT!
SMASH IT!

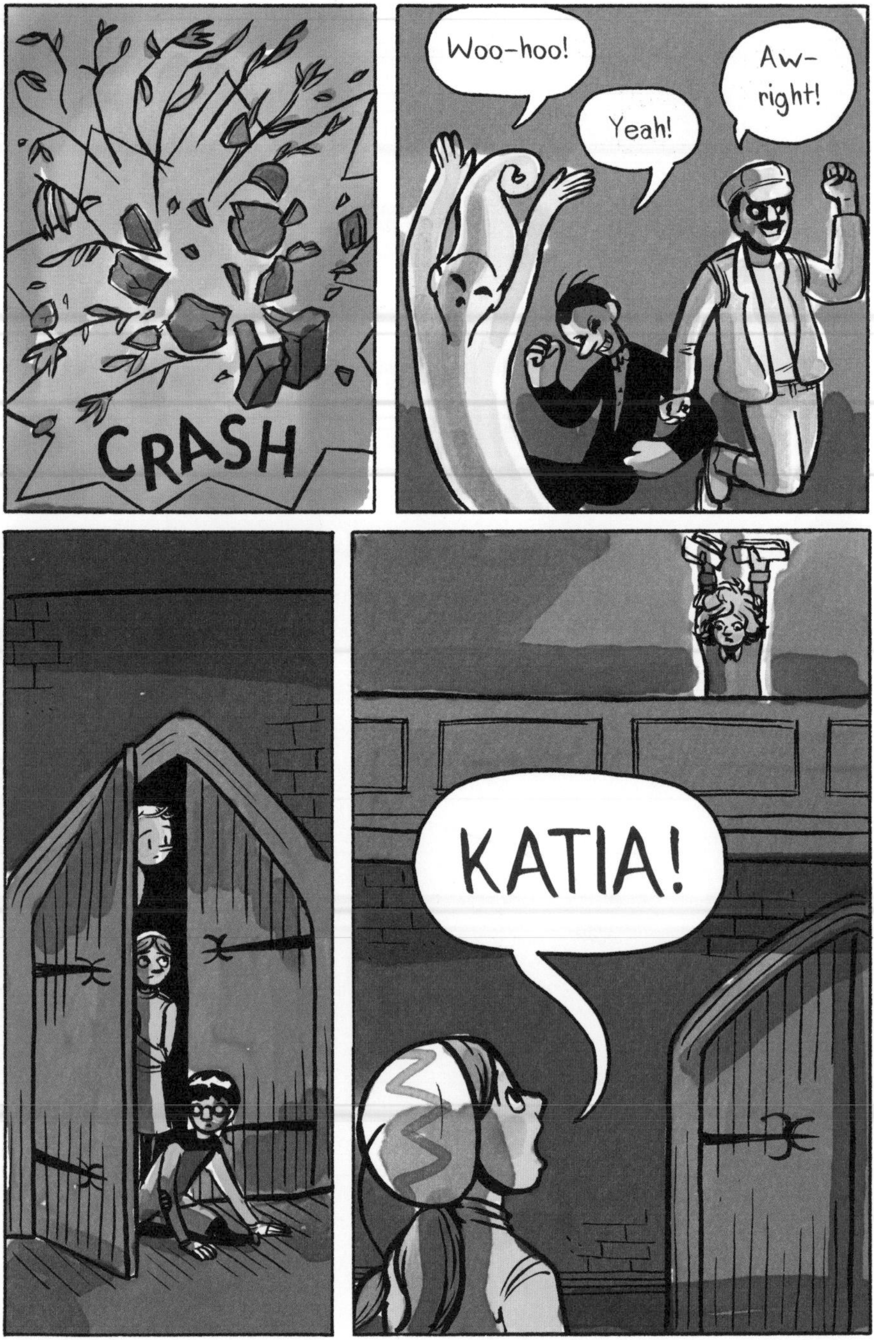
CRASH
Woo-hoo!
Yeah!
Aw-right!
KATIA!

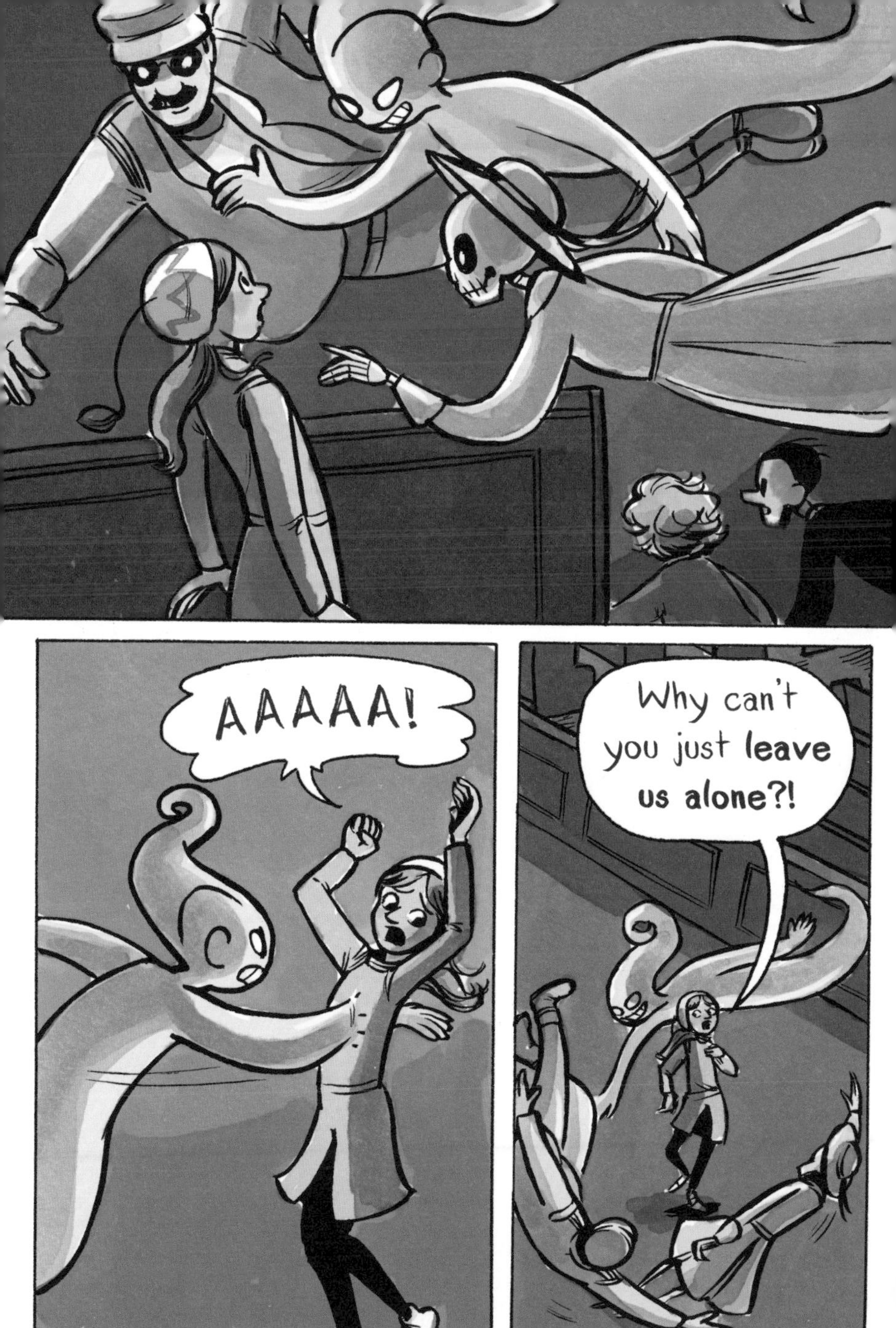
AAAAA!
Why can't you just leave us alone?!

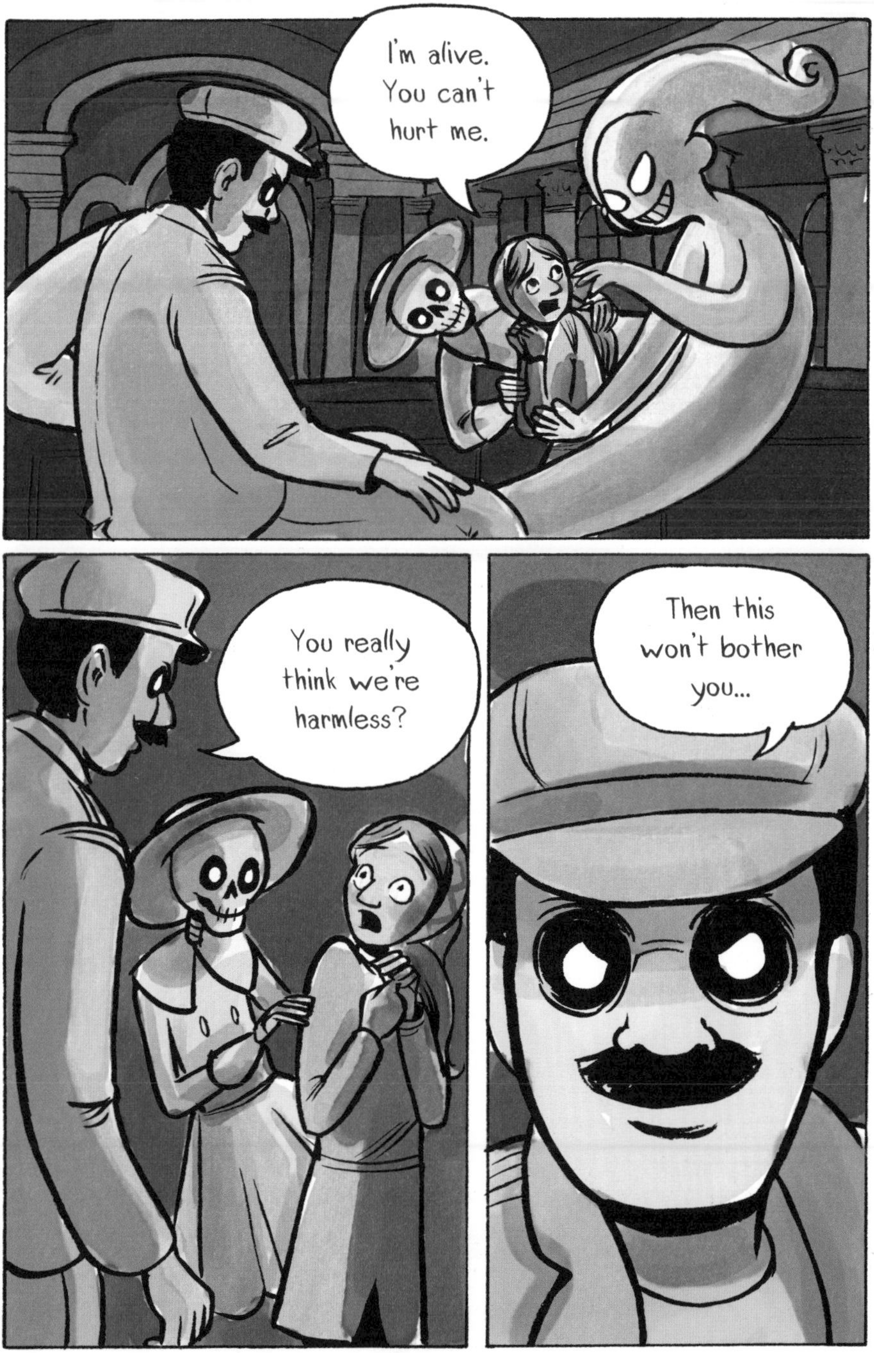
I'm alive. You can't hurt me.
You really think we're harmless?
Then this won't bother you...

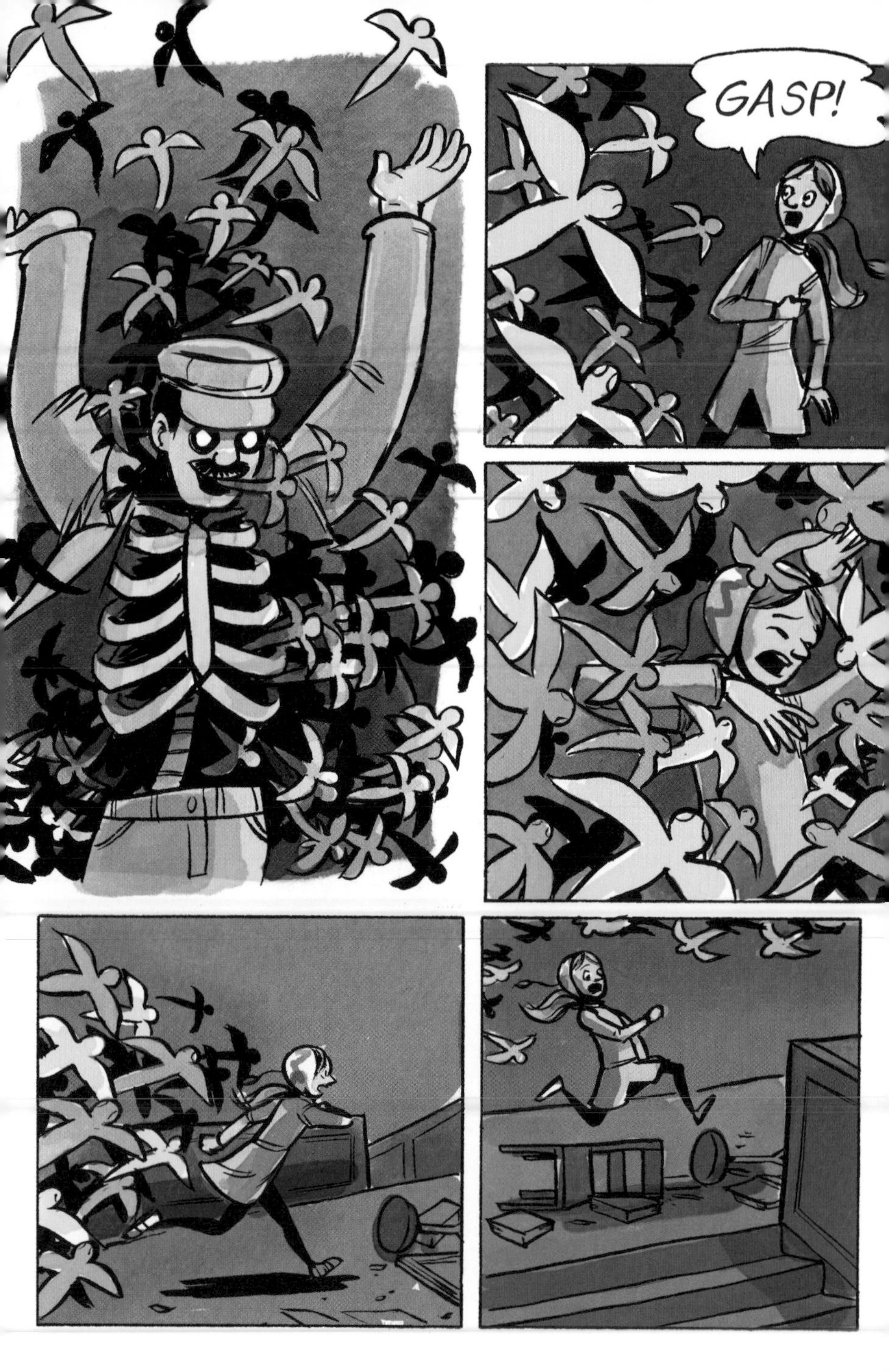
GASP!

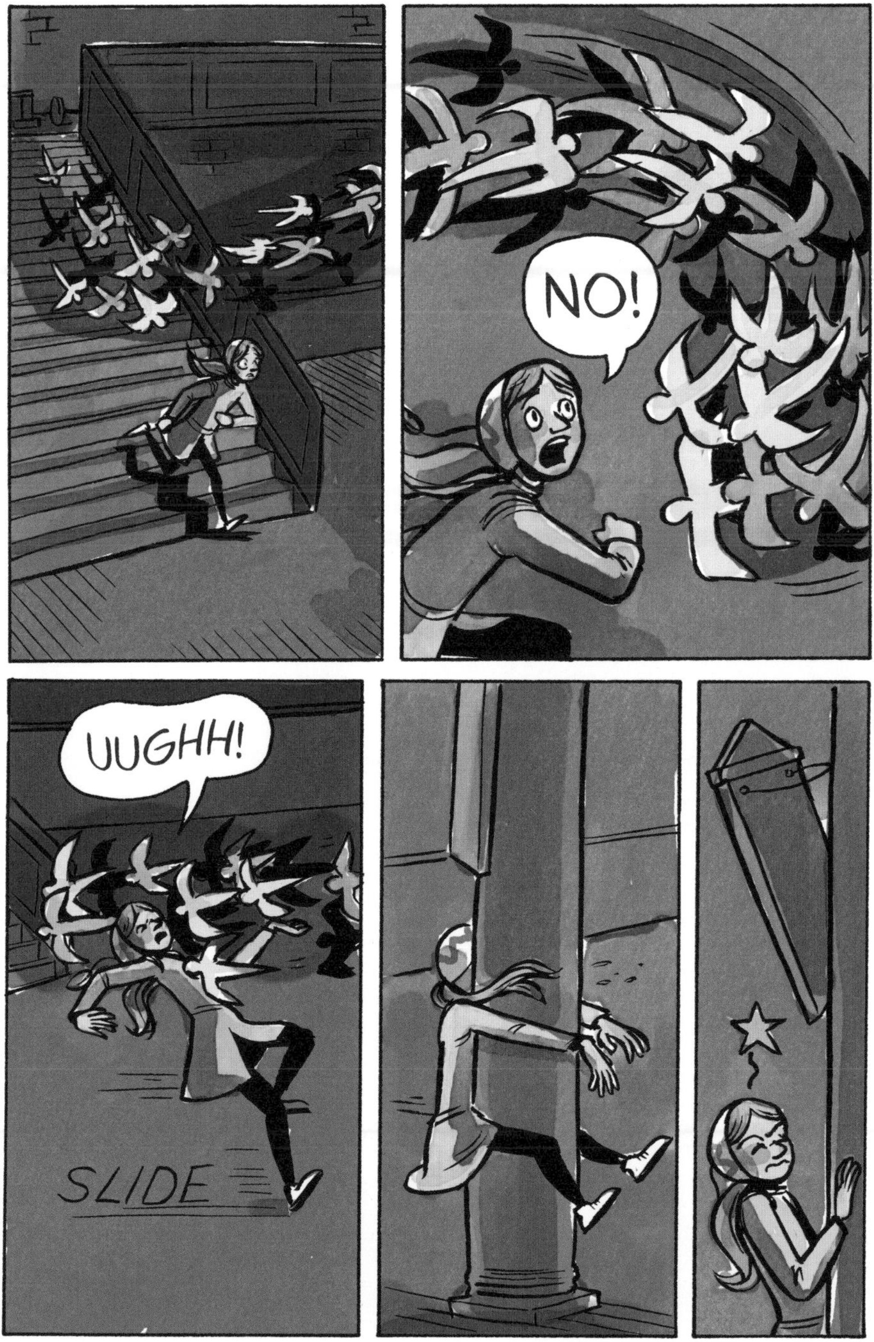
NO!
UUGHH!
SLIDE

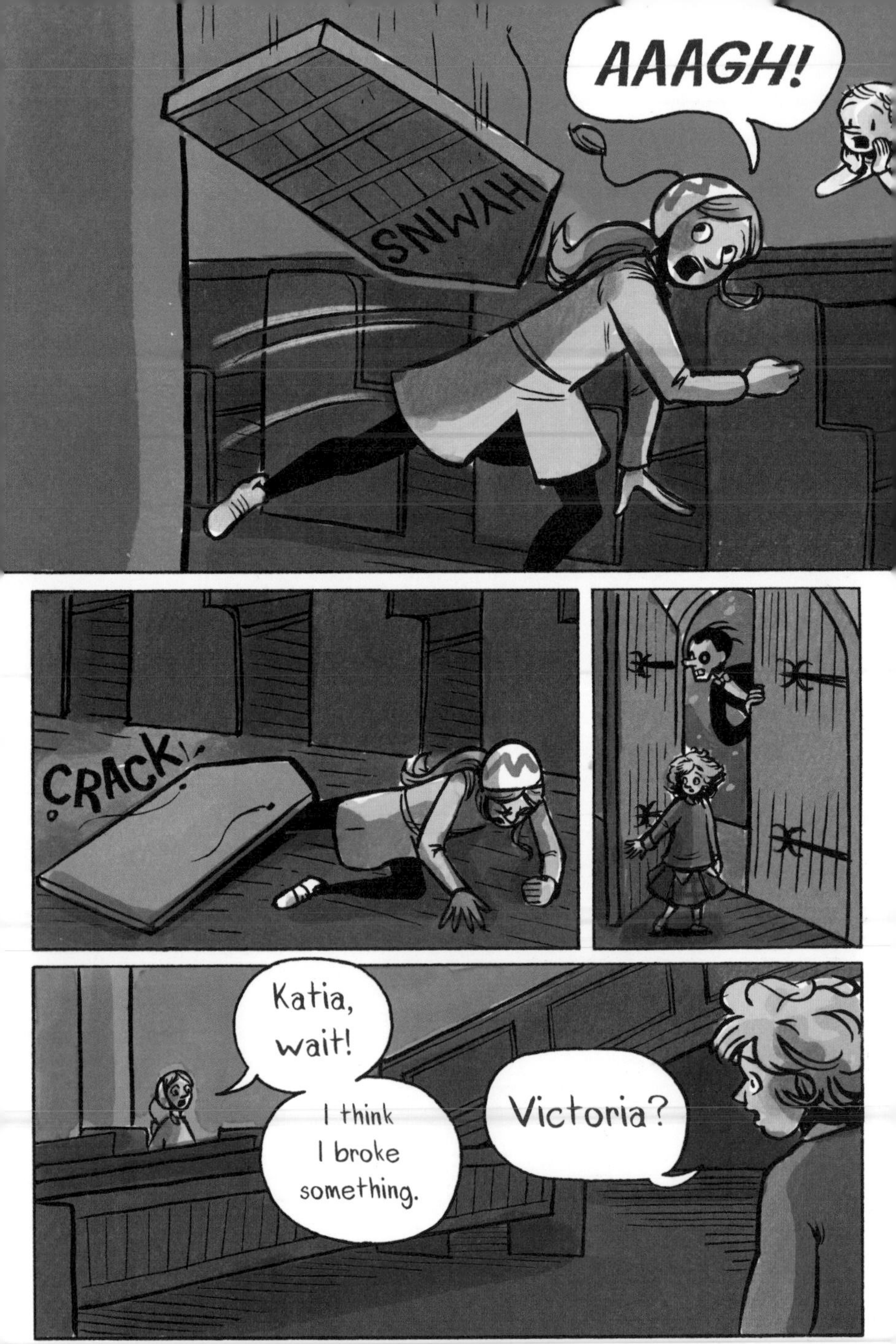
AAAGH!
HYMNS
CRACK
Katia, wait!
I think I broke something.
Victoria?

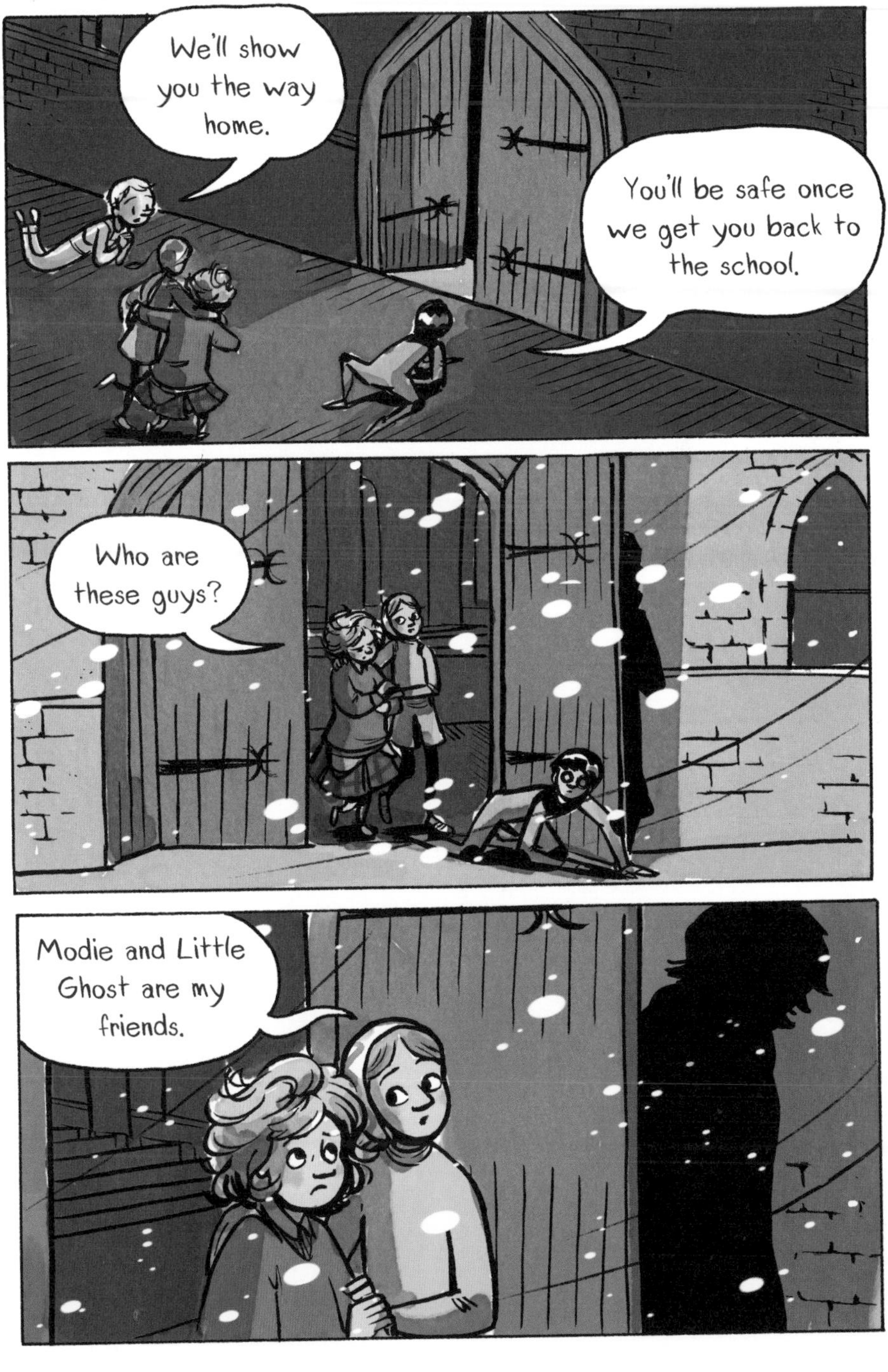
We'll show you the way home.
You'll be safe once we get you back to the school.
Who are these guys?
Modie and Little Ghost are my friends.

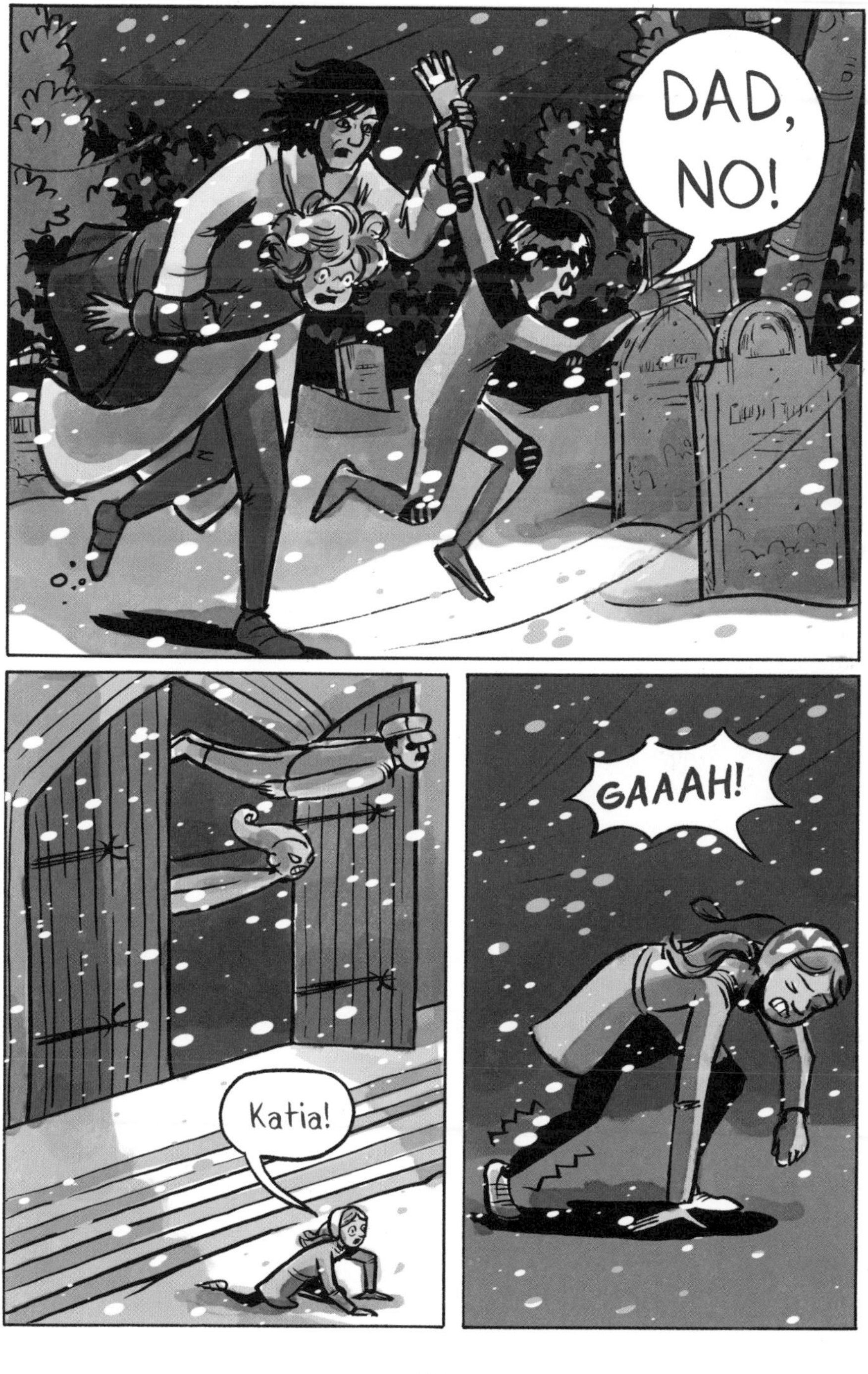
DAD, NO!
Katia!
GAAAH!

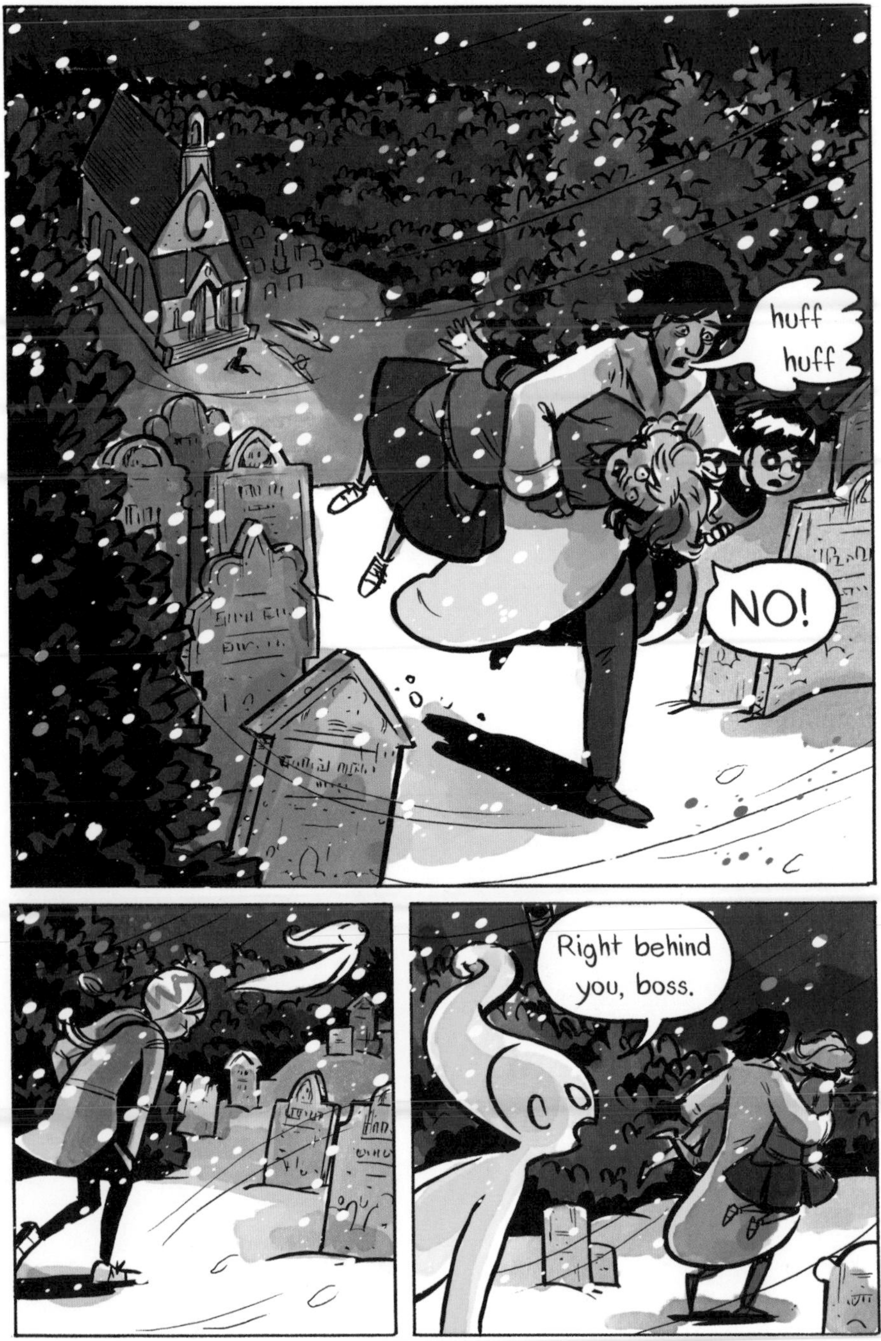
huff huff
NO!
Right behind you, boss.

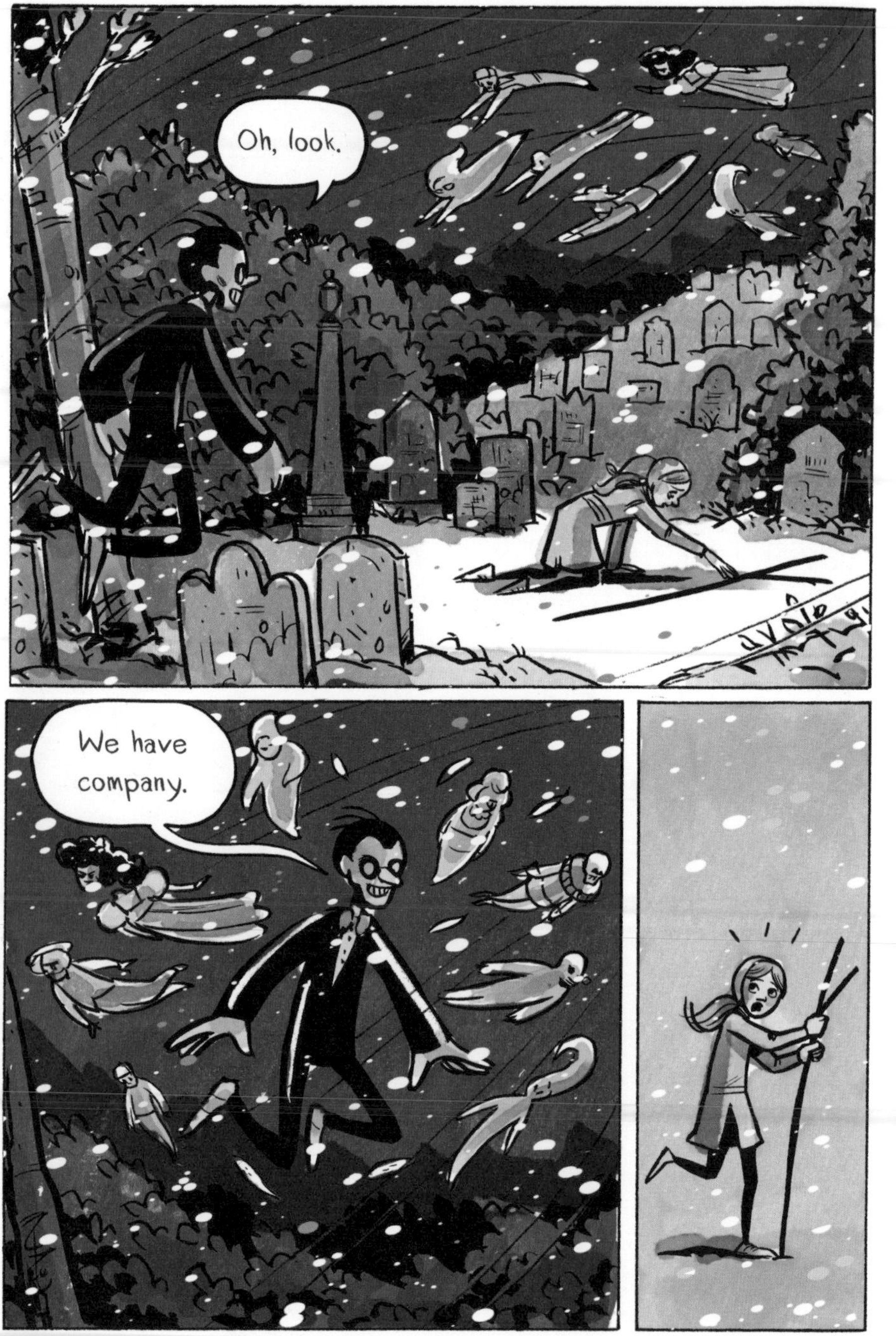
Oh, look.
We have company.

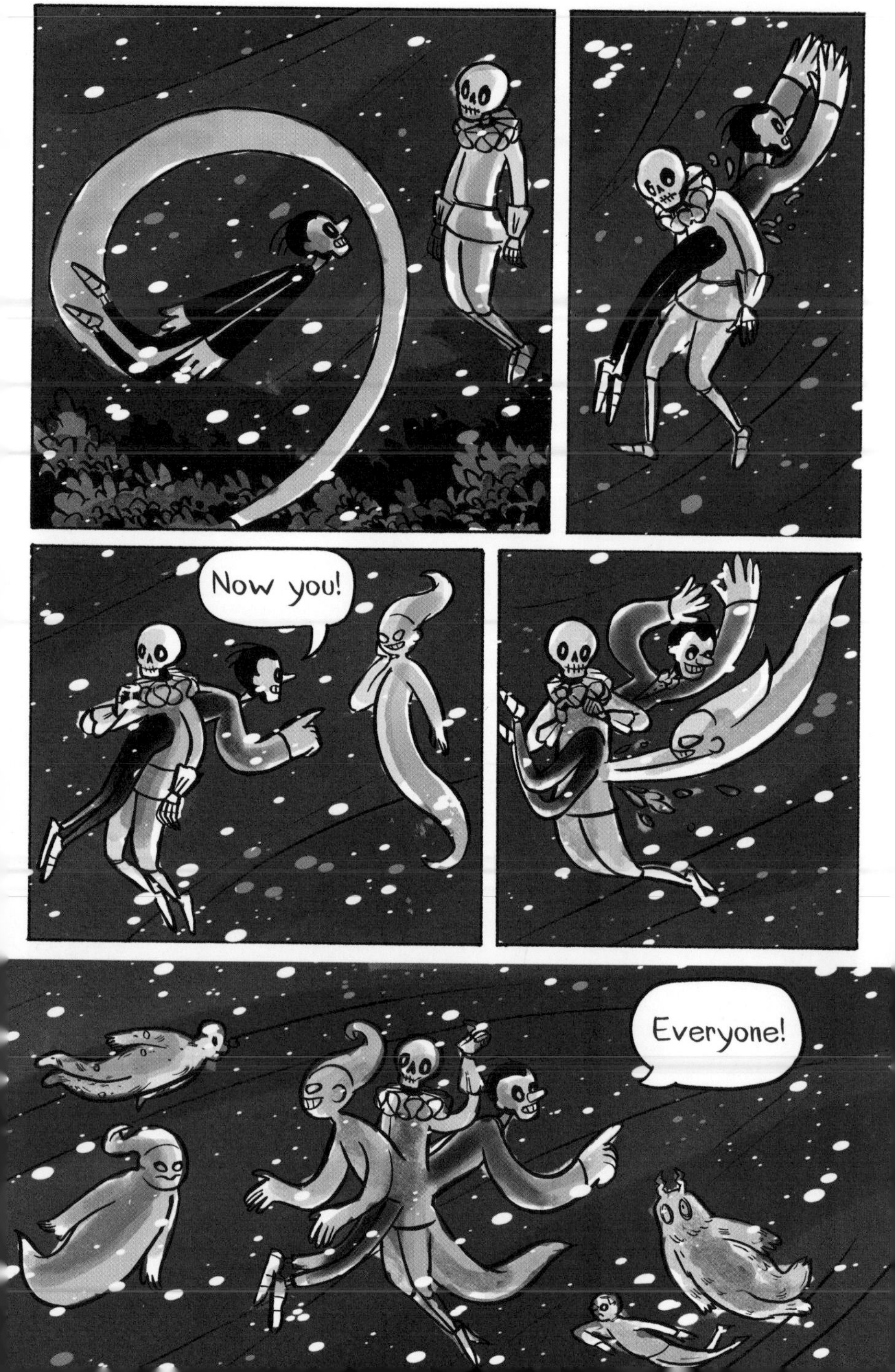
Now you!
Everyone!

157

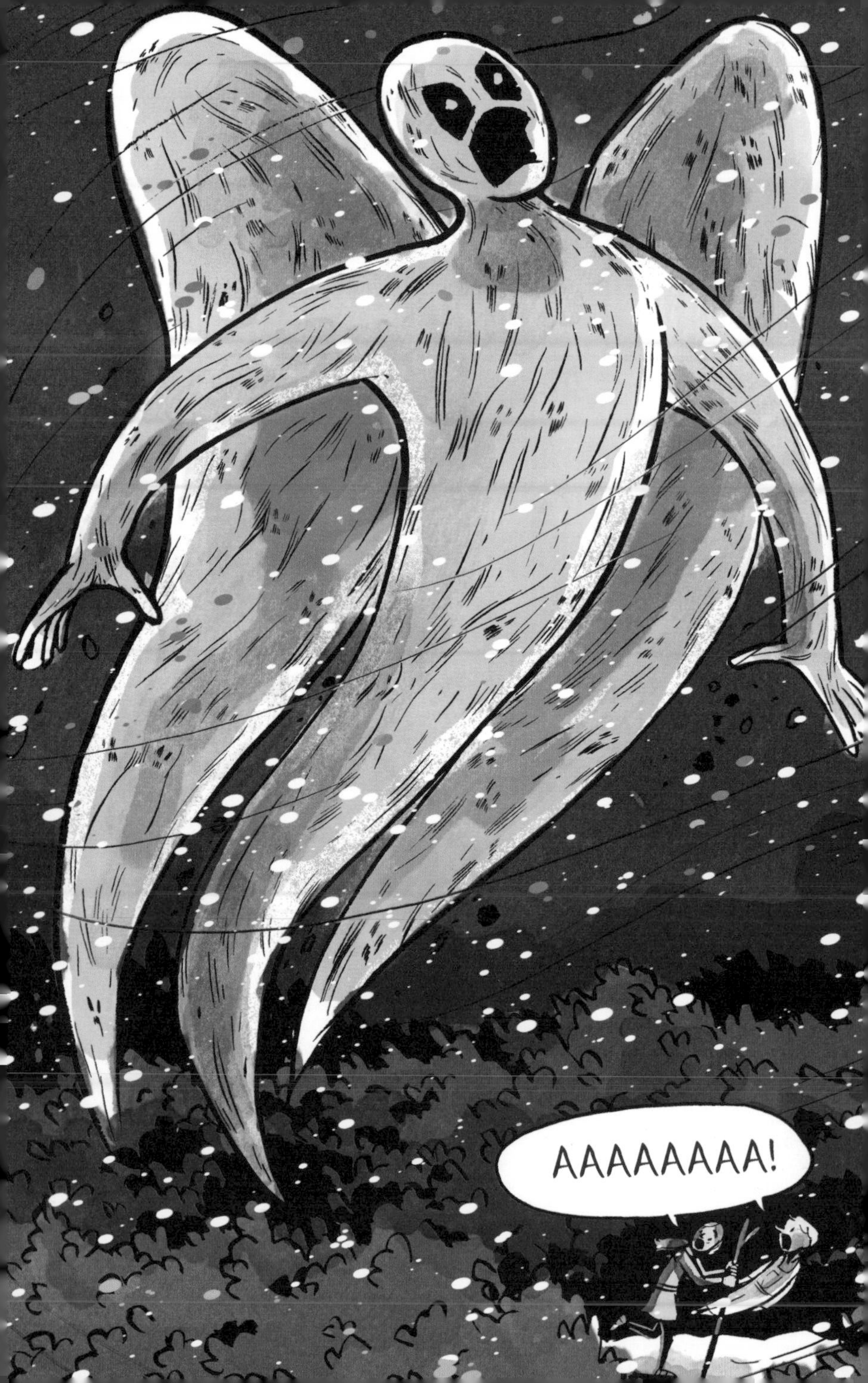
AAAAAAAA!

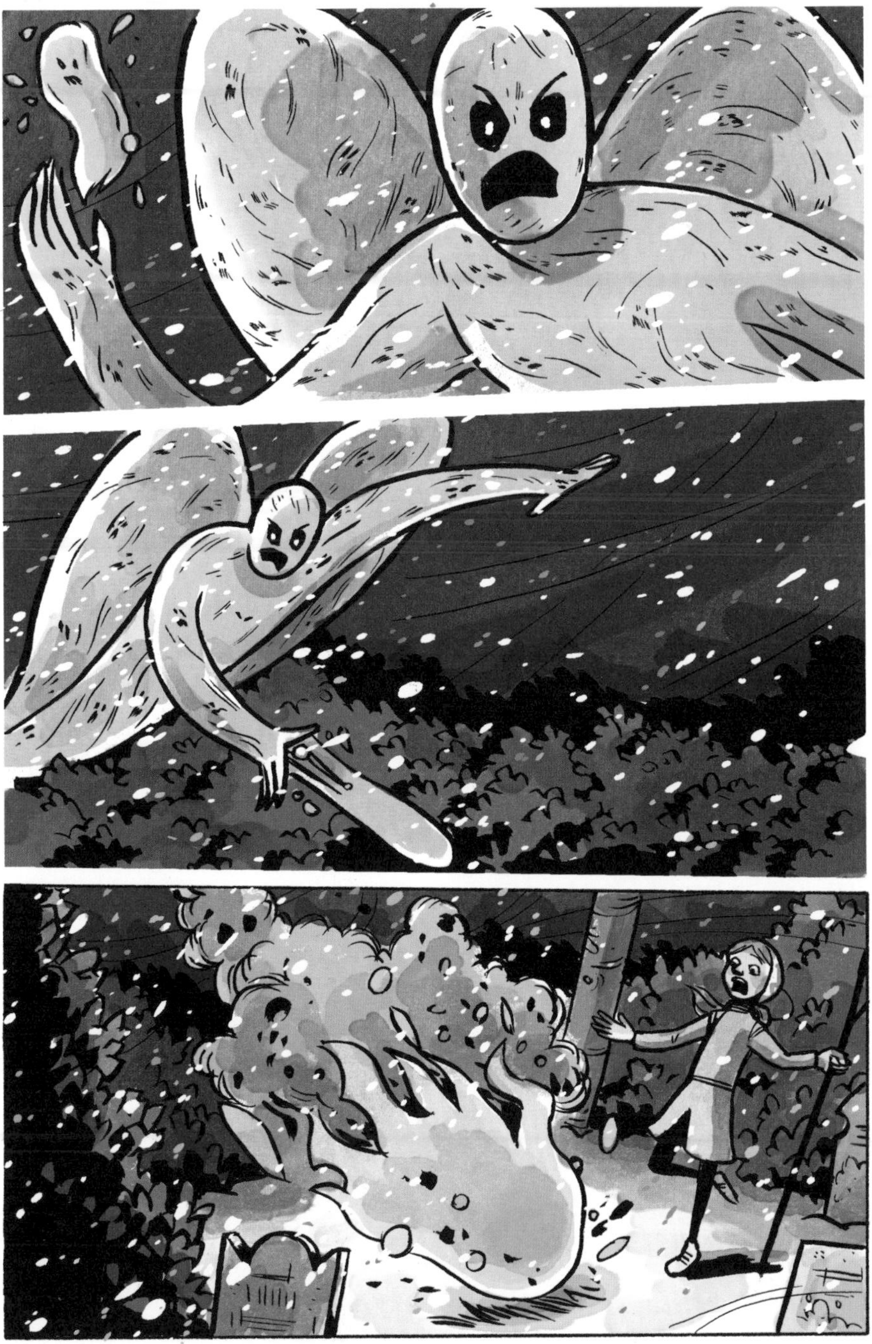

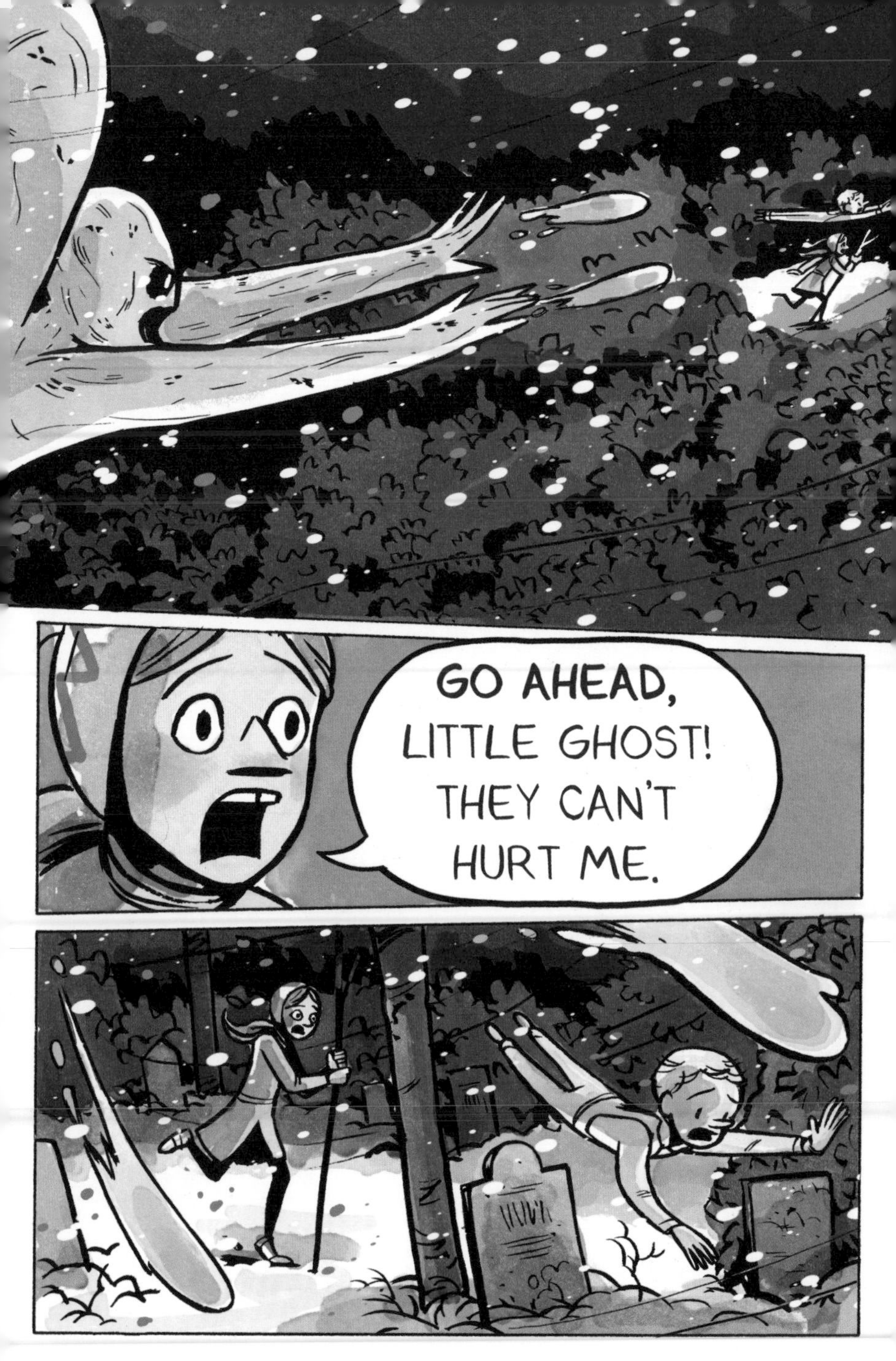
GO AHEAD, LITTLE GHOST! THEY CAN'T HURT ME.

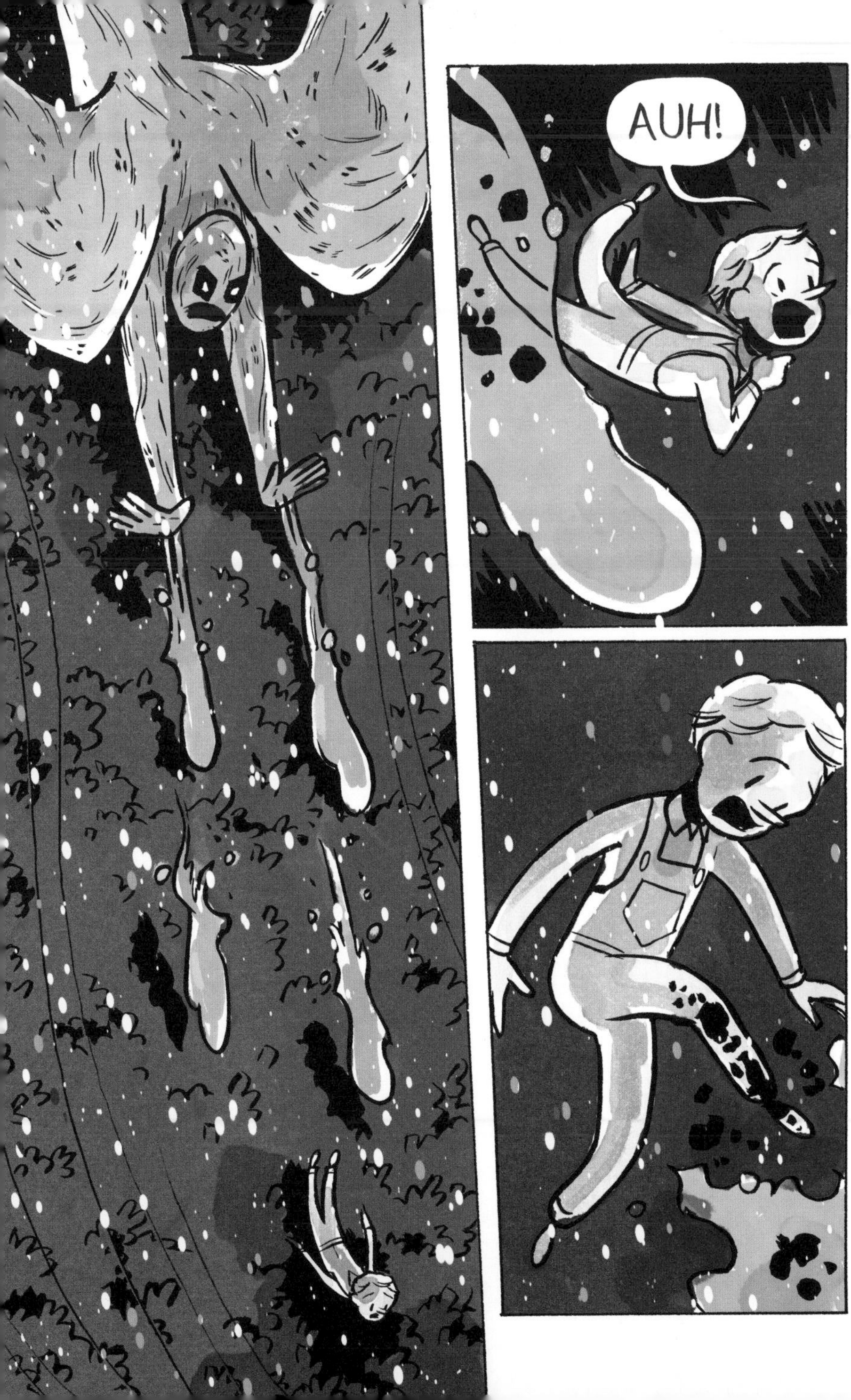
AUH!

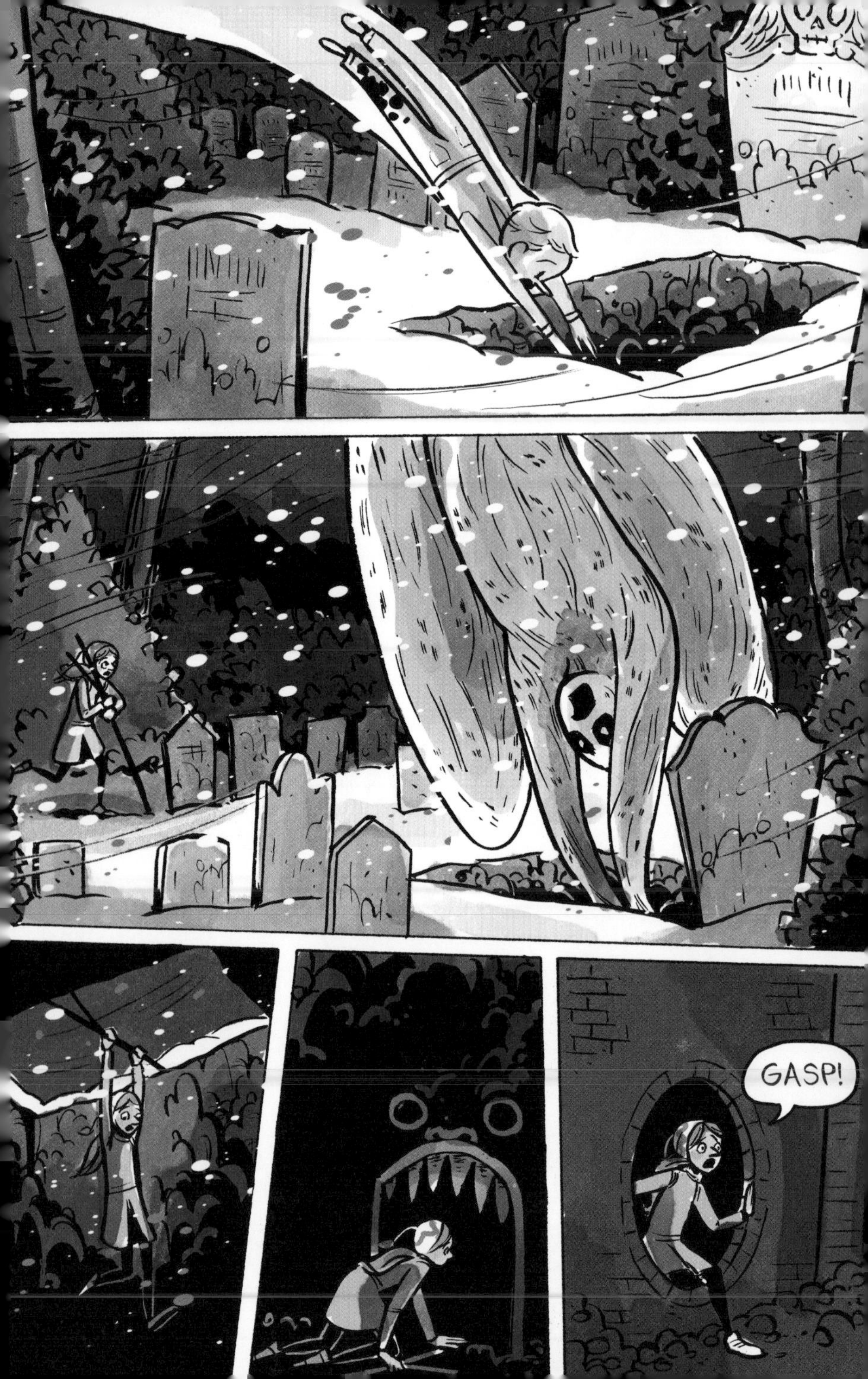
GASP!

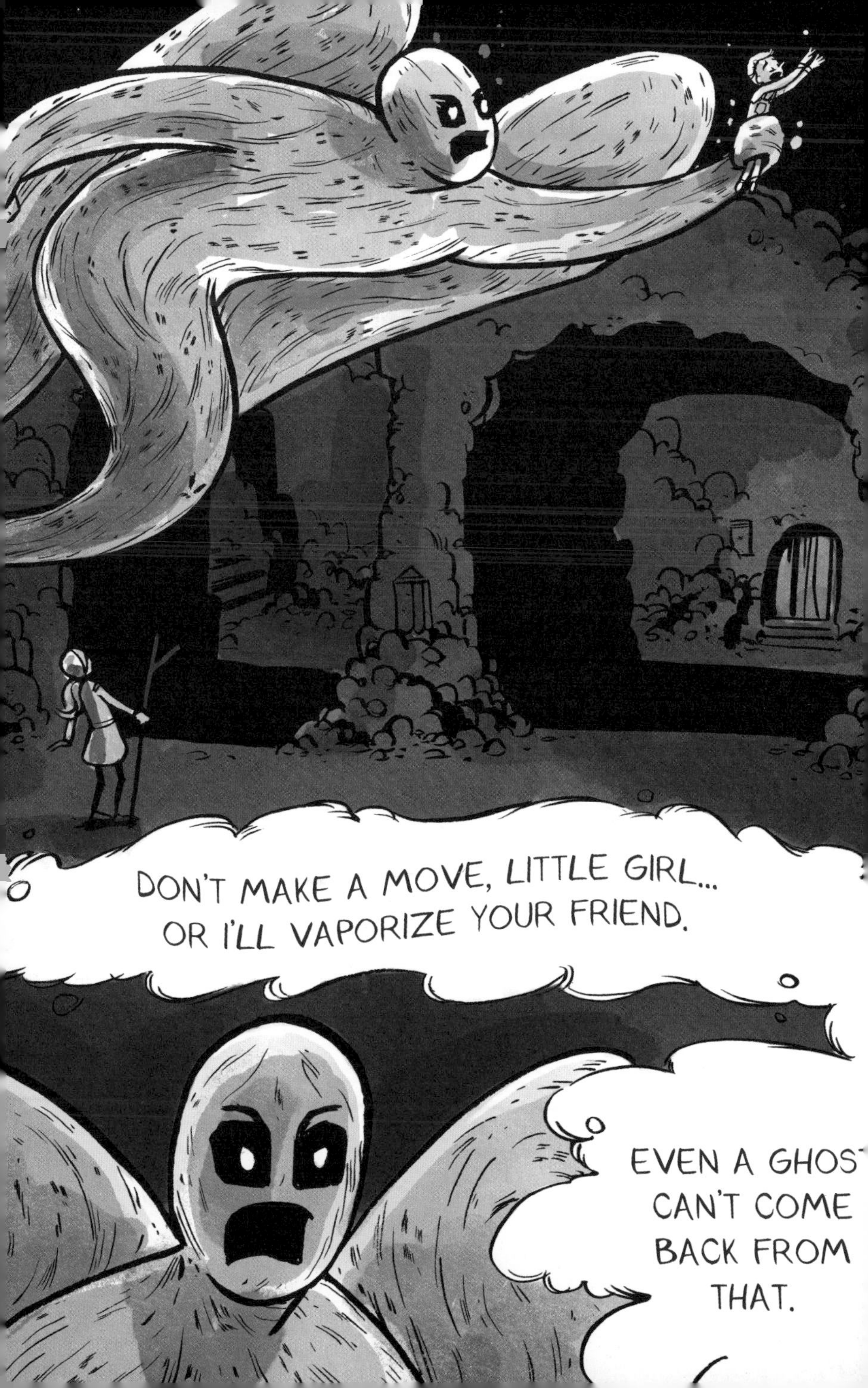
DON'T MAKE A MOVE, LITTLE GIRL... OR I'LL VAPORIZE YOUR FRIEND.
EVEN A GHOST CAN'T COME BACK FROM THAT.

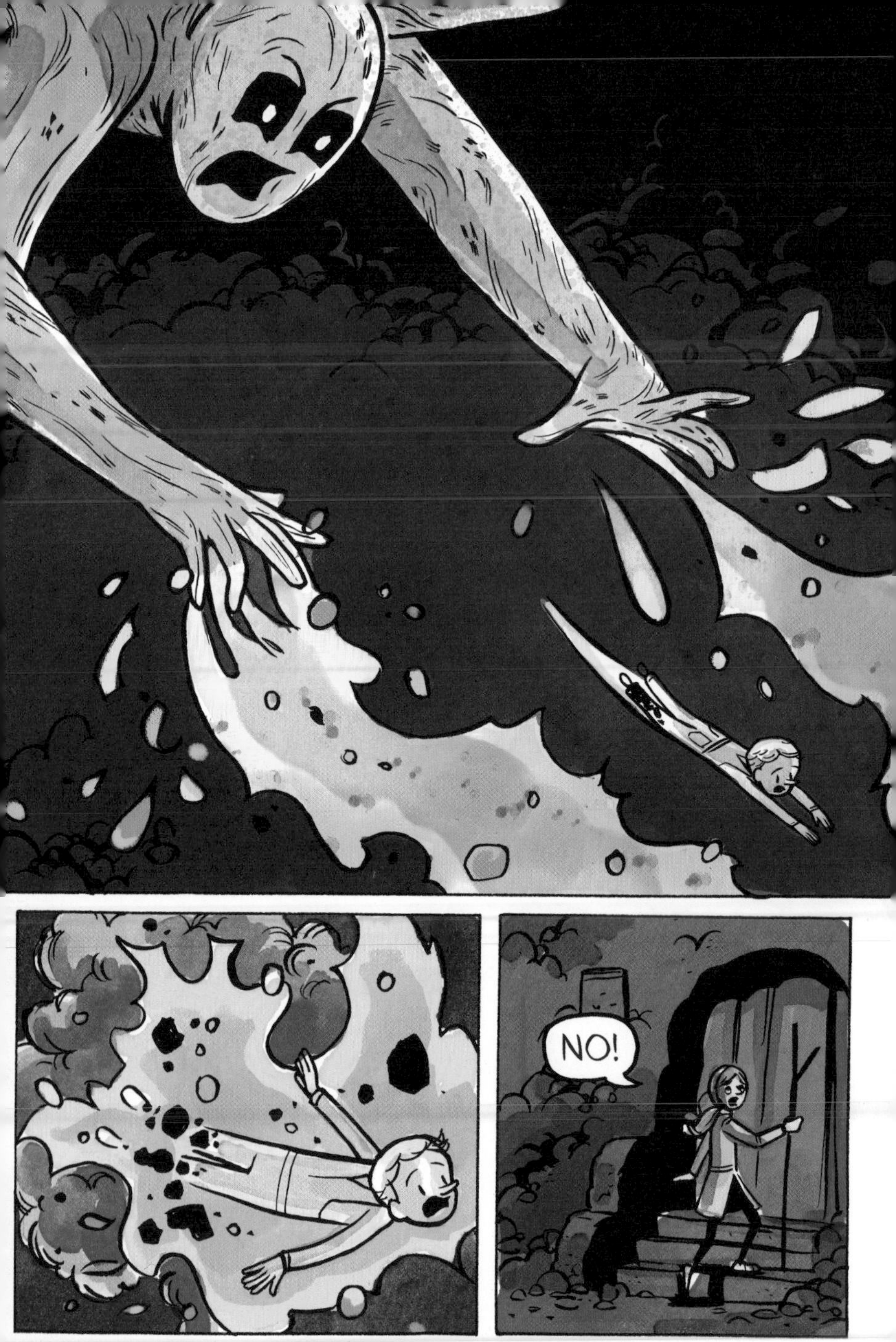
NO!

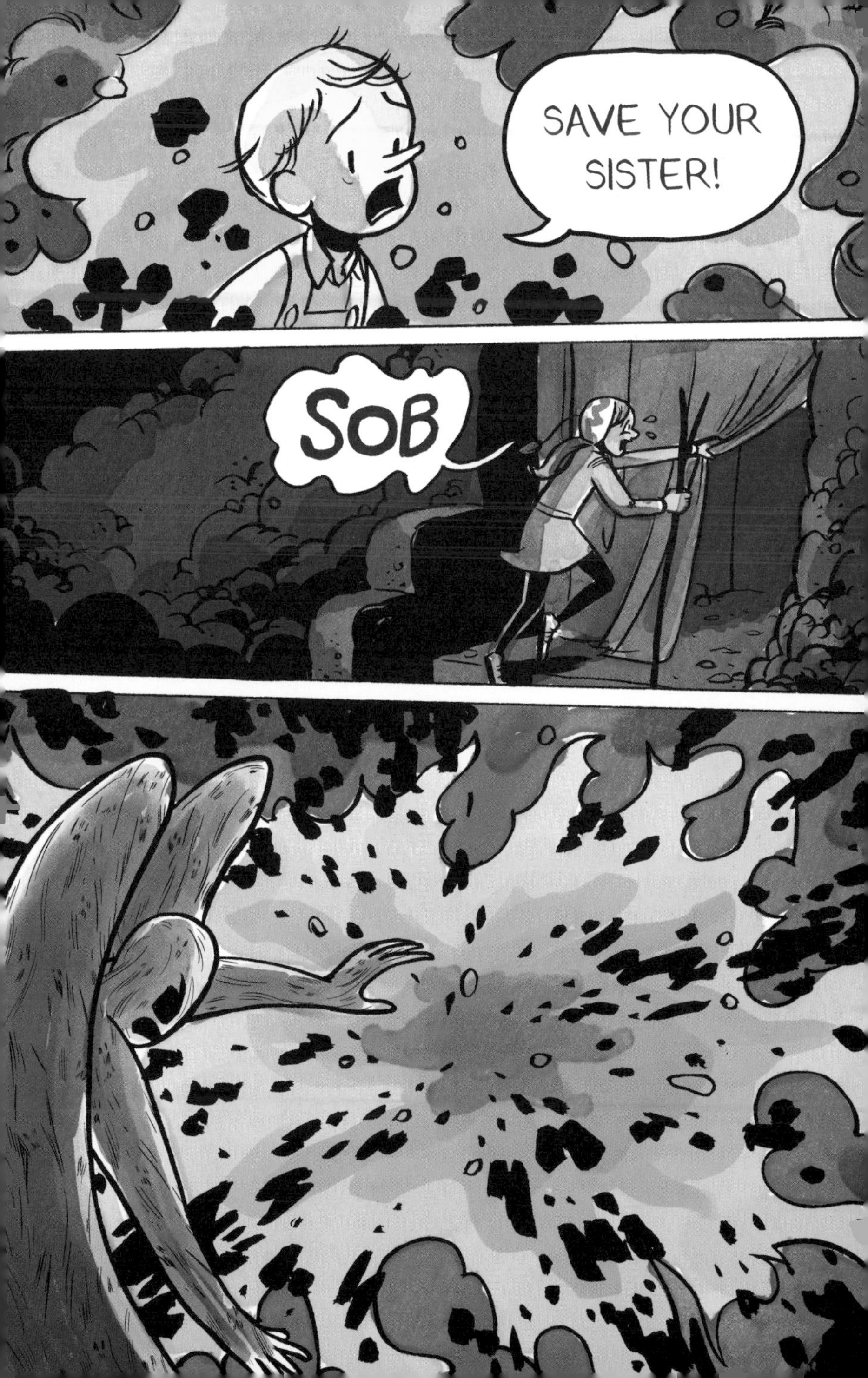
SAVE YOUR SISTER!
SOB

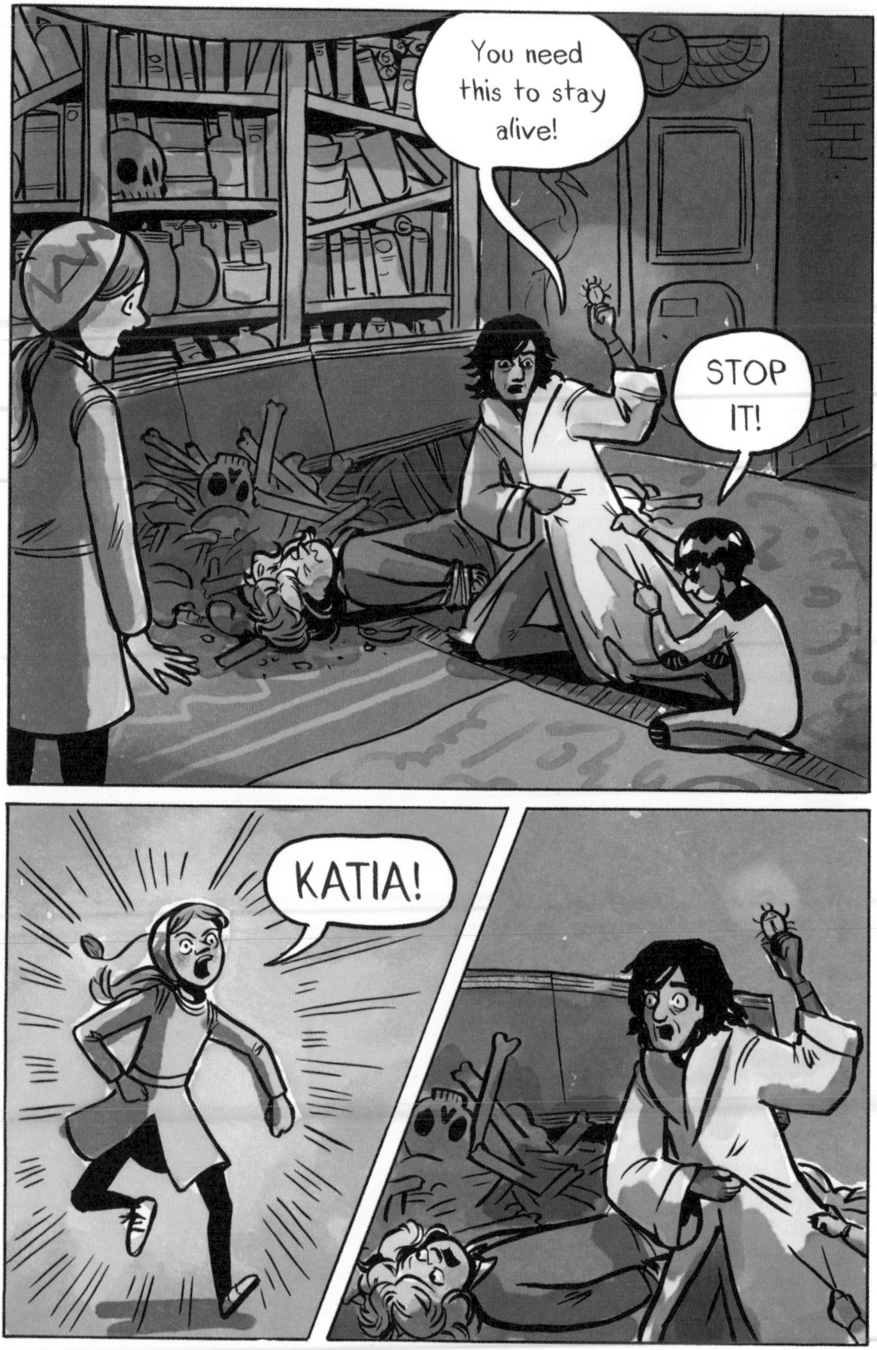
You need this to stay alive!
STOP IT!
KATIA!

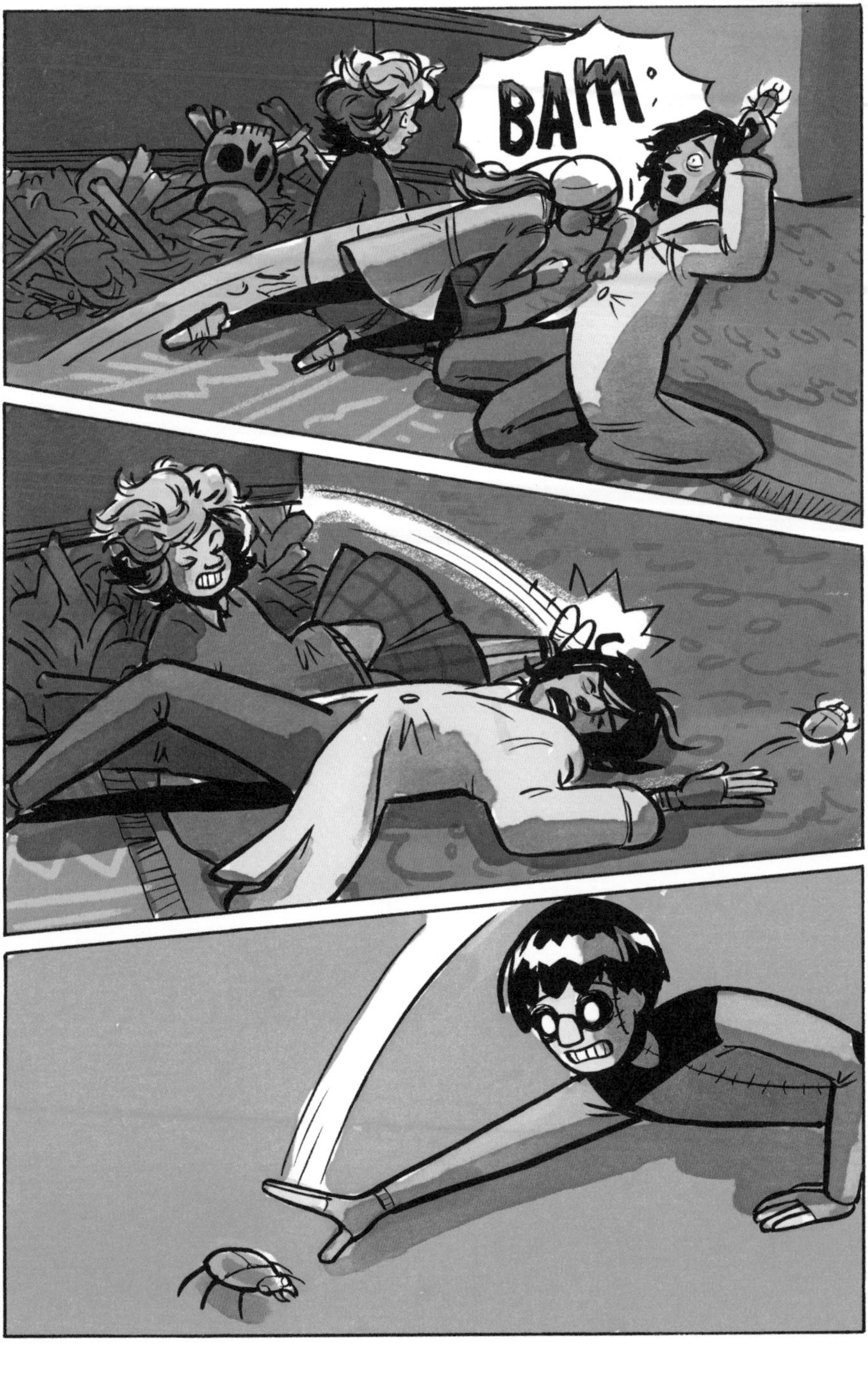
BAM

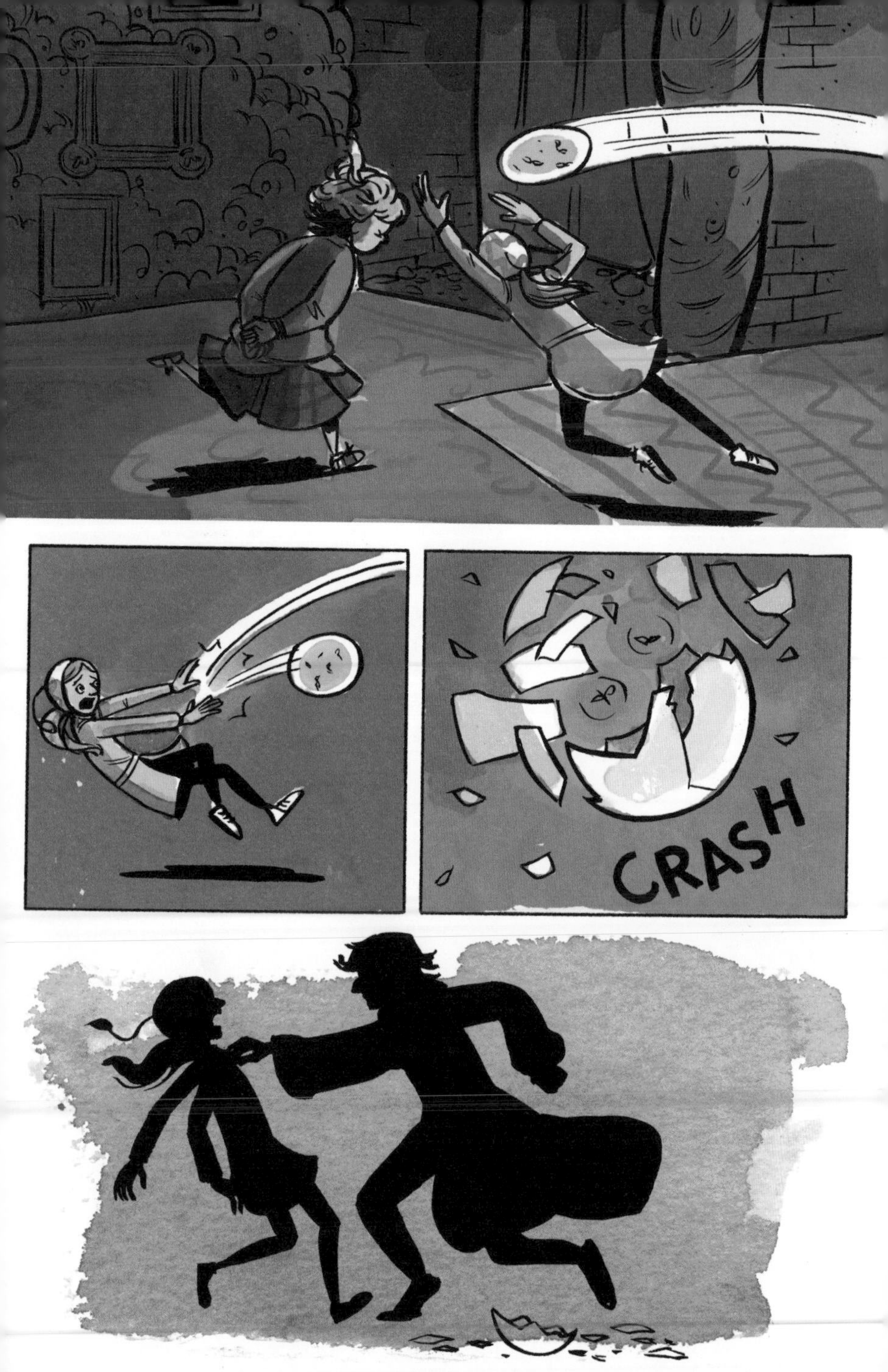
CRASH

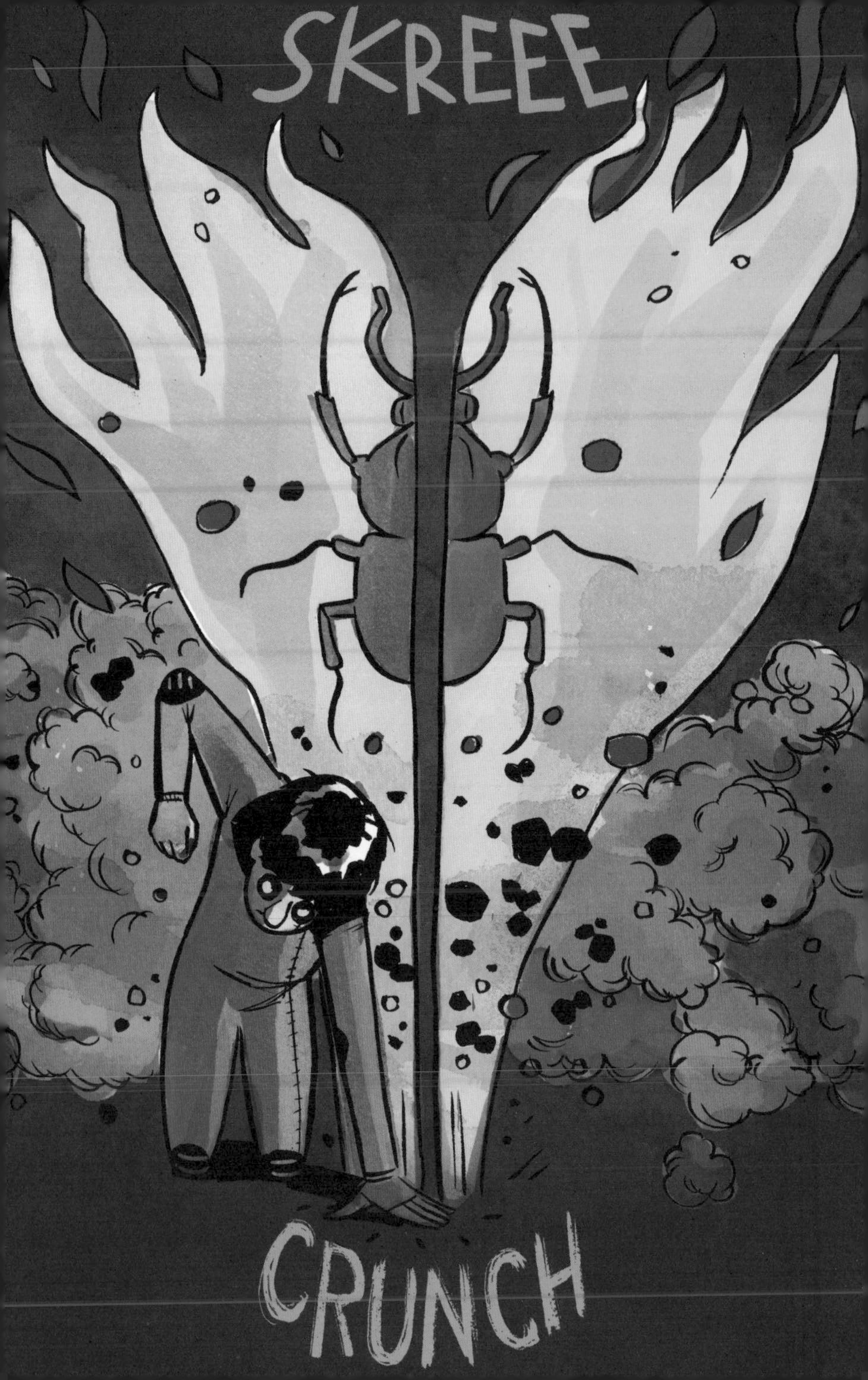
SKREEE
CRUNCH

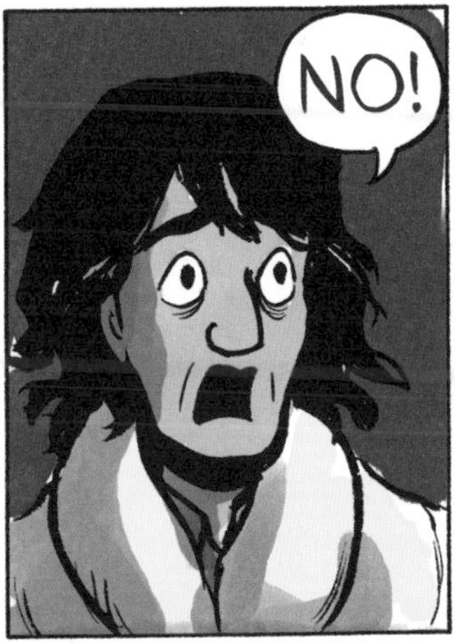
NO!

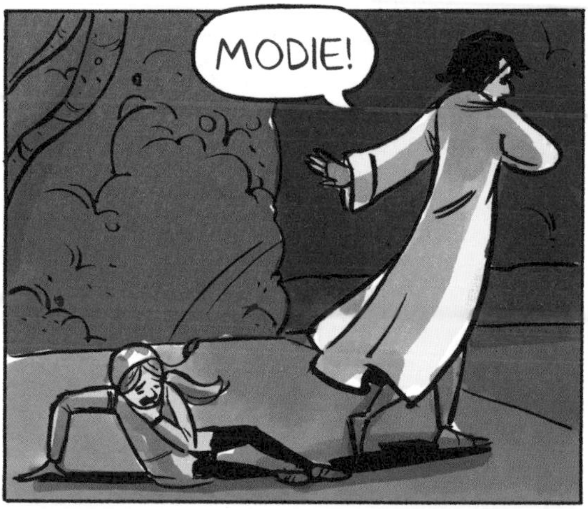
MODIE!

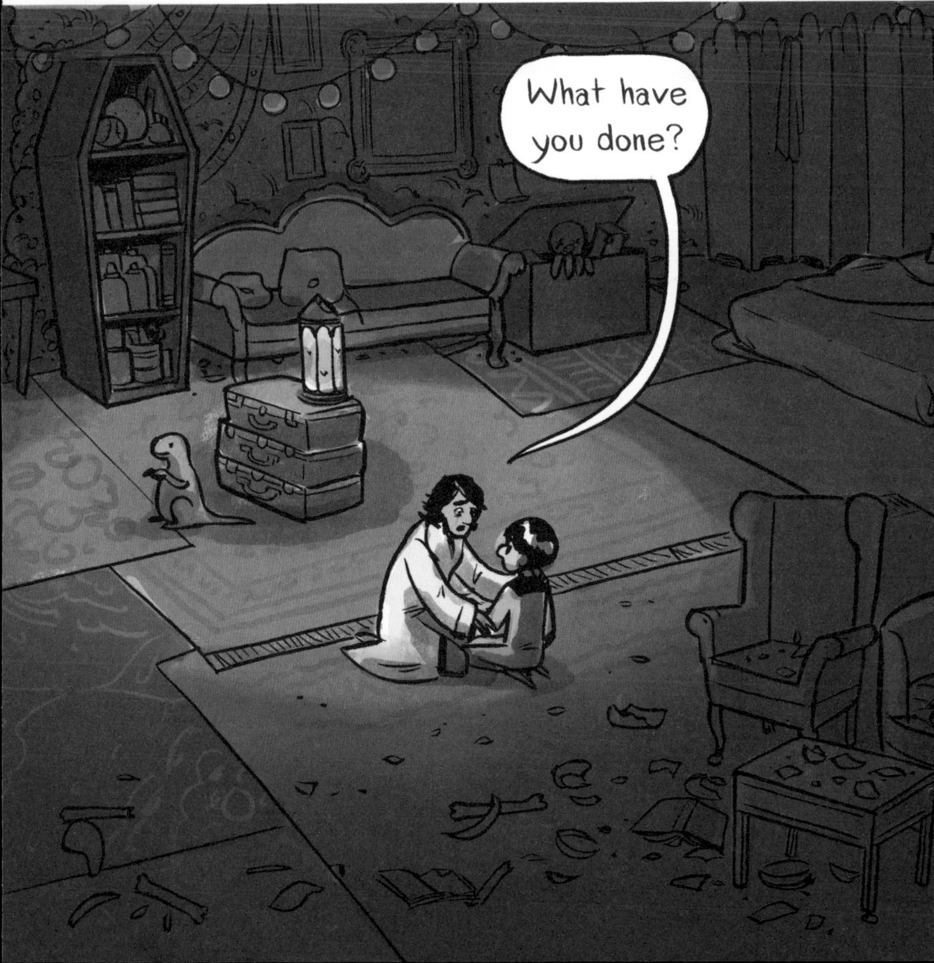
What have you done?

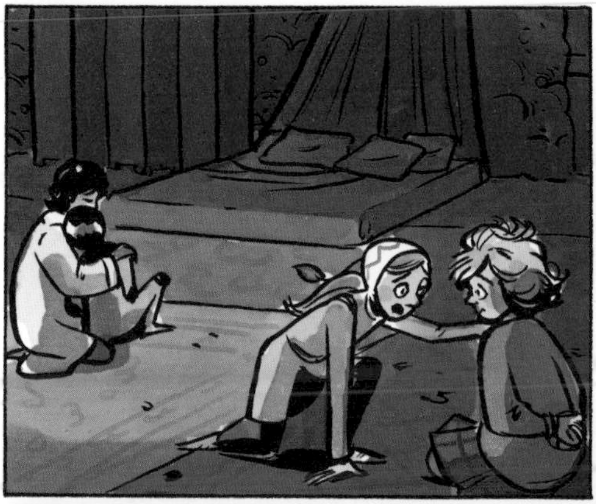
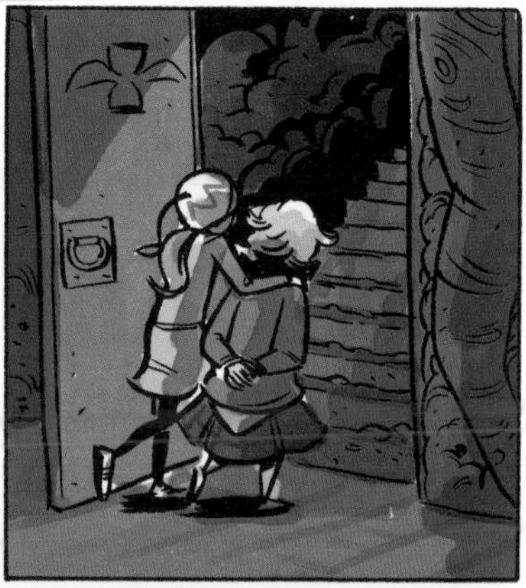
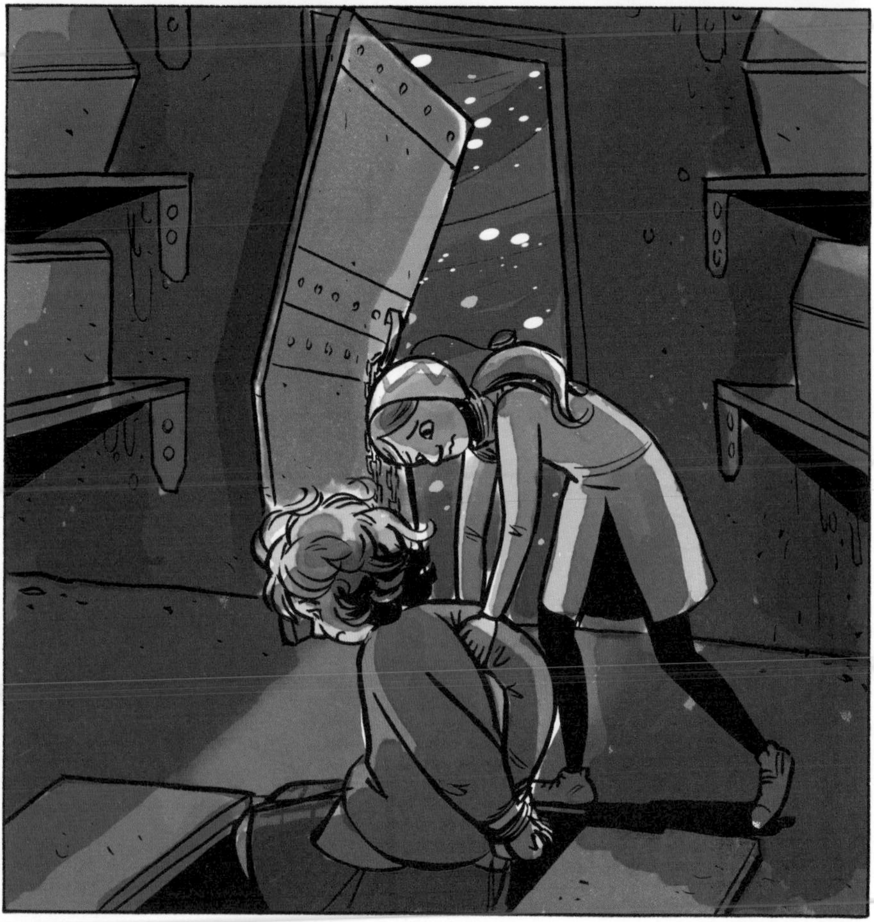

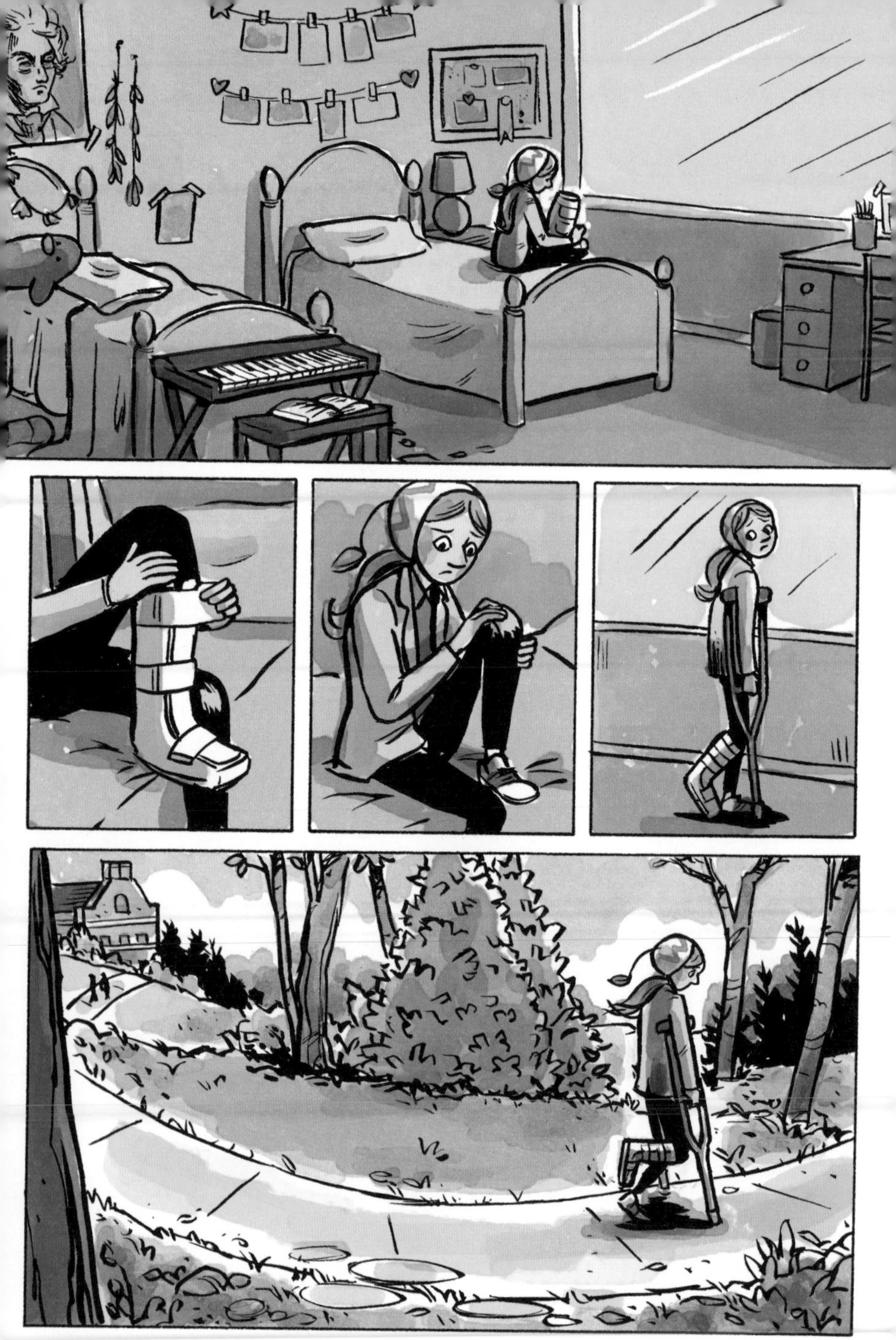

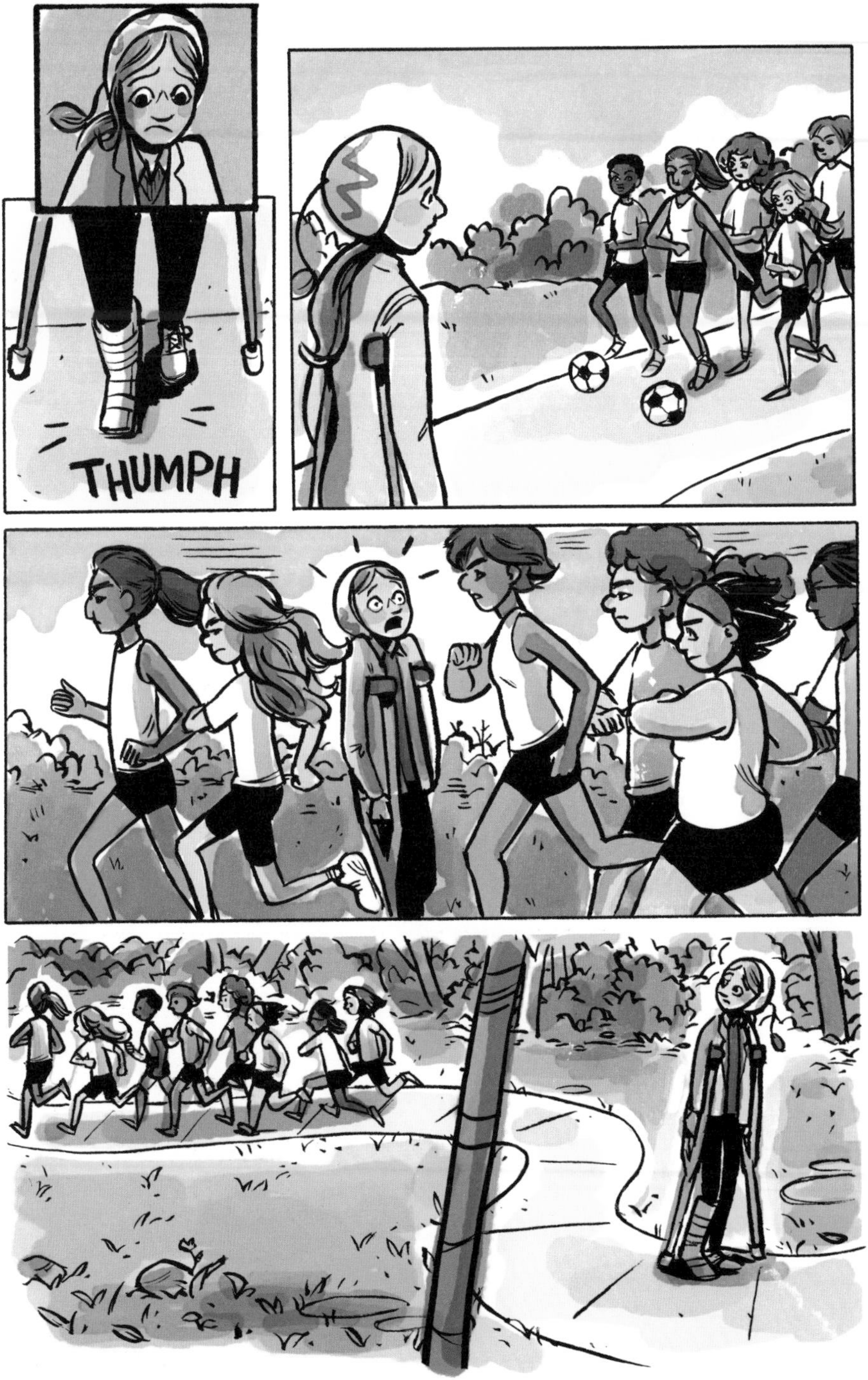
THUMPH

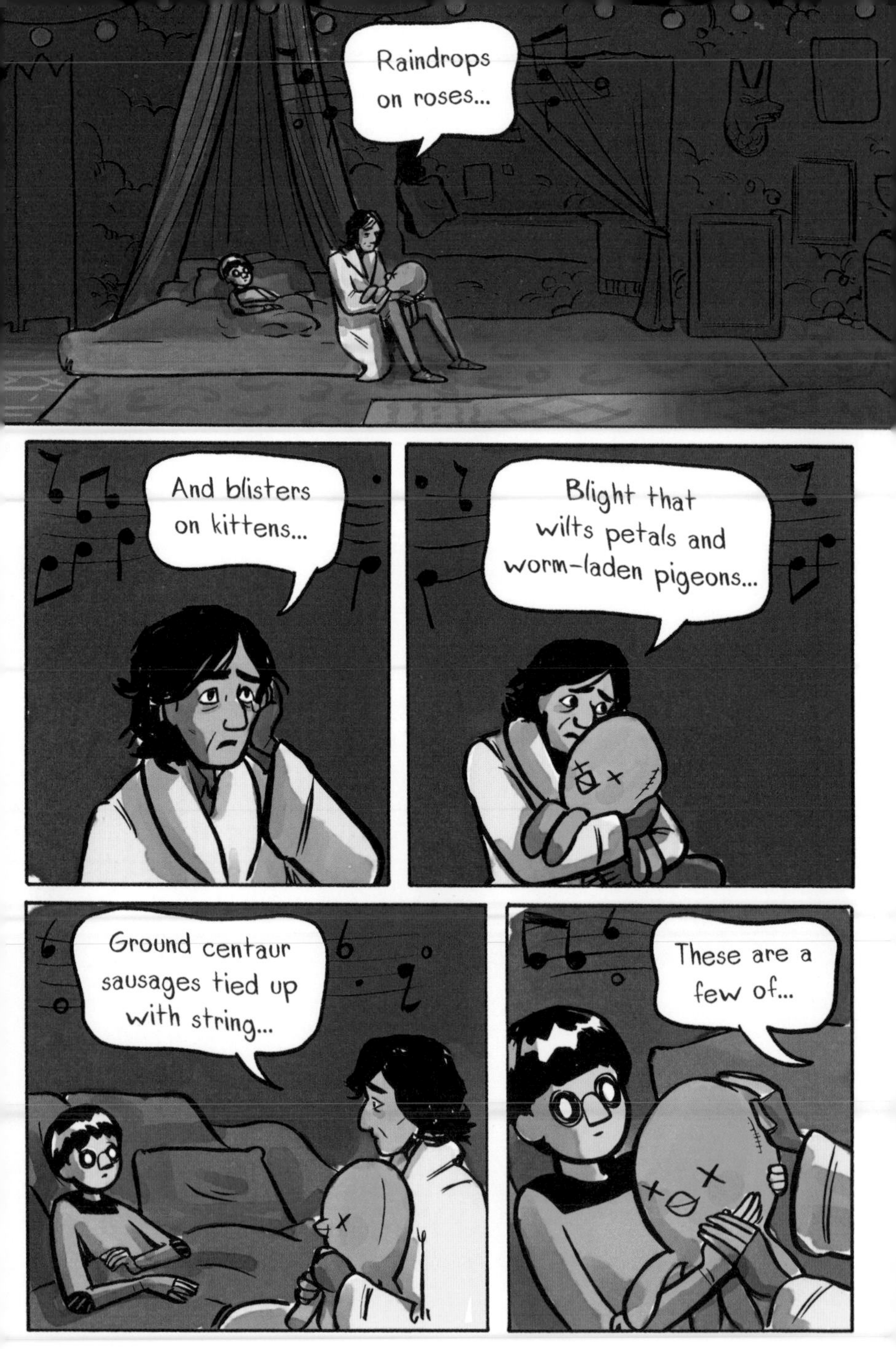
Raindrops on roses...
And blisters on kittens...
Blight that wilts petals and worm-laden pigeons...
Ground centaur sausages tied up with string...
These are a few of...

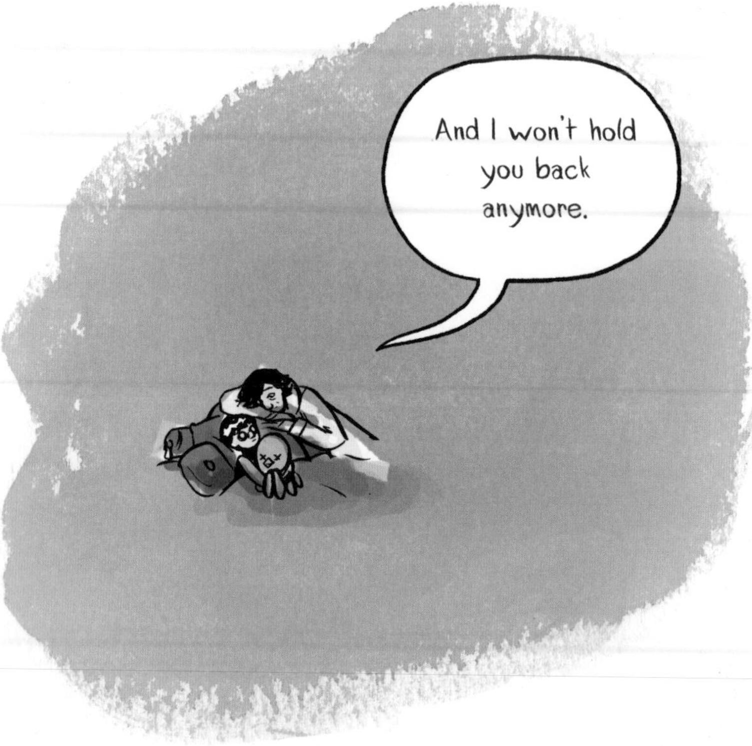
And I won't hold you back anymore.

Seven months later . . .

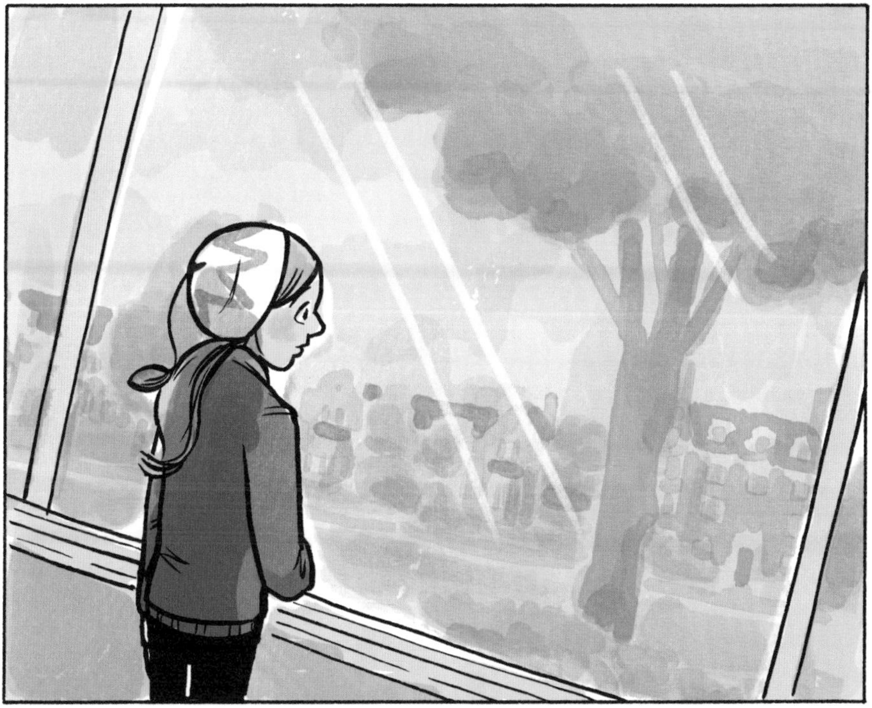

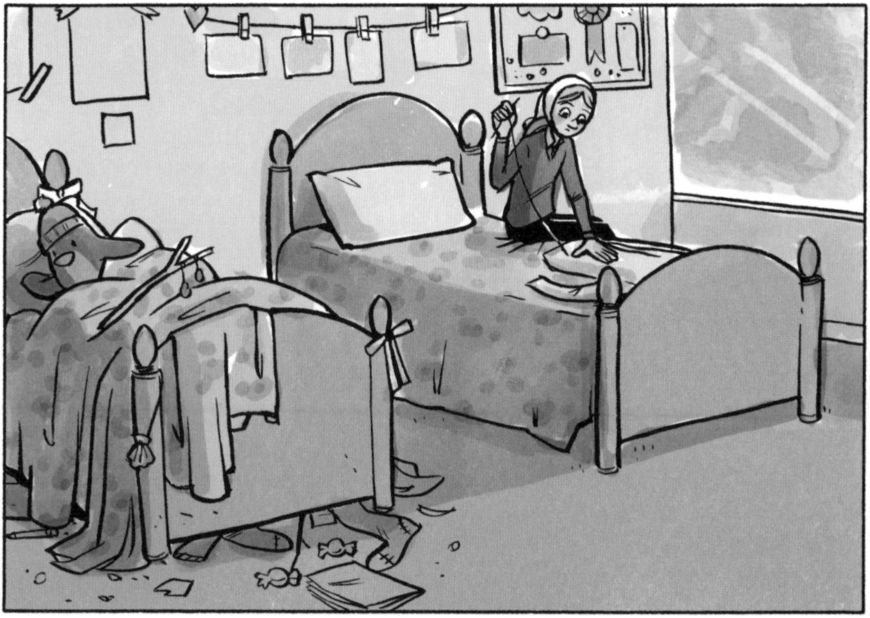

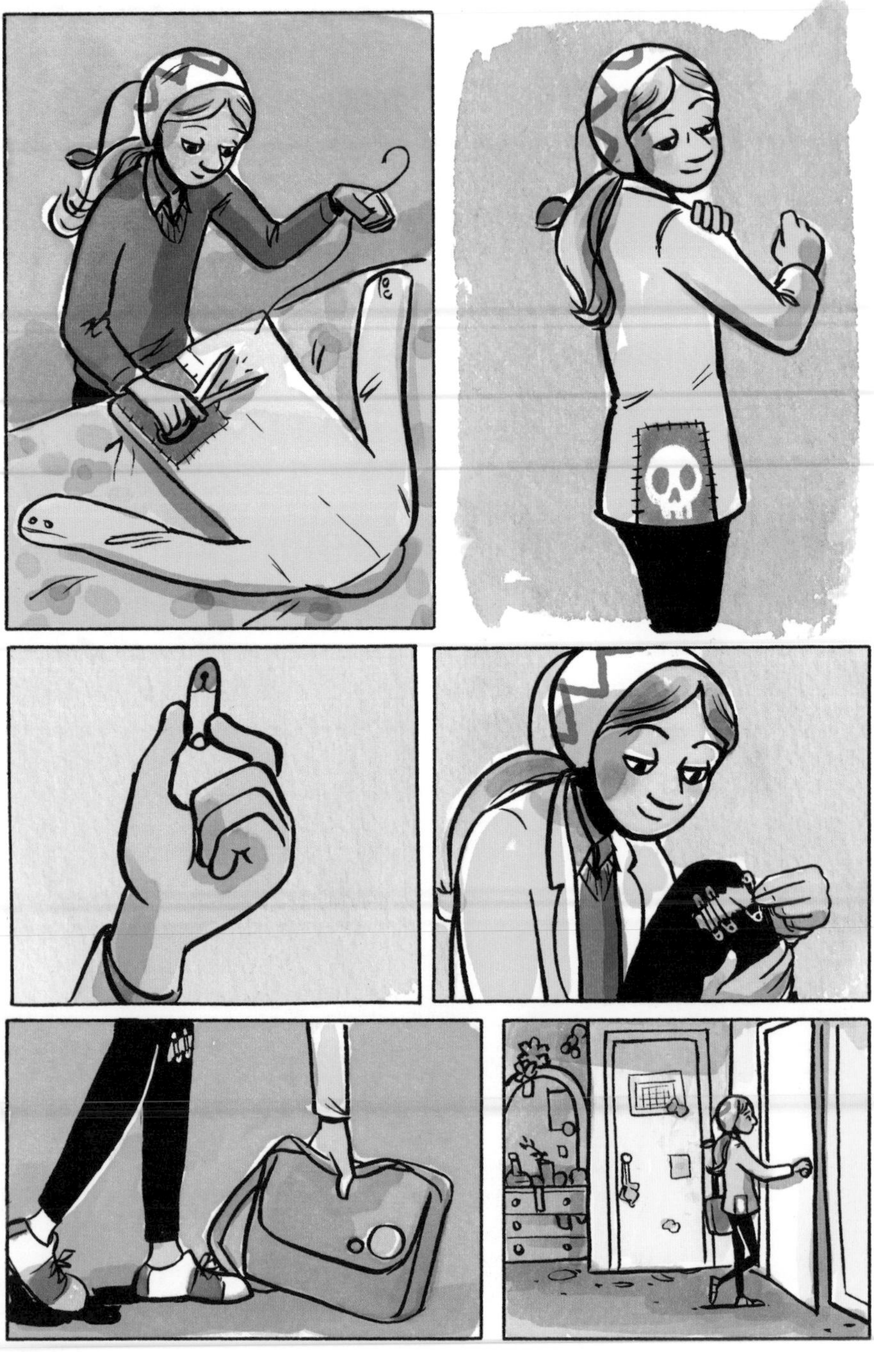

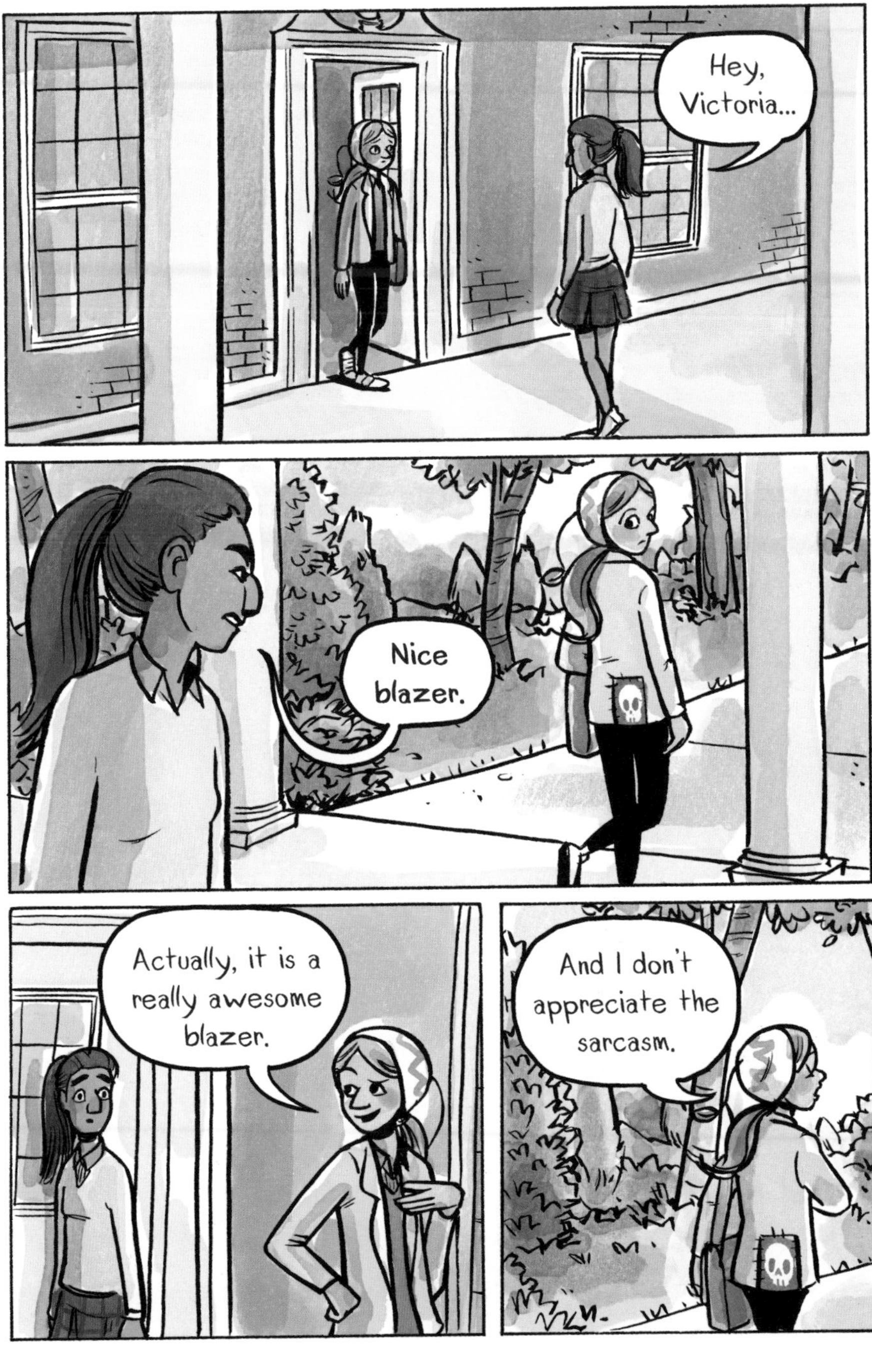
Hey, Victoria...
Nice blazer.
Actually, it is a really awesome blazer.
And I don't appreciate the sarcasm.

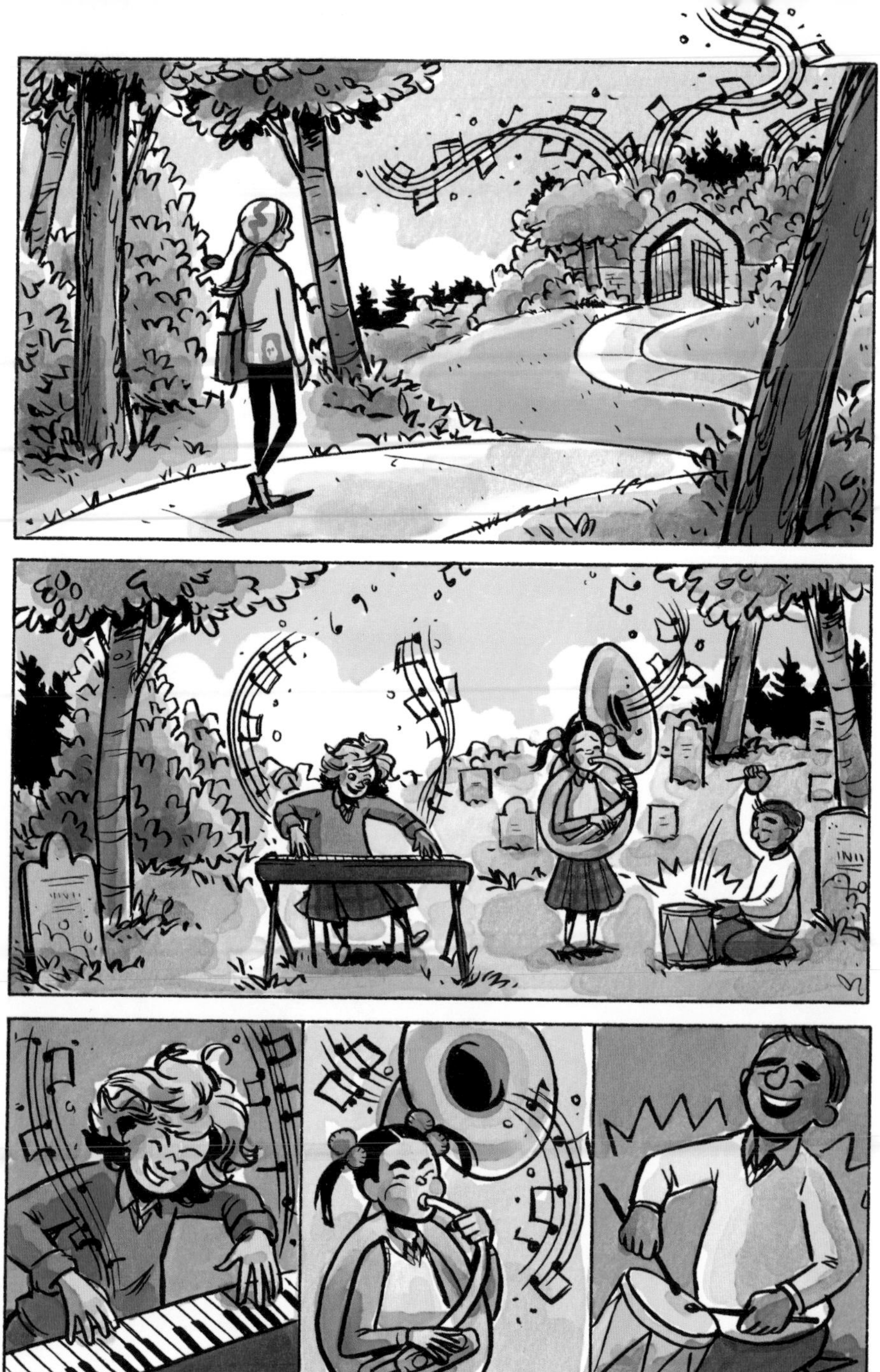

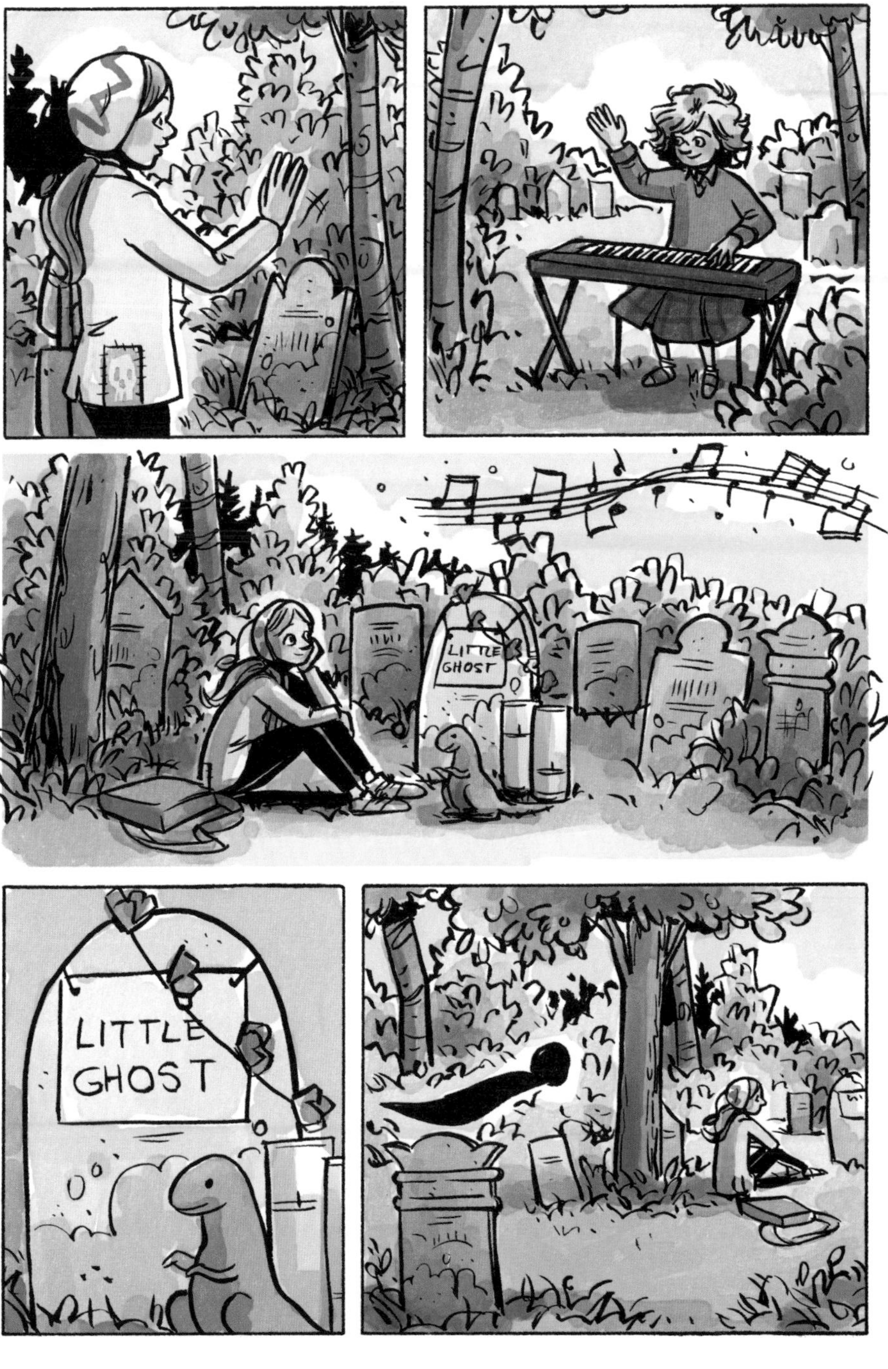
LITTLE GHOST
LITTLE GHOST

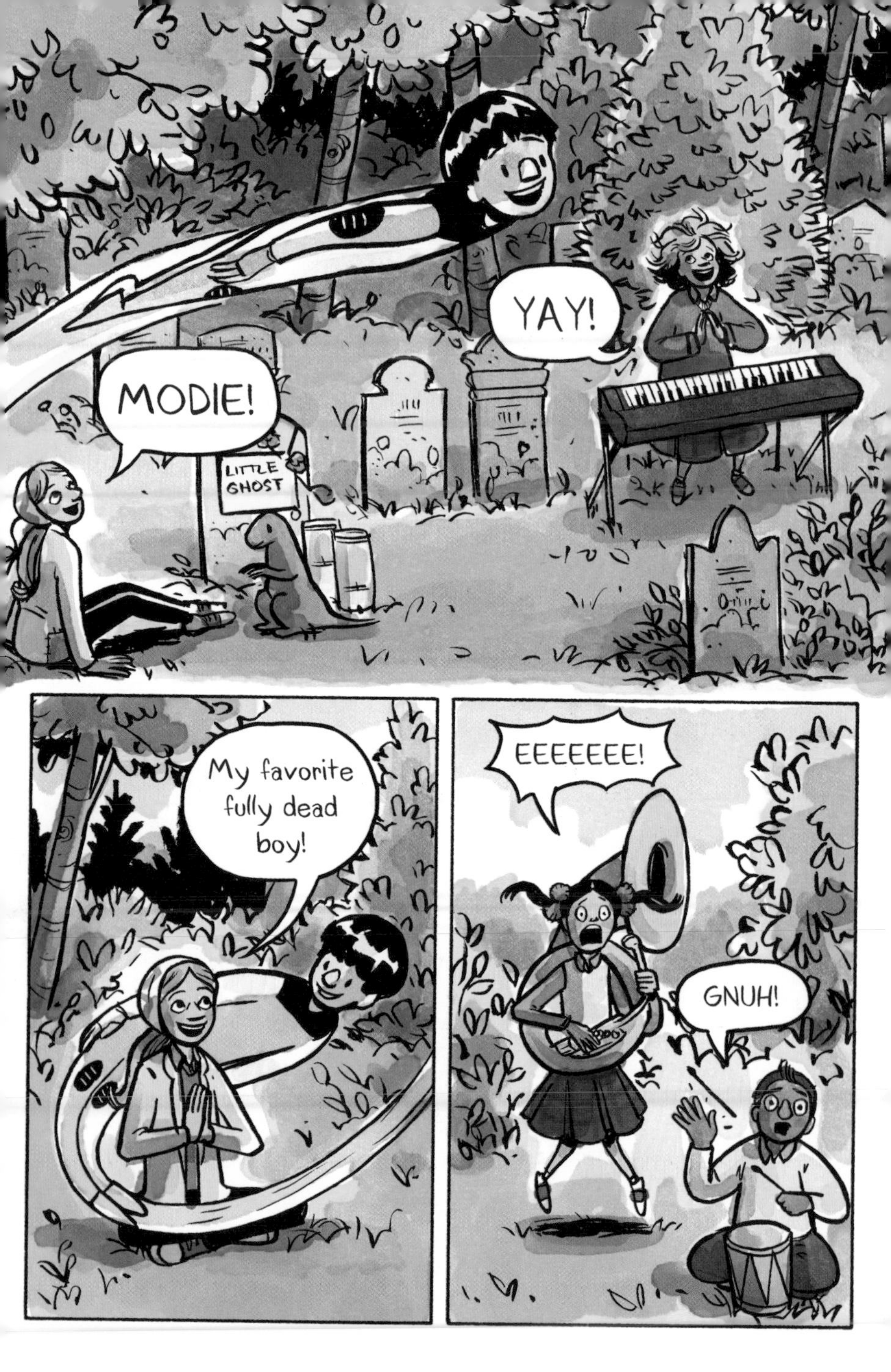
YAY!
MODIE!
LITTLE GHOST
My favorite fully dead boy!
EEEEEEE!
GNUH!

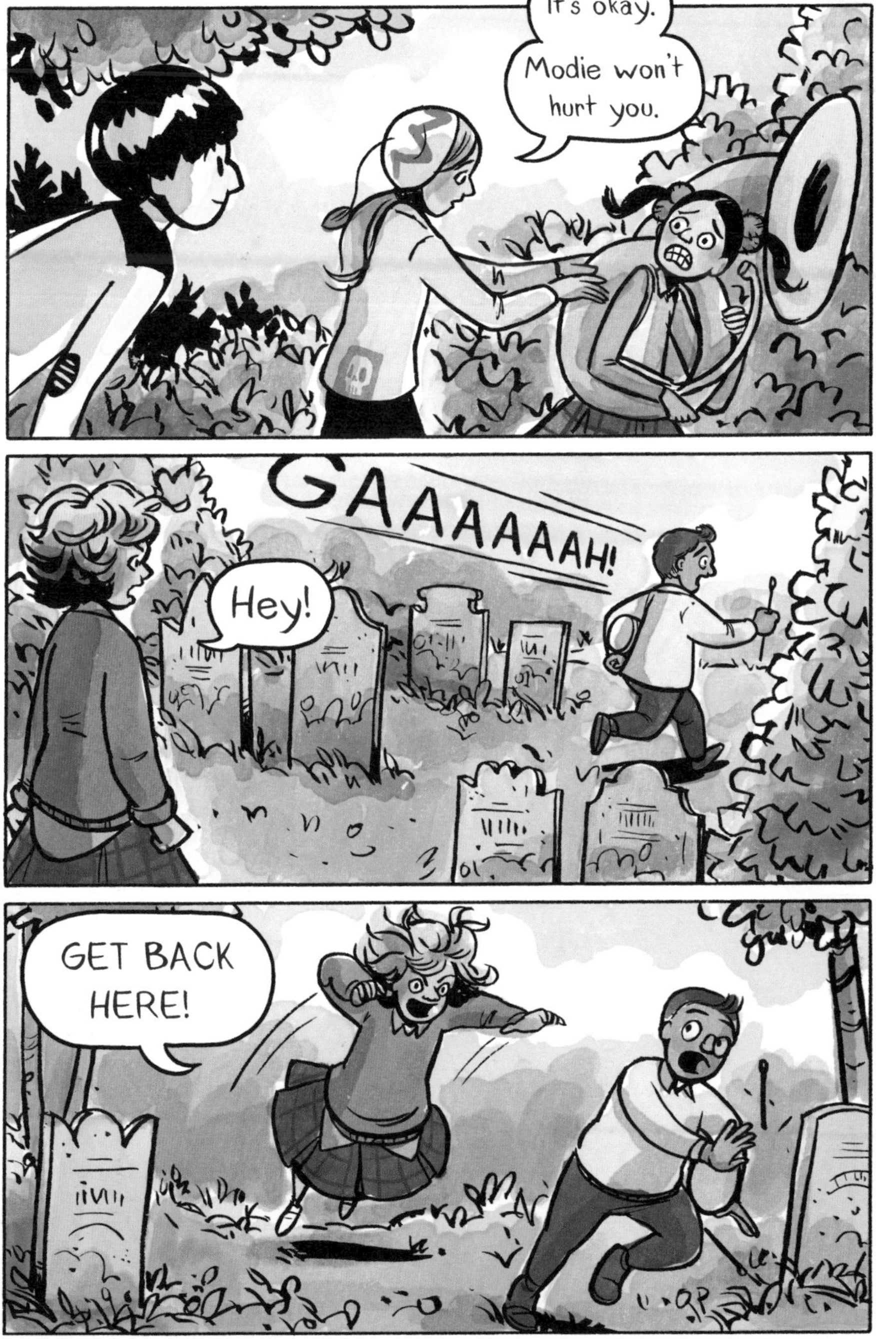
It's okay.
Modie won't hurt you.
GAAAAAAH!
Hey!
GET BACK HERE!

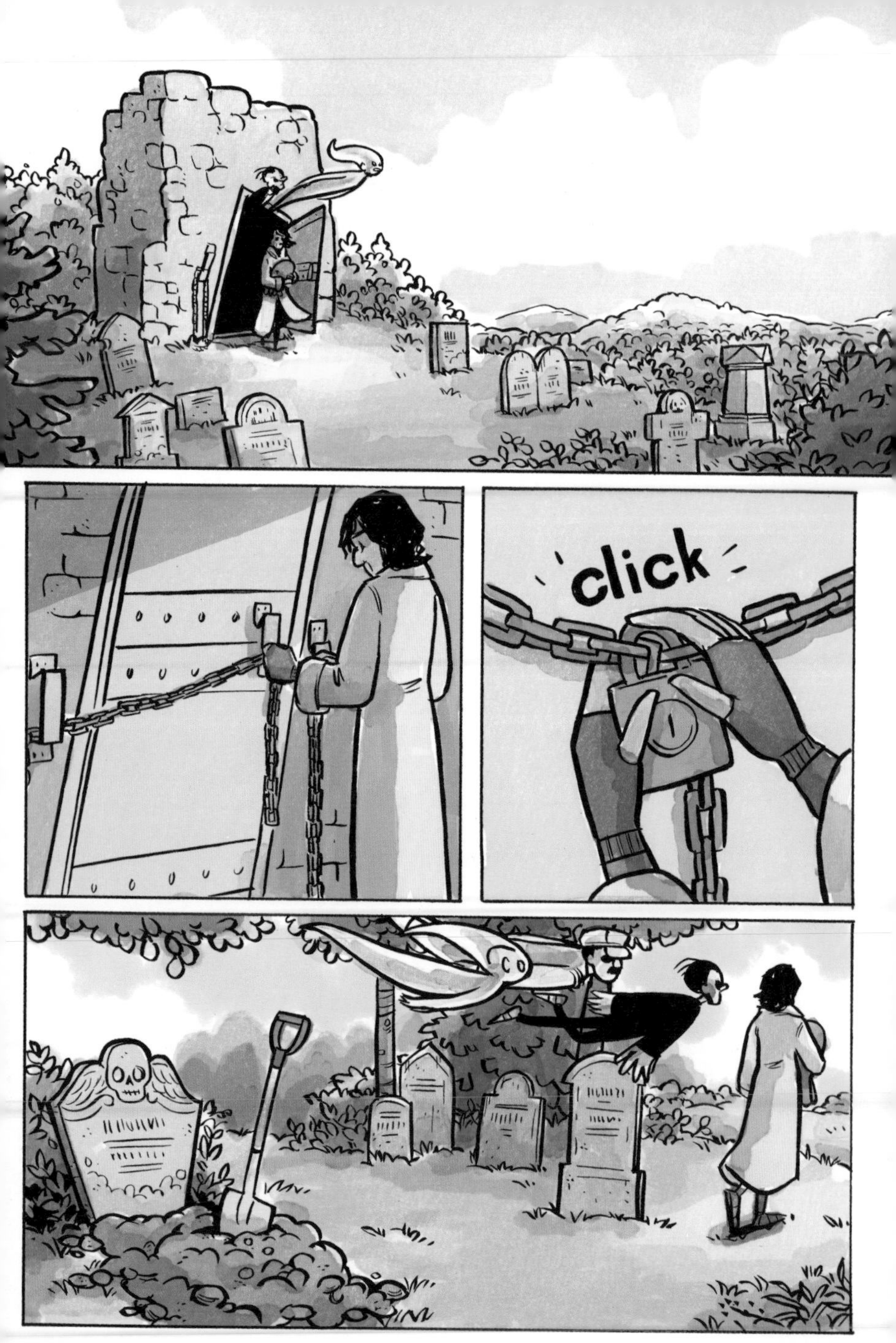
click

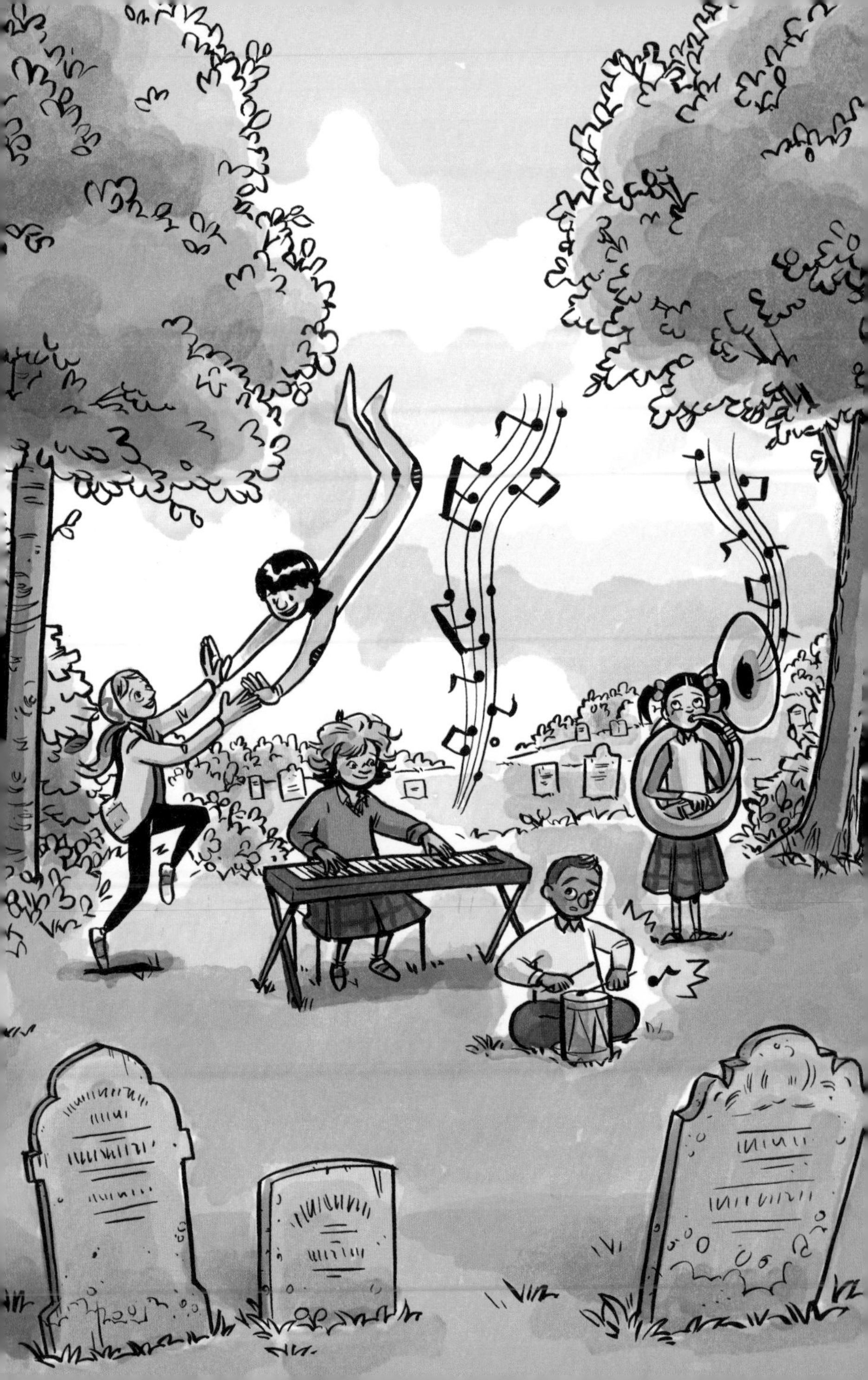